I MUST CONFESS

I MUST CONFESS

by Rupert Smith

CLEIS
PRESS

Published in the United States Cleis Press Inc., P.O. Box 14697, San Francisco, California 94114.

Printed in the United States.

Cover design: Scott Idleman
Cover photograph: Getty Images
Cleis logo art: Juana Alicia
10 9 8 7 6 5 4 3 2 1

For Marcus

and in memory of
the real Mark

*Thanks to Jessica Brighty, Tim Clark,
Patrick Fitzgerald, Tony Peake and Tony Roberts*

CHAPTER ONE

I was born a month premature. Even as a baby, I was ahead of my time.

My mother said she always knew I'd end up in show business. As I lay in the incubator, hovering between life and death, the nurses watched my every movement. Even the other babies seemed to be straining to catch a glimpse of me. Every day they expected me to die, and every day I refused to give up the fight. By the end of the first week, the crowd round my incubator had become so big that the ward sister had to let people in ten at a time to see me; even the consultants had taken an interest. Sometimes I think that the only thing that got me through those difficult days was my determination not to disappoint my public.

It's hardly surprising with a start like that I should end up starring in the most famous hospital series ever seen on television. Throughout my life I've spent more than my fair share of nights in or beside hospital beds, and now I make a living out of it, twice a week, as the star of the award-winning *Patients*.

But I'm getting ahead of myself. When I was born, hardly anybody had even heard of television, let alone of me. My first brush with fame ended the moment the doctors pronounced me well enough to leave the incubator at the tender age of ten days. And so began a life that's taken me from the heights of fame to the depths of despair, from obscurity in a small working-class town on the outskirts of London to the front page of every magazine and newspaper in the world.

When I announced that I was planning to write my autobiography, there was a great deal of speculation (not all of it kind) as to why I had chosen exactly this moment. Why had I kept quiet for all those years when the press were banging on my door demanding interviews? Why did I, the most publicity-shy star of the sixties and seventies, suddenly decide to open my door in the nineties? Was it, as some of the 'newspapers' reported, that I was simply cashing in on my huge success in *Patients*? No, the real reason is that I love the truth. The only thing that matters – that has ever mattered – is being myself as a person, whatever the cost. Over the years that belief has cost me dear – as you'll see.

The first thing I'd like to clear up is the so-called mystery of my name. Yes, I was christened Mark Young, and took the name Marc LeJeune as a young star in the sixties. A lot of nonsense has been written about how I tried to conceal my real identity, which betrays a complete ignorance of one of the first laws of show business. Nobody accused Marilyn Monroe or Judy Garland of trying to hide their real identities. It's just that we recognized the need to give the public what they wanted, what they still want: glamour, mystery.

My home was nothing special. We lived in a small house with a little yard and double garage at the front and a neatly tended garden at the back – the typical British working-class family home. We weren't poor; my father worked in London, and my mother made ends meet with a series of local jobs, so I never wanted for any of the essentials of life. My parents were smart, sociable, among the first people to make fashionable the 'drinks parties' that had become so popular by the end of the fifties. Every Saturday evening the house resounded with doorbells and laughter, cars scrunching up the gravel drive, the clink of glasses and the glug-glug-glug of bottles.

I longed to be right at the heart of the party. As soon as I could walk, I tiptoed out of bed and crept across the landing to the top of the stairs where I would sit and watch the fun in full swing down below. By the time I was three, watching was not enough. I've never been one of life's observers. So one Saturday night I made a grand entrance down the stairs in my pyjamas just as my father had put a record on the gramophone – it was 'Don't Let The Stars Get In

Your Eyes', a song that's stayed with me for the rest of my life. I pushed my way through a forest of stockings and slacks, climbed up on to the window seat that formed a small stage just behind the living-room curtains, and popped into full view as the guests laughed and applauded. It was the first time I had faced an audience, and I was hooked. I remember the staring faces, the sharp glitter of the women's jewellery through a cloud of smoke, the discomfort of the lights in my eyes. I wondered for a moment what to do next, and then started to take my pyjamas off. By the time I had finished my striptease and was doing a series of gymnastic manoeuvres in the nude, the audience was divided. Some of the livelier partygoers were cheering, whistling and even stamping their feet. The rest of them were quiet and embarrassed, looking away or loudly tutting. My mother jumped to the rescue, picked me up and whisked me away upstairs as father went round with the cocktail-shaker.

The next day the atmosphere in the house was heavy. When I tried to climb on to Dad's knee for a cuddle, he pushed me away; never again did he show me any form of physical affection. When I went to bed, I heard my parents arguing downstairs in the kitchen.

My relationship with my parents was, in many ways, ideal. My mother was a warm, spontaneous woman who loved clothes, parties and people; she's the one I take after. My father was quieter, more distant – the typical British working-class man – and a deep thinker. He believed in traditional values – that a woman's place was in the home, that black people belonged in Africa, that the unions were nothing but trouble. When my mother announced that she had taken her first part-time job he hit the roof and they didn't communicate for nearly two weeks. When we got our first television, he would switch off if there was a 'nigger' or a 'pouf' on the screen. This meant that for many years I was entirely ignorant of the careers of Nat King Cole, Liberace and Johnny Mathis.

The striptease incident wasn't the only hint of the future that angered my father. One summer Sunday afternoon, when my parents were drifting around the house pale-faced and red-eyed as usual, I was sitting in my room drawing (I've always loved art), endless pictures of princes and princesses, illustrations to the books that I'd learned to read. All the princesses looked like my mother, with sweeping blonde hair and blue eyes, but dressed in huge crinolines with crowns perched on their heads. The princes were square-jawed and handsome like Robert Taylor, Mum's favourite film star. After an hour of this, I got bored. Mum was snoozing in her armchair in the living room; Dad had drifted off to the pub.

I sometimes think that if I'd had brothers and sisters, my life would have turned out much simpler – there would have been someone around to keep me out of trouble. But only children like me have to rely on their own powers of imagination. I went into the bathroom. Strictly speaking, it was forbidden territory: mother kept all her beauty accessories in a cupboard above the sink, terrified that I would drink her eyeliner or swallow Dad's razors or drown in the toilet bowl. But what I did that afternoon had longer-lasting repercussions than anything Mum had envisaged.

Today everyone dyes their hair – pop stars, actors, even footballers are all familiar with the bleach bottle. But when I was a child it took guts for a man to work with his appearance. I coloured my hair for the first time that quiet Sunday, partly inspired by my mother, whose timeless sense of chic I had always admired, and partly by my discovery of a promising young movie actress. Her name was Marilyn Monroe, she'd just appeared in a film called *All About Eve* (not in the starring role) and I was one of the first people in Britain to recognize her importance.

I was standing on the bathroom stool, stretching over the sink and rooting around in the beauty cupboard, when my eye was attracted to a picture of a glamorous blonde woman, a hybrid of Mum and Marilyn. I stretched up, grabbed the box and pulled it out, bringing a few bottles of nail varnish clattering into the sink with it. Thanks to my advanced reading skills (school reports said I had the ability of an eleven-year-old at the age of five), I scanned the directions on the packet, and started squirting the stinking blue liquid directly on to my hair. Two minutes later, every tress was covered in bleach, and I delved back into the carton to find the little plastic rain hat. After another happy hour spent drawing, I washed the dye out – by this time it had started stinging my scalp. I can still remember the excitement of bending over the bath with the shower hose running over my head, watching the chemicals swirling down the plughole, not daring to look at my hair. I wrapped a towel around my head turban-style and stood in front of the mirror. There was one stray lock of hair falling down over my forehead – and to my delight it was not just blonde but WHITE.

I ran downstairs to surprise Mum, but it was I who got the surprise; just as I reached the hall, the front door opened and my father walked in. He stopped. I stopped. We stared at each other, neither one of us saying a word. I fully expected him to hit me, and I sensed that if I turned my back or showed any sign of weakness or remorse, he'd have grabbed me and given me the leathering of a lifetime. But I had to stand my ground and be a man, to make him proud of me however much our two worlds may have differed.

He turned, took off his coat and went into the kitchen. When Dad found us half an hour later, I was sitting on Mum's knee as she brushed out my beautiful long blonde hair in front of the fire.

My hair wasn't the only thing that made me stand out at school. At the age of five I still looked much, much younger than my years, and the other kids seized on this. Then there was my name – Mark Young. For years my nickname was 'Baby' Young or just 'Young' Young, which the boys would chant for entire lunch breaks as I made my way around the playground, oblivious to their taunts. I learned at an early age that there were some people who would mask their attraction under the appearance of hostility.

For this reason, I found it easier to play with the girls. I've always preferred the company of women. I love women, everything about them – their hair, their clothes, their conversation, their sense of humour. It was natural for me to gravitate towards the people that I found most attractive at school. But the mixing of the sexes, even in a co-educational primary school, wasn't encouraged. In certain areas there was strict sexual apartheid. Complain as I might, I had to play football with the boys on a Wednesday afternoon instead of netball (for which I had greater aptitude). On one occasion, my father gave me a serious talking-to about the virtues of being a man's man, of playing the game and being tough and brave. To please him I tried to join in the boys' war games, but ended up in the role of the beautiful Nazi spy who leads our brave soldiers to their doom.

After girls, my next big discovery was cinema. I'd seen my first film just before I started school – Disney's *Cinderella*, a film that captivated me. After that, I plagued my parents with requests for trips to the pictures; by the time I was seven, they'd grown tired of my nagging and would simply give me the money to go on my own. Thanks to an understanding door policy at the local Odeon, I enjoyed the great final flowering of Hollywood from the comfort of my regular Saturday-afternoon seat, and entered a fantasy world from which I've never emerged.

I'd watch whatever film was on, sometimes staying to see it again and even on one occasion (*Gentlemen Prefer Blondes*) three times, at the end of which I was hauled out of the Odeon by an angry father and brought home to a distraught mother who was convinced that I'd been kidnapped. And films brought the first love into my life: a girl named Tina, who shared my passion for Marilyn Monroe and with whom I'd sit and hold sticky hands throughout long, happy Saturday afternoons. Although in reality we were scruffy little kids from the local school, in our minds we were movie stars. After the cinema we'd go to her house and act out scenes from our favourite film of the day. On many occasions brunette Tina was Jane Russell to my Marilyn.

Tina's parents were happy to tolerate our games, grateful to me for playing with their daughter, a shy, withdrawn girl; only I had seen her potential. We dressed up in her mother's extensive wardrobe of cast-offs, sang along to her collection of film soundtracks and improvised our own romantic melodramas 'on location' around the house and garden. Our only problem was the lack of a leading man. I could never take the role – it would have upset the delicate balance of my relationship with Tina.

Tina's older brother Nigel was once disastrously persuaded to join in with a jungle picture that we were 'filming' on the bombsite that adjoined the garden; his subsequent stories (all lies) of precocious sexual shenanigans swept round the school within days and ended my friendship with Tina.

On the first day of my secondary education, Mum straightened my new school cap on my head (my hair had long since returned to its natural colour) and Dad gruffly shook me by the hand and exhorted me to 'play the game'. I was prepared for the worst. This was not the genteel grammar school where gifted boys were cosseted and prepared for certain academic success. My future lay in the rough and tumble of the secondary modern, an environment where intelligence and individuality were punished as often as rewarded. Within two days I had been singled out as a figure of fun; my reputation had preceded me, and before long the familiar chants of 'Young' Young were haunting me once again (can you wonder that I was eager to change my name when the opportunity arose?). While my fellow students played football or sneaked down to the newsagent to buy cigarettes, I drifted around the library, the empty classrooms and the further corners of the playing field where nobody could be bothered to follow me.

I was not the only one who existed on the fringes of the school society. There were other freaks and oddballs who were eager enough to make friends – the fat boys, the strange spindly creatures with too many teeth and thick glasses, the halt and the lame – but I ignored them as they trailed in my wake. However, there was another solitary figure who fascinated me. I couldn't understand why he was always alone. Like me, he was neither hideous nor deformed nor did he smell. He was tall for his years, an accomplished athlete, with a greasy quiff that was dangerously long by school standards. I was determined to find out more. The playground grapevine furnished me with a brief personal history. Until the previous year, he'd lived with his parents near Manchester, suffering the regular indignities heaped on him by an alcoholic father. When his mother could no longer tolerate her husband's violent temper and blatant infidelities, she threw him out. Two days later, the repentant father turned up, drunk and morose, begging to be allowed back in. He stank, he hadn't changed his clothes and had been thrown out by his floozy who had quickly tired of his incessant drinking. Father and son confronted each other on the doorstep as mother wept hysterically in the toilet. Finally son dispatched father with a swift head-butt which left him unconscious outside the front door. He never returned; the parents divorced and he and his mother moved back down to her London home.

This legendary act of domestic violence had earned its perpetrator the nickname 'Nutter'; real name Hugh Cole. There was something about him – his solitude, his air of suppressed violence, his history of family tragedy – that drew me. After weeks of following him around the school trying to engage him in conversation, I eventually ambushed Nutter in a remote corner of the playing fields one frosty afternoon in November when both of us should have been attending the Remembrance Day service. I trailed him from the hall during a silent prayer, past the kitchens to the deserted field where he loved to walk for hours, staring out across the rows of houses.

That was where I found him, leaning against the low perimeter fence, one foot resting on a broken wooden slat, chin in hand, gazing into the distance. It was a cold, sunny afternoon, the frost still lying on the shady side of the field, and Nutter's breath rose about him like smoke. I stood and watched him for a while, too nervous to approach, until he slowly turned and saw me. He didn't walk off, but slouched against the fence with his thumbs tucked into his belt loops, squinting into the sunlight.

'Why aren't you in church?' he asked with a sneer.

'Why aren't you?' I replied, boldly.

'Man,' he said (he was the first person I'd ever heard talk this way), 'That's for squares.' He stared at me for a long time and I coolly stared back, wondering what it was he put on his hair to make it so shiny. Finally he laughed, placed an arm round my shoulder and started walking me round the playing field.

For the rest of the afternoon, Nutter quizzed me about every aspect of my life. He wanted to know all about my relationship with my parents, particularly with my father; he wanted every detail of the famous hair-dye episode (a local legend that hadn't even passed him by); he demanded a list of exactly which singers and films I liked. It was on this point that we disagreed, and we hotly debated the relative merits of Marilyn Monroe (this was the year of *Bus Stop*) and the recently dead James Dean, whom Nutter idolized and resembled. I had never seen a James Dean film, but promised that I would catch *Rebel Without a Cause*, then playing at the Odeon, by the following Monday.

Much depended on my reaction. James Dean, according to Nutter, was the spokesman for our generation, the first person to articulate the failure of our parents to create a world fit for their children to live in. What fascinated me more was the relationship between Dean, Natalie Wood and Sal Mineo. When I reported to Nutter on Monday afternoon he was pleased with my review and encouraged me to assume the role of the Sal Mineo sidekick, although I had naturally envisaged myself as Natalie. It was enough; I was accepted as Nutter's best (and only) friend. During the cross-country run that afternoon, we took a short cut through the woods and stopped in a circle of bushes to smoke a cigarette (his mother gave him a tobacco allowance) and rehearse lines from the film. At last I had found a leading man.

From my parents' point of view, I couldn't have made a worse friend if I'd tried. They had never liked Tina, whom my father described as 'a sad case', but at least she could be passed off as a girlfriend. Nutter was completely beyond the pale. They disapproved of his mother, who, as a divorcee, would never be invited to their drinks parties. They disapproved of Nutter's greased-up hair, and they reserved special scorn for his Northern accent. On the one occasion when he was invited to our house for tea, he sat silent throughout the meal while my parents made prying enquiries about the state of his family life, which I fended off as best I could. As soon as we had polished off our tinned mixed fruit, Nutter and I dashed upstairs to my bedroom and leafed through my stash of movie magazines and shared a cigarette leaning out of the window, blowing the smoke into the garden.

I never asked him back. By the age of twelve, I was ashamed of my parents. Nutter's house was Liberty Hall by comparison, and it was during one of my first visits that he solemnly announced that he was going to 'initiate me'. He crouched in front of the record player, opened the doors of a small wooden cabinet and brought out a stack of 78s. Removing one of them from its sleeve, he placed it reverently on the turntable. For the first time in my life, I heard the music of Elvis Presley.

I can't remember exactly what that first record was. Nutter insisted that it was 'Heartbreak Hotel', but I'm convinced it was 'Love Me Tender'. He watched me like a hawk for the two or three minutes' duration. When the song ended and I was about to speak, he silenced me with a gesture and replaced the record. Song followed song until I had heard the entire Presley output to date – seven or eight songs. I knew that I was hearing the sound of the future. Nutter was one of the first people in Britain to own Elvis's records; he was one of the pioneers who brought rock & roll across the Atlantic. For me, it was the beginning of a revolution.

I found a mail order outlet advertised in one of his fan magazines and regularly invested my pocket money in the new seven-inch singles that were gradually replacing the 78. During our regular trysts in the school playground I would present Nutter with the latest batch of records – titles by Eddie Cochran, Gene Vincent and Buddy Holly which he grudgingly accepted and eventually came to expect. Soon we were the greatest authorities on rock & roll music in the United Kingdom.

But there were other interests that were demanding my time. At the end of the first year, all the boys had to choose a Friday afternoon 'recreational' activity – extra football, scouts or the cadet force, who paraded in military uniforms up and down the playground and were occasionally bussed out to a rifle range. I had no interest in football, and as for the scouts and the cadets, I had no intention of making a fool of myself in a uniform or being shot at by my schoolmates. The alternatives, reluctantly offered, were three hours of 'private study' (sitting supervised in a room with the school's asthmatics, myopics and overweight) or the new, burgeoning drama society, run by magnetic English teacher Mr Phillips. This was the obvious choice for me, but there was a problem: joining the drama group was tantamount to standing up in front of the whole school and announcing that you were a 'pouf'. There was also my parents' reaction to consider; ever since my stage début at the age of three my father had done everything possible to quash my dramatic inclinations.

Nutter was the only one whose good opinion I craved. He would have opted for football; he loved the game and could have captained the school team. Unfortunately, his unpopularity meant that he and I were always the last to be chosen for any sporting activity. With a little gentle persuasion, I convinced him that acting was a viable alternative to football. Was not his hero James Dean a serious student of theatre? Was not Marlon Brando a worthy role model for a would-be rock & roll star? Finally (the clincher) was not Elvis himself pursuing a parallel career as a film star? When Nutter announced his decision to join me in the theatre, shock waves reverberated around the school – and the prestige of the drama group was considerably increased. We were joined by a few other creative students, and by the end of the summer we were keenly looking forward to our first rehearsals.

Let me introduce my drama teacher, Mr Phillips, a man who was to have such a profound influence on my life – not all good. He was a senior member of staff, respected by colleagues and feared by students, a brilliant pedagogue who laboured tirelessly to instil a love of poetry into the thick heads of boys who regarded the subject of English as slightly cissy. Bernard Phillips – or 'Phyllis' behind his back – was a gentleman of the old school, elegant, witty, urbane and well dressed, a youthful sixty-year-old with long, manicured fingers, neatly dressed white hair and pale blue eyes which gazed witheringly over a pair of gold-framed lunettes. Rumours abounded that Phyllis was 'queer', that he seduced students in his flat and was interested in the drama group only as a means of getting his hands on more boys. It was the typical reaction of the philistine English male confronted with something beautiful and high-minded – a reaction that I myself had been provoking since my first date with Mr Peroxide. If Mr Phillips was privately homosexual, he certainly never allowed his tastes to influence his dealings with students. In my eyes, he was the epitome of refinement and intellectual grandeur which I, at the age of twelve, could never hope to attain. But I set myself the task of learning everything I could from that wise, silver head.

The play that Mr Phillips announced as our first production was an ambitious choice: Shakespeare's *Antony and Cleopatra*. I knew nothing of the play. The Elizabeth Taylor version was a long way off, and nothing in my education had acquainted me with Roman history or the works of our greatest poet. But from the moment we were issued with our pocket-sized 'acting editions' (heavily edited so as not to offend the tastes of the times) I knew that I had formed a special new relationship. Nothing has ever stirred me as much as Cleopatra's speech from Act One: 'Eternity was in our lips and eyes/ Bliss in our brows' bent, none our parts so poor/ But was a race of heaven.' The moment I saw those words, I was determined to have the role.

Mr Phillips's original plan had been to produce *Antony and Cleopatra* with girls from our 'sister school' in the female roles. But he was easily persuaded otherwise. At the first audition, I insisted on reading not for the role of Caesar (which he had offered me) but for gipsy queen herself. When he heard my rendition of 'Ram thou thy fruitful tidings in mine ears/ That long time have been barren' I could see that the battle was won. Yet still he dithered; decisiveness was not one of our director's strong points. I was prepared. I knew from a brief scan of the introduction that, in Shakespeare's time, the female roles would have been taken by boy actors. Who were we, I argued, to stand in the way of tradition? Phyllis immediately announced that our production of *Antony and Cleopatra* would be 'historically correct'.

I could only play the part of Cleopatra with the right Antony opposite me – and nobody would do but Nutter. Further down the list a few concessions were made to the original notion of co-ed casting: the parts of Octavia, Iras and Charmian were given to girls. This didn't trouble me; the main point had been conceded. Perhaps I would have put up more of a fight had I known that, way down the *dramatis personae*, lurked the asp who would bite me.

From the moment I began to rehearse the role of Shakespeare's greatest queen, I knew that destiny had plucked me out for a career in the theatre. I threw myself into the production body and soul, and even took a perverse pride in the fact that my playground nickname had changed from 'Baby' Young to 'Queen' Young. My appearance assisted me: I still looked younger than my years while others were falling prey to the curse of acne and greasy hair. Mr Phillips was generous in his praise, and even Nutter admitted that it wasn't too difficult to imagine me in the role of the 'triple turn'd whore' to whom he, as Antony, would lose empire and life.

This was to be no ordinary schoolboy mangling of Shakespeare. Mr Phillips summoned up the spirit of 'old Nile' with every resource that our small theatre (a sparsely refurbished old gymnasium) had to offer. The school orchestra was pressed into service, yards of sheeting were painted by conscripts in the art block to resemble the exotic hangings of the Egyptian court and bedchamber, while our wardrobe ransacked the local fancy dress shop for gleaming armour, swords and togas. My costumes were hand-stitched by Phyllis himself: diaphanous creations draped around my shoulders and hips, leaving my midriff bare. Nutter started referring to me as 'Little Sheba'.

An entire term was devoted to rehearsals. While the rest of the cast were drilled to be word perfect, Nutter and I were gently coaxed and nurtured in hour upon hour of after-school workshops. 'You must make the audience forget that you're adolescent boys,' insisted Phyllis. 'For two hours, they must believe that you are the greatest lovers in the history of the world.' This made Nutter uneasy, and finally, after an evening in which Phyllis coached me in the art of straddling Nutter's supine form after one of the many banquet scenes, he stormed out muttering inaudible oaths and was not seen for the rest of the week. It took a larger-than-usual packet of 45s to persuade him to return.

Finally I had to let my parents in on the secret. They'd accepted without question that my evenings were spent studying, at the cinema or at friends' houses, but as rehearsals progressed, I was sure that even my father would admire my performance as Cleopatra. Surely Shakespeare was one of the great English traditions that he'd fought to preserve?

One night after dinner I presented my parents with two tickets for the opening night of the show. 'What's this?' asked Dad, grimly. I explained that it was a surprise, that I'd been 'discovered' and was about to launch myself on my chosen career. The reaction was not enthusiastic. The theatre, to them, was little better than embracing a life of crime. They sat tight-lipped while I outlined my plans for the future.

Nothing they could say or do, short of actually locking me in my room, was going to stop me. Eventually, they were persuaded to accept my acting career – although they would never encourage it. Mr Phillips himself intervened on my behalf at a parents' evening, gently persuading Mr and Mrs Young that they had an exceptionally talented son who would surely bring them fame and glory, and considerable amounts of money.

Finally, the big night arrived. Rumours – the very best sort of pre-publicity – were circulating that various of the performers would appear nude, that there were sex scenes, that Nutter and I would kiss on stage. None of it was true (Phyllis would have been incapable of anything so dangerous) but it ensured a complete sell-out, and the promise of an extra performance if demand continued.

The dress rehearsal was a disaster. Phyllis reassured us all that this was a good omen for the first night, but as I sank to my death amidst chaos and confusion (Nutter had once again stormed out, objecting this time to my over-zealous attempts to revive him during the 'I am dying, Egypt, dying' speech) I wondered whether anything could really justify this much suffering. It was a question I was to ask myself many times in the future – and the answer always has to be yes, as long as the public wants you.

Ten minutes before curtain up, Nutter and I stood backstage surveying the audience through a chink in the wings. There were my parents, in the front row. Mrs Cole, Nutter's mother, had stayed away. And ranged from side to side of the auditorium were our hateful school chums, slavering with prurient adolescent curiosity. Nutter was morose, resigned to the indignity he was about to undergo – he had long since decided that the stage was not a fit place, even if sanctioned by the likes of James Dean and Marlon Brando. 'Please,' I whispered, 'do this for me. I'll never ask anything of you again.'

'Okay, Little Sheba,' he replied, and wandered off to prepare for his entrance.

The performance itself went by in a blur. I've always found that during my greatest stage successes, I'm scarcely aware of what's going on around me, possessed by something greater than myself.

I remember my first entrance, dressed in a bikini with a gold cloak slung over my shoulders and gold sandals, surprising my Antony as he relaxed in the traditional Roman bath (Nutter's costume in this scene consisted of a loin cloth and several coats of baby oil which I had agreed to apply when he complained that Phyllis's hands shook too much). I heard a gasp from the audience, looked down to see my parents' white faces, then remembered the cardinal rule that Phyllis had impressed upon us – never look at the audience. I fixed my gaze on the school clock above their heads, took a deep breath: 'If it be love indeed, tell me how much . . .'

The audience was quiet – respectful of the words of Shakespeare, astonished by the artistry with which a group of simple schoolboys had interpreted the immortal lines. But as scene followed scene I was dimly aware of a restlessness spreading throughout the hall. At the end of Act One, as I writhed on the sofa in a green sheath dress and gold turban intoning 'Oh happy horse, to bear the weight of Antony', I distinctly heard coughs and sniggers from certain sections of the audience. I glanced down to where Mr Phillips sat in the prompt position with the orchestra, but he merely beamed and signalled encouragement. It was enough, and I continued to writhe.

In Act Two disaster struck. Phyllis had designed a beautiful balletic interlude, when, to the orchestra's scraping and blowing, we enacted the famous erotic speech of Cleopatra in which she recalls how 'I drunk him to his bed/ Then put my tires and mantles on him, whilst/ I wore his sword Philippan.' These lines had been cut from our schools' version, but Mr Phillips had reinstated them as a series of tableaux in which Antony and I performed a *pas de deux* as we exchanged clothes. There was nothing remotely shocking about it – the whole dance was performed behind a gauze that was waved by the Roman soldiers to suggest a dream – and it was only due to a wardrobe misunderstanding that I was wearing nothing under my costume. As I shimmied out of my dress and reached to accept the toga from Antony (which was intended to preserve my modesty) I found nothing was on offer, and was left standing in only my high-heeled gold sandals. I turned to see Nutter with his costume rucked up between his legs in grave danger of pulling his Y-fronts down, and suddenly realized, from a chilly draught blowing from the wings, that I was in the nude.

All hell broke loose. With a curse, my father jumped to his feet and dragged my mother out of the hall. I grasped the gauze from one of the soldiers, created an outfit for myself and attempted to continue the scene, but it was too late. Shrieks of laughter, whistles and cries rendered the music inaudible. The curtain began to close, operated, as I saw from the corner of my eye, by the headmaster. I struggled to make the front of the stage only to be pushed into the wings by brute force. And where was my leading man? He had disappeared, leaving his toga and his sword Philippan in a heap on the ground. I stormed back to the dressing room only to be confronted by the sight of Nutter, my Mark Antony, locked in a clumsy embrace with the treacherous fourth-form girl who had foolishly been given the role of Octavia. Caesar's virgin sister indeed! She stood crushed against the wall with her hand rammed down Nutter's pants and her tongue down his throat.

This was the final straw. Robbed of my greatest role, held to ridicule by a crowd of fools and now betrayed by my best friend, I burst into tears and rushed from the building, straight into the arms of Mr Phillips. Frightened and confused as I was, I dared not go home to face my parents; my father, I told Mr Phillips, was a violent man and would almost certainly beat me, or him, if we were to confront him after what he had just seen. Poor Mr Phillips was understandably distraught; faced with a hostile public, he didn't have the courage to stick up for what he believed was right and beautiful. And so the kind old man took me back to his flat and put me to bed. When I awoke in the morning, my school uniform (retrieved by Phyllis from the dressing room) lay neatly folded beside me. The length of chiffon in which I had been wrapped when I fell into Mr Phillips's arms was nowhere to be seen. I left before he awoke and made my own way home, let myself in before the house was stirring and went to bed. I was too ill to return to school before the end of term.

My parents' response was swift and barbaric. I was forbidden from any further theatrical 'adventures', threatened with everything from the juvenile courts to electric shock treatment and warned that any involvement with Mr Phillips or Nutter would be very severely punished. 'If you don't grow up and start behaving like a man,' said my father, 'you won't be my son any more. Do you understand?' I understood. He was ready to throw me out on the streets.

Everything after Cleopatra was a let-down. In retrospect I recognize that our production was groundbreaking: 'underground' theatre long before such a thing existed. But at the time I felt frustrated, even defeated. I started to keep a diary. These volumes capture the bleak depression that settled on me as the New Year began.

Friday 12 January: Compulsory football all afternoon. Drama group 'suspended', everyone blames me. Nutter ignores me, actually enjoys the game, scores twice. Suddenly he's everyone's friend.

Saturday 13 January: Nothing on at pictures, only stupid war films. Went to town hoping to see N. Saw Gill (the dreaded Octavia) and her friends hanging around outside the Golden Egg. They laughed at me but I ignored them. Got caught nicking H&E from Smiths. Manager took me into office, threatened police, let me go when I cried.

Sunday 21 January: Stayed in bed all day. Mum and Dad don't care. So bored.

Wednesday 7 February: Talked to Nutter during lunch break. He's finished with Gill, he says (she doesn't know yet, ha ha). Told him I had some records for him, he was pleased. Went to Boots and nicked Little Richard LP, will give it to him soon (if he deserves it).

Monday 19 February: Half term at last. Went round to N's house, his mother out. Gave him Little Richard LP, he said I was his best friend after all and he blames Phyllis for trying to turn us both queer. I said our friendship was clean and pure, reminded him of Sal Mineo. Smoked cigarettes. It rained all day.

Tuesday 5 March: Saw N after school walking down road with Gill's friend Jane. Holding hands. How dare she?

Wednesday 6 March: Off school. Too sick to get out of bed. Made myself puke, Mum wanted to send for doctor, I said no doctor could help me.

Friday 12 April: At last! Drama group meets again for first time in months. Phyllis 'under strict supervision' from headmaster, he warns me – choice of plays not his, rehearsals to be monitored by prefects. Ph. says it's like Nazi Germany, promises me lead role in all productions.

Thursday 18 April: Nutter refuses to join drama group. Says he's 'too busy' to get involved, which means he's too busy seeing Jane. How dare she hold him back?

Friday 26 April: First rehearsal for *Journey's End*, R. C. Sherriff, stupid play about war, head's choice of course. No women in it at all. Still, my part quite good, Phyllis says uniforms will look nice. Haven't told Mum and Dad.

Saturday 4 May: Big rehearsal all morning for *JE*. Told Mum and Dad I was in special detention for breaking a window during a football game. Dad seemed quite pleased. Rehearsal went well. Phyllis took me for lunch at Golden Egg afterwards, told me I was the most talented young actor of my generation.

Thursday 16 May: Nutter hasn't been at school all this week. Mrs Cole came in to see headmaster today. N's in trouble for playing truant. Went to see him after school, he says he's finished with Jane because she 'wouldn't', although by the look of her I'd say she already has. It's his birthday soon, don't know what to get him.

Monday 3 June: One month exactly before first night of *Journey's End*. Extra rehearsal tonight for my big speech at Phyllis's house. Goes well, he says I'm developing splendidly. Gives me a glass of sherry! Home late. Told Mum and Dad I'd been out with 'the gang' drinking coffee. Dad smelt alcohol on my breath, called me 'a terror' and laughed. Nutter's birthday tomorrow.

Tuesday 4 June: N's birthday (fifteen). Went round to his house after school and gave him bottle of whisky I'd 'borrowed' from Dad's cupboard. N very pleased, gave me some. His mum gave him a guitar! He tried out Elvis poses in bedroom.

Monday 1 July: Final week of rehearsals. Costumes came today, they're great. I have two, formal uniform with puttees, epaulettes, etc., and nightshirt for hospital scene. Phyllis practised tying bandages on me today.

Wednesday 3 July: First night!!! Headmaster came to dress rehearsal last night, no changes. Show went well. Nutter didn't come. Phyllis very pleased, gave me a lift home afterwards, dropped me off at end of road. Long talk in car before I got out. Told Mum and Dad I'd been out with Gill (joke). They believed me. Asked Dad for advice on where to take girls on dates.

Friday 5 July: Last night of *Journey's End*. Hospital scene very good tonight, saw girls crying in audience. Phyllis crying too afterwards, wanted to take me back to flat for 'nightcap'. I said no. Head and cronies came backstage to compliment us. Nutter still didn't come, too busy practising guitar he says, doesn't want to see me 'playing at soldiers'.

Friday 19 July: Last day of term. Phyllis embarrassing in class, hands out prizes to all best pupils (I get three of the five prizes). Nutter didn't turn up again today. Wasn't at home either. Left him a note.

Sunday 4 August: Nutter says YES! At last! Can't wait!

What Nutter had finally agreed to, after weeks of pestering, was my long-cherished plan for a camping and cycling holiday. I'd secured my parents' permission by telling them that Nutter and I were taking Gill and Jane with us 'in separate tents, of course' (they didn't believe that bit and were convinced that we were going away for a week of sexual intercourse). What finally persuaded Nutter to agree was my suggestion that he could cycle with his guitar slung over his back, that we could sit around the camp fire every night drinking and singing songs just like Woody Guthrie (Nutter's latest hero).

One Saturday afternoon in early August we set off on our bikes, Nutter with his beloved guitar and several panniers stuffed full of booze, me with the tent packed on my back and the rest of the provisions, clothes, penknives and torches overflowing from my saddle bag. It had been my intention to cycle as far as Dorset and back, stopping off at the end of every day's ride in a suitable site where we'd pitch the tent, strip wash, cook a meal and sit under the stars. In fact, we never got further than a field outside Aldershot which we shared with a couple of elderly horses. We stopped there on the first night and Nutter immediately started drinking, leaving me to struggle with the tent and prepare the food (which we ate straight from the tin). By nine o'clock, Nutter was incoherently drunk, strumming tunelessly before collapsing unconscious in the grass, half a bottle of whisky clutched in his hand with which he had been attempting to play slide guitar in between swigs.

I managed to drag him bodily inside the tent. As he lay there snoring, the tent became unbearably stuffy with the smell of alcohol and adolescent male bodies. I couldn't sleep. Nutter, however, was as good as dead. My dream of long, intellectual conversations under canvas evaporated. I lay there with the torch trained on Nutter's sleeping form, contemplating the troubled upbringing that had turned a talented teenager into a self-destructive, reckless alcoholic. Finally, with the torch balanced carefully on my rucksack, I undressed him and put him inside the sleeping bag.

The next morning I awoke to the sound of rain drumming down on the canvas. I was alone in the tent; Nutter was nowhere to be seen, and his clothes had gone with him. To my relief, his guitar still lay propped against the side of the tent – he couldn't be far. I scrambled outside and lit the tiny primus stove, boiled a billy can of water and brewed up the coffee, the smell of which brought the wanderer back to the hearth. He accepted the coffee, drank it in hunched silence with his back to me, silent except for the occasional grunt in response to my questions. Finally he turned round, looked me in the eye and said, 'What actually happened last night?' I was at a loss for an answer. What did he think happened last night? 'I don't remember going to bed,' he said, and added, more pointedly, 'and I don't remember taking my clothes off.' I just shrugged and told him I'd called it a day long before he'd finished drinking and playing his guitar, that I'd been fast asleep when he'd finally come to bed.

He was suspicious and grumpy for the rest of the day, refusing to carry on with our tour, preferring to wander the perimeters of the field with his guitar. By lunchtime I found him happily playing a tune to the two old horses, who were munching grass and eyeing him with a detached interest. He'd cheered up enough to share my spam sandwiches, but turned down my suggestion that we should search for a stream in which to bathe.

Nutter was never the same with me after that night. He grew sullen and wary, reading into my most innocent gesture some hidden meaning. At the time I was bewildered and hurt; with the benefit of hindsight I realize what he was afraid of. Nutter was more sexually precocious than me – I believe he'd had his first experience before he left the North, and had continued with his subsequent dates. It was Nutter, too, who had instructed me in the schoolboy art of self-abuse, and insisted on a full report as soon as I had achieved my first 'wank'. Now, it seemed, he was one step ahead of me again. He suspected – and I can now see why – that I harboured homosexual longings for him. I can't blame him. The intense erotic climate of *Antony and Cleopatra*, the long afternoons listening to Elvis and sharing cigarettes, and now the suspicion that I had undressed him as he lay sleeping – it all added up to a persuasive case against me.

If anybody was guilty of attempted seduction that summer, it was Nutter. After a wasted day in which he'd done nothing but mooch around the field with his guitar and ever-present bottle, we finally went to bed for our second night under canvas. As I lay in my sleeping bag, Nutter undressed in front of me then stretched out naked, daring me to make the first move. Nothing happened, but from then on I knew that there was more to our relationship than simple friendship. The next morning he was even worse, and moodily announced that the holiday was 'doing him in' and he was returning home. I had no choice but to pack up and follow him. We didn't see each other for the rest of the summer.

Rejected by my best friend, I faced the prospect of a new term without enthusiasm. I was vulnerable and lonely, isolated from my parents and full of strange new feelings. There was only one person who was willing to listen to me – the ever-present Mr Phillips. Perhaps he wasn't the best influence on an impressionable young man, but he was my only refuge, and I ran to him. Of course, there was another play to rehearse, and another, and another. For the rest of my time at school, I was only truly alive when I was on stage. Emboldened by the success of *Journey's End* and once again in the head's good books, Phyllis embarked on ever more audacious productions. And I was always the hero: Doctor Faustus in Marlowe's masterpiece, Nicky in Noël Coward's *The Vortex* ('Dear Noël was so interested to hear about your performance,' Phyllis told me – he had been in correspondence with 'the Master' for many years).

My mother and father remained in complete ignorance of my stage career, a situation I was happy to encourage. They believed that I was past my 'difficult' stage and now busy dating girls at every available opportunity. True, I never brought any of these girls home ('Don't suppose they're the type you'd want your mum to meet,' said Dad) but that bothered nobody. At the age of sixteen, I was leading a double life – something that most of my contemporaries would not begin to do until their twenties.

Phyllis saved me from going completely off the rails. Had it not been for the discipline of learning lines and rehearsals, I would have been out looking for trouble, like Nutter. But Phyllis was a tyrant, and instilled in me a belief in the necessity of hard work and diligence. Useful lessons to learn! And, as I would later find, rare enough in show business. So, night after night, I went up to Phyllis's flat to be coached through my lines, and to learn – about art, about theatre, about films I had never heard of during my Saturday afternoon pilgrimages to the Odeon. Together we read texts that were forbidden in the school library: Oscar Wilde's *Ballad of Reading Gaol* was the first I remember, followed by Shakespeare's Sonnets, *Lady Chatterley's Lover* and the novels of Genet, from which Phyllis had me read to improve my French. Finally he announced that I was ready to appear in his most ambitious production to date, the one that would bring us to the attention of the theatre world, a play by his hero Jean Cocteau. Phyllis was planning the first schools' production of *Orphée*.

To understand this daring scheme, it's important to realize that by the age of sixteen I was physically and mentally more mature than the piping child who had 'boyed the greatness' of Cleopatra. I was a young man, with (as Phyllis put it) a ballet dancer's physique and the perfect skin that I was so fortunate to keep from childhood. The role of Orpheus, the man-god, the artist with whom Death herself falls in love, was simply waiting for me. But was I, a schoolboy amateur, ready for this greatest of modern roles? Phyllis conceived the production as a dance drama, 'total theatre', both physically and intellectually demanding. I naturally assumed that the star part was mine – but Phyllis, to my astonishment, insisted on an audition.

At first I was crushed. Was anyone else capable of playing the role? Had Phyllis nurtured another protégé? He made me do my homework, studying Cocteau's graphic work in a rare copy of *Le Livre Blanc* with which he presented me, poring over stills of the film version of *Orphée* starring Jean Marais. I began to understand just how demanding the role would be.

The night of the audition arrived. I had been preparing for days, learning my speech off by heart, committing to memory the exact details of Cocteau's drawings which I planned to recreate in *tableaux vivants*. I reported to Phyllis's flat determined not to leave until I had secured the part. Phyllis poured two large whiskies and told me to prepare myself while he changed out of his school tweeds and into his pyjamas and dressing gown (all silk).

I've never had any problem with auditions. I've given some of my best performances for an audience of one, focusing all my energy on the producer who's casting me. But I've never given myself so completely as I gave myself to Mr Phillips that evening – I'd never known before what it was to need a role as badly as I needed Orpheus. I strode into the spotlight and began my speech, strumming an imaginary lyre as I did so. My French accent was appalling – it was many years before I became fully bilingual – but what I lacked in technique I made up for in passion. By the end, as I pleaded for the return of Eurydice, Phyllis had tears in his eyes.

But I had only just begun. Now came the dance drama, a style for which I've always had a natural aptitude. Without music I began to move, pouring every nuance of my troubled sixteen-year-old self into a spontaneous display of rhythmic athleticism. Inspired by the Cocteau drawings with which I was so familiar – and reliving another private performance many years ago – I began to take off my clothes. First my blazer, then my school tie, my shirt, my shoes and socks, my grey flannel trousers and finally my pants. I had almost forgotten that there was anyone watching me as I went into the last, frenzied movements of my dance, finishing off prostrate on the floor.

I was roused from my artistic euphoria by a slight dig from a slippered toe against my ribs. Phyllis stood up, extended a hand and helped me to my feet. It was the only physical contact there had been between us. 'Dear boy, you are my Orpheus,' he said in a tremulous voice as I dressed. 'Perhaps you had better leave.

I have ... work to do.' I ran home and confided to my diary:

Wednesday 5 February: Good night with P. Got Orpheus and present of £10. Best yet.

After this sensational start, rehearsals for *Orphée* were an austere business. It was a small cast, with few set pieces and little to distract from the central focus – me. I knew this would be my last school performance, and I wanted to give them something to remember. Night after night in my bedroom I rehearsed in whispers, creeping around the room, finally falling into bed exhausted but more often unable to sleep, sitting at the window smoking, thinking about Nutter. He had taken to full-time truancy since the summer holiday. I'd see him occasionally hanging around the town with one of his girls, smoking and flirting. Sometimes he'd acknowledge me, but more usually he'd just carry on with his business, knowing that I was watching him. During that last year at school, I almost began to hate him.

With the pressure of rehearsals and the misery of not seeing Nutter, I became confused and detached. Mr Phillips was my one contact with reality, constantly praising me and presenting me with gifts. But I felt as if I was going mad. I started shoplifting, stealing ridiculous things – pencils, rulers, batteries, sweets – coming to my senses with a stash of useless swag in my coat pockets which I would immediately ditch in the nearest bin. As spring turned to summer I was oppressed by a sense of impending disaster. I drank whenever I could – small amounts, but enough.

The end of term came at last, and with it the twin climaxes of the school year: sports day and the Leavers' Festival, of which our production of *Orphée* was the centrepiece. Nutter had returned to the fold to train for the sports, competing in the long-distance events (all those hours chasing girls around town had obviously kept him in trim), and was happy to let me come running with him (I needed all my stamina for the play). I had never known him so happy and talkative, enthusing about music and how good he was getting at the guitar, his plans to move to London and get a record deal. I felt that we had unfinished business. We had to talk, and I knew how to make him.

I waited for the hottest day of the year. It was the Saturday before term ended; sports day was on the Tuesday. I called round at Nutter's house by prior arrangement to take him out training; he would run, I would cycle alongside him. I'd brought water, chocolate, towels – and, unbeknown to Nutter, a bottle of brandy (a gift from Phyllis). We started from his house at a steady pace and reached the towpath that ran out of town alongside the canal. It was an appalling day to be running: there were clouds of flies, the canal stank and the heat was unbearable. I was comfortable enough on my bike, but Nutter was fading fast. 'I need a rest,' he announced after half an hour's solid running, but I was merciless. 'Not yet. You can rest at the next bridge! Come on, you can do it!' The next bridge was a good ten minutes' run away, well out of town where the canal cut a course through the scrubbily wooded fields.

When we finally reached our resting place, Nutter was purple-faced and soaked with perspiration. 'Well done!' I shouted, all cheerful encouragement as he sank to the ground. 'You deserve a drink!' He thought I meant water, of course.

'If bloody only,' he groaned, lying prone as I parked my bike against the tree. 'I could kill for a drink.'

'You don't need to do that,' I replied, producing the brandy from my saddle bag like a rabbit out of a hat. He sat up and laughed, took the bottle and drank deeply, forgetting that it's not a good idea to slake your thirst with spirits after a five-mile run. It hit him quick and hard, just as I knew it would. Now was the time for our talk.

'How's your latest flame?' I asked in a matey tone.

'She's great, yeah,' he replied, already slurring.

'She's really sexy.'

'You reckon?'

'Oh yes. Best-looking girl in her year. Everyone says so. You're a very lucky man.'

'I wish.'

'Everyone's jealous of you and her.'

'Really? Well they've got no reason to be. Give me that bottle again.'

'Keep it. Why, what's the problem.'

'She's frigid, isn't she?'

Somehow I'd seen this coming. Half the boys at school made the same complaint; by their account, uncooperative girls were either frigid or lesbians.

'What do you mean?'

'She won't, you know. I ought to just make her.'

'That's right.'

'I'd show her.'

It was the moment I'd been waiting for. It had been easier than I'd expected. I reached out for the brandy.

'Here, give me a swig.'

As I grasped the bottle, Nutter grabbed my hand. It was then that I allowed him to seduce me.

I remember my first sexual encounter as something beautiful – two young men, friends and comrades, fulfilling the unspoken love that had always existed between them. In the short term, however, the results were disastrous. After I'd led him back to his house and deposited him half-conscious, I heard nothing more from him.

But as I've found so many times, a door never closes without somewhere someone opening a window. And so it happened that, hot on the heels of my first great love, I embarked on a second, more mature relationship – with a woman.

I'm getting ahead of myself again. Before the summer holidays that officially liberated me from school, there was the final week of celebration. Sports day passed off without incident – only a slight disappointment that Nutter, a hot favourite in the 1500 metres, had once again failed to show up. And then it was my turn to be in the spotlight with the long awaited, for-one-night-only production of *Orphée*.

The headmaster had taken his eye off the ball at a very early stage in rehearsals. Never having heard of Jean Cocteau, he assumed that Mr Phillips's latest whim was to revive a dusty fragment of classical drama, a genre from which no danger could be anticipated. He'd sat in on our first read-through, dozing intermittently as I intoned Orpheus's bizarre fragments of poetry with as little expression as possible. When it was over he clapped his hands, muttered, 'Splendid, splendid,' and disappeared to the staff room. But, as he was to learn, words alone do not theatre make.

By the time Phyllis's advanced staging ideas had finished with *Orphée*, there was little trace left of the poetic niceties of Monsieur Cocteau. The curtain rose on a chorus of 'Death Angels', a selection of the football team's more robust members who had been drilled and bribed by Phyllis with surreptitious alcohol. They stood in line, their uniform leather jackets, caps, boots and white cotton jockstraps matching the Cocteauesque frieze that Phyllis had executed across the rear wall. Any reaction from the audience (parents, governors, local journalists and school-leavers) was drowned by the deafening chunk of *Götterdämmerung* blasting over the antiquated PA.

The Death Angels dispersed upstage to be succeeded by a secondary chorus of Maenads – six girls whom I had recruited from the Golden Egg – whose role consisted of running around the stage in a screaming frenzy then collapsing at the foot of a flight of stairs. It was down these stairs that I made my entrance, hoisted from the top of a concealed and very rickety stepladder by the unseen Mr Phillips. Wagner faded into silence as I processed down the steps, trailing a long white toga behind me, a lyre (of spray-painted plywood) clutched to my chest. There was total calm for a moment as the audience watched, spellbound.

Suddenly, with a scream, the Maenads arose and attacked,

fighting me to the floor (with more force than was strictly necessary) and symbolically ripping me to shreds – a preliminary re-enactment of the classical myth, said Phyllis. When the sated nymphs finally dispersed, I was revealed, naked save for a flesh-coloured pouch, covered in stage blood which had been applied during the ruck. I staggered downstage, my broken lyre hanging together by a few pitiful strings, before adopting a crucifixion pose as the Death Angels bore me off into the wings to be sponged down by Mr Phillips.

I never performed on that stage again. I could vaguely hear the shouts from the audience, the stamping of feet and scraping of chairs as people rushed for the exits. Phyllis, I think, had seen it coming, squeezed my hand and said, 'Looks like we've done it again, dear boy.' Those were his final words before the headmaster dragged him off, shouting insane threats about the police.

The dressing room and auditorium emptied as if by magic. What was this force that could terrify as well as delight? As I wandered around the empty school hall, I dimly perceived that the evening had been a triumph as well as a disaster, that sometimes it was the duty of the artist to shock as well as to entertain. It was my first experience of political theatre, a movement for which I would later become a figurehead.

Empty? So I thought. But I was not alone. Still sitting in the back row was a young woman – a girl – watching my every move. I strained to see her, this quiet creature who had witnessed my solitary meditations, but as I approached she made to flee the hall. 'Stop!' I commanded, still in character. She stopped. 'Come here!' She came, head bowed, a humble votary at the altar of art.

And she looked strangely familiar. 'Who are you, child?' I coaxed.

'Sue Cole. And I thought you were brilliant.' I bowed and bestowed a smile on her which, I noticed, made her blush.

'I will never set foot in this building again,' I announced, leading her by the hand as I made a valedictory tour of the theatre that had been my second home for so long, touching the curtains, the windows, the chairs in mute farewell. But all the while I was wondering 'Sue Cole? Sue Cole? Why is that name so familiar?' As I reached the stage and prepared to deliver an impromptu eulogy to my school days, I was struck dumb by the realization: she was Nutter's sister.

I had been dimly aware of another child around the house during the long afternoons that I spent with Nutter, a sort of shadow that he occasionally referred to as his sister. But beyond that I had no memory of her – this child, now nearly a woman. Nutter never spoke of her. But then I began to realize that she had been there all along – Sue peeping into the living room as we listened to Elvis, Sue squirreling away the empties so we wouldn't be discovered by Nutter's mum, Sue taking charge of Nutter when I brought him home drunk from our cross-country run. The more I thought about it, the more I realized that Sue had been Nutter's guardian angel, a small, luminous presence who watched over her brother and his friends, never pushing herself into the limelight, just quietly watching and loving.

It also occurred to me that, as Nutter had refused to speak to me on the phone, refused to answer the door when I rang, ignored all my letters and even left my gifts unacknowledged, that Sue could be the peacemaker, the bridge-builder.

There was silence between us as I stood on the stage looking into her upturned face, my speech suspended by a series of rapid, profound calculations. 'Please, go on talking,' said Sue. 'I could listen to you forever.' How had I been unaware of her beauty for so long? I jumped down from the stage, leaving the insanity of Phyllis and his infernal visions behind me, and descended feet-first to the real world of men and women. I took her hands in mine and, holding her gaze, asked her to go out with me.

I learned a lot from Sue that summer, not only about her brother – who, it seemed, was hastening his departure to London having got a girl pregnant. But also I learned about myself – the Mark that others saw. Unwillingly, Sue told me the terrible rumours that had gained currency around the town: that I was Mr Phillips's 'bum chum', that I was in love with Nutter and had tried to seduce him. They painted my mother as an alcoholic and my father as a pitiful bar prop who couldn't control his wife and son.

Well, I thought, I'll show them. Part of me wanted to leave, to turn my back on everyone and let them think what they wanted. But there was another part of me – the better part? – that was determined to make them eat their words. Besides, where else could I go? At least I still had a bed at my parents' house – although it hadn't been a home for many years.

So Sue and I began to go out together. She was a popular girl, with lots of friends who spent most of the summer holiday organizing parties and going to dances. And we went to every single one of them. We were always the first to start the dancing, the last to leave the floor when Sue would shyly suggest that we 'go somewhere' to kiss. Her passion surprised me, and also her mania for secrecy. Not for me the privacy of the bedroom or the alleyway – if we were lovers, let the world know!

After we had been going out for a week, I took Sue home to meet my parents. Her quiet charm won them over immediately; nothing was too much trouble. Strange how quickly they changed from the distant, troubled figures of my adolescence to warm, companionable adults offering lifts home and extra pocket money. My father was so eager to put the car at our disposal that soon I had him waiting for us from the moment we arrived at a party until the time we decided to leave. As the summer progressed, we stayed out later and later.

The welcome was not so cordial *chez* Cole. I was reluctant to visit, and finally Sue had to insist. Nutter was not at home, which came as no surprise. But evidence of his feckless existence was everywhere – the scattered record sleeves (among them the recent, unacknowledged gifts from me), the crushed clothes, the empty cigarette cartons. But never Nutter himself. Why was he avoiding me? Why, now that I had proved to everyone else that I was a normal, healthy teenager? What was it that he feared from me – or from himself?

Sue's agenda for our relationship was different from mine. I was shocked by the rapidity with which she changed from an innocent, blushing schoolgirl barely on the brink of womanhood to an irrational, clinging creature who watched my every move like a hawk. Her demands became ridiculous, rapacious. Although younger than me, she was as sexually precocious as her brother, expecting the physical side of our relationship to be consummated within a matter of weeks. Finally the ugly truth came out.

'Why won't you do it?' she asked, her face a mask of exasperation, as we broke from a long-held kiss during which she'd manoeuvred my hand to her breast.

'You're only fifteen,' I replied.

'So what?'

'I don't want to spoil you.'

'I want you to.'

'How can you know that?'

'All the girls have done it.'

I was shocked, although hardly surprised.

'And they say that if we don't do it soon it's because you're a . . . you know.'

So that was it. I was an experiment, a subject for discussion between Sue and her friends. Without further words, I left the house, pausing only to collect a few of the more expensive records I had lent to Nutter. Sue, Nutter, the whole clan of Coles, were out of my life.

But there was one final confrontation before my separation from that doomed family. I spoke with Nutter – briefly, without feeling – as we both sat on the platform of the local railway station weeks later, as summer gave way to the autumn of 1962. It was a month after the death of Marilyn Monroe – and with her passed my childhood. We were waiting for the same train to take us away – from our homes, from each other and from ourselves – to London. There was little left to say.

'What did you do to Sue?'

'Nothing.'

'She's been crying a lot.'

'Oh. Where are you going?'

'London. I'm sick of this place. I'm going to join a band.'

'What about your girlfriend and the . . .'

'None of your business.'

There was a pause. Then I asked 'Where will you stay?'

'Don't try to find me.'

'Don't flatter yourself.'

Another pause. 'What about you?'

'Oh, I have a place to go.' This was true. Only the previous week I had received a letter from Mr Phillips containing £30, an address and a set of keys, asking me to join him as a guest in his new home in the capital. He had left the school – or been asked to leave, depending who you believe – and was ready to embark on a theatrical career. And he wanted me by his side.

The train rolled into the station as Nutter and I parted in silence. He walked down the platform to find a seat in a second-class smoker, lugging his guitar behind him. I stepped aboard first-class and watched my childhood slip quietly away down the tracks.

CHAPTER TWO

I left home with nothing but my stage experience, and arrived in a city poised on the brink of revolution. As yet, London hadn't begun to swing; it needed only the catalyst that would set the sixties in motion and make it the centre of the world.

I had no academic qualifications, no 'CV', no means of earning money, but not for one moment did I think of turning back. Not even as I stood on the platform at Waterloo, surrounded by strangers, vainly searching for one last glimpse of Nutter. There was nothing for me at home, and ahead of me – everything.

Luckily, I wasn't friendless in the big city, and pulled from my pocket a letter from Phyllis containing detailed directions to his house. Unsure of my way but trusting, I picked out a well-dressed gentleman and asked him the way to an address in SE1. He took me by the arm, led me to a café and bought me coffee, explaining my route and asking all about my new life and prospects. 'If you should wander from the path, lad,' he said, producing a card from his car coat, 'feel free to give me a call.' Londoners were friendlier than I had feared.

Conscious of the need to save money, and delighting in the warm late summer sunshine, I decided to make my way on foot. Leaving the shadow of the great glass-roofed terminus, I emerged on to Waterloo Road, a blur of double-decker buses, black cabs and sports cars, alive with the cries of the stallholders, who brought colour to dusty arches. And there before my eyes was the Old Vic Theatre, like a great temple from antiquity. Would I one day walk that stage with Olivier, Gielgud? I hurried past.

As I neared my new home, the colours and sights of Waterloo receded and I stepped back into the nineteenth century, where blackened Victorian houses stood crazily between huge, rubble-filled craters, the unhealed wounds of the War. Where once were church spires and pleasure gardens now towered huge cranes, slowly, painfully rebuilding a shattered community. Between rows of tiny shops I finally found my street, a narrow lane of ancient terraces in the heart of the Elephant and Castle.

Timid souls might have been dismayed by that dingy street and the strange, lost old folk who shuffled along the pavements. But not me. I took a deep breath of sooty air, marched up to the front door and rang. A net curtain dropped behind the grimy window, and within seconds Phyllis was hustling me indoors like a mother hen.

The flat – or 'maisonette' as I soon learned to call it – was smart and compact, if less *de luxe* than Phyllis's previous accommodation. His furniture (fine old pieces, many valuable) was ingeniously arranged in the smaller space, the highly polished rosewood and mahogany glowing with a deeper lustre for its plainer setting. He gave me the grand tour: a small bedroom where the vast antique bedstead took up most of the floorspace; a living room that housed a leather suite and copious books, the walls crammed with Phyllis's priceless collection of prints; the 'galley' kitchen (how well I would soon know that room!) and spartan bathroom; and finally, the small back yard that Phyllis promised would be 'a little bower of bliss' within a year. 'Now,' he said, hanging my coat and taking my small bag of belongings, 'you must make yourself completely at home.'

The first thing that struck me was the bed dilemma: there was only one. Of course Phyllis didn't expect me to sleep with him, but as yet I was unacquainted with the great traditions of 'bedsitland'. 'I could do with a nap,' I said, stretching and yawning – that would give me an immediate answer.

'Oh, dear boy, why didn't you say?' said Phyllis. 'I'll make up your bed on the sofa at once. Unless of course you'd prefer . . .' I understood immediately, and opted for the sofa (not forgetting that the offer of the bed remained open, if unspoken, should the need arise).

Phyllis tucked me into my sleeping bag and sat on the edge of the sofa, sharing a glass of whisky and massaging my tired feet. Just as I had slipped into a deep, peaceful sleep, I was jolted awake by a crash and an oath that seemed to come from inches above my head. Shaking myself into full consciousness, I realized that the noise (now mawkish song) came from the street. The disadvantages of the sleeping arrangements were about to become horribly clear to me. The window of my basement bedsit looked out on to a tiny area, separated by a few railings from the street where the night traffic of drunks and lost souls was even heavier than in the daytime. Within a few days, I had become accustomed to the local sounds – the sirens and pneumatic drills that formed an urban dawn chorus had little power to wake me. But there were nights when my nerves were bad, when I crept from my room to share the peace and warmth of Phyllis's bed. There I slept largely undisturbed. But my main memory of those first months in London is one of constant fatigue.

Not only was I sleeping badly, I was working harder than ever before. My position in the household was not that of sponging parasite – I had to earn my keep, and was glad to do so. Cheerfully I undertook the domestic duties of which Phyllis, frail since the shock of his removal to London, was incapable. From the moment I rose I dusted, swept, washed, painted, brushed and polished, under the critical eye of my landlord. His standards in the domestic sphere were even more rigorous than in the dramatic, and soon the hitherto dingy maisonette was restored to its original splendour. It was work I loved (had fate dealt me a different hand I might have made a fortune from 'doing up' old property), but under my patron's supervision it became arduous.

There was the vexed question of my uniform. Phyllis had asked for 'a few additional favours' in return for my bed and board (which, believe me, I was already earning in full). One of these was that I should wear certain clothes around the house – nothing bizarre, just the leather jacket and jeans, with optional white

T shirt, that he loved. At first I rebelled. I've never liked being told how to dress, and this uniform seemed pointless and impractical. But then I reasoned with myself. First, there was my overwhelming sense of gratitude to the man who had first recognized my talents. Was it so much to pander to the eccentric whims of an artistic old man? But more than that, there was something in me that responded to the demand, that saw in this strange *ménage* a dramatic challenge. Soon, the kitchen floor was my stage, the mop and bucket my modest props and the skimpy 'uniform' my wardrobe.

Being nice to Phyllis brought rewards. After a dirty morning washing down walls in the bathroom, I suggested that it would be more practical if I left my jeans off and worked in jacket and briefs only. Phyllis was delighted, and later took me out for dinner. When he asked if he could sketch me for a series of studies that he was working on, I happily obliged: posing as a sleeping sailor *à la* Cocteau was far easier than sweeping carpets.

Inevitably, this hothouse atmosphere became oppressive to a healthy, energetic boy of sixteen. I hadn't come to London to work as a glorified skivvy – and there were bigger stages to conquer. At first, I took to exploring the immediate vicinity, fascinated by the teeming variety of life right outside my window (now clean and polished). Here the old world rubbed shoulders with the new. The cockney barrow boys, still dressed in the cloth caps and 'gor blimey' trousers of the music hall stage, were always ready with a cheeky 'Morning, guv!' as I passed by. But on the building sites that peppered the area, where new high-rises crowded to fill the bomb sites and to cover the crumbling slums, the workmen were more brazen, more aggressive. ''Ello, darling!' they'd shout, mockingly, as I passed by. Or they'd whistle and call names – the names of the hateful playground. And always the ghostly parade of senior citizens, drifting around an area once familiar, now a strange new jungle of skyscrapers and subways.

I was never short of company: working men from the building sites would stop by the pubs before going home to their wives, eager for a drink; shop girls and office workers milled around the steamy interiors of cafés sharing sandwiches and gossip. But, young as I was, I knew that there was another world – the *beau monde* of artists, intellectuals and beauties – where I more truly belonged. It was calling me from across the Thames; dared I answer?

Phyllis was a fiercely protective guardian, taking seriously his responsibilities *in loco parentis*. He forbade journeys beyond a certain limited territory, and most specifically discouraged any thought of venturing into the West End. No sooner does anyone tell me not to do something than I long with all my heart to do it, and I knew that it was in the West End that my new world lay waiting to be conquered. In a matter of weeks, when I had more fully got the lie of the land, the magnetism of that forbidden country became too strong to resist.

But before I plunged head-first into a new world and made it mine, there was the small matter of my parents to settle. In the eyes of the law, I was still a minor (people forget how very young I was when I began my career, hence the often-repeated misunderstandings about my age). Mum and Dad didn't want me back at home – in truth they were glad to see me started on the road of life. But they had misgivings about my new situation, particularly about my relationship with Phyllis. When I left home, it was technically without their permission; they knew from experience that they couldn't stop me. I hadn't thought it necessary to spell out the details of my new lifestyle – Mum and Dad had made it abundantly clear that they disliked Mr Phillips, and privately suspected him of leading me astray. I told them only that he had helped to find me a flat in London; I didn't mention that he also lived there, nor that he had refused my offer of a financial contribution to the housekeeping. Of course, I paid my way in other currency, but they would never understand the niceties of that arrangement.

Soon after I had moved, I received a letter from my father informing me that he and my mother were coming to visit. I had hoped to wait a little longer before extending the invitation, but they were naturally loving parents, eager to see their child safe and happy in his new life.

The date was soon – very soon. Phyllis received the news with chilly disdain; he hated my parents, blaming them for his dismissal from the school. (There may have been some truth in this; Mum had often mentioned that 'the authorities should hear about your Mr Phillips'.) I saw no reason for a confrontation, and persuaded Phyllis to make an 'awayday' of the Saturday in question, a favour easily granted after I posed as a dying slave for a new series of drawings, and hoovered the living room in a jockstrap.

Phyllis left early on Saturday morning, travelling to the South Coast to visit friends who ran a discreet *pensione*. My parents were due at eleven o'clock; I had exactly two hours to prepare for their arrival. Unwilling to cause them undue worry, I made a few rearrangements in the décor; Phyllis's fine collection of prints and photographs would only have confused them, and the recent drawings for which I had modelled, fine works in themselves, were not to my parents' bourgeois tastes. Then there was the library. Unlikely as my father was to scan the bookshelves, there was no point in leaving anything to chance, and I squirrelled away any titles that might have raised his eyebrows (carefully noting their original positions; Phyllis loved a tidy bookshelf). My mother had excellent taste in interior décor, preferring the clean lines of post-war modern to the baroque flourishes and frills favoured by Phyllis. Mirrors, cushion covers, valances and floral arrangements were stripped and stashed, the Lalique lampshades replaced by plain paper ones that I found in Woolworths.

Finally I was ready to receive Mum and Dad in my smart, unostentatious flat. Eleven o'clock struck, and the doorbell rang. As I marched forward to welcome them, my chest expanding with pride, I noticed from the corner of my eye one final, missed detail

– a framed, signed photograph of Joan Sutherland hanging in the hallway. Just in time I whisked it away and opened the door to my dear parents.

The interview went better than I had expected. Mum and Dad were interested in every detail of my new life, opening cupboards, testing the bed, perusing the bookshelves. 'It's lovely, dear, really lovely,' said Mum, passing from kitchen to bathroom with a look of vague irritation on her face – the look she wore when she was searching for something that she couldn't find. 'You've done well, lad,' echoed Dad, turning over a copy of *The Seven Pillars of Wisdom* that I'd decided not to remove.

The inspection complete, they sat down edgily on the sofa and accepted a cup of tea and a biscuit. Questions came thick and fast. 'Who's the landlord?' 'How much are you paying?' 'Where's the money coming from?' from Dad. 'Have you got a girlfriend?' 'Are you eating enough?' and 'Why haven't you hoovered under the bed?' from Mum. They loved me, God knows, and they cared about me – but I couldn't wait to get them out of the flat.

After a long hour I bustled them out of the door in search of lunch. A strained meal in the Waterloo Kardomah passed without event as I parried each question with vague answers, not exactly lies but avoiding too much truth. When I saw them off, they were friendly, almost affectionate. 'Get a job, son,' said my father on parting. 'Make us proud of you.' I promised him that I would.

As the train took my parents back to sleepy suburbia, I pondered my situation. It was two o'clock. Phyllis was away, at least until the morning. I strolled out of the station towards the river, the great boundary of my territory. On this side, the grim monotony of life with Phyllis. On the other – who could tell? Somewhere out there was my future. And somewhere in that maze of unknown streets was Nutter.

What was to stop me? I walked a little further, setting foot on the bridge, enjoying the sunshine and the breeze off the river. I walked a little further. I was half-way across, suspended between my old life and my new. Did I hesitate? Did I hell.

An unseen hand pushed me onwards, and I fairly flew the last hundred yards over the bridge before landing, breathless, on the Strand. I had no idea what I was looking for, knowing only the vaguest details about the West End, most of them learnt from the Monopoly board. Nutter had talked endlessly about 'Soho', his personal Mecca, where (he believed) sex and music overflowed from the coffee bars, pubs and night clubs that lined every street. It was thither that I was drawn, as if in a dream. Along the Strand I floated, dimly aware of the matinée audiences shuffling into the theatres that lined that once glorious street. Past Nelson, past the National Gallery, past the bookshops of Charing Cross Road where colourful volumes spilled out on to the pavements (I recognized some of the titles from Phyllis's library). Past the Hippodrome and the Palace Theatre – names from a fairy tale. I had the strangest sensation – a mixture of the smell of freshly roasted coffee, the cheap scent of a blonde woman beside me, the shock (to me) of seeing her arm-in-arm with a black man – that I had found what I was looking for.

Nothing happened on that first visit – nothing that the casual observer would have remarked. I wandered through a maze of streets, noticing the shops stacked with favourite records, the pubs where conversation and laughter roared, the handsome 'types' that lined every lane. But inside me, something clicked. I wonder how a young priest feels when he first hears the call of God and discovers his vocation? I'm not religious (although I'm a deeply spiritual person), but I imagine it's something akin to what I felt as I first penetrated Soho.

I reached Piccadilly Circus and jumped on a bus. Within minutes the colour had drained from life and we were back in Kansas – in my case, Elephant and Castle. Time had flown. It was well past seven. I hurried to the house and set about repairing the havoc I had wrought in Phyllis's over-decorated nest. Pictures went back on to hooks, books were returned to their shelves, swags and tassels and bibelots came out of hiding. Soon it was *maison Phyllis* once more – and for the first time, it revolted me. This padded cell, this decorated prison, how drab and dismal compared to the sights of Soho! Here I seemed sucked of energy by the soft comforts that Phyllis loved so much. Out there, in the clean, cool streets, among the sharp young men of the West End, I felt alive, invigorated. Finally, I was satisfied with my handiwork. Even eagle-eyed Phyllis would never detect the change in his surroundings. But would he detect the change in me?

After that first taste of freedom, I wanted more, more, more. Did Phyllis know that I was sneaking across the river at every opportunity? Certainly he was sullen with me, sometimes downright nasty, but I could always win him over by leaving the bathroom door open in the mornings when I took my shower, snuggling up with him at night to share a hot chocolate. But one thing was sure to me now: I needed my new life in the West End more than I feared the consequences of disobeying Phyllis.

At first my visits were cautious; I'd sit in a café, or I'd browse the record shops. I seldom ventured into the pubs; I still looked much too young to be served. But as I grew more accustomed to my patch, I became bolder. I struck up conversations with people on the street, with the friendly fruiterer who sold me a banana (with a cheeky smile and a joke), or the distinguished customer in a book shop who helped me to find the novels of Christopher Isherwood. I was eager to make friends and to learn. And of course the best place in the world to do those things was in the bars.

In those days, pubs and bars were civilized places where you could enjoy a drink, a chat and a cigarette without being deafened by music or assaulted by drunks. Soho was famous for the variety and quality of its pubs, many of them haunts for intellectuals and artists like myself. But it wasn't in these rarefied circles that I felt at home. I was drawn to earthier company – the 'hoofers' and showgirls eking out a living in theatreland, who loved nothing so much as a party. I've never been a snob. I chose not the academics and intellectuals, but followed my instinct for the young, bright and energetic. History would show how right I was.

There was one bar that I made my very own. It's gone now, swept away in a welter of sex shops and wine bars. But for me, it was a second home. Second home! What am I saying? It was the first place where I had ever felt truly at home.

I discovered it one grey, freezing afternoon when seeking shelter from the coldest winter on record in a bookshop off St Martin's Lane. I was a favourite with the manager, a dear Australian who specialized in militaria and was always happy to warm me up with a drink in one hand and a leather-bound volume on corporal punishment in the other. On the day in question, trade was slow (it was never brisk) and my friend decided to shut up shop. It was five o'clock – earlier than I had intended to go home to Phyllis's unpredictable temper, but with only enough pennies in my pocket to pay the bus fare, I had little choice. Besides, I was hungry.

Trevor, my Australian friend, sympathized with my situation (he'd heard enough about my landlord's eccentricities) and offered to buy me a drink and a sandwich 'at my club'. Now Trevor was not the sort to have 'a club' – despite his impressive war record he would not have been welcomed at the Garrick or the Athenaeum. But he buttoned his raincoat, pulled down the shutters and, umbrella under one arm and my hand over the other, marched me at a smart pace down Charing Cross Road, made a sharp right and bundled me into an unremarkable little side street that led back in to Leicester Square. 'Here we are, son,' he said, stopping in a dark doorway. 'Welcome to the club.'

There was no sign, not even a light to suggest that we had 'arrived' anywhere. But Trevor pushed the street door open and led me into a dimly lit hall, up some shoddily carpeted stairs to a landing. Two doors faced us. One was blank. The other, in shaky metal lettering, spelt out the word 'Members'. Trevor rang a doorbell and we were admitted.

The interior of the club (it was always just called 'the club', although officially it was La Bohème) belied the shabbiness of its approaches. It was dimly lit with a welcoming red glow. Plush and gold wallpaper gave it a rich, luxurious feel – just like something from a film, I remember thinking. It was a small room, with a curved bar along one wall, three or four tables, some banquette seating and a window carefully concealed behind thick, colourless velvet drapes. Pictures of sporting heroes and movie stars lined the walls, with pride of place given to Marilyn (I felt an immediate pang). Trevor led the way, descending a few steps from the door to the bar, and I followed, conscious of every eye upon me. I paused, smiled, and continued my descent.

There were, maybe, a dozen patrons in the club that night, and every single one of them bought me a drink. Even the barman, Tommy, bought me a drink (an unheard-of occurrence, I was informed, but Tommy and I struck up an immediate sympathy). Fortunately for me, I was used to liquor – remember, I'd started drinking at a very early age, otherwise they would have carried me out of there on a stretcher. Trevor was amazed at my capacity and boasted that he'd introduced 'a valuable new member' to the establishment. He was so happy that night, his tiny eyes shining out of his sweaty little face with sheer pride.

It was not the décor or the booze that impressed me most about the club, but the clientele. It was a democratic mix: all ages and types rubbed shoulders in that little room, and for once the crippling class-consciousness of post-war England seemed forgotten. Soon Trevor and Tommy weren't my only friends: there was Paul, a one-eyed 'odd job man' with a splendid collection of tattoos who'd sustained his injury in 'a fight with a Maltese pimp'. When we were flush, we'd stand each other drinks, but more often we'd accept hospitality from the older customers who befriended us.

There was Charlie, Tommy's best friend and 'companion', a hopeless drunk who tried, night after night, to tell me the secret of life but who always lapsed into incomprehensible slurring just as he was getting to the good bit.

Phyllis, of course, knew nothing about my West End life. He was aware that I was going out on my own, and retaliated in the only way left open to him, with sulks, scenes and a thousand petty acts of grudgingness. Mostly I kept him sweet: he was at heart an affectionate old man with too much time on his hands, prone to temper but quick to forgive. I felt sorry for him. His 'new career' had failed to materialize as his health gave out, and he didn't have the heart to embark on fresh theatrical projects. His memory of our school stage triumphs was enough – and I was always happy to fan the flame of his devotion to that memory, acting out favourite scenes, 'rehearsing' for hour after hour as Phyllis watched his ambitions slip ever further beyond his grasp.

It was not Phyllis's career, but mine that was on the rise. It was a magic time to be young, and I was in the right place at the right time. Sooner or later, my lucky chance would come along. And I saw that lucky chance walk through the door of the club one evening as I sat drinking with Paul.

It was a busy night – a royal film première had just taken place in Leicester Square, and the pubs, clubs and cafés were full of black-tie revellers. Even our club had an elegant air; Tommy had placed a framed picture of the Queen in pride of place above the bar and draped red, white and blue bunting around the windows. (Remember, this was before Swinging London and the fashion for Union Jacks – like so much else, that was a trend that started in La Bohème.) Paul and I were stationed at the corner of the bar where we could keep an eye on the new arrivals, hoping that we could 'charm' a friendly stranger into buying the round. Suddenly there appeared at the top of the stairs a striking figure of a man, neat and tidy in his DJ and bow tie, his hair and nails expensively maintained (I've always had an eye for grooming). I didn't recognize him at first, although soon enough he'd be on the cover of every magazine in the world.

The big stranger descended the stairs, followed by a couple of friends, laughing and joking, obviously 'high' on the atmosphere of the night and the special magic of the club. I leaned forward on my stool and bingo! I was staring straight into his eyes. He didn't come over right away; I think he was shy and uncertain of the 'form'. He went with his friends to the other end of the bar, and bought drinks. Shortly, Tommy came over to us and whispered in Paul's ear: 'Gentleman down there wants to buy you a drink.' We looked over, and there was one of the strangers – not the one I had noticed – waving and grinning at Paul, who slipped off his barstool and rolled up his T shirt to show off his tattoos to their best advantage. I lit a cigarette and sat alone.

My patience was rewarded. After a few minutes I felt a gentle touch on my elbow and there at my side was the gentleman in the dinner jacket. 'You look like you could do with a drink, young man,' he half whispered. 'What'll it be?' I asked for a rum and coke and watched as he pulled out a crisp new five pound note from his wallet to pay.

Soon we were chatting away like old friends. He had a way of bringing me out, getting me to talk about things I'd never told even Phyllis before. My ambitions as an actor, my interest in rock & roll music, even my search for my 'lost' friend Nutter – it all came spilling out. (I omitted to tell him of my domestic problems.) He was a good listener, attentive, interested, inviting confidence. Drinks appeared as if by magic; I became animated, effusive, singing and reciting for all the world as if I was auditioning for a West End show. My new friend (I didn't know his name yet) laughed at my jokes, applauded my songs and patted me on the back and the knee in mute encouragement.

'So you want to get into showbiz, do you?' he asked, after I had been rattling away uninterrupted for hours.

'Oh yes, more than anything in the world.' I blush now to think of how naïve and gushing I must have seemed – a young, untried talent taking its first breathless steps on the road to success.

'Do you realize how much hard work is involved?' he asked, placing a hand on my shoulder.

'I'm ready to work for it,' I said.

'I do believe you are. You've got what it takes. You're the most talented youngster I've met for a long time. Not since . . .' He fumbled his words and was silent.

I was intrigued. 'You seem to know a lot about the business, er . . . What did you say your name was?'

That was when he told me his name, who he was and what he did. I'm not the sort of person to drop names – and this is certainly not a 'kiss and tell' autobiography. Suffice to say, he was the manager of the biggest, most famous rock & roll band in the entire history of popular music. And he, HE!, was telling me that I was the most talented person he'd met since – well, we all know who.

Here at last was my chance to learn something useful about my chosen profession. That's how I've always regarded the celebrities that I've met – and over the years, I've met them all – as a golden opportunity to sit humbly at the feet of the immortals and learn. It would never have occurred to me that my new friend – I'll just call him Brian – would 'do' anything for me. But if he'd only let me into his mind for a moment, that would be enough.

Brian was forthright, almost stern, in his advice. If I was serious about the profession, he said, I should concentrate on music. That was the art form of the people, the future; theatre was a dead end. All the big stars of the future would be pop stars – bigger stars, he added, with a sweeping gesture that took in the portraits of Marilyn, Lana, even the Queen herself, than 'all of these'. It was as if someone had read my mind. How could the theatre, that stuffy domain of old men like Phyllis, possibly touch the hearts of the *real* people? Surely the future was in the hands of the young, the boys who, like Nutter, had tasted life's bitterness at an early age, who could put the twentieth-century blues to the beat of rock & roll. This was how Brian put it, and I heard every word. Goodbye Cleopatra, goodbye Cocteau, hello Top Twenty!

But first, there were some hard lessons to learn. 'You're talented, Mark', said Brian. 'You belong on the stage. But you'll never get anywhere looking like that.' I was shocked! I thought of myself as a snappy dresser, and certainly I fitted in with the other young men in the club. It was the uniform of youth, a look that Nutter and I had developed: long hair greased up into a quiff, white T shirt, black leather jacket, jeans and work boots. But this wasn't good enough for Brian. 'You look like a hooligan,' he said. 'People don't want greasy little oiks from the Dilly. They want a bit of style, a bit of class, a bit of tailoring. Suits and ties.' He fingered a satin lapel. 'Get your hair styled. Smart jackets cut short. Fitted trousers. Show off your bum, boy. That's what they want.' And he gave me a rough, appreciative squeeze. It was the best advice I ever received in my life.

The evening ended with a challenge. If I could show that I meant business, Brian would 'see what he could do' for me in terms of a band, a gig, even a record deal. 'Everything's there if you've got the guts to grab it,' he said as we climbed the stairs together. 'Show me what you're made of and then we'll talk.' He stepped into a waiting car and disappeared.

But how? How could I transform myself into a stylish, sophisticated star? That kind of look costs money, and money was the one thing I didn't have. How many talented young people have foundered on those very rocks?

I knew what I wanted and where to find it. So it was to west Soho that I bent my footsteps, seeking out the as yet obscure shops and 'boutiques' that would soon be the epicentre of a fashion revolution. Carnaby Street, Foubert's Place and Broadwick Street were still just obscure names in the *A to Z*, waiting for the wave that would sweep them on to the shores of immortality. They were quiet streets in those days, with discreet shop windows displaying a few carefully chosen goods. Just across the road in Savile Row, tailors were turning out the formal styles that British men had worn for centuries; but here, in these unremarkable little streets, there was a European invasion going on. The cuts were French, Italian and *modern*.

There was one shop I kept coming back to. It wasn't the biggest or the flashiest – a less discerning shopper would have walked straight past it. It had a modest frontage, with one large circular vitrine. Behind that, beautifully framed and lovingly placed on a podium draped with black velvet, was a photograph of – me! Not me now, but the me I wanted to be: a young man with shaggy hair cut in a fringe, a sharp little round-collared buttoned-up shirt, a pearl grey jacket that barely came down to his waist, straight-legged tailored trousers that ended in pristine black boots. He stood – I stood – leaning against the bonnet of a sports car, his hips thrust towards the camera and a knowing look in his eye. I could have been looking in a mirror.

I glanced around in search of further enlightenment, and found a discreet sign above the door: *Homme*. I wanted to burst in directly, scoop up armfuls of clothes and rush off to the nearest hairdresser. For a few days I dithered around deciding what to do, searching for cheap versions of the clothes I'd seen in the *Homme* window. But finally my patience snapped. There was nothing else for it, I had to go and try them on. After walking up and down the street half a dozen times, I entered Aladdin's Cave.

It was a dark interior, filled with racks and shelves that disappeared into the gloom. Here and there a little spotlight pierced the darkness to pick out one specially displayed item, accompanied by a neat handwritten label – in French: 'La chemise, £10', 'Le pantalon, £15'. And in pride of place, ranged against one wall on a long table like an altar, a single pair of very brief white underpants: 'Le caleçon, £5/10/-'.

The bell above the door had rung musically when I entered the shop, and soon from a door behind the counter emerged a figure whom I took to be the proprietor. He was small – shorter than I am, and at first glance not very much older. But on closer inspection I saw that this was a gentleman well into his forties, if not fifties. All that could be done to skin to halt the ageing process by way of astringents, moisturizers and exfoliants had been lavished on his face, which gleamed where it caught the light. His neatly trimmed, dark brown beard and moustache outlined a shapely little pink mouth. And to top it all off, he had a luxuriant head of chestnut hair, full at the sides, on top and on the back – and most obviously a wig. He was eccentrically dressed: a long silk smoking jacket over an open white cotton shirt and (when he emerged from behind the counter), no trousers. His feet were encased in kid slippers.

He nodded coolly at me as I browsed between his displays, watching me like a hawk. I was used to being looked at: my years in the theatre and, more recently, as an habitué of the club had accustomed me to appraising stares. But this was a new experience. It was not a friendly look, nor was it hostile. It was calculating, penetrating, as if this strange little man were assessing me for some secret purposes of his own. The situation would almost have been sinister, were it not for that wig.

After two minutes of silent staring, he offered his assistance. 'Can I help you with anything? Or are you just having a good look round?' He had a beautiful speaking voice, the obvious product of theatrical background.

'I'd like to try a few things on, if I may,' I replied, indicating a jacket, shirt and trousers that had caught my eye. He whipped out a tape measure from some fold of his *deshabillé* and applied it to my physique with a practised ease. Drawers were opened, and from the fragrant lining paper there emerged the most beautiful clothes I had ever seen – *my* clothes, I felt, forgetting for one delicious moment the money problem. He ushered me towards a cubicle in the corner of the shop and discreetly drew the velvet curtain, waiting to witness my transformation. As I was half-way through my change, I remembered that I needed shoes. 'Could I possibly try on a pair of those black boots as well, size seven?' I asked, overlooking the fact that I was already stripped to my pants. He whisked across the shop and handed me the boots with, I thought, a slightly shaking hand.

I finished dressing, revelling in these borrowed feathers that could never – could they? – be mine. Suddenly a thought came to me, as I remembered the dreadful state of my Y-fronts (underclothes I had brought with me from home, purchased by my mother). I had forgotten *le caleçon*. 'I'm so sorry,' I explained, 'but I simply must try some on. Perhaps you could give me some advice on the best styles?'

'Certainly, sir,' he replied. 'Excuse me one moment while I fetch a special selection for you from the stock room.' He disappeared.

I don't know what happened in the next few seconds, but suddenly I found myself running, running from the shop, bursting through the door and hurtling (as fast as the boots would allow) down the street. No sooner had I heard the shop bell jangle behind me than I collided with a crash into the arms of an oncoming stranger. Stranger? No! It was the manager from the shop. In one swift movement he grasped my wrist, twisted my arm behind me and marched me back indoors.

Where before he had been all politeness and deference, now he was callous, insulting. 'Come on, you little slag,' he said, bustling me through the door (which he bolted behind him, turning the 'Open' sign to 'Closed'). 'You didn't really expect to get away with that one, did you? Do you think I was born yesterday?' Suddenly I woke up as if from a horrible nightmare. I saw everything so clearly: my moment of temporary insanity, my flight from the shop, and the obvious fact that my captor had anticipated my exit by nipping straight through the basement door to apprehend me like a common thief. It was a terrible shock, and my knees gave way underneath me.

'Where . . . where am I?' I murmured as the shop span around me. 'Have I had another of my fits?' It wasn't the first time I'd blacked out in a shop and come to with a cache of apparently stolen goods about my person. 'Oh God, it's getting worse and worse,' I continued. 'The doctors say that one day . . . one day . . . I'll just never get better. They say that one day I might just . . . drop . . . down . . . dead!' I could keep the emotion back no longer; tears brimmed over my eyes, down my cheeks and splashed on to my new jacket.

My assailant was unmoved. 'Spare me the amateur dramatics,' he rasped, his voice very much more common now than the plummy tones in which he had first solicited my custom. 'It's all so bloody predictable. Although I like the terminal illness bit, that shows a spark of originality. So, what are we going to do? Shall I call the police straight away?'

I realized that I was dealing with a hardboiled cynic. I might as well face the music. Brushing the tears from my eyes and pushing back my ruffled hair, I looked up at him from the kneeling position I had assumed when I first collapsed. He was hardly a threatening figure: his little white legs, hairy tummy (peeking through where his robe had parted) and most of all *that wig* made it impossible to fear him. And yet there was something imposing about him. Unlike Phyllis, whom I had long ago learned to 'manage', this was someone much, much stronger as a person. 'I'm sorry,' I breathed, looking up at him through wet lashes. My mouth was dry; I had to lick my lips to get the words out. 'Please don't call the police. I'll do anything.'

'Anything?'

'Yes, anything at all.'

I could hear the cogs going round in his mind. But when he finally spoke, it was not at all what I had anticipated. 'Perhaps we can do business, you and I. You've got guts. You've got looks too, the sort of looks they'd kill for. You've got the body. But have you got the mental capacity? I wonder if you're as stupid as you seem?'

That was provocative, certainly. 'I know what you take me for,' I began, 'but I'll have you know that I'm a singer with a band and

I've got friends in very high places who will make damn well sure that nothing happens to me.' I stood up and looked straight into his eyes. They were cold and expressionless. Or was that a tiny crease of amusement? Or just crow's feet?

'So you're a singer, are you? Well, well, well. I wondered if you might be. A singer. Hmmmm.' He walked around me, pondering. 'What kind of songs, exactly?'

'Pop songs. Rock & roll. Rhythm and blues.'

'Why don't you sing me one?'

'What?'

'One of your repertoire. One that you perform with your – what was it? Your band?'

'I can't sing just like that, you know.'

'No, I don't suppose you can. And I don't suppose the band can play. And I don't suppose your friends in high places can really do very much to keep you out of borstal, can they?'

'Don't be ridiculous. You don't know what you're talking about.'

'That's just it, I think I do. What a shame. I thought for a moment that there was more to you than meets the eye. But it's all skin-deep, isn't it? Pity. If you weren't so incredibly stupid I might think that you had a future.'

I was shocked by this rough handling, but at the same time exhilarated. Here was a man who saw me not as a plaything, who wasn't blinded by my talent or my looks, but who spoke to me as one professional to another. 'All right,' I admitted, 'so I tried to steal from you.' It was what he wanted to hear, even if it wasn't true. 'So, I'm a petty thief, a criminal, if that's the way you want it. Go ahead and call the police. Let them take me away. It's what I deserve.' I was warming to my theme. He began to look at me with a little more interest.

'But can you blame a starving man for stealing a crust of bread? I'm like that man. I'd do anything I need to do to get my career off the ground. And if that means breaking the law, that's a price I'm willing to pay. I need those clothes because I've got an audition.

I've got no money. So what can I do? Would you really expect me to put the law before my career? Well I'm sorry, but that's something I just can't do.'

'I see.' There was silence for a moment. 'Well, thank you.' More silence. Then he laughed, rubbed his hands together and fished around inside his gown for a pair of glasses.

'Okay, this is the deal. You want to work; I'll help you. As for the clothes . . .' I prepared to say farewell to my beautiful new wardrobe ' . . . You can keep them. But you'll have to earn them.' I was too dazed to understand, and stood there like a goldfish with my mouth gaping. 'Hello? Yes? Anyone at home? Is it a deal?'

I shook myself into full consciousness. 'Yes. Of course.'

'Now, what's your name? I'm Nick Nicholls.'

'Mark Young.'

'Oh dear.' He extended a white, manicured hand which I shook with genuine warmth and gratitude. 'You saw the picture in the window? I took that photograph. It's a sideline of mine: photography, journalism, public relations – all part of the package. Now, this is where you come in. I'm looking for a new face. The face of the future. The boy you saw in that photograph is done, finished, *disparu, fini.*' He snapped his fingers and stamped a little foot.

'So, you get your clothes and you keep your reputation intact, and I get your exclusive services as a model for my clothes and my shop. And if it works out in front of the camera, you'll get a nice glossy portfolio of ten by eights to take round to all those booking agents and managers that are interested in you and your . . . band, was it?'

I blushed and stuck my hands in my pockets.

'That is not how we want the *Homme* man to look, thank you very much,' snapped Nick, leaning forward to yank my hands out of my pockets and gently cuffing me under the chin. 'And we have to do something about that horrible, hid-ee-*ous* hair. What do you say?'

Was this destiny? Or was I selling my soul to the devil? For what? A set of fancy clothes and the promise of publicity? Under the circumstances, I had little choice.

When I finally emerged from *Homme* it was nearly midnight. I had learned a lot more about Nick Nicholls and his plans for me – plans that had been waiting for just the right person to come along. I learned, among other things, that Nick was a close personal friend of Brian. 'We're all club members, dear,' he told me, before recounting tales of the parties that he'd attended at Brian's home. I learned that Nick was a man of genuine vision, who could spot talent a mile off. 'I've picked up some pretty rough diamonds in my time,' he said, 'but I can always see the sparkle, however deep the shit.' I saw a selection of his photography – brilliant, innovative work that captured the very spirit of sixties youth, light years removed from Phyllis's effete doodlings. Some of it was highly experimental, daring material. 'My private work for special clients,' he explained, hoping that I'd agree to model for him. I also left the shop with a new haircut (executed by Nick as I sat swathed in a dust sheet) and taxi fare in my pocket.

Phyllis was waiting for me when I got in. 'Where have you been? Who have you been seeing? What's happened to your hair? Where did you get those clothes? Why didn't you call?' It was an ugly scene, with Phyllis in tears begging me not to leave him; but finally he tired and I slipped off to my couch.

I couldn't sleep. For the first time since I'd arrived in London, I felt that I'd really *arrived*. Nick had invited me for dinner at the weekend, promising to introduce me to a group of friends, 'all of them in the business', who could do something for my career. I could hardly wait for Saturday to come.

I was super-attentive to Phyllis for the rest of the week, only leaving home to buy food or take the old man for an airing around the block. I spruced up the house, cooked him nice meals, read to him and, of course, modelled for him. It was a pleasant few days – 'Just as I'd always dreamed it would be, dear boy, if only you hadn't gone and cut all your lovely hair off!' Phyllis was happy, life was easy, and there was nothing to stop me from strolling out of the house on Saturday afternoon, leaving Phyllis contentedly dozing after a huge lunch and half a bottle of wine.

I jumped on the underground and made my way straight to Holland Park, where Nick resided in a handsome mansion block, set well back from the noisy main roads on a pleasant garden square. He ushered me in and sat me down in one of the huge brown leather sofas that dominated the front room. All around me was evidence of Nick's photographic sideline, boxes of prints, some of them even more artistic than those he'd shown me in the shop. 'No time for browsing just now, young man,' he said. 'I want your undivided *attention*' (he pronounced it the French way).

'This is a very important evening for you. Do you understand? A very important evening.' (As if I needed reminding!) 'So no tantrums, no sulks, and definitely no rifling through the guests' coat pockets while nobody's looking. Do I make myself clear?' I nodded. 'There's half a dozen very valued friends coming over tonight to have a look at you. I haven't told them much, just that there's a new project I'd like to interest them in. They're investors, you see. People with capital and influence. People we most definitely do not want to piss off.' Nick's insults were just a way of showing affection.

The plan was simple enough. The guests would arrive at seven to be served cocktails and food, Nick would tell them all about me and my talents, then I would be brought out, amid much fanfare, from a hiding place elsewhere in the flat. During the foregoing, I was to sit quietly and wait. Nick himself was going to 'style' me for the evening, 'And I don't want you looking a mess, so don't fidget about.'

And so I waited. Once Nick had dressed me, from the *caleçon* to the shine on my shoes, there was little for me to do but sit in his bedroom leafing through his extensive collection of art books. I could hear brief snatches of conversation, laughter, the sound of glasses and plates being laid out and taken away, but I was barred from the party. Once again I was the three-year-old child longing to join in with the grown-ups.

But at last, well after ten o'clock, my moment came. 'We're ready for you,' said Nick, all businesslike as he made a few final adjustments to my hair and tie. 'Now remember what I said. Don't let me down.' He stood back to survey his handiwork and looked pleased, if stern. 'You'll do very nicely indeed.'

Nick preceded me into the drawing room and silenced his guests with a slight cough. '*Messieurs*,' he began, 'I'd like to introduce the young friend I mentioned this evening. *Je vous présente* . . . Mark.' He opened wide the door and gestured me into the room. There was a sharp, collective intake of breath and then silence. Through the cigar smoke, through the glare of the lights that were shining in my eyes, I could vaguely make out a small crowd of faces, among them Brian, who winked and grinned when he caught my eye. 'Walk up and down!' hissed Nick in my ear, once the initial impression had registered. And so I paraded around the room as if I was on a Paris catwalk, stopping every so often to strike an attitude. The reaction was electrifying. Where there had been silence, there was suddenly a hubbub of voices. 'Oh Nick! Oh la la! Oh, he's divine! You've done it again! Where do you find them, you clever thing? Oh I can't wait, I simply cannot *wait* to see the photographs!'

And I couldn't wait to see my photograph either – plastered across billboards 20 feet high in Leicester Square!

The rest of the evening was a great success. As the guests settled down, I was introduced to each – charming, professional men, of a class I had never met before, easy in their manners, clearly used to money and to the best that money could buy. And they, in return, were enchanted by me. One or two of the older guests – older even than Phyllis – took the opportunity of Nick's temporary absence from the room to offer me a luxury hotel for the evening or a trip to the countryside, 'Just us for the weekend, don't you see?', before

Nick unceremoniously cut in and hustled them out of the flat.

When the last guest had gone, I expected – I don't know – congratulations, kisses, a celebratory bottle of champagne or a pair of cufflinks. But not from Nick; he was never big with the gestures. 'We've got a lot of work to do,' he said as I stood poised to accept his thanks. 'No time to lose, no time to lose.' Finally, after he'd dashed around the flat removing empty glasses and clearing ashtrays, he saw me standing forlorn in the doorway. 'You did well,' he said. 'Get yourself a drink from the kitchen. Now let's get down to business.'

The 'business' that Nick had in mind was my first professional modelling assignment. Not allowing for the fact that I might be tired after such an arduous evening, Nick led me downstairs to 'the studio', a converted guest room in which he had erected a small 'throne', a selection of backdrops and an impressive array of cameras, lights and tripods. 'Hop up,' he said, even curter than usual, and began fiddling with his equipment. With the flick of a switch, a row of arc lamps above my head came on, then a pair of blindingly bright lights ranged on stands on either side of me. With a 'whoomph!' Nick tested out his flash; I was blinded, and staggered a little on my platform. 'You'll have to get used to this,' he said. 'You're going to spend a significant amount of your life in front of the camera.' How right he was – and how little he really knew about my future!

At first I felt strange, yet aroused. I loved the way Nick disappeared behind the lens, the way he jumped up to 'pose' me, handling me as if I were nothing more than a piece of animated sculpture. But I was stiff, awkward, uncertain. Gradually, however, my inhibitions slipped away. I grew to love the camera – and it's been the one great love of my life ever since that strange night in Nick Nicholls's shabby little studio.

We shot many rolls of film – images that would become icons for a generation. No other pictures capture so perfectly the impatience, the arrogance of youth. There I stand in my new clothes, a faraway look in my eyes, a slight sneer around the mouth . . . I knew so little of the world, but expected so much. And while I relaxed in front of the camera, the effect on Nick was nothing short of a complete metamorphosis. The curt, rude manner was abandoned, and suddenly there emerged a warm, seductive personality, a flatterer who could get the very best out of his model. I forgot his strange appearance, his many unpleasant-nesses – and, to tell you the truth, I actually began to find him attractive.

We carried on taking pictures well into the night, and by the small hours of the morning I had given my all. Finally Nick switched off the lights. The spell was broken, and he was once again a prickly little man with a beard and a wig. I picked up my clothes from where they had been flung around the studio, folded them neatly and trotted off for the sleep of exhaustion.

From that night on, my life was no longer my own. I was public property – as I've remained to this day. In the morning Nick presented me with a set of five glossy enlargements that would do nicely for 'front of house'. The rest of the pictures, he said, he'd be developing and 'sending out' over the next few days. I was as pleased as Punch, and even more excited when Nick instructed me to report back on Monday afternoon to begin 'rehearsals'.

'What for? A show? What kind of show?'

'Wait and see, child. Wait and see. Now go home to mother.' He patted me on my behind (an irritating habit that he would sometimes do in company) and saw me off the premises.

I couldn't help thinking about Nutter. He was the one who'd left home with his guitar slung over his shoulder, on his way to become a star. And who had got there first?

For the rest of the weekend, I was in a frenzy of preparations. The show that I envisaged was a rock & roll spectacular, drawing fully on my theatrical background. I was the first artist in the field to blend those two areas – rock & roll and theatre – although others would come along ten years later and lay claim to the idea. As with so many things, I was too far ahead of my time.

I spent hours on end practising songs and routines in the front room of the flat, imagining myself on the stage of the Marquee or the 100 Club, or any of the other 'gigs' that were springing up all over London. I imagined the screaming fans, the popping flash-bulbs, the raw energy of my performance. In reality, the only audience I had was Phyllis, who was anything but appreciative of my efforts. He regularly interrupted rehearsals with his screaming temper, complaining that I was neglecting my household duties, threatening me with eviction. But I didn't care. What was my home, my security, compared to my future? Finally I had my routine all worked out. I'd start with 'Heartbreak Hotel' as a nod to my 'roots', then I'd go through an R&B medley, a selection of favourite songs from the movies ('The Girl Can't Help It', 'Anyone Here for Love?', 'Diamonds are a Girl's Best Friend') before the climax, a spine-tingling rendition of 'Love Me Tender'. It was a twenty-minute slot – perfect for top billing on one of the spectacular rock & roll revues that were then touring the country.

When I arrived at Holland Park on Monday morning, I was abuzz with creative energy. Nick was more brisk and businesslike than ever. 'Now, do you want the good news or the good news?' he snapped. What could he mean?

'Sit down and concentrate. First of all, I've got you a show. No, I said sit down! It's an important showcase for you, with all the most important agents and critics in town. Investors, boy, investors. Thanks to your friend and mine,' (here he winked) 'we've got a nice little bit of money behind us for this particular extravaganza.' So, Brian had been as good as his word! He'd booked me into a top-line cabaret venue – where? The Talk of the Town?

'Remember, this is a private affair. We're not ready to go public yet. You've got to learn how to handle an audience in an intimate setting before you get out there on the bigger stages.'

Maybe it was one of the cabaret clubs of Mayfair, Chelsea? I begged Nick to tell me where I was to make my début.

'La Bohème.'

La Bohème! I was outraged – that dump where I had spent so many fruitless hours propping up the bar talking to losers like one-eyed Paul and drunken Charlie! But gradually Nick brought me round.

'Think about it for a minute. It's a place you feel relaxed in. It's the perfect size – intimate, full of atmosphere. And it's discreet.' Also, as I discovered, it was on friendly terms with the local constabulary and therefore less prone to raids. All this was kept from me at the time.

Perhaps it was destiny that brought me back to La Bohème. Was it not there, after all, that I'd first met Brian? Wasn't it there that Marilyn herself had seemed to greet me from the walls, as if to say in her unforgettable, breathy voice, 'Welcome home, baby . . .'? The more I thought about it, the more I realized that La Bohème was the only possible venue for my first, 'secret' live appearance. I cheered up immediately.

But there was another surprise that would cheer me up even more. Nick took me into his study – a labyrinth of filing cabinets, dusty box files and bureaux with secret compartments – and presented me with a fat brown envelope. 'Your first instalment.' I tore it open and inside were four five-pound notes – more money than I'd had in my life. Only a few days after my first modelling session, and the rewards were pouring in already. At last I was a professional!

I started telling Nick about my plans for the act. I was just launching into the first verse of 'Heartbreak Hotel' and doing my best Elvis impersonation when Nick raised a commanding hand. I 'dried' completely. '*Ab-so-lu-ment* no. No, no, no! That sort of thing won't do at all.' I didn't understand: wasn't I supposed to be launching myself as a pop star? But Nick had other ideas, new ideas. I, he said, was aiming myself at a different market – a more 'adult' market, who wanted solid show business values. I mentioned to him that I had a selection of songs from the movies in my repertoire, and was about to give him my up-tempo rendition of 'Diamonds'. But Nick silenced me again and handed me a short typewritten list.

The Street Where You Live (My Fair Lady)
I've Never Been in Love Before (Guys and Dolls)
Maria (West Side Story)
It's De-lightful

Not the sort of material I had envisaged at all! I respected Nick's judgement, but I was hurt that so little interest had been shown in my work. It was then that I learned one of my hardest lessons in the school of show business: you've got to give the people what they want because at the end of the day it's the public that comes first. I've kept that lesson close to my heart for the rest of my life.

And so I threw myself into my new routine body and soul. Fortunately, I had no need of singing lessons, being blessed with a fine, expressive tenor voice that had a pleasing 'untrained' quality about it. And I was quick to pick up the routines that Nick taught me to go with the songs. Hadn't I been dancing in public since the age of three?

As the date for my début approached, I was brimming with excitement. Even Phyllis was showing an interest 'in the theatrical possibilities of cabaret'. There was only one fly in the ointment: an empty feeling that nagged away inside me, a hunger that no amount of praise could satisfy. Lying awake one night, I realized what it was: I couldn't enjoy my triumph to the full unless Nutter was there to witness it.

Hadn't we dreamed, all those years ago, of stardom? Hadn't we whiled away those afternoons in his bedroom, those long happy nights under canvas on our never-to-be-forgotten summer holiday, planning our careers, promising that we'd always be there for each other? And now here I was, on the brink of success, without my oldest friend beside me. I promised myself that I would move heaven and earth to get Nutter to the show.

But where was he? I'd heard nothing of him since we parted (barely friends) on the station platform. I swallowed my pride, and penned a letter to Sue. I was friendly, forgiving, unwilling to rake up a bitter past. Others might have vowed never to speak to Sue or Nutter again, but I have always believed in giving people a second chance. I told her about my new life in London, my career as a model-singer-actor, my forthcoming residency at one of the West End's most exclusive supper clubs. I sketched for her the kind of circles I was moving in – the parties, the dinners, the air of wealth and sophistication – I even hinted at the identity of my close personal friend Brian. And I invited her to be my guest on my opening night, a privilege of which even suburban Sue can't have missed the significance. A few days later I received a reply, and, to my delight, she agreed to come – on condition that her brother could chaperone her in London. Bingo!

She also said that she looked forward to seeing Mr and Mrs Young at the club. I wrote a hasty note back explaining that my parents were sadly unable to attend as they were currently travelling through Italy.

Show time finally arrived. I was sick with nerves. Normally I breeze on stage without a care in the world – *if* I'm happy with my vehicle. But that night my instincts were warning me of something. I should have listened to them.

La Bohème was packed, mostly with Nick's investor friends, including Brian and a gang of his hangers-on, and kindly Phyllis, uncomfortable among this fast crowd. Where were the journalists from the 'fan' magazines that Nick had promised me? What was I doing performing to this gang of corpses when everything in me was reaching out to youth, youth, youth? As I scanned the crowd from my 'dressing room' (in reality the seldom-used ladies' toilet),

I was relieved that Sue and Nutter had broken their promise to come.

Then they walked in the door. I wanted to run. Nick pushed me on to the stage.

The moment the spotlight hit me, I went into my routine, but I was an automaton, without passion. I aimed at a spot somewhere just above the bar, determined not to make eye contact with anyone – particularly not with Nutter. After the first verse of 'The Street Where You Live' I began to feel better: the music was working its magic. Jim, the house pianist, winked at me, and I gave just a little bit more.

By the end of the song, I was actually having fun. My voice had warmed up, and the audience liked me – there was a discreet jostling at the front of the stage which, given the average age of the crowd, was the equivalent of teenybop hysteria. The next song was one of my favourites from *Guys and Dolls*, Sky Masterson's soaring ballad 'I've Never Been In Love Before', just the sort of number that I could really 'put across'. I shut my eyes and thought of Marlon Brando in the film, I thought of Nutter in the audience – that was enough. As I hit the high notes on 'But this is wiiiiiine that's all too strange and strong/I'm full of foolish song/And out my song must pour', I was in another world. And somewhere in the back of my mind, I coolly made a note of another important lesson: if you give, give, give yourself to an audience, you can rise above even the most unpromising circumstances.

At the end of that number, I sensed a restlessness in the crowd. I had given them so much, and yet they wanted more. I could see Nick furiously gesturing to me from the side of the tiny stage, and remembered the next section of the routine: I removed my jacket and tie and undid the top two buttons of my shirt. Once again, the faces at the front of the stage were beaming. An elderly gentleman handed me a handkerchief from his top pocket to dab the sweat from my forehead, neck and chest; when I handed it back he gave me a bashful glance like a lovestruck schoolgirl.

As I launched into 'Maria' I took myself on a little tour of the tables (which didn't take very long in the cramped spaces of La Bohème), stopping to sing to a few lucky patrons, cheekily drinking from their glasses or puffing on their cigars. One or two of them took advantage of my proximity to unbutton more of my shirt; others slipped notes and cards into my pockets. I regained the stage intact (just) for the final climax of the song, threw my arms open in an all-embracing gesture and took the applause as my shirt, now fully undone and damp with sweat, dropped to the floor.

There had been some disagreement in rehearsals about the grand finale; Nick had suggested that I should continue to disrobe, a suggestion which I found frankly bizarre. Now I saw the sense of the idea; it was what the audience wanted, and who was I to deny them that pleasure? Many of them had come to know of me through the medium of Nick's marvellous photographs – and those enduring, classic images were now *my* image. So as Jim banged out the introduction to 'It's De-lightful' I clambered up on to the lid of the piano and removed my boots. By the end of the first verse, both socks had come off. Finally, I wriggled out of my trousers and rolled around on top of the piano in my *caleçon*. Jimmy didn't miss a beat, although I'm sure he slowed down; the end of the song just never seemed to come. Eventually I jumped down from the piano, possessed by a frenzy of elation; I knew the audience – and bigger audiences all over the world – was mine. I took my bow as dozens of elderly hands reached out to help me off the stage (or out of my *caleçon*, I was never sure which) and ran back to the dressing room.

The last thing I saw as I turned to wave goodnight to my audience was the ashen face of Nutter. Our eyes met for a fraction of a second before he turned and, dragging Sue with him, rushed from the club and once again out of my life. Jealousy is an ugly emotion.

The next morning I was sick and remorseful. The evening had ended after a long, boozy party. I can't remember how much champagne I drank. Nick took me back to Holland Park for another modelling session 'while the muse is fluttering around your shoulders', of which I remember next to nothing. All I wanted was to creep home to Phyllis, pull the blankets over my head and sleep.

I expected the worst when I returned to Elephant and Castle, but for once Phyllis was all charity. 'You poor, deluded child,' he said, struck by my grey face and bloodshot eyes. 'What have they done to you?' I mumbled some vague story and then burst into tears; I've often found that a major professional triumph leaves me emotionally vulnerable. 'It's all right now. You're home. You're safe.'

Phyllis put me to bed and nursed me through the next two days as I fell prey to all sorts of ridiculous regrets. He confirmed my worst fears, that I'd prostituted my talents, made a fool of myself in front of some of the most influential men in town, lost my oldest school friend and nearly (he said) lost the love and respect of the one man who truly cared for me – Phyllis himself. After listening to this catalogue of my woes, all I wanted was to be cradled like a child. As Phyllis rocked me in his arms, I fell into a deep, healing sleep.

The next day, however, he was less obliging. He had been 'disgusted', he said, by my 'pornographic display' and feared that I was being exploited by a 'sex ring'. It was the language of the Sunday papers that Phyllis clandestinely loved to read, and hardly rang true from a man who had forced teenage schoolboys to parade in drag and jockstraps. But there was truth in what he said, and he knew that he'd hit me where it hurt. I too was uncertain about Nick's motives, nervous about the kind of attention I was getting. And while Nick had taught me many valuable lessons about show business, I couldn't dismiss Phyllis's assertion that 'the man's a pimp'. Phyllis warned me that there were no short cuts in the theatre; that if I wanted the kind of real, lasting success that my talents truly deserved, I had to pay my dues. Nick, he said, was offering me a quick, one-way ticket to obscurity.

And so, for a while, I came back under Phyllis's wing. I even agreed to find a job. The manager of the local pub was happy to take me on as a pot boy three lunchtimes and three evenings a week for a small but sufficient wage. I knuckled down, disciplined myself and observed life from behind the bar, noting down the character types that I'd use in later performances. Phyllis was delighted; when I returned, exhausted, from a shift at the pub, it was the most I could do to wolf down some supper and fall into bed.

This state of affairs lasted for three weeks. Then, one morning, I happened to collect the post and found a fat, brown envelope addressed to me. I tore it open, and inside was forty pounds – more than the total amount I had earned at the pub. And there was a note.

First instalment on photo sales. Well done: you're a star in the making. Lots of plans. Call soon. *A bientôt*. NN.

Forty pounds! A fortune to a boy of my age. And plenty more on the way, by the sound of it. How could I continue to wear myself down in drudgery when destiny was calling so loud and clear from the other side of London? As soon as Phyllis was out of the way, I called Nick.

He was in great good humour, making no reference to the fact that we hadn't spoken for so long. 'Glad you rang,' he said. 'I'm taking you to a party tonight. Some people I want you to meet, you'll like them. Your sort of people. Pick you up at nine!'

If he'd offered me a million, he couldn't have seduced me more effectively. Fun, glamour – just the things I'd been missing! I longed to get out of the house, out of SE1, if only for a night; I fully intended to kick up my heels for an evening and return to my job the next day. But I just wasn't meant to have an ordinary life. Fate kept getting in the way.

I told Phyllis I was working late at the pub, and waited for Nick on the corner of the street. He was punctual, rolling up in his sporty little car on the dot of nine. 'You look immaculate!' he remarked as we sped away, feeding an appetite for praise that had been starved in recent weeks. As we sped through the city, I could feel myself coming back to life; the adrenalin was pumping through my veins, I was singing, happy to be alive. Maybe Nick was bad for me – but it felt so good!

I didn't know where we were going, didn't care. Finally we stopped in St John's Wood, at a handsome house far grander than any I had ever entered before. 'Just be your own sweet self,' said Nick, ushering me through the hallway where my coat was taken by a butler. 'Everyone's dying to meet you.' And there was colour, life, YOUTH! Young people, beautiful people, sexy, just like me. They thronged the floor, dancing, shouting, laughing, flirting. If I can pinpoint one moment in the sixties when the youth explosion really began, it was then; as I walked into that party something just seemed to click, and life would never be the same again.

A drink was thrust into my hand, and I was whirled around the room. Everyone seemed to know who I was, to like me; and they were all 'in' something – models, singers, actors, writers, journalists, designers, painters, politicians. I danced with a beautiful, blonde-haired girl who span me so much I flew, dizzy and unstable, into the arms of a handsome young man who span me back the other way. I was kissed a thousand times, and whenever I took a sip of my drink the glass was magically refilled. Nick was at my elbow all the time, making introductions, oiling the wheels, ensuring that I had the time of my life. 'Look, there's Mandy,' he said, pointing to my blonde dancing partner. 'I wonder if Christine's with her? Oh yes, here she comes. Christine,' – he presented me to a striking brunette in a tiny black dress – 'this is Mark.' Christine kissed me and took me to meet 'my friends', a distinguished collection of foreign gentlemen, one of whom slipped an arm round my waist and took me for a tour of the building. As he spoke no English, and I didn't speak a word of Russian, our conversation was limited to sign language, but when I returned to the party an hour later I felt I had made an important new friend. Mandy and

Christine were delighted that I had been such a hit with 'the attaché'.

When Nick drove me home that night, filling me in with little snippets of gossip about my fellow guests (Mandy and Christine, he informed me, were 'in terrible trouble' with the government), he congratulated me on being the life and soul of the party. In the next few days I was deluged with invitations, and I accepted them all.

Something was changing in London. The city was waking up from a long sleep, shaking off the misery of the War and the dreary decade that followed. Everyone was full of energy and new ideas – and I was at the centre of it all. Nobody had more fun, nobody laughed harder or danced longer or went to more parties than I did. Was I running away from something? A secret sorrow in my past – the disappointment of my parents, the loss of Nutter? I don't think so. I was just young and beautiful and very much in demand.

People were so generous then, not just with money but with advice, introductions. I had many 'protectors' vying for my attention (and, happily, filling my pockets along the way) – so many, in fact, that even the ultra-*mondain* Nick began to display his first signs of possessiveness. At one party, I was about to leave with a new friend (I can't name him of course, but he was a high-ranking minister in the brand new Labour government) who had excellent contacts in Wardour Street and was hoping to get me a part in a film. I didn't hesitate; surely what was good for me was good for Nick, my mentor and manager. But as we were getting our coats, Nick swooped down on us, frostily demanding, 'And where are we going?' before giving my new friend a barrage of his most unpalatable abuse, naming him a pervert of the deepest dye who would have me 'squirrelled away to Bangkok', never to be seen again.

My swain fled. 'Do you know that he just happens to be a very important member of Her Majesty's Government?' I began, but for once Nick surprised even me. He reached into his jacket pocket and pulled out two tickets for the boat train to Paris.

Paris! The very word sent shivers down my spine. Within minutes we were back in Holland Park throwing a few clean clothes into a bag before jumping into a taxi for Victoria. After just one performance in a tiny West End club, I was on my way to the top. And Paris – city of light, the home of romance, couture and cabaret – was waiting for me.

'Say goodbye to all that, Mark Young,' said Nick as we boarded the ferry, waving his arm at the dingy little coffee stand that served bedraggled British passengers, badly dressed, huddling against the cold as they waited for their passage. 'And say *bon soir* to a new life and a new you!'

As the boat pulled out of the harbour and I watched the white cliffs of Dover receding until they were a dirty smudge on the black circle of our cabin porthole, Nick surprised me again by popping open a bottle of duty-free champagne and pouring two glasses. '*A votre santé*,' he said, becoming more and more French the further we got from England. 'How I long to show Paris to you. And how I long to show you to Paris.' It was a magical moment – the thrill of my first foreign travel, the rush of champagne, the promise of a new life – and Nick captured it in a roll of film that he shot right there and then in our cramped cabin.

Dozing through the French countryside while the train sped from Calais, I woke in time to spruce myself up before we reached Paris. I splashed water on my face, brushed my hair, cleaned my teeth and arranged the beautiful silk cravat that Nick had presented to me on our departure. Emerging from the *toilette*, I felt every inch a man of the world.

Paris was a revelation. So much more beautiful than London, the streets teeming with women who had stepped straight out of the pages of *Vogue*, sleek, groomed panthers compared to the over-made-up, pudgy provincials who passed for beauties in

London. And the men – they wore hipster slacks, loafers, brightly coloured knits and even carried little clutch bags, the kind of outfit that would have provoked a murder in the Elephant and Castle. Nick booked us into an exclusive hotel a stone's throw from the Gare du Nord, where the desk clerk smiled politely to *Monsieur Nick* and showed us to our double room (with double bed) without batting an eyelid. There was no time to settle in – Nick wanted me to experience my first *petit déjeuner parisien* at a pavement café beside the church of St Vincent de Paul.

As I tasted the *café au lait* (ambrosia compared to the dishwater of London caffs) and bit into my first *pain au chocolat*, I happily contemplated the fact that Mark Young, the timid, friendless schoolboy who lived with a demented old man in squalid south London, had come an awfully long way in a very short time. Here I was in the heart of the fashionable world, sipping coffee as a handsome waiter smiled and winked at me as if it was the most natural thing in the universe.

'A *centime* for your *pensées*,' said Nick.

'I was just thinking how far I'd come,' I replied.

'Indeed you have, *mon cher*. I'd hardly recognize you as the little thief who tried to rob me one afternoon in Soho. No, don't interrupt, I'm not blaming you. I was impressed. I recognized a spark of talent. How right I was.'

'Indeed, how right you were.'

There was a pause. I felt that Nick was about to make some announcement that was of great importance to my future. The silence hung in the air for one minute, then another.

'You've changed, Mark.'

I didn't deny it.

'I've watched you grow and blossom. You're like a butterfly that's emerged from a chrysalis. A new person. Unique. Beautiful.'

'*Mais oui*,' I replied, hazarding a little of the French I was already picking up (I have a gift for languages). The waiter looked over again and smiled, striking a match and lighting a pungent cigarette.

'And a new person must have a new name, a new identity. A name that the world will remember. A name that expresses the new you, the real you.'

Nick pushed a small black box across the table towards me. I opened it, and inside was a heavy silver identity bracelet. I pulled it out of the box and held it up, where it caught the strong morning sun. For a second, I was dazzled by the light. Then, screwing up my eyes, I read the engraving, beautifully rendered in a flowing italic script:

Marc LeJeune

The rest of my long weekend in Paris was a delight. Nick took me to the best boutiques, the best restaurants. And always he had his camera. He photographed me relaxing in the Tuileries, clowning around the Palais Royal, posing against classical statues in the Louvre. There were portraits, casual studies, and an extensive portfolio of shots that he took each afternoon when we returned to our hotel room for siesta.

I was in love with Paris and half in love with Nick; how could I not love a man who had done so much for me? Who had even given me a new name, a name that finally set me apart from the lonely child who was mocked and chased around the playground? That wasn't me any more. Now I was Marc LeJeune, actor, singer, model, sophisticated international man of mystery. I would have said *oui* to anything Nick suggested. In later years I would pay for my openness, my trust, but how can a young man on his first visit to Paris not believe that the whole world, like him, is in love with life itself? *Je ne regrette rien.*

On our last evening, over dinner in Montmartre, I agreed to sign a contract that would formalize the business arrangement that had existed for the last few months. In return, Nick made me a solemn promise: international fame by the end of 1965. I could hardly believe what I was hearing, but why should I doubt it? Wasn't he only telling me what I had secretly known all along?

When we returned to England we set about a punishing round of auditions and interviews. I was out of action for four days in a private ward where Nick paid for the best dental surgeon in the UK to perfect my smile (early portraits show that my teeth, prior to 1965, were slightly crooked at the front). I hardly saw Phyllis – I was spending less and less time at his depressing little flat, despite his increasingly pathetic attempts to blackmail me into staying by claiming that his health was failing. I didn't have time to care for a pitiful old man; and when he really needed me, I wasn't there for him. But now is not the right time to tell that story. I was too busy and too excited to think about anything else except my career.

Nick was astonishingly proficient and well connected. Producers, casting directors, designers, photographers, columnists – all of them came running when Nick snapped his fingers. Offers of work arrived every day, but Nick turned them all down. We were waiting for something big, something special. 'There's no point flogging your arse round provincial rep for four pounds a week,' he explained when I missed the chance to play my first love, Shakespeare. 'We can do better than that. You've got to believe in me.' And I could afford to wait; there were plenty of friends to 'sub' me until the real money started to roll in.

But I've always been impatient, and the agony of waiting for that 'something better' was telling on my nerves. True, there were endless parties to take my mind off things, a throng of famous names to meet and a gruelling modelling career to pursue ('I can't get enough of you into my lenses,' said Nick). But still the big break eluded me.

Finally, when I was on the brink of being lured by Phyllis into another bout of respectability, Nick made a great announcement. 'It's happened at last,' he said, 'the opportunity we've been waiting for. Fame by the end of the year, I think we said?' (It was February 1965, a depressing winter.) 'Let's revise that. I think we can count on immortality by August. You're on TV.'

Television! The medium to which I truly aspired, the one which

I understood most fully. But when Nick described the job to me, I was disappointed. It wasn't a lead in a dramatic series, or a witty comedy. It was an advertisement. I rebelled and sulked and told him he was a fool. How wrong I was.

There's one strange footnote to this chapter. I owe so much of my early career to the brief intervention in my life of the man I've called Brian. After that one-night-stand in La Bohème, when I changed the future of rock & roll on a tiny makeshift stage, I never saw him again. I was bitter for some time, hurt that he'd broken a promise so easily given. It was with great shock and sadness that I read, in 1967, of his death by suicide.

CHAPTER THREE

Before 1965, TV commercials were amateurish affairs with little artistic flair; no performer of my calibre would ever have considered appearing in one. Nowadays we're used to seeing superstars promoting everything from trainers to toilet paper, but in the sixties the only 'stars' of commercials were anonymous, second-rate actors who'd do anything for money. That was about to change.

There was a groundswell of talent in the advertising industry – names who would dominate the media for the next twenty years. Suddenly, adverts were art, and I was the first bona fide British star to elevate the lowly commercial to its current status. The job was one of the most influential campaigns of its time (what we'd now call a 'lifestyle' campaign) advertising healthy eating. Remember, this was long before British people were conscious of what they ate; I was instrumental in introducing the idea of dietary fibre to a nation more used to chips and gravy. The product (in case anyone reading this is too young to remember!) was a brand new breakfast cereal called Bran Pops, and I was cast as the healthy, active epitome of young British manhood – or, as the adverts had it, the 'Regular Guy'.

Bran breakfast cereals had always been regarded as a joke, a food for the elderly and constipated. In the Regular Guy adverts we were tackling a deep-seated British taboo about the human body, educating a nation about health and establishing one of the most enduring images of the sixties. I still get fans who ask me to sign autographs not as Marc LeJeune but as 'the Regular Guy'. Far be it from me to dismiss the fame that Bran Pops brought me, and the pleasure that the advert brought to millions!

The Regular Guy campaign started in the press. Nick and I were called to the first meeting with the advertising agency 'creatives' in a dingy office on Greek Street, where we were shown drawings and 'storyboards' and introduced to the woman who was to be my co-star in the campaign, a stunning blonde named Janice Jones. In many ways she was my perfect match, epitomizing all that was contemporary in women's grooming as I did in men's. She was a little older than me and looked it; late nights, hard drinking, heavy make-up and teenage childbirth had seen to that. But she was full of life, exuding an irresistible sexual energy that no man (apart from Nick) could ignore.

Our first task was to model for a print campaign that would introduce readers of newspapers and magazines to the Regular Guy and his girl. Of course, I was an old hand at modelling – I'd been a professional for well over a year now, and my photographs featured in some of the most important collections in the country. But I was disappointed when we showed up at the shoot to discover that we would be working in a freezing old warehouse in Chelsea with a photographer who looked as if he'd just stepped off a building site. He was a sleazy, unclean character who chainsmoked and stank of drink – but, it turned out, a genius. On that first afternoon he photographed Janice and me running and jumping in front of a stark white backdrop, in outfits provided by a team of stylists who created the uniquely sporty look that would soon be seen on every British high street. I enjoyed myself and gave my best. For one shot, I had to carry Janice – sweeping her off her feet with one strong, graceful movement – and I knew we'd created something special. I remember the moment well. I was wearing a white tennis shirt, my precious silk cravat, navy slacks and pumps; Janice was wearing a short powder-blue mac and a polka-dot headscarf. I heaved her into the air, smiled insouciantly as Janice gave a little scream. Thus was born one of the icons of the swinging sixties.

But after the shoot, I felt depressed. The whole job, I told Nick, was stupid; I was being made to look foolish, I'd be associated forever with a laxative product and had been saddled with an unprofessional co-star who totally lacked charisma. I don't know why I was so negative; perhaps it's a feeling that other artists share when they've finished an important piece of work. I didn't realize that the creative sum would far transcend the parts, that every element of the campaign – my looks, Janice's easy sexuality, the overtones of health and carefree enjoyment – would coalesce into a powerful social statement. (My misgivings about Janice, however, were not misplaced.)

Three weeks later Nick summoned me to his West End 'office' – a café just off Long Acre that he had 'adopted' for business meetings. I ordered a coffee and sat down moodily. Without a word, he produced from his attaché case a small stack of magazines and thumped them down on the table in front of me. *Woman's Own, Woman's Weekly, Health and Strength* – I forget the others.

'What are these?' I asked, hardly daring to believe the suspicion that was forming in my mind.

'See for yourself. Read them.'

I picked up the first one and started feverishly flicking through it; I could find nothing but page after page of knitting patterns, recipes and romantic fiction.

'Inside back cover,' said Nick in his driest tones.

And there I was. In glorious black and white, the simple, timeless image of me whisking Janice into the air, under the single line of copy 'He's a regular guy'. At the bottom of the page there was a small, hardly noticeable picture of a packet of Bran Pops and a few lines of sound dietary advice in eight point type. It was magnificent. I could hardly believe my eyes.

'Look at the others,' snapped Nick, stemming my confused flow of thanks and praise. And there it was in every one – inside back cover, full page. I was overwhelmed.

'Well?' said Nick, a mischievous little twinkle around his eyes. I could see that he was as excited as I was; small beads of sweat were visible around the edge of his wig.

'Very nice,' I replied, all *sang froid*. 'Not bad.'

Then we could contain ourselves no longer. We both shrieked and jumped in the air, hugging each other, oblivious to the disgusted stares of the other customers.

I ran straight out of the café to a newsagent and bought a dozen copies, dashed to the post office and mailed them to my parents.

Fame came fast, and I was ready for it. I laugh when I read of other stars who say they found it difficult to adjust to their first experience of celebrity. To me it was the most natural thing in the world. I was recognized everywhere I went, observed, discussed and criticized, and I loved it. After the magazine campaign came the billboard campaign – close-ups of my beaming face with Janice gazing in adoration. 'He's a regular guy' became a national catchphrase in playgrounds, on buses, even in the House of Commons. I received a half-bashful letter from my father telling me to 'show them all' and to 'stick at it' and saying how much 'your mother and I are looking forward to meeting your girlfriend'. Like millions of others, they believed that the Regular Guy and his girl were real.

And soon it was hard even for me to believe that Janice Jones and I weren't 'an item'. We were photographed doing everything together – shopping, eating in cafés, walking in the park, relaxing by the pool. I regarded what we were doing as just a job; but Janice, naïve and unstable as she was, found it harder to separate the fantasy from the reality.

Let me give you some idea of Janice Jones, the woman. Physically, her image endures: the archetypal blonde bombshell, uncannily similar to my own beloved Marilyn but with none of her softness, intelligence and vulnerability. Janice had the looks and the figure for sure, but there was a hardness in her, a reckless streak, something that at times looked very much like madness. She was tall – at five foot ten almost taller than me – with long, long legs and a perfect hourglass figure (remember, this was 1965, before Twiggy had 'banned the bust' and before feminists had 'burned the bra'!). She wore her hair in a deep fringe, backcombed up from the crown and severely nipped in at the neck; sometimes for evening dates she'd put it all 'up' in a chignon, combing her fringe over one eye in a voluptuous 'peek-a-boo'. She had great skin – a disastrous skincare regime hadn't wrought its havoc yet. And she was always flawlessly groomed, her make-up as perfect as a doll's face, her clothes just so. Yes, on the surface Janice Jones was the perfect mate for the Regular Guy.

But there was more to Miss Jones than met the eye. Firstly, she was a two-fisted drinker. She could drink Nick, me and any other man under the table. Her 'tipple' was anything that was available: wine, spirits, even beer (which women did not drink in those days) were poured down indiscriminately. She was hopelessly unpunctual, but somehow she always managed to shine the moment the camera turned on her. And she was prone to terrible depressions, crying jags that could last for days and which, I was fast discovering, revolved largely about her failure with men, her estrangement from her family and the difficulties of raising a three-year-old child.

Janice's personal history was not a happy one. I could see so much of myself in her – the self I could have been without the advantages of a loving home background and some lucky breaks. Janice had been drawn to the stage at an early age, had performed in plays, musical revues and even films. But her parents had disapproved of her career, and, when she announced at the age of sixteen that she was pregnant, turned her out of their house. Janice drifted to London, living at first with the father of the child and later, as money came in from modelling jobs, in a series of flats and bedsits. She never stayed anywhere long; irregular personal habits combined with her noisy baby made her an unpopular tenant even in liberal London. Now at the peak of her career, she could afford a decent flat, a live-in maid who also acted as a nanny to little Noel, and gallons and gallons of booze.

Noel was an uncanny creature. I remember him sitting in studios where Janice would park him during shoots, watching the flashing lights with a solemn expression on his pale face, as quiet as a mouse while we were working. But as soon as Janice picked him up to go home he would howl as if his heart was breaking. It seemed that Noel, too, had show business in his blood. Little did I know back in 1965 that I was 'Uncle' Marc to a household name in the making!

Nick and Janice never got on. Nick was a man's man, uncomfortable in the company of women, and fiercely critical of Janice's personal eccentricities. 'She's a cut-rate Jean Harlow,' he'd mutter, 'and she's going exactly the same way.' He told terrible, vindictive stories about her sexual life which, if they were true, added a criminal cachet to her already considerable chic. Janice, in turn, grew to fear and despise Nick, and would go out of her way to avoid him. She started asking photographers if Nick could leave the studio during shoots, claiming that he 'inhibited' her, which added to the friction of this crazy, creative time.

I regretted the day that I gave Janice my home number. She'd phone me at all hours of the day and night asking for advice about her latest trauma, telling me how much little Noel needed a father figure in his life, how much she was looking forward to our next job. At first I was flattered – what man wouldn't be flattered by the attentions of one of the world's most beautiful women? But soon Janice's attentions became a burden, particularly when Phyllis got to the phone first.

Phyllis – there was another thorn in my side. He was dismissive of my work; it was not what he regarded as 'serious'. To him, the modern world was 'hideous', 'vulgar', 'insincere', where to me it was daring, exciting and fun. He hated the fact that I was 'publicly associated with a trollop'. He told me I was wasting my talent, for he failed to understand that the boundaries between art and commerce were collapsing and that the new era – the Pop Era, of which I was an icon – was with us.

Finally we were ready to take the Regular Guy into the television studio to make our first commercial. The studio (a cleverly converted railway arch near King's Cross station) was booked for a Friday – just one day. I spent the whole week in preparation, trying on clothes, having my hair done, enduring a regime of facials and massages: I wanted everything to be perfect. And most of all, I wanted my parents to be proud of me. For so long they had disapproved of my work; here at last was something that they could boast to their friends about. So I invited them up to London for the day to meet 'the gang' and to watch as we made television history. Once again I met them at Waterloo – under what very different circumstances from their last visit! They seemed to have shrunk. Were those timid little figures who emerged from the train really my parents? And they treated me with a strange deference due solely to my sudden fame. As we walked to the taxi rank, my mother caught sight of my enormous image on a billboard above the station clock and practically genuflected.

Caterers had been brought into the studio to provide a slap-up 'brunch' for the cast, crew and guests. Mum feebly complained that they'd had breakfast before they left, but after a couple of glasses of bucks fizz (common enough now, but unimaginably elegant then) she perked up and became her outgoing, sociable self. I was glad of a drink myself – I had been secretly dreading the first meeting between Mum and Dad and Nick and Janice. Nick was in full managerial mode, smoking a cigar and wearing a suit; he was polite, distant, imposing. Janice was a different matter. She greeted my parents like long lost friends, kissing my mother on the cheek and embracing my father, who underwent a complete personality change the moment he felt the impress of my co-star's ample bust. He became jocular, raffish – and actually affectionate towards me. 'She's a smasher,' he whispered in my ear. 'If I was twenty years younger I'd have her off you!' Never before had we engaged in this kind of rough, man-to-man humour. I felt ten feet tall.

Leave it to Janice, though, to take things too far. 'Oh, Mrs LeJeune,' I heard her gush to my mother, 'Marc is the perfect man. So attentive, so romantic. Don't be too shocked if he has a little surprise for you some time soon!' Just then, as Janice was topping up my mother's glass and knocking back her umpteenth drink, little Noel appeared out of nowhere and tugged on Janice's dress. She looked round and for one split second anger flashed across her face. Then she collected herself, beamed down at the child and said, 'Oh, what a sweet little boy! What's your name, precious? Someone take him away and give him a sweetie!' Noel shuffled off and hid under a table.

By the time brunch was over, my father had taken on the role of a jaunty retired colonel, twirling imaginary moustaches and beaming with blurry bonhomie at the assembled crew. My mother was dashing about blabbing to anyone who'd listen, telling tales of my mischievous childhood and how she'd encouraged me on my first steps to stardom.

The shoot took a little over four hours. That's nothing by today's standards, but at the time I was amazed that it could take so long to produce a thirty-second film. In between 'takes' I relaxed with a coffee and a cigarette while Janice grazed through the leftover hospitality. By the end of the shoot she was plastered, screaming and hooting as I whisked her around the studio, even at one point heaving a breast out of her low-cut dress and exclaiming to the astonished crew, 'Get a load of these Bran Pops, boys!' My father nearly choked.

Despite Janice's best endeavours, the shoot was a great success and ensured our TV immortality. Edited and dubbed, it was a little masterpiece – 'a national treasure' as I recently saw it described in a learned article on advertising art. We're even in a museum – part of the Museum of the Moving Image's collection of classic commercials. It's primitive enough by today's standards, shot in black and white with no special effects, just a boy and a girl and a song, the immortal 'My Guy' by Mary Wells that became a hit thanks to Bran Pops and launched the Motown sound.

We finished at seven o'clock, and I saw my parents off with fond farewells (Janice, fortunately, was having a lie-down at this point and couldn't embarrass me any further). Stepping out of the studio, we were surprised by a small but vocal gang of girls who screamed when they saw me and had to be fought off by Nick and my father. I went back indoors to have a stiff drink and prepare for the 'wrap' party.

It was quite a bash. Nick had rounded up every journalist he knew and invited them all to dinner at an Italian restaurant on Villiers Street, whither we repaired in a fleet of limousines as soon as Janice had recovered sufficiently to be baying for more booze. Once there, we let our hair down and partied in true sixties style, eating, drinking and dancing till dawn. I spent much of the evening trying to fend off Janice's amorous advances as she breathed alcoholic fumes into my ear and told me how much she loved 'Mummy' and 'Daddy' and how she hoped one day that Noel might call them 'Grandma' and 'Grandad'. I fled to another table and chatted to a group of journalists, trying to distract their attention from the antics of my co-star, who was now doing one of her party pieces – standing on a table and singing 'Burlington Bertie' at the top of her tuneless voice, slurring, staggering and occasionally pulling her skirt over her head and screaming, 'Look at my lovely legs, everyone! Aren't they lovely, my lovely legs!' Finally she grew quiet and passed out with her head in her supper. (After this incident, Nick always referred to Janice as 'Pizza Face'.) Little Noel, fortunately, didn't witness any of this; it was only the next day that we discovered he'd been left behind at the studio.

It felt wrong, strange, leaving the party and returning to my absurd home in Elephant and Castle. Nick put it so well when he dropped me off at the end of the street, just as a milk float was rattling past the sleeping houses.

'You don't belong here, Marc.'

'I know.'

'This is no place for a star.'

'But where can I go?'

'We'll have to see about that. Goodnight.'

'Good morning, you mean!'

He drove away, and I crept into the house, unwilling to wake Phyllis, who would undoubtedly rain on my parade.

I slept through most of Saturday, and made myself as pleasant as possible to Phyllis as he passed me, wordlessly, in the kitchen or the hall. He was in one of his silent phases – preferable to his ranting, vindictive moods, but only just. I had no idea that these were the symptoms of a galloping mental illness about which I could do nothing. I went out that night with Nick and some friends, happy to escape from the stifling atmosphere at home. A storm was brewing; when would it break?

It broke the next morning. I was rudely awakened from my beauty sleep when the door burst open and there stood Phyllis in his disgusting pyjamas, hair sticking up and his dentures not in yet. He threw something at me – a stack of newspapers, I discovered, as they hit me on the head and tumbled to the floor. I rubbed my eyes, hardly certain whether I wasn't dreaming the whole ugly scene, and sat up. 'Go away!' I mumbled.

'I will not go away until I've got an explanation! Look! Just look!'

I picked up the nearest newspaper – the *News of the World*, Phyllis's favourite weekend reading. 'Well? Well? What have you got to say for yourself?'

'What are you . . .' I was about to protest. Then I saw. Splashed across the front page was a photograph from the party on Friday night: Janice with her skirt in the air while I sat at a table near by. Somehow the photographer (who should never have been allowed into the party in the first place) had caught me looking as if I was hopelessly drunk (I was simply tired after a hard day's shoot) with my arm around one of the crew (a lighting technician who had been kind enough to ensure I looked my best all day). Taken out of context, the picture looked bad, very bad. And the copy that accompanied it was positively inflammatory. IRREGULAR

HABITS OF THE REGULAR GUY it screamed in huge block capitals, before a catalogue of excesses that would have made me laugh under different circumstances.

Move over Mick Jagger – *this* is the latest, lowest excess to which today's teenage idols have stooped. NO! It isn't a scene from a new dirty movie to come out of Soho – this is real life!

At a West End party on Friday night model Marc LeJeune, star of the cereal ads, made merry with his co-star and wife-to-be Janice Jones to celebrate their first TV appearance.

'Regular Guy' Marc, 20, shared a joke and a drink with another bachelor friend while lovely Janice (38–24–36) entertained in her own special way. 'I'm so ashamed of my boy,' said Marc's mum earlier that day. 'Since he ran away from home he's fallen in with a bad crowd. I'm so scared that he'll end up hooked on drugs or worse.'

'Marc's a figurehead for tomorrow's generation,' said manager, boutique owner and 'beefcake' photographer Nick Nicholls. Looks like Marc needs an early night and a bowl of Bran Pops!

Of course it was all lies. I knew that, my parents knew that, but how could Phyllis and the rest of the world be expected to know? I could imagine the scene at breakfast tables all over Britain as eager readers tutted and clucked over each salacious, mendacious detail. 'And what do you think that's going to do for sales of Bran Pops?' asked Phyllis, his voice dripping with the most evil sarcasm. I hadn't thought of that! The image of the nation's healthiest breakfast cereal had been dragged into the gutter. I'd be sacked, even prosecuted. I'd never work again. I had to speak to Nick.

'Isn't it marvellous!' he cooed as soon as he picked up the phone. 'Couldn't be better. Well done!'

I pinched myself. Suddenly my world was upside down. Was everybody mad, or just me?

'Have you seen the papers, Nick?' It wasn't just the *News of the World*. There were reports in practically all of them, written with varying degrees of bitchiness.

'Of course I have! It's fantastic.'

'What on earth are you talking about?' I screamed *sotto voce*, unwilling that eavesdropping Phyllis should witness my discomfiture.

'Now we've really made it. You're big news. The phone hasn't stopped ringing.'

Slowly, patiently, Nick explained himself. The reporters – invited by him, of course – had been fully briefed to expect a story. Nick had even fed them lines – 'irregular habits' was his work, I discovered. And why? For publicity. 'Everybody loves the Regular Guy,' he said, 'but he's a bit tame, a bit squeaky clean. People don't want their heroes to be too perfect these days. They like a bit of excitement. And that is exactly what we're going to give them.'

Nick was a PR genius. While other managers would do everything in their power to keep their clients out of the Sunday papers, Nick was doing his utmost to get me in. And if that meant that I was portrayed as a tearaway, a bad boy, who was I to complain? It never did James Dean or Marlon Brando any harm. Suddenly I was Britain's answer to *Rebel Without a Cause* (sweet irony!) and *The Wild One*, the first homegrown rock & roll rebel icon.

Phyllis, however, was unimpressed when I explained that my tabloid coverage was part of a carefully orchestrated PR campaign. 'I won't have it, do you hear me?' he hissed. 'Any more trouble and you're out. And don't try to wheedle your way out of this one. I mean it. You've let me down, Mark. You've let me down very badly indeed.' Phyllis rushed from the room in tears. I couldn't be bothered to follow him, my head was still spinning. But I knew he was serious. Phyllis wasn't one to make idle threats, at least not in his sane, lucid interludes. I had come to depend on him as a rock of stability amidst the madness and glamour of my new life. I had also been delighted to discover that he had made me his legal heir.

But what could I do? The work was flooding in: interviews, personal appearances, photo calls soon became a matter of course. And each occasion was attended by an ever-increasing horde of screaming female fans. My biggest 'gig' that summer was opening a shopping mall, the first of its kind to be built in Britain, situated just across the road from Phyllis's flat, in the heart of the Elephant and Castle. It was a symbol of all that was bright and new in London, rising above the dingy streets like a giant temple of consumerism.

A limousine collected me from Phyllis's house and drove a few times round the block before depositing me at the entrance to the mall. Traffic came to a standstill, teenagers rushed and screamed and grabbed, cameras clicked and whirred. We were even on the news. I cut a ribbon, kissed Janice (bad-tempered, as she'd been kept away from the bottle all day), signed a few autographs then made my escape in a waiting getaway vehicle. Little did the thousands of fans realize that 'home' was only just round the corner!

They found out soon enough, though. One day I was shocked to find a group of three girls sitting on our doorstep. I assumed that they were local kids until they started screaming 'Marc! Marc!' every time I went near the window. Within a week there were regularly twenty or thirty fans cluttering up the narrow street. Phyllis was horrified and called the police, who arrived with journalists. The resultant coverage in the *South London Press* ensured that dozens more fans arrived every day. Soon we were under siege, requiring a strong-arm escort to and from the front door. Phyllis stopped leaving the house and stayed mostly in his bedroom. Fans scaled the wall and set up camp in the garden. And with each new excess, Nick was ready with a story for the papers.

Poor Phyllis, the pressure was beginning to tell. I didn't realize that he had a weak heart, and that more than anything he needed peace, quiet and constant nursing. If I'd known how my fame was hurrying him to his grave, I would have moved heaven and earth to help him. But brave Phyllis suffered in silence.

Nick was right about one thing: there's no such thing as bad publicity. After the shock of my *News of the World* exposure, I entered a new league of stardom. It was the kids who put me there, but it was the press who nurtured me. Soon I was the darling of the teen magazines, and my face was plastered over every bedroom wall in the country. They loved me, my wholesome, outdoorsy image with its spicy hint of naughtiness, my will-they-won't-they relationship with Janice, my readiness to give them a quote on any and every subject under the sun. Nick brilliantly placed me at the very heart of the teenage revolution, creating a buzz that the magazines lapped up. He issued press releases that were reprinted almost word for word in a dozen syndicated titles. 'Man of the world Marc loves dancing, shopping and long drives in the country,' ran one of his more memorable efforts.

Only 18, he's already travelled across four continents, and is now living in London where he's working on his first record album. 'London's the place for me!' says cheeky Marc, whose French father was a war hero. 'Everything I love is right here!' Does he mean blonde bombshell Janice Jones, co-star and constant companion? Baby-faced Marc won't tell. 'I'm not ready to settle down yet,' he says, lighting a cigarette. 'There's so many things I want to do.'

It rattled on in the same vein for 1500 words. In another feature, Janice was 'interviewed' (via Nick) about her health and beauty secrets. ' "I only eat fruit and drink water before six o'clock in the evening," says Janice, a trained dancer. "I keep in shape with a daily exercise programme. It's all about toning and stretching!" she smiles.' Ironic, considering this was a woman who kept her figure by swallowing two 'black bombers' every morning and sticking her fingers down her throat after every meal.

I've always believed in giving credit where it's due, and I have to say that I might not have become famous quite so soon had it not been for the tireless efforts of Nick Nicholls. What was it that drove him on? Was he experiencing the thrill of success vicariously, through me? Was he simply a consummate professional, content with his 'cut' of my income and the satisfaction of a job well done? Or was there a more sinister side to his interest in my career? Only time would tell.

And time was the one thing that was in short supply. As 1965 rolled into 1966, I was working every second of every day. There was no time for relaxation. Even the parties were work, making sure that I was seen in the right places with the right people. And what people! A few snapshots from that time: drinking champagne from Dusty Springfield's shoe after we'd danced the can-can down Oxford Street; hosting a party for George Best (who briefly dated Janice) at the Kensington Roof Gardens (I never knew George well, but I became very close with a member of the England World Cup squad); crashing the *Top of the Pops* backstage party and posing for photographs with Jimmy Savile, both of us puffing on a cigar; being chatted up by a humble, self-effacing young American who introduced himself only as Warren. And everywhere I went, the fans came too.

For the second Bran Pops campaign, we decided on a whole new image for the Regular Guy and his girl. It was 1966, that strange, transitional year between 'mod' and 'hippy' styles, when the clean-cut looks that I'd created only a year before were being replaced by something looser and more flamboyant. The tailored, pegged pants and sharp jackets of yesterday were giving way to brightly coloured 'flares' and puff-sleeved shirts, accessorized with flowing scarves and chunky jewellery. Nick and I spent night after night literally at the drawing board, sketching out the cuts and lines of a revolution in male fashion. Even my haircut changed. The deep-fringed, pudding-bowl style that Nick had given me was 'out'; now I wore it parted at the side, flowing down over one eye and curling well over my collar at the back. And for the creation of this new look I was introduced to the most famous hair salon in London – in the world – a name that is synonymous with sixties styling.

Willy Frizz, society crimper, ruled over the world of hair from his fashionable King's Road salon. Here you got not only the best *coiffure* but also the best gossip in town, rationed out by the eccentric Willy himself. Of all the characters I had met so far in my odyssey through London, Willy Frizz was the wildest – a 'screaming queen' we'd have called him in those days, whose mannerisms and outrageous vocabulary made Phyllis, even Nick, look 'butch' in comparison. His Francophilia, too, was considerably more pronounced than Nick's. '*Oh, mon trésor!*' he screamed when I first stepped into his salon. 'Just wait till I get my hands on your *cheveux*!' He wore his own grey hair in a trademark teased tangle – an 'afro'. Silk shirts in daring hues – tangerine, plum, lime – were undone to the belly button. A record-player in the corner of the salon blasted out Willy's favourite records, everything from Motown to Mahler (the outcome of one's hairdo depended greatly on Willy's current choice of music). And in Willy's, drugs were the norm. The man himself gobbled back 'pep pills', 'diet pills' and 'downers' like sweets, handed them to clients or accepted them in payment. When I think of Willy Frizz's legendary salon, I remember the blaring music and the sound of pills rattling across the floor as another handful was shaken into his screeching mouth.

I met many stars at Willy's. Everybody who was anybody was trimmed and teased in his Chelsea hair headquarters. Pop stars rubbed shoulders with royalty, criminals chatted to ballerinas. It was a magnet for journalists, who would try almost any ruse to get an appointment; Willy had an uncanny sixth sense for snoopers and would unceremoniously chuck them out. Only the *crème de la crème* of the press were welcomed. One such was a gossip columnist who had a brush with fame back in the sixties (readers with long memories may remember the name Paul 'Pinky' Stevens, whose daily column for the London *Evening News* practically set the city's agenda at the time). Since those heady days, Pinky has sunk into deep obscurity (his was not a lasting talent), but in 1966 he was the golden boy of the British press, and I was happy enough to be on easy terms with him as we sat under the driers at Willy's.

He was an attractive, easy-going personality (I thought) – but more of Pinky Stevens later.

After my first appointment at Willy's, I returned home pleased as Punch with my new look. But a terrible shock awaited me. I hadn't been back to the flat for a few days – parties, appointments and dates had kept me on the go for over seventy-two hours. During that time, Phyllis had taken a turn for the worse. Dozens of fans were surrounding the house (I signed autographs and kissed a few cheeks as I arrived), making it impossible for Phyllis to leave; in fact, he'd barricaded himself in the kitchen. When I breezed into the house shouting a jaunty 'hello!', the first thing I noticed was the smell. This led me to the kitchen, where I found the old man naked and filthy, crouched under the table clutching a carving knife. When he saw me he cowered and whimpered, making feeble passes with the blade. 'No one home! No one home!' he jabbered. 'They want to kill me!'

'Who wants to kill you?' I asked, gently taking him by the wrist and disarming him.

'All of them! But I won't die! I won't die!' He shrieked with laughter, muttered something incomprehensible and then suddenly stopped, his eyes glazed over, staring into space. As I led him to the bathroom, I noticed two empty bottles of gin shoved rudely into the bin.

After a dreadful hour, I had Phyllis clean and tucked up in bed. He slept peacefully, seemingly unaware of his recent outburst. The fans were happy enough to disperse when I asked them nicely; I suspected, however, that they had taunted poor Phyllis cruelly. For the first time, I realized that my beloved guardian was sick, possibly near death. How much had he suffered, quiet and alone, while I was out enjoying myself? How could I make amends for the terrible humiliations he'd undergone? I called in the doctor, and prepared myself for bad news. Phyllis was suffering from acute depression, I learned, and anxiety attacks associated with cardiac arrhythmia.

Too much stress, or a sudden shock, could send him into permanent dementia or even kill him outright.

The situation was aggravated when, a couple of days later, our household was increased by the addition of a bull terrier bitch puppy, a gift from Nick ('dogs are quite *de rigueur*' he told me, and he was right; the waiting room at Willy's often resembled the champion's ring at Crufts). Little Sugar (as I named her after one of my favourite Marilyn roles) was as good as gold with me, but she hated Phyllis. She worried at him, barked and even bit him, and seemed to reserve her toilet-training 'accidents' for those moments when Phyllis was sure to step in it.

I had to do something to make it up to Phyllis. After all, I owed him everything. He'd been the spark that ignited my talent. He'd taken me in when my parents threw me out. And for all our differences, he'd been my best friend. And what had I given him in return? Nothing but heartache.

I knew that what he wanted more than anything was for us to live together 'as friends' – that was his oft-repeated dream. And now that his life and sanity were slipping away from him, there was less chance that he would ever see that dream come true. What could I do but ensure that the old man enjoyed a taste of happiness before he . . . It was too awful to think of. I decided to devote my energies to giving Phyllis the time of his life.

When he'd recovered from that terrible episode with the carving knife, I spent many a spare moment casually chatting with him as he lay in bed resting. I'd bring him snacks and cups of tea or drinks, then I'd lounge on his bed in my bathrobe, talking about old times. I started modelling for him again; it was so wonderful to see his long-dormant artistic genius flaring back into life as he posed me first as a martyred saint (bound to the bedstead), then as a revelling satyr. I allowed him intimacies – kisses, caresses and more – that he had never dared to ask for before. Phyllis blossomed under my care. The colour returned to his cheeks as he flushed with excitement, but I had to be so careful that he didn't fatally 'overdo' it during one of our jolly afternoon romps.

In fact, to my amazement, Phyllis seemed to be getting better and better. Soon he was up and about again, even taking Sugar for a walk along the river. This was not what I had expected at all. Instead of a dying man, suddenly – to my inexpressible joy – I had a hale and hearty, active, amorous pensioner on my hands.

Clearly, my unorthodox treatment was working. And if the mild 'giggles' that we'd allowed ourselves made him so much saner and stronger, think (I reasoned) what a more energetic approach to our relationship might achieve. I took to wearing my old leather jacket again, and even bought a nifty biker's cap and boots to go with it. I strode around the house in this outfit while Phyllis chased me; this was the man who a few short weeks before had been unable to manage the stairs to the bathroom. Our friendly, man-to-man romps on the bed were lasting longer and becoming frankly taxing of my energies. He had the vitality of a lovestruck young man. I simply couldn't believe what my innovative treatment was achieving.

As time wore on, he became more demanding. Soon our innocent dalliances weren't enough, he craved stronger stimuli. Exhausted, I was forced to trawl through Soho's specialist clothing shops seeking out costumes and props that would satisfy his ravenous appetite for novelty. Our home life, never orthodox, now became downright bizarre as I dressed myself in hoods, masks and chains, 'disciplined' Phyllis with a studded leather belt and a vicious 'paddle', allowed myself to be restrained with velvet ropes for which Phyllis had a thousand and one uses. Friends and colleagues remarked on my sunken eyes, my drawn expression; Willy Frizz complained that my hair was greasy and lifeless ('*comme un cochon*', as he put it). But I was willing to make almost any sacrifice to save Phyllis.

As in so many things, I was ahead of my time in this radical 'homoeopathic' approach to Phyllis's illness. But alas! I lacked the support of a conservative medical establishment, and was forced to proceed without professional supervision (the doctor, a stick-in-the-mud GP, still insisted that Phyllis needed nothing but rest, and that any stress was dangerous). Should I have listened to his advice? Would Phyllis still be alive today? Maybe. But he would have lived a long, unhappy life, unfulfilled and bitter. At least he died a happy, happy man.

The end, when it came, was as quick as it was unexpected. After nearly a month of our new regime, by which time I was frankly running out of ideas, we were indulging in a gruelling game of horsey up and down the living-room floor. First of all, Phyllis would 'ride' me as I panted, reared and whinnied, naked except for the leather 'bit and bridle' that I wore. Then we'd change places, and Phyllis would trot around as I sat astride his back and occasionally spurred him on with a smart cut of the whip. Just as he was about to take the first jump (he'd insisted on setting up a small steeplechase of chairs and coffee tables) he reared, snuffled and collapsed. 'Bad horsey,' I shouted, assuming that he was 'refusing' the fence in order to provoke my anger. 'Giddy up, boy! Giddy up!' I whacked him across the haunches with my cane. There was no response. I dismounted and stooped to examine him.

All I remember of that terrible moment was his twisted, crimson face, the tongue bursting out of his mouth, the staring eyes. It was too much; I blacked out, and came round with an awful start an hour later.

As soon as I was able, I dashed to the phone and called an ambulance, but by the time it arrived (many minutes later) it was too late. Who knows, those few, fatal minutes may have cost Phyllis his life. The paramedics took the pitiful body away on a stretcher; I'd dressed him in a decent pair of pyjamas, eager that he should have some dignity in death.

This was my first date with death. Over the years, I'd lose many loved ones, but Phyllis was my earliest, bitterest loss. 'You don't know what you've got till it's gone' goes the song. How true. Only when the house was empty did I realize the terrible void that Phyllis had left in my life, my heart. If it hadn't been for little Sugar, constantly begging for attention, demanding walkies, I don't think I would have made it. Certainly, life with Phyllis had never been easy; we'd fought almost constantly, and his demands had grown ever more pettish and bizarre. But now I realized that, deep down below the surface of our daily lives, there ran a current of pure, self-sacrificing love. I'm not ashamed to say that I loved the old man, not just as a son loves his (surrogate) father, but as a young, passionate boy loves an older, stronger, more experienced man. It was the Greek ideal, of which Phyllis had spoken so much in the early days. Without it, I was vulnerable, alone.

But how quickly the vultures gathered to pick over the bones! While I should have been left to the quiet dignity of grief, I was assaulted on all sides. First of all, there was the coroner's inquest, which recorded an open verdict. A strange decision! If ever there was a death by natural causes it was this, an old man, with a history of mental and physical ills, paying the price for a brief game of snowballs in the winter garden of his senility. I was called in for hour upon hour of questioning – I who had done nothing but nurse Phyllis in the last weeks of his life! I nearly broke under the strain, and spent most of the time in tears. Certain 'marks' had been found on Phyllis's body (how could I shame the dead by revealing details of our life together?); and there was the question of the 999 call. The coroner had 'established' (how I fail to see) that the time of death was long before the time of the call. Unbelievably, fingers began to point at me as some kind of culprit in Phyllis's death.

Needless to say, the moment the police arrived at my house, the press were there to report every detail. Now I began to see the darker side of fame, the terrible hunger that feeds on pain, heartbreak and tears. What was this strange delight they took in my grief? For the first (and only) time in my life I wished that I was just plain

Mark Young again, living an unremarkable life away from the glare of publicity.

Of course, nobody would come right out and accuse me of anything. The law, perverse as ever, prevented that outrage while persistently treating me as suspect number one in a murder case that didn't exist. One by one, my so-called friends became distant. One frightful afternoon *chez* Willy Frizz I suffered the indignity of having my hair washed and hacked by a spotty-faced junior. I knew that I would be in social and professional Siberia until this confusion was cleared up. Each day, I was summoned back to the police station and forced to go over the details of Phyllis's last days, to reveal the most private habits of a man whose memory I respected more than I valued my own freedom. I know now that I was a fool. By protecting Phyllis I was, in effect, lying to the police and getting myself into very hot water indeed. But it's a mistake I'm not ashamed to have made.

Eventually there was even some talk of charges being brought, which would mean a trial, a barrage of negative publicity and the end of my career. During this horrible time, when I was most in need of support, I received a hideous shock from beyond the grave. Too ill to attend the funeral, I'd nevertheless managed to drag myself along to the solicitor's office for the reading of the will, determined to do all in my powers to execute Phyllis's final wishes. He had, as I knew, left me everything; but how little that 'every-thing' turned out to be! A few books, some valuable furniture (which had to be sold to pay bills) and the tenancy of the flat. The tenancy, that is, not the ownership. How deceived I had been! Phyllis's maisonette, 'my one possession, dear boy, my refuge and my dowry', was his in name only; it belonged to the local council. I didn't even have the comfort of property ownership to see me through my mourning; all I could cleave to was a complete Shake-speare and a few second-rate pornographic drawings.

Just as I had steeled myself to face ruin – prison, after all, couldn't be any worse than the hell I was living in – suddenly, without explanation, the investigation was suspended. Phyllis's death, which had been a matter of serious police concern, was now a closed file. When I reported to the station for my daily grilling by the detective inspector on the case, I was told by the desk sergeant to 'run along and be a good boy', I wouldn't be required again.

I'll never know what evidence had come to light to exonerate me from those terrifying false charges. But I realized straight away that Nick had a hand in my release. I phoned to tell him the good news, but he knew already and requested an immediate interview at his house.

Nick's cold, calculating business sense under the most distressing circumstances will never cease to amaze me. He explained that the police had been made to 'see sense', that he had 'a friendly chat' with a friend in Scotland Yard ('a great admirer of yours, by the way') who had been easily convinced that my continued persecution could do no good in the long run. How right he was! The conviction of an innocent man would only bring the force further into disrepute. I was delighted at first, but I soon realized that there was a price to pay for my freedom.

Without his assistance, Nick was quick to assure me, I would have been in prison by the end of the year. Thanks to him, I was free to carry on working as if nothing had happened. He, Nick, would get me back on my feet and continue to manage my career, but only on certain conditions. 'Don't rock the boat, Marc,' he threatened in his silky, insinuating way. 'A little harmless scandal is one thing, but a queer murder is a different matter. You've been a silly boy, but we'll put that behind us now. Play the game my way and we'll all be fine. But remember: you're in my hands now.'

I was happy to agree. How could I do otherwise? And the first condition of my liberty was that I should go and say a personal thank you to Nick's friend (my fan) in Scotland Yard, the high-ranking police commissioner who had struck such an important blow for truth, liberty and human rights.

It was hard to return to work so soon after my bereavement, but I knew I must. And, to my surprise, it saved my sanity. They speak of the power of 'Doctor Theatre', the miraculous healing force of our profession that I was feeling for the first time. And Nick was at hand with just the right prescription: job after job after job. The time had come to 'cash in' on my success in the Regular Guy adverts which had established me as a star, a force to be reckoned with; added to that was the novelty value accruing from my recent brush with notoriety, all of which made me irresistible to producers. Once again I was 'making the rounds', but this time, it was I who was doing the picking and choosing, considering the rival attractions of a dozen powerful, influential industry figures eager to work with me.

The vehicle I chose with which to announce my professional comeback was a stage play – yes, I, Marc LeJeune, who had turned my back on the stage, decided that the theatre was ready for me once again. After the dull-as-ditchwater tedium of the fifties, the theatre in the late sixties was once again the home of artists and innovators, where the moral and sexual issues of the day were debated in bold dramatic gestures. For my début on the West End stage I selected a script from the many that had arrived at Nick's office, a tense, brooding thriller entitled *Kill Me, Darling*. I was teamed with a top-flight supporting cast, all of them names familiar from the television, and a brilliant (if untried) director. We were booked for a short out-of-town run before our London opening in only six weeks time.

Kill Me, Darling was a daring blend of sex and violence, the like of which had never been seen on the British stage. I played Gary, a wealthy young playboy who is drawn into an obsessive sexual relationship with a much older woman, the beautiful French novelist Arlette (played *con brio* by my dear friend Noele Gordon). The action took place in Arlette's suite at Claridge's, her *château* in France and the Old Bailey, where I was tried for her murder after a fatal accident on a punt. The sensational climax of *Kill Me,*

Darling, in which Arlette's jealous lesbian sister confessed to the murder, thus freeing me to marry my home-town sweetheart, had audiences literally on the edge of their seats every night.

We got a wonderful reception in the provinces, where theatre-goers are more honest in their appreciation of a fine dramatic entertainment. When we opened in London at the Savoy Theatre, excitement had reached fever pitch. Advance publicity ensured a full house for weeks to come, and had spewed up a forest of newspaper coverage, most of it bursting with enthusiasm. But every so often I'd notice with dismay the voice of carping criticism – that cancer that eats at the heart of every democracy. A week before we were due to open at the Savoy, I read this in the *Evening News*:

What does it take to make a star these days? Not much, if the ecstatic reaction currently greeting out-of-town performances of lame whodunnit *Kill Me, Darling* is anything to go by. Lead Marc LeJeune is better known for his appearance in the scandal sheets (and, of course, for his famously regular bowel movements) than for his acting ability, but has turned his recent misfortunes to good effect with a sell-out tour. Londoners will have a chance to see for themselves when *Kill Me, Darling* staggers into the Savoy next week . . .

The Friday before we opened I saw another pustule of malice in the same paper.

Lock up your grandfathers! Marc LeJeune, star of laxative commercials and police reports, is bringing his special brand of acting to the Savoy in *Kill Me, Darling* (opens Tuesday). Expect queues of elderly gentlemen and teenage girls stretching back to Trafalgar Square for a few nights to come!

It didn't take long for me to figure out that these 'reports' were from the poison pen of Paul 'Pinky' Stevens, a man who, in our occasional meetings at Willy Frizz's King's Road salon, I had thought was my friend. What had I done to upset him so much?

Nick was philosophical. 'At least they spelt your name right and said there'd be queues,' he said.

Despite Pinky's best efforts, *Kill Me, Darling* was a triumph. 'Marc LeJeune takes the thriller into completely uncharted territory,' raved one review, while another praised 'his uncanny ability to deliver any line, however absurd, with the kind of boundless enthusiasm one usually sees only in small children and animals'. 'LeJeune: the new Novello!' began a report that Nick submitted to *Vogue*, *Harpers* and *The Tatler* (it finally appeared in a much edited form in *The Stage*). But it wasn't just in the artistic sphere that *Kill Me, Darling* was a success. It played for three months to good houses, ensuring a bountiful return for the investors and proving my pulling power as a West End star. At the closing night party, Nick thrust a new contract into my hand: never again, it seemed, would I be out of work.

We rang down the curtain on *Kill Me, Darling* on a Thursday evening in February 1967; the following Monday I was back in rehearsal preparing for an even more challenging role, my comic début in the farce *There Were Three in the Bed*. So far, my experience had been limited to dramatic roles: the tragic grandeur of Cleopatra, the dark genius of Orpheus, the triumphant innocence of Gary. But here was a new side to me – a talent for light comedy. I confess that I was nervous as we went into rehearsals for *There Were Three in the Bed*, doubting my ability to match the brilliant supporting cast. But I needn't have worried: at the end of the first readthrough the actors, the director, even the wardrobe mistress were in stitches. I had swapped the mask of tragedy for the mask of comedy with ease.

There Were Three in the Bed is, in retrospect, among my best work. There was nothing experimental or daring about it: this was classic, timeless English farce. The script had the brilliance of Molière, the insouciance of Coward, the pathos of Rattigan. I played Ben, a roguish young fashion designer used to getting his way with the women he works with, until one day he falls under the spell of a mysterious young model, Magda, protégé of the elderly Russian couturier Count Mushkin. At a weekend party at Mushkin's vast country estate, Magda and Ben are surprised in bed by Andrei, Mushkin's handsome young son and Magda's official fiancé – and Ben's exact double. A fast-paced comedy of mistaken identities ensues, before Ben, Magda and Andrei run away to Cap d'Antibes in Mushkin's private yacht.

It was a happy production, and I was glad to discover a kindred spirit in the actor who played Andrei, a *molto sympatico* colleague and friend who was my constant support through a difficult production that stretched me in every direction. Once again we 'tried out' in the provinces before coming to London, and the familiar pattern emerged. We had full houses, the public and press loved us – everywhere but in London. Just as we were toasting the first night reviews at our hotel in Cardiff, Nick came in clutching the *Evening News*. Once again, Pinky had dipped deep into the vitriol.

Connoisseurs of exquisite theatre will be thrilled to know that Marc LeJeune, idol of the pink poodle brigade, is once again London-bound in a new vehicle, the tantalizingly named *There Were Three in the Bed*. Mr LeJeune, we are told, is flexing his comic muscles after the dramatic excesses of *Kill Me, Darling* emptied out the Savoy Theatre some weeks back. The producers of *Three in the Bed* must have heard the bellows of laughter from the stalls and decided to put them to good use. Opens 6 April.

I was hurt, I won't deny it, but it hurt a little less this time. Whatever lies he told about me, one great truth remained: I was an artist with a growing reputation and an adoring public, whereas Pinky Stevens was a two-bit hack on a despised tabloid newspaper. I was a legend in the making; he'd be wrapping tomorrow's fish and chips.

But the ignorant sniping of the critics couldn't spoil the success of *There Were Three in the Bed*. By the time we came to London, word of mouth had ensured a sell-out, and the whole of the West End was abuzz with excitement about this brilliant, sexy new farce.

'Andrei' and I were the talk of the town, besieged every night by stage door johnnies bearing gifts and invitations. I still have fond if rather guilty memories of the beautiful matching monkey-skin coats that were presented to us by one infatuated admirer (with a sweet little matching coat for Sugar); we were certainly noticed when we made an entrance into a chic night club wearing those!

And this was the pattern of my life for the next year. Nick drove me hard – I think he realized that work was the only medicine for me. He worked almost as hard as I did; in no way did I begrudge him the fifty per cent of my earnings that he took as his 'cut'. We were a formidable team, clawing our way to the top of the tree, upping our prices with every new job. Nick ran my diary, my wardrobe, even my social life. He kept a close watch over my friendship with 'Andrei'. 'Remember,' he'd caution, 'you're brothers, nothing more.' Soon, Nick and I were working so closely together that it became necessary for me to move to Holland Park on a permanent basis; I'd been more or less living there anyway since Phyllis's death. Reluctantly, I bade farewell to my old home – home only to ghosts now – and installed myself and Sugar in Nick's spacious apartment.

There were more plays; I can hardly remember some of them now. There were television appearances – Lulu, Cilla, Petula all welcomed me as a friend and a guest. My duet with Cilla surfaced on BBC2 recently as part of a night wittily entitled *Musical Hell*, and we certainly 'raised hell' with our raunchy rendition of 'It Takes Two'. But the more successful I became, the more the pressure started to build. I badly needed a holiday, to heal myself after the terrible events of the last twelve months, to muster my artistic powers on which such demands had been made. I argued with 'Andrei' shortly after we finished in *There Were Three in the Bed*; his reliance on me had gone beyond a simple professional attachment and was blossoming into something unhealthy. Now he was out of my life.

But it wasn't just work that was getting me down. There was another factor pushing me ever closer to the edge – Janice Jones. Although we hadn't worked together for months, Janice and I were still 'man and wife' in the minds of the public; the adverts were on television many times every day. And Janice, with time on her hands and money to burn (or to drink) had fallen into the error of believing her own publicity. She wanted so desperately to 'make it real', to have me for herself. I was happy to be her friend, to tolerate her fantasies if it made her feel better; and after all, she'd been a staunch ally during the negative publicity following Phyllis's death. (Nick had placed a story about our impending betrothal in several of the newspapers, brilliantly diverting attention from the hints of impropriety in my relationship with the deceased.) She'd also kept in touch with my parents, developing a friendship with 'Mummy' and 'Daddy' that delighted them. But that was never enough. Janice wouldn't be content until she had me body and soul.

Before I knew it, I was the object of a persistent campaign of harassment and intimidation. Janice, frail as she was in many things, was implacable in this one obsession. Sometimes she was wheedling, pathetic, calling me on the telephone to cry and wail and bemoan her lot. Those, believe it or not, were the good times. On other occasions she was violent, turning up at Nick's house at 3 a.m. (drunk of course) and punching a hole through the window when we wouldn't let her in the door, putting unspeakable things through the letterbox, even attempting to kill Sugar in an insane traffic 'accident'. But that wasn't the worst. There were times when she was just downright mad. She'd phone the flat at four in the morning, and we'd hear nothing on the other end except occasional laughter, whispered nonsense, drumming. Of course, we'd put the phone down, but that didn't bother Janice; when we picked up the receiver ten, twenty, thirty minutes later she was still there, drumming and cackling away. Occasionally she was her sweet, sane self, meeting me at a party and pretending that nothing had happened. I wondered what effect it was having on poor Noel.

On top of all this, I had to contend with the malicious attentions of Pinky Stevens (I now featured in his column on an almost daily basis) and the intolerable pressures of working and living with Nick Nicholls. I don't know which was worse. Pinky made me look a fool, deriding my every effort and lampooning me under a variety of childish epithets ('the killer kid' was a particularly hurtful one that sticks in my memory). But there was no escape from Nick. It wasn't just that he worked me hard; no professional minds that. It was his way of constantly reminding me of my obligations to him, his harping on the past, that made me feel like a caged beast. Whatever request I made, for time off, for new clothes, for some say in the choice of work I was doing, Nick would reply with a tasteless reference to my recent bereavment, or to Scotland Yard. And if I complained about the way he ran the business – about the fact that he still expected me to model for 'private' photographic clients, in particular – he'd simply laugh. 'I wonder if Pinky Stevens would like to run a little portfolio of my pictures,' he'd say. I had no control over Nick. There was no love in the man. He craved two things only: money and power. I gave him both.

Things came to a head one afternoon in the early spring of 1968. I'd had a bad week with Nick: he'd forced me to attend another of his occasional 'investors' parties', a very different and more sordid affair than that glamorous night so long ago. And I was depressed by yet another bitchy remark in Pinky's column, a total misrepresentation of an unfortunate scene he'd witnessed in the Waldorf when Janice Jones had chosen to execute one of her embarrassing performances during tea (she hadn't, I need hardly add, been drinking tea alone). I was struggling through rehearsals for yet another play, a second-rate romance that hadn't even been guaranteed a West End run.

I was depressed, and not looking forward to meeting Nick and Janice at Claridge's to discuss our next Bran Pops commercial. I was sick of Bran Pops, sick of the Regular Guy and the stupid, shallow fame that commercials had brought me. I hated Janice, I hated Nick, I even kicked Sugar when she stopped to squat in Hyde Park. And London was unbearable, full of unaccountable crowds seething around Oxford Street and Mayfair, great unwashed hordes of longhairs. I literally fought my way to Claridge's and stumbled, crushed and sweaty, into the lounge where my colleagues awaited me. They'd obviously been arguing – Nick and Janice were incapable of civil social relations – and were eager to take it all out on me. 'You're late, Marc,' snapped Nick before I'd even said hello.

'Leave him alone!' slurred Janice before bestowing a wet, sloppy kiss on my mouth (I immediately recognized whisky sours). Sugar was no help; cowering in a corner, she laid a small but very smelly turd behind one of the parlour palms.

Nick was in combative mood. 'You two have got to get your arses in gear,' he began. 'You don't seem to realize it, but in the next month we've got to shoot two more TV commercials, you've got a mini-tour of supermarket appearances and you, Marc, have a number of personal engagements with investors. I want both of you where I tell you to be and when I tell you, not breezing in twenty minutes late like some poncey movie star.'

I tried to keep my cool (Janice was practically unconscious). 'I'm sorry, Nick,' I explained through clenched teeth. 'I've had a bad day. Forgive me.'

But Nick was not in forgiving mood. 'A bad day? That's rich.'

'What do you mean?'

'I mean, Marc, that you've been having a "bad day" now for some weeks.'

How dared he? Whatever personal tragedies I had undergone (without compassionate leave, I might add) I had never given less than 120 per cent to all my professional engagements. 'I resent that slur,' I said, and rose to leave. Unfortunately, the chair became entangled with Sugar's lead and forced me to sit down again rather abruptly. Sugar yelped as I trod on her foot.

'I've told you before, Marc,' continued Nick, '*you* do not resent

things with *me*. We have an understanding, don't we? You listen
to what I say and you damn well respect it.'

'It's very hard to respect a man who uses blackmail to maintain
his hold over a rising star.'

'You should have thought of that before you killed Phyllis.'

That was it. That was the foul insinuation he had been saving
up for this moment of crisis. I was speechless, devoid of words.
Once again I struggled to my feet.

'And you should have thought of that before you became such a
popular Nick Nicholls model.'

I suddenly saw my situation very clearly. I had a choice. Either I
sat down, accepted Nick and his 'terms', worked hard and enjoyed
the financial rewards while sacrificing my personal liberty, my
integrity. Or I broke the bonds, flung his filthy accusations back in
his face and took the consequences, come what may. There was
not a moment's hesitation in my mind.

'Do your worst. You and I are through. Goodbye, Janice.'

I marched out of the hotel, leaving Nick, Janice and even little
Sugar staring after me in appalled surprise.

I had no idea what I was doing, where I was going, but suddenly,
as I stepped out of Claridge's into the bracing spring afternoon, I
felt giddy with freedom. The nightmares of the past – of Phyllis,
of Nick, of Janice, of the other vultures who were tearing me apart
– evaporated. I strode into the street, mad with excitement. And
the rest of the world seemed to share that excitement! Everywhere
I looked there were young people racing towards the hotel, to greet
me as I stepped out into a new chapter of my life. Let them come,
I thought! Let it all come!

I stepped out to face these harbingers of a new life, and found
myself swept along in a current over which I had no control. Faster
and faster the crowd surged down Brook Street, carrying me along
with it. At first I assumed that there must be a sale at Selfridges,
and that these were keen bargain-hunters. But as I took stock of
my situation I saw a strange new uniform: tatty denim jeans, long

hair, beards and moustaches on the men, beads and headbands on the women. These were England's first 'hippies', and they had claimed me as one of their own.

The noise and mayhem grew more intense as we poured into Grosvenor Square, now a forest of placards and banners: Troops Out of Vietnam Now! Down with Uncle Sam! Yanks Go Home! Kill the Pigs! I felt as if I'd walked into an insane asylum where the lunatics had taken over.

A group of uniformed policemen came charging towards me. My first reaction was one of panic: I'd been discharged from the recent police inquiry, but for one second I feared that some new, damning evidence had come to light. Then I realized that they were advancing with truncheons flailing, aimed not just at me but indiscriminately at the crowd to my right and left. I screamed and ran across the square, ducking and diving past scenes of pitched battle that turned this exclusive West End address into a living hell. I made for the American Embassy, where, I assumed, I might find shelter. How wrong I was! As I made a desperate leap for the stairs and the safety I hoped to find inside the doors, my collar was grabbed by a sturdy police officer who picked me up like a rag doll, swung me through 180 degrees and carried me bodily towards a waiting police van. 'Pigs! Pigs!' screamed voices all around me. I had one final vision of a sea of angry, frightened faces before I was pitched into the back of a police van that moved off, sirens blazing. Darkness and the smell of alarmed human bodies surrounded me.

Gradually I came to my senses. My eyes grew accustomed to the Stygian gloom of the 'pig van' and I could see maybe half a dozen fellow travellers. One of them, a woman by the sound of her voice, began singing 'We Shall Overcome'. We rode along, for all the world like a works outing to the seaside enjoying a jolly sing-song. I began to enjoy the press of humanity, the closeness, even the earthy smell and touch of the man who was pushed against me. Finally the van stopped, the doors were thrown open by a pair of brutal, ugly cops, and we were bundled out at Paddington Green police station. I brushed myself off, smoothed down my hair and prepared to be recognized. I turned to face my neighbour, now standing in a half-huddle at my side on the pavement, blinking in the light. It was obvious that he had been severely kicked in the stomach – he was bent over, clutching himself in agony. I put a hand on his shoulder to help him up. It was then, as he looked up at me with pain and supplication in his eyes, that I recognized this scruffy, hairy creature.

'Nutter!'

For a moment, his face was cloudy, incomprehending. Then the light dawned.

'Christ! Mark!'

'Nutter, what the hell is Vietnam?'

CHAPTER FOUR

That day in March 1968 marked my rebirth as a political person. For twenty years I'd drifted along like flotsam on the tides of history, happily pursuing my own career, oblivious to the greater world of injustice that lay beyond. I admit that I was woefully ignorant of current affairs. I blame Nick, and before him Phyllis, who had worked me too hard and kept me away from realities that, they felt, didn't concern me. But that all changed in one day. If anyone feels the need for a crash course in reality, I'd recommend a night in the cells.

I won't dwell on the details. I know that police practice has changed a lot in thirty years, and young people today would never be subjected to the terrible violations that we suffered in the hours of darkness. Suffice to say that when I was released in the morning, I was a changed man. I'd learned a lot – about Vietnam, about American fascism, about the scandalous collusion of the British government in military atrocities. And I'd seen the 'pig state' in action as I was brutally assaulted by one power-crazed police officer after another. Blinking in the daylight, I saw the world through new eyes. Nutter scratched his beard and threw a comradely arm round my shoulder. 'Are you with us?' he asked, fixing me with his cool, steady gaze. Once more I was a lonely teenage schoolboy, Nutter the more experienced hero.

'Yes,' I answered. 'Together we will fight. Together we will win.'

I couldn't go back to Nick, that much was clear. So Nutter and his friends invited me to 'crash' with them until things were 'cool'. How could I refuse? I felt immediately at home with their relaxed attitude to life, their warm spontaneity. How different from the bitchy, artificial world into which Nick was trying to force me!

The communal house was a decaying property off Portobello

Road, an area that had once been genteel but was now crumbling into dereliction. The 'pig landlord' had been trying to evict them for over a year, Nutter proudly told me, but they now enjoyed squatters' rights and rent-free accommodation while the 'fascist lawyers' wrought their ultimate expulsion. The exterior of the house gave little away: peeling paintwork around brown, dust-caked windows, a yard where a few spindly daffodils flowered, a rainbow painted on the fanlight above the door. But inside! Floors were strewn with brightly coloured rugs, whole walls blazed with collages from the pages of magazines and books. There were no doors between the rooms ('We all share the space,' said Nutter) but occasional bead curtains. Across one doorway a blanket was hung, from beyond which came the unmistakable sound of sex. 'That's Julian enjoying himself again,' said Nutter with a weak smile. Everywhere there were new, tantalizing smells – vegetable curry from the kitchen, patchouli from the living room, and a bouquet of natural animal aromas from the bathroom. Occasionally a cat would stroll in from the garden. It wasn't a clean house in the way that my mother would have understood.

After the guided tour I sat down in the big, bright front room and was formally introduced to the rest of the household. The women I already knew from the cells – Anna, a large, dark-haired woman in a full-length kaftan dress, and Barbara, a short, boyish creature who spoke in a barely audible monotone and would never look me in the eye. New arrivals were Howard, a tall, fuzzy-headed, spindly-limbed man squeezed into tight black jeans, and Julian (I'd already heard him 'at play'), who strolled into the room stark naked and proceeded to roll a joint. (Later he was joined by his friend, dazed but fully dressed, who, it transpired, was the local milkman who had only called at the house to settle the bill.) These four shared the house – and much more – with Nutter.

It soon became clear to me that personal relationships between the five were anything but simple. Nutter and the Anna woman were having an affair of some sort; that was obvious from the possessive way that she draped herself across his lap. But occasionally she'd drape herself elsewhere – across Howard, across Julian, even across Barbara. Nutter restricted himself to half-hearted caresses of Anna and the familiar, affectionate gestures of old friendship that he bestowed on me. Julian was physically familiar with everyone (although with Nutter he was guarded). Barbara lavished her most ardent passions on the nearest cat. I had wandered straight into the heart of the alternative lifestyle.

At first I was shocked. I realized what a sheltered life I'd lived: my erotic experience was confined to my doomed relationship with over-eager Sue, my tragic love for Phyllis and the demented attentions of Janice Jones. Here, however, love and sex sloshed around like dirty bathwater. All my puritan, working-class values rose up against the sight of Anna, a joint in one hand and Nutter's thigh in the other, as she playfully tickled Barbara with her outstretched foot (Barbara blushed a frightening dark purple and laughed hysterically but totally silently). Julian arranged himself on a scatter cushion, leaving nothing to the imagination. And Howard sat cross-legged on the floor, his spidery limbs folded neatly in front of his pot belly, smiling contentedly like a fat little Buddha. (Howard, I later discovered, was a 'sex guru' who took credit for 'liberating' the entire household.)

Later, after several joints had been passed around, Anna disappeared to the kitchen to prepare some food. I was sober (drugs have little effect on me), but the others, even Nutter, were nodding off. I went to help Anna, and found her chopping an unidentifiable white substance into a saucepan. She beamed at me and carried on, seemingly uninterested in making conversation.

'So, how long have you and Nutter lived here, Anna?' I asked.

'He moved in last year, babe. Before that it was just me and my old man.' (I assumed she was referring to Howard.)

'And the others?'

'They come and go. There's no hassle here.' She beamed woozily and continued chopping. There was a minute's silence.

'And what does Nutter do these days?' I asked, trying to be friendly.

'Mostly grass, a little acid. I've got him off the booze.' Again, the beam split her face and she chopped in silence.

'It's so good to see him again after all these years.'

For the first time, Anna seemed interested in something I'd said. 'You've met him before, have you?' she asked.

'Of course. Let me explain. I'm his oldest friend. I . . .' (I paused for effect) ' . . . am Marc LeJeune.' I laughed, anticipating her amazed reaction.

'Great, babe. Could you pass that jar of miso?'

She had never heard of me.

The meal, when it was finally ready, was a strange textureless soup that tasted vaguely of onions. This was my first experience of vegan cuisine, an acquired taste. There was so much about this strange new world that I found incomprehensible, even disgusting – not least the food. Their domestic arrangements, their casual approach to sex . . . all of it I mistrusted and even feared. Little did I know that in a few short months I would be sharing their tastes, living their life – living it more fully, perhaps, than any of them had ever dared.

I returned to Holland Park late that night to find Nick up in arms. He railed at me for my 'unprofessional behaviour' in storming out of Claridge's in a 'queeny tantrum' (his vicious phrase). Janice, he reported, had reacted so badly to my departure that she had spontaneously leapt across the bar, wrested a bottle of whisky from the wall and pumped the entire contents down her throat by rhythmic applications of the optic to her lips. Even now she was recovering in hospital after a stomach pump ('And the cost of that little escapade will come out of your account, I assure you').

'Don't hassle me, Nick,' I said, softly.

'I beg your pardon?' He folded his arms across his chest, pulled himself up to his full height (just over five foot six) and puffed his chest out, looking like an absurd little duck with a pom-pom hairdo.

'You crack me up, man.' I could see that my new tactic of non-violent resistance was enraging Nick. He looked ready to explode. 'Chill out.'

That was the final straw. He stormed across the room, his dressing gown falling open to reveal purple *caleçon*. 'What is this shit, Marc? What silly little ideas have you got into that tiny mind of yours now? Will you be good enough to inform me? Or do I have to phone my friends in Scotland Yard and see whether they can find answers to these and other questions?'

'Go ahead,' I drawled. 'I've just spent one night in the pig pen. I don't suppose another would hurt me.' With that I drifted off into my room and shut the door, laughing too much to hear the familiar litany of threats and abuse that continued for a good ten minutes before the ringing telephone summoned Nick back to his usual chilling politeness. That was the end of that – for now.

Nutter was never the best of correspondents. I'd given him my number, my address, but true to form he failed to get in touch. Good old Nutter! He hadn't changed. Fortunately, I'd taken a note of his address. (There was no telephone in the house. Howard had described it, with one of his beatific grins, as 'The Heart Attack Machine'.) So I dropped Nutter a line explaining how happy I was that he had met such a great group of friends and that I would be paying him a call on the following Thursday.

I turned up as arranged and was glad to discover the house ablaze with light. At least they were in, a fact that could be easily discerned from the thick vapour of marijuana that drifted down the street. There was no door bell – no doubt Howard had a good reason for avoiding that engine of Satan as well – so I let myself in. Music was blaring from the front room, I had a brief vision of an enormous red dress flitting across the end of the hallway before I made my way to the kitchen. The lights were on, the smell of

Anna's cooking gave stiff competition to the sweeter smells of intoxication, and I assumed it was safe to enter.

And there was Nutter, sitting with his back to me, helping himself to a generous 'toke' on one of the joints that were permanently on the go in this Liberty Hall. He threw his head back and exhaled a great groan of pleasure: it must have been particularly good grass. I waited until he seemed to have come round a little, then gave a discreet cough. Nutter looked round with a happy, stoned smile, recognized me and practically jumped out of his skin. 'Oh shit! Anna, get up!' he yelped, leaping to his feet then thinking better of it and hiding himself behind the table, but not before I had noticed that he was in a certain amount of personal disarray. As he righted his trousers, Anna emerged from beneath the table to welcome me with her usual grin.

'Hello, babe!' she said, as if nothing had happened. 'Why don't you make us all a drink?'

I turned on my heel and marched smartly out of the room. I would have slammed the door, had there been one to slam. I was upset – I have always believed that sex should be an intimate act between two people, not the kind of ugly public show that Anna made of it. But as I stood leaning against the wall, trying to control my breathing, I had little time for reflection. Once again there was a flash of that red dress across the hall, disappearing for a second then just as quickly returning to confront me. Here was a new apparition, half woman (the crimson lake skirt was buoyed up on a crinoline, the feet exquisitely shod in silk court shoes), half man (the torso was bare apart from a ruff of red feathers around the neck).

'Oh it's you,' it said. 'Come and help me with my eyelashes.' It was Julian.

I followed him behind the blanket curtain, whence I had heard the sounds of carnal abandon on my first visit. In the middle of a chaos of clothes, beads, books, records and what looked very much like a pair of feet sticking out from under a sheet, there was a large, gilt-framed mirror artfully arranged on the floor to reflect the light from a single bedside lamp back into Julian's face. 'I can't get the fucking things on straight. Come on, you're an actor. Give us a hand.'

At last I felt on home ground. I forgot my recent shock and became the professional. If there was one thing I had learned about in my years in the business, it was stage make-up. 'You're not letting the glue dry enough before sticking them on,' I said, whipping the errant lashes off his face (they'd slid half-way down his cheek), 'and you've powdered too soon. Where's your cleanser?' Julian lamely proffered a jar of Vaseline. 'Cotton wool?' I demanded. An old sock. It would have to do. I'd achieved miracles with less in the dressing rooms of certain provincial theatres. With gentle strokes I removed the haggish make-up from around his eyes, reglued the lashes and fixed them with a deft precision that left him gasping. As I knelt before him, I could feel an exploratory hand roaming around my lap, which I deterred with a knuckle-crushing twist of the thighs. 'You'll do,' I snapped, all clinical authority. 'Now will somebody please tell me what's going on?' I was aware that my voice sounded high, strained, like a schoolteacher who knows she's under threat from an unruly fifth form.

At that point there was a stirring from beneath the pile of sheets, and the feet scrambled into life. Moments later a tousled head appeared, opened its eyes, mumbled, 'Fuck!' before disappearing beneath the bedclothes. None of this Julian noticed.

'It's the big night tonight! Every freak in town will be there! You've got to come, it'll be a scream!'

'What will be a scream?'

'It's the Release benefit at the Roundhouse, man!' said Julian, then 'Tally Ho!' as he leapt across the room, heedless of his expertly applied lashes, and joined his friend beneath the sheets. I withdrew and decided to leave them – all of them – to their own devices. But I encountered Nutter in the hallway, lurking sheepishly outside Julian's room. He greeted me with an interrogative smirk. 'That's cool,' he said. 'That's cool.'

'What is cool?'

'You and Jools getting it on. Great.'

'Nutter, I see that the gap between us is greater than ever. I have not been "getting it on", as you put it, with Julian or with anybody. Now I'll say goodbye. Don't try to find me.'

And with that ironic echo of his own words I turned for my grand exit from a house that had become repulsive to me. But the spark of an old friendship hadn't died for Nutter; he wouldn't let me slip through his fingers again quite so easily. He grabbed me, roughly but firmly, by the upper arm. 'Cool it! Hey, I'm sorry, man. I'm sorry. I didn't know you were . . . watching. Look, it's okay. Don't go.'

I wavered. How dare he think I was 'watching' him and Anna?

'Please. Don't go, Marc. Stay. I want us to . . . talk. You know, old friends, man . . .'

That was the limit of Nutter's articulacy, the fullest extent of his ability to express emotion, and tantamount to a declaration of everlasting love with a bouquet of red roses thrown in. I stopped in my tracks.

'Very well. I'll stay. We'll talk.'

There was no turning back now.

The Roundhouse was the legendary venue in Chalk Farm, once a mundane tram terminus but now, in 1968, the throbbing heart of London's underground scene. It was thither that we – Nutter and I, followed by the whole rag-tag household – made our way by bus (to the tight-lipped horror of the other passengers, one or two of whom obviously recognized me from the telly). The crowds were dense. Where did they come from, these creatures of the night? But it was with them that my destiny lay. This was youth on the march! And how soon they would look to me for leadership.

Release was a voluntary agency devoted to helping those poor souls who had got into trouble with drugs, particularly those who were being persecuted by the law. To celebrate this fundraiser (I doubted whether the collective mass between them could raise much over £100) everyone had decided to get riotously stoned. I was to see much puke, many near-deaths, that night. Two sturdy matrons in St John Ambulance uniforms prevented any actual loss of life, and coped with the worst of the mopping and swabbing. Little thanks they got for it! ('Nazis,' muttered Howard, who took exception to any kind of uniform.)

There was no formal programme for the evening's proceedings, no seating, in fact very little that I recognized from my own professional background. What passed for entertainment was a rolling smorgasbord of performance, some of it on the stage, some of it in the audience and in the quieter, darker nooks and crannies of the old building. There was a self-destructiveness, a seeking after oblivion, in these crowds of young people yearning for louder music, stronger drugs, new 'kicks' of every description. Did I see danger in the dark corners of the Roundhouse that night? And if so, did I heed the warning?

At first I was stunned – literally – by the volume, the light show, the sea of writhing bodies. I stuck close to Nutter, unwilling to lose him in this amorphous, stoned mass. Someone handed us a drink (was it spiked?) and we made our way through the crowd, hoping to find a sheltered spot where we could discuss old times and our plans for the future. But everywhere we went Anna popped up, kissing Nutter or embracing me and telling us what a good time we were having. She was making me 'uptight', I felt out of place, *de trop*. But gradually I relaxed, let go of my inhibitions and allowed myself to 'go with it', as Nutter kept advising me as he massaged my shoulders. Eventually we escaped the attentions of Anna and found ourselves on the edge of the stage, revelling in the lights and music and telling each other how happy we were to have found each other again. 'I love you, man' admitted Nutter, as he flung an arm around my neck, missed and slumped in my lap. They were the words I'd waited many years to hear.

While Nutter succumbed to whatever had been slipped into our drinks, I took time to survey the scene. I've always been an observer. Even when I'm up to my neck in a situation, there's a cool, detached part of me looking down and taking notes. So while the madness and the music swirled around me, I took stock. There was a freedom here, not just in the crazy clothes (or lack of them) and the free-love games of kiss and grope. This was a greater freedom – from the pressures of work, of business, of boy-meets-girl. I realized what had happened to me – what I'd allowed to happen to me – since I'd moved to London. I'd become a commodity, a product, while my real talents went unrecognized. And it wasn't just since I'd moved to London, I understood with a sudden flash of insight. Even as a child, my parents had forced me to be what *they* wanted me to be, not what I wanted to be. I was their only son, their hope for the future, the father of their grandchildren. Everybody I knew – Mum and Dad, Phyllis, Nick, Janice – had used me to fulfil their own needs. And here I was, surrounded by people who were pursuing their own fantasies, their own appetites, in a loving, caring environment. Why shouldn't I be part of it?

So lost in thought was I that five or more hours slipped by before I was roused from my reverie by a gentle hand on my shoulder. 'You looked so sweet, the two of you,' said a familiar voice, 'like two little fluffy bunnies. Was it a good trip, darling?' I looked up, peering back into reality from the bottom of a well. (Like many deep thinkers, I often find that I literally lose myself in thought.) There was Julian, his dress in tatters, his feathers but a memory, but his eyelashes still glued securely to his drooping eyelids. 'And look at Nutter!' he continued. 'Beautiful! You lucky thing. I've been trying for years!'

Something was being insinuated. 'Firstly,' I replied, 'I am stone-cold sober, and have been all evening. Secondly, my friendship with Nutter is far too serious and adult for someone of your obvious limitations to understand.' I rose to my feet, but my legs must have gone to sleep, for I staggered and almost plunged headlong through a massive bass speaker.

'That's right, darling,' drawled Julian, deftly righting me and helping the still semi-conscious Nutter to his feet.

'We'll be quite all right now, thank you!' I said, dragging Nutter towards the door. I wouldn't trust any of this gang of vultures to take care of him in his condition. I knew how vulnerable he could be when 'under the influence', and intended to protect him by spending the night in a comfortable hotel where he could recover unmolested and enjoy a decent bath and breakfast before returning to his squalid 'pad'. But wouldn't you know it! There, blocking our path with arms outstretched was the large, floral form of Anna.

'There's my baby boy!' she cooed, practically snatching Nutter from my side. 'Time for beddy byes! Was he tripping? Was it beautiful? Did he see nice things? Come on, lover, home we go.' She bestowed on me one final, patronizing smirk. 'See you on a pink cloud some time, babe!' And with that they were gone.

The Roundhouse was a sorry sight, filthy in the daylight, almost silent save for the rhythmic sound of a few unconscious revellers being slapped around the face by the stalwart St John Ambulancers, still cheerfully working their way through this sea of human debris. I stumbled into the morning, crawled into a taxi (what Howard would have made of this shameless materialism I neither knew nor cared) and thus ended my first night in the deep, deep underground.

When Nick got wind of my new life and my new ideas, he became genuinely scared. And there's nothing more dangerous in this business than an unscrupulous small-time manager who sees his meal ticket slipping away. He became devious in his determination to keep me sweet, to keep me working. But it wasn't just me he was fighting, it was the whole course of history. There was revolution in the air – you could feel it every time you opened a newspaper or stepped into a London street – and nothing Nick Nicholls could do was going to stop it. He offered me more money (a reasonable rate for the amount of work I'd been doing) and I accepted. He gave me presents – clothes, meals, jewellery – things I no longer craved. His promises became wilder and wilder: 'Your own TV series next year, I think, don't you?' 'A major motion picture deal!' 'Front cover of every edition of *Vogue*!' The empty words of a desperate man. Nick knew that he was losing me, and that no amount of bribes would keep me.

Then there were the threats, Nick's favourite business tactic. He was shameless, saying openly that he would tell the police I was a murderer (as if anyone would believe such a bizarre story), that he would release to the newspapers certain photographs that would put an end to my career. I simply smiled. After all, if Nick revealed me as a murderer and a pornographer, he revealed his own complicity in the very same 'crimes'.

One day, he summoned me to dinner at the Ivy with greater gravity than usual. He was at his most masterful and charming, plying me with the best wines on the menu, ordering the things he knew I loved – lobster, asparagus – and complimenting me on my appearance. He was witty, urbane, flirtatious – far from the raging, threatening little tyrant who, I knew, lurked beneath that dapper exterior.

'I was speaking to dear Bernard Delfont the other day,' he announced breezily. 'You know, he's a very big fan of yours. He says you're the brightest talent on the scene at the moment. He says you should go far.'

It was good to see that someone had been paying attention. 'Tell me more,' I said, licking the butter from an asparagus spear.

'He said, and I agree, that you're the only artist who really bridges the generation gap, who appeals to the kids but who also gets the mums and dads. He says, and I agree, that you're uniquely gifted. What were his words? Talented, exciting and beautiful.'

'I see. And to what, pray, is this leading?'

'But he stresses the danger, and I really couldn't agree more, of compromising yourself by meddling in things you don't understand and that can only harm your public image.'

'By which you mean, keep away from the hippies.'

'By which I mean, you . . . you dear, sweet, misguided boy, that I have a very nice new job for you, something that will ensure your success for a good few years, if you'll just knuckle down and do it.'

'Oh yes, and what is it this time? A regional tour of *Pardon Me But You're Sitting On My Face*?' I was bitter, sarcastic. 'Or an advertising campaign for toilet paper, perhaps, which would be only right and proper after I've had the entire nation crapping itself for the last three years?'

Nick was unruffled. He smiled, suddenly reticent. 'No. It's not that.' He ordered another bottle of wine, drank a glass with impenetrable calm, smiled and lit a cigar. He was trying my patience with another of his pointless mind games. I cut through to the heart of the matter.

'So what is this job?'

'Job? Ah, you're interested all of a sudden. Well, it's a marvellous job. The sort of thing that any young actor would give his eye teeth for. West End show, movie deal in the bag. But you're right. I don't think it's right for you after all. I don't think you've got the right attitude for this sort of thing any more. And who's to say if you've got the talent? It takes more than just a pretty face to play Shakespeare.'

'Shake – '

'Excuse me a moment!' Nick cut me short, stood up and waddled off to the lavatory, trailing his cigar in the air as he went. I waited for five, ten minutes. Finally he sat down with an infuriating little pussycat smirk on his face as he toyed with his food and avoided my gaze. I could have cheerfully ripped his wig off and plunged him face-first into the buttery mess on his plate.

'You mentioned Shakespeare, I believe.' I was a miracle of restraint.

'Oh, yes. A great favourite of yours, isn't he?'

'You know how much I love him. How much I've longed to play him.'

'Perhaps you've mentioned it once or twice.'

This was too much. 'Do you want me to walk out of that door, Nick? Because I will. And believe me, you'll never see me again if I do.'

'There's no need for scenes, dear boy,' he said, warming up and suddenly enthusiastic. 'I've found you something simply splendid. The job of a lifetime. And it's yours – if you're ready to make a serious commitment to your career and stop dicking around with a bunch of drug addicts.'

'They're not – '

'Now listen and learn. Stoll Moss want you for the lead in their new show. Major West End opening, no provincial shit. So let's not ask any questions and let's just keep out of trouble till the ink's dry on the contract, shall we?'

'What's the part?'

'Hamlet.'

Hamlet! The part that every young actor feels born to play. But how much more did I, with my Shakespearean training? I was careful not to show any enthusiasm, but my heart was thumping so much that my voice must have wavered.

'Hamlet! Well, that's a pretty good gig, I'll admit.'

'I should bloody well say it is, boy! And it's not just any old bloody doublet and hose deal that nobody's going to go to, either! This is Hamlet for the 1960s, a sexy Hamlet, a rock & roll Hamlet! This is Hamlet with balls! What do you say? Do you think you're man enough?' Nick recharged my glass with champagne. It was a critical moment. I sipped and pondered.

How much I had changed! There was a time when I would have jumped at the mere mention of *Hamlet*, would have signed any contract out of sheer excitement at playing Shakespeare's most challenging role. But I'd learned to be cautious. It's a sad fact: the young, the talented have to become distrustful, to develop a sixth sense for self-preservation. And despite my strong spiritual belief in the ultimate goodness of human nature, I was well aware by now that Nick Nicholls was nothing but a con man and a schemer.

So I relaxed, enjoyed my champagne and smiled, quickly reviewing the potential pitfalls of this glowing proposition.

'Mmmm . . . Hamlet, eh? I see . . . Interesting . . .'

To my intense satisfaction, Nick was now puffing on his cigar and checking the back of his head for stray hairs – a sure sign that he was anxious. I caught his eye, but he looked quickly away, collected himself and resumed the persuasive grand manner.

'Yes, Marc, *Hamlet*. You've heard of it, no doubt. Perhaps even studied it at school. Phyllis was a great one for Shakespeare, wasn't he?' He hissed the name of my dead benefactor, seeking to depress me with bitter memories.

'Oh yes,' I replied brightly. 'I'm very familiar with the play. It's one of my favourites, and so of course I've read it several times. Now tell me, Nick,' (by now he was twitching again) 'what sort of production would this be, exactly? The full text, four hours, with a classically trained cast in the Old Vic? Would that be the sort of thing you had in mind?'

Nick resorted to bluster. 'Four hours, don't talk out of your arse, boy. What audience is going to sit and watch you droning on for four hours? We're in show business, remember, so we've got to put on a show.'

My bluff was working. In fact, I'd never read *Hamlet* – opening the complete Shakespeare that Phyllis had left me brought back too much grief. 'I see.' I narrowed my eyes, rested my chin on my hands. 'Do tell.'

'It's . . . well . . . it's a new version of the play. An up-to-date version.'

'In what way, up-to-date, exactly?'

'You know . . . it's a mmmszkl.' Nick contrived to take a gulp of wine, suck his cigar and smooth his beard all at the same time.

'What was that word again, Nick? That last one? I don't think I heard it aright.'

'A musical.'

'Ah. A musical.'

'Yes, a bloody musical. What are you suddenly getting so snippy about? Musicals were all the fucking rage with you not so very long ago, weren't they? *West Side Story*, you did that a treat didn't you? Remember that little show? Remember those nice pictures Uncle Nick took after the show? Lovely they'd look all over the papers with your Mum and Dad's Sunday morning tea and toast, wouldn't they?'

I was used to this sort of mindless filth, the deluded ramblings of a sick brain. 'Tell me more. I'm intrigued to know just how you're intending to turn *Hamlet* into a West End musical comedy. What's the name of the show, for instance?'

Nick was turning puce under my expert goading. For one crazy moment, the hope leapt up in my heart that he'd simply burst a blood vessel and drop down dead in front of me.

'*Danish Blue.*'

'Come again?'

'*Danish Blue*, all right? Danish, as in Prince of Denmark, Blue as in blue movies. Sexy, sophisticated. Sit down!'

I had drained my glass, wiped my fingers and carefully folded my napkin and was now preparing to leave.

'It's the chance you've been waiting for, you ungrateful little bastard! Sit back down this instant! They've written a fantastic rock score. It's a vehicle for you, it'll make you into a star!' I was half-way out of the restaurant. Nick had to shout. 'They're offering you fucking piles of money, you little shit! Come back this instant! Come back! Come back!'

I could still hear him shrieking from the street.

Strange how much in my life has depended on being in the right place at the right time. Just as I left Nick stewing in the Ivy, I turned the corner into Long Acre and there, tripping daintily down the street, was the unmistakable figure of Julian, trailing clouds of chiffon and a small gaggle of amused children and their abusive mothers. He blew kisses as the women shouted insults; when they saw me approaching they hushed their noise (I was always treated with respect by the public) and went about their business. Julian was about to kiss me in gratitude but I sidestepped his embraces and fell in beside him.

'Fancy meeting you here,' he giggled, obviously stoned.

'And where are you going? I thought Howard disapproved of the West End.'

'Oh bugger Howard,' said Julian, and sniggered at the appalling image. 'I'm going to the Outer Space darling!'

I must have looked dumbfounded. 'Haven't you heard? It's the latest thing, darling. Everyone's getting into theee-ah-tuh!' He pronounced the word like Tallulah Bankhead. Julian may have been grossly effeminate, but he was amusing. 'We've all joined the avant-garde. We're going to be in showbiz, we're all going to be big stars, Just! Like! You!' He pirouetted off down the street and out of sight. I found him draped artistically around a lamp post at Seven Dials.

'You are coming, aren't you? Moska said he particularly wanted to meet you.'

'Moska?'

'Moska, darling, Moska! The great underground superstar director! Don't you read the press at all? We're all going to be in his next show! And he's dying for you to be in it too so be a good boy and just follow me.'

Julian frogmarched me along Tottenham Court Road; by now we were well out of my usual West End territory and heading towards the depressing hinterland of the Euston Road. Suddenly he stopped, teetered for a moment on his heels and pulled me into a doorway. 'This is it! The gateway to the staaaaaaaaaaars!'

Destiny comes in strange disguises. There was nothing promising about the prospect that faced me: the side door of a modern, post-war pub, already seedy in the afternoon light, and the dim view of a few determined drinkers supping up the last of the lunchtime session. But Julian led me up the stairs to a deserted pool room which a shaky handwritten sign proclaimed to be 'The Outer Space: Theatre Workshop'. Inside a small, sparsely built figure in a long white shirt, black leggings and bare feet jumped, turned and stopped, jumped again, turned, bowed and leapt. I saw flashes of a narrow, lined, tanned face with a peculiar bird-like profile, framed by corkscrew curls that hung from a sadly thinning crown. The hands were long and thin, permanently held in oriental gestures, miming a fan, twirling together like a bird in flight. Had he seen us? I thought so; Julian evidently thought not, as he was holding his breath, his hands clasped under his chin in adoration.

Finally the dance was over, the dancer bowed one final, deep reverence and then seemed to wake from a trance and notice our presence. He held out his arms and bounded towards us, still maintaining complete turn-out and the full range of Balinese hand gestures. He embraced Julian and kissed him on both cheeks, then, as I held out my hand to shake his, he executed an elaborate curtsey and remained grovelling before me for nearly a minute, while I studied the wide centre parting that ran from forehead to nape, revealing generous amounts of scalp on the way. Finally he rose, clasped my hand in both of his and spoke in a voice strangely accented (French? Russian?).

'One great artist greets another,' he announced. 'I am . . . MOSKA!' I felt for a moment as if I ought to kneel, but soon recovered myself. 'Pleased to meet you. I am Marc.'

'I know you. I see you everywhere. I see you too,' he tapped the centre of his forehead, 'in here. For long time I say to myself, with him I must work, with him I will create great work. I see in him what the world does not see. I recognize in that beautiful boy the soul of an artist.'

Balm to my soul! At last someone had recognized that there was more to me than the cheap exploitation of my good looks. How long, I'd asked myself as I cried with frustration in my prison-bedroom at Nick's, would I have to struggle in the mire of commercialism before somebody plucked me out and gave me my wings?

When would I find what I needed most – a mentor and a teacher, someone who sought to develop me, not to exploit me? And here, this strange creature in a dingy little room had answered my prayers. I didn't know what to say, but held on to his hand.

'I feel the spirit stirring in you, Marc' (he pronounced it 'Mahrrrrk'). 'We were meant to meet. Let us work, now.'

I glanced at Julian, who had tears rolling down his cheeks. Moska guided me to the centre of the floor, let go of my hand and stood facing me, breathing deeply and loudly through his nose as he elegantly extended his arms above his head. I mirrored him. After a series of gentle movements of this kind Moska astonished me by leaping, suddenly and unexpectedly, into the air and into my arms. I caught him and held him like a baby (he was surprisingly light) to prevent his falling painfully to the floor. This was my first experience of a theatre workshop and the elaborate regimen of 'trust exercises' that began each rehearsal.

We carried on like this for nearly an hour, throwing ourselves at each other, falling into each other's arms, lying prone and being lifted ceiling-high on fingertips. It was pleasant, relaxing and invigorating, a far cry from my experience of rehearsals, a mechanical recital of lines and 'hitting your mark'. Finally we broke; Moska reached for a packet of cigarettes, sat crosslegged on the floor and motioned for Julian and me to join him. There had been no discussion so far of our working together, just an easy assumption (based on my obvious suitability for this type of work) that we were already collaborating. Instead, Moska answered Julian's eager questions about his recent tour of the Far East where he and his company had performed a show called *Psychosis*, 'an exploration of male sexuality and the American imperialist ambitions in Southeast Asia'. The tour, he said, had been 'a triumph', the highlight being the desertion of an American soldier from a base in Korea to join the company (and, it seemed, to become Moska's favourite until the military police caught up with him in Dubai). 'The spirit is strong in the East,' said Moska, brandishing his cigarette like a dainty geisha. 'I learnt much from their traditions. In the West, theatre is all corruption and death,' (how this struck a chord with me!) 'while in the East it is beauty and light and colour! This you will see in our new show,' he announced. 'Through movement, music and spectacle we will open the hearts and minds of the people!'

So it seemed I had found my longed-for teacher. Moska may have been eccentric and even reviled (the critical establishment treated him as a joke – how typical! – and dismissed the Outer Space as 'the Waste of Space') but to me he oozed truth and beauty at every pore. I accepted him as he had accepted me – as one artist will always recognize another. At the moment, that was enough. I didn't need the details of contracts, opening dates, wages – it satisfied me to know that, finally, I was growing as an artist. When I left the Outer Space, night was falling. I kissed Moska's hand and called him 'master'. Wordlessly, he gestured me from the room.

Even before I put the key in the lock at home, I could hear voices raised in a screaming argument. How they cut through the mood of the afternoon! I came crashing back down to earth as I recognized Nick and Janice engaged in one of their famous cat fights. I paused on the landing, did a few breathing exercises before letting myself into the flat, hoping to make a quick escape to my room and enjoy my own space. Of course, I failed.

'Here he is!' screamed Janice, hurling herself through the living-room door and into the hall. 'Now you can tell him yourself! Go on!' She looked terrible, her blonde hair flat and ungroomed with a generous inch of roots, her face puffy. She stank of alcohol, days and days of alcohol. Here was the corruption and death of the Western tradition in one pitiful victim's body. I silently took Janice's hand in mine (just as Moska had done to me) and she burst into tears like a frightened child.

Nick stomped along behind her. 'What a pathetic sight. The

Regular Guy and his girl – a hippy and a lush. Not a good advertisement for Bran Pops. Oh dear no!'

Janice braced herself again. 'Tell him, Nick!'

'Oh, I'm sure our Marc will be delighted at the news. He's turned his back on all that dirty commercial stuff. They've axed the Bran Pops campaign, dear boy. No more Regular Guy.'

'They can't do it!' squealed Janice, red-eyed and wild. 'The public still wants us!'

For once, Nick was right – I was glad to see the back of a job that had become a burden and an embarrassment. But my heart broke for Janice. For months she'd lived only for the few moments that we worked together, when she could recapture the hope and innocence of our early days, when the world was at our feet and we were the most envied couple in town. I had grown since then, but poor Janice was trapped in the past, clinging to a fantasy that would never let her go.

'You'll find work, Janice,' I said, trying to comfort her. 'You're still the most beautiful girl in the business.' Nick snuffled with suppressed laughter, and to tell the truth I cringed when I surveyed the tear-stained figure before me, no longer sleek but bulging around the waist, the breasts less firm than in the days when she'd happily pop them out for the cameras. 'There's so much more that you can do!' But what, I wondered, stroking her shaking hand. Inspiration struck. 'Hand modelling, for instance! You have beautiful hands, and your nails just need a manicure. Think of all those adverts for washing-up liquid! Hands that do dishes can be soft as your face . . .' I looked up into Janice's open, frightened face, her skin rough and patchy, the broken veins showing through the hastily applied base. Nick was laughing quite openly now as Janice, shaking and sobbing, seemed to collapse, all the fight gone out of her. She slunk to the door and let herself out of the flat, tottering dangerously down the stairs. 'And don't come back!' yelled Nick. My heart was breaking.

The street door slammed and Janice was gone. I could feel the rage boiling up inside me. I was ready to kill Nick Nicholls for what he had done to that poor, broken butterfly. How he gloated over his victims! How secure he felt at the centre of his web! And if I turned on him, caused a scene, broke a few bones, wouldn't it just strengthen his hold over me? Nick, I knew, would go to the police at the first sign of trouble. Instead, I practised a technique that I'd learned from Moska: I visualized a beautiful Japanese garden, pink cherry blossom and tinkling streams, and flooded my mind with peace. I went to my bedroom and meditated.

I discovered to my horror the next morning that Nick had placed advertisements in the *Stage* announcing 'Marc LeJeune reveals all in *Danish Blue* – Shakespeare for the Age of Aquarius – Hamlet learns to Rock & Roll!', as well as a venue, even a date on which I was to open in this debased travesty. I was furious, but once again I let peaceful colours wash through my mind, concentrated on my breathing and was ready to face a new challenge in a spirit of creative equanimity.

'I'm so sorry that you wasted your money,' I said to Nick as I dropped the newspaper on to his desk. 'Let's remember our time together as something beautiful.'

Nick shot me one of his looks, the kind that once had me cowering in fear and eager to please. They no longer worked. 'I'll be out all day,' I said, hoping to avoid a scene. No such luck.

'You will be in meetings with me all day, young man,' he breathed, 'talking to producers, directors and publicists. We have work . . . to . . . do . . .' He could hardly get his words out; I could sense the anger coming off him in waves of bad, blocked energy. I tried to keep visualizing sky blue, coral pink, grass green, but Nick was still a powerful force, dragging me back to his vicious level. For a moment we faced each other in silence. Then I spoke, calmly.

'Let me go, Nick.'

'Not on your life.'

'We've worked together well. We had our time. It's passed. Now I must move on. I'll never forget you.'

'Damn right you'll never fucking forget me, you ungrateful little shit.' Nick was actually spitting now, flecks of saliva glittered in his beard. 'You will drop all this crap and come back to work today or I will make you sorry you were ever fucking born, Marc. Do you understand me?'

'I understand you and I pity you, Nick.' I tried to lay a hand on him to calm and heal him, but he knocked it away.

'What's the matter with you? Are you on drugs? What have they done to you? This is everything we've worked for, everything you've ever wanted. Why do you think I keep pulling you out of one scrape after another? Because I believe in you. Because, despite the fact that you are so lacking in the brain department, I still believe that you have talent! And now you expect me to sit here and watch you throw it all away? Well I won't let you.'

I was impressed. For once, Nick was being honest, finally recognizing that I was an artist in my own right, not just a piece of meat to be paraded before a hungry public. But it was too late.

'I'm sorry,' I said. 'I don't want to hurt you. I must have my freedom. If you really believe in my talent, let it grow, let it flower and fly. I appreciate all you've done for me, but I can no longer work in the decadent, corrupt traditions of Western theatre. I have found a new world, Nick,' (he was practically crying with fury by now) 'and I must follow my heart.'

Suddenly, Nick was calm. 'If you leave me now, Marc,' he said, standing, 'you must understand three things. Firstly, we will never under any circumstances work together again. Secondly, I retain absolute rights over all the work we've done of whatever kind. And thirdly, you agree never to seek any kind of financial settlement from me. If you agree, you can shake my hand and you're free to go and throw your career down the pan. Or you can stay, we can work together and I'll forget all the problems you've caused me. What's it to be?'

There was no question in my mind. Why did Nick think he could lure me with money? I held out my hand in a gesture of farewell. He understood. 'Just one moment, then, before we say goodbye,' he said, rummaging in his drawer. 'You want to be absolutely, legally free of me, don't you?' I nodded. 'So let's have it in writing. No arguments, no unpleasantness. Just sign here.' It was a simple document, formalizing the conditions that Nick had spelled out to me before. I signed and dated it, shook Nick's hand and went to my room to pack a few belongings. When I left the house with a hold-all and a few carrier bags, Nick said goodbye with a friendly smile and a wink. 'Good luck for the future, mate!' he shouted after me as I skipped down the stairs. Who would have expected him to be so reasonable?

I went from Holland Park straight to the Outer Space, where Moska was holding another class, this time for his whole company. There were many familiar faces there – Julian, of course, Anna, even Nutter – as well as a handful of performers whom Moska introduced as 'my *corps de ballet*', a collection of thin, beautiful men and women who were warming up and stretching amidst clouds of cigarette smoke.

When I appeared in the room with my bags, the strain of a recent parting must have shown in my face. Anna swamped me in a huge motherly embrace, and for once I found her emotional openness (which had sickened me before) strangely comforting. I knew that I had a home, I had friends. I was learning to relax and take life as it came. Even Nutter was warm in his greeting, although I could see that he was nervous in this new company.

We had gathered at the Space for a 'workshop'. I was expecting a script and a readthrough, but when I asked Moska about the show and my role in it he simply beamed, made a few expressive hand gestures and scampered across the room to join the dancers. 'Don't worry,' said Julian, 'this is how he always works. The show has to evolve out of improvisation. Just relax.' He handed me a joint, and I was grateful for the wave of peaceful wooziness that it imparted.

The initial exercises completed, we sat in a large circle on the floor and began the 'guided trip' that initiated Moska's method. First of all we joined hands and closed our eyes and hummed. Then we played 'word catch', throwing random phrases across the circle to each other. Nutter was squirming with embarrassment, but soon the drugs calmed him and he sat there laughing to himself. Then came the class proper, a welcome opportunity to actually do something rather than just sitting about. Moska put us into pairs (I was partnered with Anna; Moska himself took Nutter) and began to lead us in a dance, the only accompaniment a rhythmic clash of finger cymbals. There were no formal steps, but I improvised a casual foxtrot while Anna ground her pelvis in a figure-of-eight pattern. We were not a comfortable partnership. After we'd tottered inelegantly round the room for a few minutes, Anna gripped me firmly by the hips and jammed our groins together.

'You've got to learn to relax, Marc,' she whispered in my ear. 'You're so tense. Move your hips with mine, babe.' She began her pelvic grind again. 'White middle-class men are so uptight about their bodies. Come on, feel the rhythm. That's it. Round and round and round and round . . .' I glanced across to Nutter, who was mutely suffering a similar mauling from Moska, but was too stoned to care. 'Try and be a little less Western in your thinking,' murmured Anna in my ear. 'Go with the flow, baby . . .' Julian, sailing past in the arms of one of the ballet dancers, deftly inserted the ever-burning joint into my mouth. I took a long, deep drag, and another, and another. I began to see why, in underground circles, cannabis was such a popular drug – it completely inhibited any sense of embarrassment at the foolish pranks that comprised so much of the lifestyle.

The dancing lesson over, we sat down once again for a 'rap session' – a discussion of the news and views of the day that would 'inform' the show. And there was only one subject on people's minds: the events in Paris. It was May 1968, a month that would go down in history. For the first time that afternoon, Nutter came alive, recounting with enthusiasm a narrative of street violence, barricades, sit-ins and strikes that had turned Paris into 'a battle-ground in the struggle'. How different from my memories of the city where I had wandered, so innocent, at the side of that *grand boulevardier* Nick Nicholls. Now the world of chic cafés, the hushed interiors where money talked while waiters whispered, that paradise of the élite was all to be swept away in the fires of the glorious revolution! This was our storming of the Bastille, our October revolution, the defining moment that marked cataclysmic change.

The day wore on in more exercises and discussions, although by four o'clock everyone (including our director) was so high that nobody could remember what anyone else had said, and we spent the last hour of rehearsal rolling around giggling. Finally, as everyone was leaving, Moska took me to one side.

'I can count on you, yes, Marc?' he asked, taking my hands in a characteristic gesture. 'To me you have become necessary, the central point of my art, my . . . inspiration.' He whispered the final word.

'Of course. I'm a professional. You can rely on me, don't worry.'

'And if sometimes my methods are a little different, you won't . . . what do your friends say? Freak out?'

'Of course not.' I was beginning to worry; there had still been no mention of money or an opening date. Just at that moment, Nutter bounded across the room and gripped me around the waist.

'Fie, wrangling queen! Whom everything becomes – to chide, to laugh, to weep! Come my queen! Last night you did desire it!' He tore me from Moska and held me in a melodramatic clinch. He had remembered! After all these years Nutter had remembered one of our greatest scenes from *Antony and Cleopatra*. All my doubts were swept away; I knew then that destiny intended me to star in this new role, and that I must not be ensnared by something as unimportant as money.

But the worm of suspicion was gnawing away in my mind. What

did Moska want from me? Was it simply a question of two creative souls calling to one another across such very different disciplines? Or did Moska have another, baser motive? My doubts deepened during a late-night conversation at home (I was sharing a room, but nothing else, with Julian). Moska, he revealed, had learned from a casual conversation in a gay bar that I, Marc LeJeune, had taken to hanging out at the house. Suddenly he had been inexplicably keen to offer parts to anyone who wanted them, to which Julian, star-struck like so many homosexuals, responded eagerly. Soon the whole house had roles in the new Moska show, on one condition: they must deliver LeJeune.

'Why is he so keen on me, Julian?'

'He thinks you're fabulous and gorgeous and so do all of us,' replied my ingenuous room mate.

'Is that all? Has he ever said anything else about me?'

'Well, yes, I suppose he has . . .' I immediately detected a reluctance, as if something was being hidden from me.

'Go on, Julian.'

'I don't know if I should.'

I was seductive, moving closer. Julian couldn't resist me. 'He said he needed a star. He said he was sick of playing to empty rooms above pubs. He wants success so badly, Marc, and he thinks you can give it to him.'

So that was it. I was confused. On the one hand I felt hurt that Moska had compromised my artistic integrity with this crass gesture towards Mammon. On the other hand I was flattered that the underground theatre had recognized me as an important cultural icon, one that could be explored and even exploited in the right theatrical setting. So who was using whom?

For the next week, I lay low, going to workshops at the Outer Space during the day, relaxing with Nutter, Anna and Julian at night. They had become like family to me: Anna the loving mother I had never known, Nutter and Julian the brother and 'sister' (his term) I had missed so much as an only child. I kept out of Nick's way; he had no way of finding me, and I thought it better to let him lick his wounds. He'd soon find a new protégé – God help him. But soon I felt the time was right to make the final break; and besides, I needed to collect my belongings from Holland Park and settle my account with Nick Nicholls Ltd.

I arrived late one afternoon. I knew Nick's hours: he was always to be found at home around this time, recovering from lunch. I let myself in at the street door and climbed the old familiar stairs, a thousand memories crowding to meet me with every step. I almost felt a wave of affection as I put the key in the lock of the flat – Nick and I hadn't always been unhappy together, I remembered, and we had achieved a lot. 'The old team!' I thought with a sigh, hoping that a friendship could be salvaged from the wreckage.

But the key would not turn. It was an old lock, and sometimes prone to stick; I jiggled the key and tried again. No luck. I took the key out, inspected it, and tried again. The lock had been changed.

Immediately, I sensed trouble. I'm an intuitive person, like so many actors. I knocked on the door. Silence.

I knocked again, louder, and listened intently. I could hear Sugar barking and yes, there was the unmistakable flip-flop of Nick padding down the tiled hallway in his leather slippers. I must have woken him from a nap. The footsteps stopped at the door; once again there was silence.

'Nick?'

'Who is it?'

'It's me!'

'Who?'

'It's me, Marc! I've come to pick up my stuff!'

'Go away.'

Sugar was barking hysterically at the sound of her lost master's voice, scrabbling wildly at the door that stood between us. 'I won't be a minute, Nick. Just let me get my books and clothes and stuff and I'll be out of your way.'

'You're too late, Marc.'

'What do you mean?'

'Remember that piece of paper you signed? I can't believe you've got the nerve to come back here after what's happened.'

'What?'

'I've got nothing to say to you, Marc. Get yourself a lawyer. Goodbye.'

I was completely at a loss. What had I signed? Did I really have no right to my clothes, my jewellery, the personal belongings accumulated over a number of years, many of them gifts?

'Let me in, Nick!' I shouted. He sensed the fear in my voice and was ruthless.

'Get out, or I'll call the police.'

'Nick, for Christ's sake, what's going on? Let me in!'

I was banging on the door in my frustration. Heads were peering round doors along the landing; Sugar was whining pitifully.

'I'm giving you a count of ten, Marc, and then I'll call the police. Run along now. Ten. Nine. Eight. Seven . . .'

There was no point in arguing. I ran down the stairs, but before I left the building I heard Nick's door open. I stopped in my tracks. Had it all been a joke?

'Oh, and Marc,' he shouted down at me, 'I'd suggest you read the *Evening News*.' The door slammed.

I stepped back on to the street in a daze, sick in the stomach. I needed a drink. I marched smartly down to Shepherd's Bush, heading for a favourite pub that I knew Nick would never be seen dead in (a haunt for the local motorcycle community). As I passed the station news stand, I was reminded of Nick's parting words: there was the old vendor as usual, crying, 'Paper late! *News* or *Standard*! *News* or *Standard*!' I thrust the money into his hand and tucked the *News* under my arm. As soon as I was settled in the pub with a large brandy inside me, I began to scan the paper.

Nothing on the front page, just the latest news from France, where the 'May Events' were spreading throughout the nation. (I'd read that later and use it in tomorrow's workshop.) Boring political news on pages two and three. Adverts. Gossip. Sport. What was he on about? A-ha, I thought, Pinky's column. But there was nothing: just a bitchy review of a new West End musical, and some idle speculations about Marianne Faithfull. Nick had been trying to frighten me. Then I noticed, in bold type at the bottom of the page, 'DON'T MISS WEST END SCANDAL SPECIAL PAGE 19'. Again, that old intuition; my palms began to sweat. With a terrible foreboding, I turned to page 19. The first thing that caught my eye was a large photograph of me from *Kill Me, Darling* (a dashing portrait in which I was holding a revolver) under the banner headline DEATH OF A REGULAR GIRL. At first I couldn't take it in. My eye glanced across the page to a smaller, grainier picture: a stretcher being loaded into the back of an ambulance, its contents covered by a sheet. I read the caption underneath: 'Dead at dawn: the body of tragic Janice Jones is removed from her London flat.'

I read the article from the beginning:

Popular actress-model Janice Jones was last night found dead in her London apartment, after her eight-year-old son Noel telephoned for an ambulance. An empty bottle of pills was found near the body, but at this stage the police are still regarding the circumstances of her death as 'suspicious'.

Miss Jones was believed to have been depressed by the end of her relationship with Marc LeJeune, her co-star in the famous 'Regular Guy' TV commercials, who is said by friends of the actress to have broken off their engagement in an 'abrupt and callous' fashion. Miss Jones' home was full of memorabilia of LeJeune: posters, framed cuttings, even a life-size cut-out of the Bran Pops star, who recently absconded from rehearsals for the million-pound West End musical *Danish Blue* and is facing legal action from former manager Nick Nicholls.

·This is not the first time LeJeune's name has been involved in police investigations. Just two years ago, LeJeune was implicated in the mysterious death of 68-year-old Bernard Phillips, his former schoolteacher and 'companion', with whom the actor was living as a lodger. Police inquiries in that case focused on the strange marks found on the dead man's body, and the unexplained gap between the time of death and the phone call to the ambulance service. The police investigation was finally dropped due to lack of evidence.

I couldn't believe what I was reading. What did Pinky care for the fact that I'd just lost one of my dearest friends – poor, fragile Janice, whose death suddenly hit me like a rabbit punch. I ran to the toilet and was violently sick.

I had to have another drink, and another, to stop myself from shaking. I read through the article again, finding yet more insinuations and lies. I was not only implicated in two deaths, it went on to say, but I was also a prostitute, a pornographer, a sexual pervert and a drug addict. Suddenly the scales fell from my eyes. This was Nick's doing. This was his revenge. He'd gone to Pinky Stevens with a story, and been handsomely paid for it. And Pinky, unaccountably vindictive and jealous as he had always been, was only too happy to print the lies. But, they would soon find, there was a price to be paid for insulting a star. I would stop them, and avenge myself, somehow. But how?

I made my way home slowly until I was shocked and scared by a woman spitting at me – *spitting at me* – at Paddington Station. The news had travelled, and I had to act fast.

Nick and Pinky, Pinky and Nick, their names chased each other round my head like rats in a trap. Together, they thought, they could break me. But inside myself I knew I was stronger, that I would fight and win. *They* had accused *me*, they who were two of the dirtiest, most disreputable creatures to crawl through the slime of the West End. How dared they?

Then it clicked. I had a plan. It meant dirtying my hands, fighting my enemies with the same weapons that they were using against me, but it would be effective. Not for nothing had I listened to the gossip of the hairdresser's salon, the green room, the theatre bar. I had ammunition and now was the time to use it.

I composed a letter to Pinky, which Julian delivered to the offices of the *Evening News* where, I calculated, its message would seem particularly clear.

'Dear Pinky Stevens,' it began, 'I was so interested to read your article about me in yesterday's *News*.' It continued:

You have put me in a fascinating position: I have absolutely nothing left to lose. You, it strikes me, have a good deal. You have called me a murderer, a prostitute and worse. But you are not the only one with tales to tell. I will expect to see a full, unreserved apology in tomorrow's edition, otherwise I will be sending details of the following to your notoriously uptight editor.

1. Your live-in relationship with Stuart. (I will also be pleased to send details of this to the headmaster of the school where Stuart teaches.)
2. Your holiday in Tangiers and your greedy consumption of hashish and young boys.
3. Precise details of Nick Nicholls's business practices, a list of his regular clients and information on the contents of his photographic library to which I now believe you to be a subscriber.

With very best wishes, Marc LeJeune

The following article duly appeared on the front page of the next day's *News*, under the headline MARC LEJEUNE: APOLOGY.

In a recent article, we suggested that Marc LeJeune was somehow implicated in the death of his former teacher and flatmate Bernard Phillips. We were mistaken in doing so, and are pleased to confirm that Scotland Yard is 'completely satisfied' that the case is now closed. We also accept that Mr LeJeune was not in any way directly involved in the death this week of Janice Jones, and we regret any implication in our report which may have suggested this. We apologize for any distress we may have caused to Mr LeJeune or his family.

That was all: no retraction of the other foul insinuations, but a clear indication that Pinky's report was nothing but lies. It would have to do: for now. But I vowed that Pinky and Nick would mess with me again at their peril. Finally I had discovered the one thing that they and their type feared more than anything else: exposure. I made sure that my parents had seen neither the original article nor the retraction.

The summer of '68! It was every bit as exciting as it's cracked up to be. I won't add another account to the vast literature that exists about this special time, I'll only say that everything you've ever read about it is true, and that I was at the centre of it all. By July, I had become a fully fledged hippy: my hair was long, my clothes were colourful, I even sported a beard for a while. I could go anywhere I chose and was seldom recognized. I was just a small speck in a warm, loving sea of humanity. That's how it seemed that summer – that summer that we thought would never end, that summer of long nights, of parties that lasted for days, of lovers that came and went, the faces I remember like snapshots, slightly faded now. The unforgettable atmosphere of the house where it all happened: the smell of food, the drugs, the cats, the great un-washed crowd that passed through that door, sometimes for a sweet, brief night, sometimes to stay for weeks at a time. Nutter, dear kind Julian, loving Anna – and of course Howard and Barbara, whom I could never warm to – were my constant companions. To-gether we laughed and loved and played like children in the garden.

But it wasn't all play. Slowly, painstakingly, the show that would relaunch my career was taking shape. Sometimes, during those long rehearsals in the Outer Space, I despaired; we were no nearer a script, a plot, or any sort of show at all. But then something wonderful happened. After weeks of aimless doodling, some-thing began to coalesce: a series of unrelated scenes, a few fragmentary lines, a handful of diverse props – a toy gun, a whip, a set of handcuffs . . . We came back ceaselessly to these same few elements, and Moska began to embellish them with more ideas, some of them insane, all of them outrageous. By now we'd done so many trust exercises that I had blind faith in Moska's judgement.

And then, God knows how, we suddenly had a show. Also, as Moska announced casually one day, we had a venue: the tiny Travesty Theatre Club on Endell Street, subversively positioned right in the middle of the West End. We would open at the end of September – a crucial date which, as historians will recall, marked the end of the Lord Chamberlain's powers of censorship over the British stage.

For many years, I'd been at the forefront of the movement to abolish this ridiculous, outmoded legislation. All of my perform-ances, from the very first time I stepped on stage as Cleopatra, had walked a legal and artistic tightrope; in my more recent work, I'd adopted subtler tactics, observing the conventional forms of thriller and farce but always stretching the content to the very limits. Sometimes I'd gone too far, hence the hostility of certain elements of the press, who saw me as a danger to their hidebound, conventional theatre. But it was thanks to the tireless efforts of me and a few others like me that, finally, censorship was lifted in 1968.

We would be the first to take advantage of the new freedom, opening our show at 6 p.m. on the day that the new act was passed, beating the rest of the West End by a few crucial hours. (There was another reason for the early curtain: the show was over four hours long.)

The first night of *Meat* – that was the title that Moska had finally settled on – will stay in my memory forever. I've been asked about it a million times by students, keen to know the minutest details of a turning point in cultural history. Did I realize, they ask, what I was doing? I have to be truthful: no, I wasn't aware of its full significance, of the magnitude that it was to attain in later years. But yes, I certainly sensed something special in the air. There was a buzz in the West End; journalists were sniffing around on every street, limousines cruised up Shaftesbury Avenue, the evening papers sold out as fast as they hit the street. We weren't the only opening in town that night: there was an American musical coming into the Shaftesbury Theatre that was also testing the new freedoms, amidst much hype. (This proved to be the vastly overrated *Hair*, a disappointing show that featured a brief flash of nudity at the end of the first act but was basically a conventional musical with a few trendy drugs references thrown in to grab publicity.)

Meat was a different kettle of fish. Our show was radical, not just in its content but also in its conception and form. Moska described it as a theatrical critique of imperialism, both sexual and political, and of theatre itself. The plot (such as it was – this was not conventional, bourgeois, 'linear' theatre) revolved around themes of the body: the body as sex object, the body as possession, the body as spectacle. 'The central image', he had said during one intense rehearsal, 'is the flesh. The firm young flesh that we desire. The flesh that bleeds and dies and rots, the flesh that is eaten and sustains life. The flesh as commodity.' Hence *Meat* – flesh as commodity. We picked up a lot of unexpected publicity in vegetarian publications, who threatened to picket us until Moska explained that *Meat* was a radical critique of a carnivorous society as well.

There were queues around the block by five o'clock. I was used to full houses, but for Moska and the rest of the company this was an unimaginable thrill. Word had spread that *Meat* was the hottest ticket in town, and Moska had given interviews to the radical press promising shock after shock. He had also made great play of my presence in the cast, how he was 'using an icon of the commercial culture as the focal point' of the new show. The popular press had been quick to pick up on the fact that Marc LeJeune was appearing in a 'sex and drugs shocker'.

The audience were ushered into the tiny auditorium. I recognized a scattering of my faithful older fans who attended my every London show, some of them chums of Nick's who had seen my very first performance at the club and had remained loyal ever since. How out of place they looked, those smart old gentlemen in their blazers and club ties, among the great hairy mass that comprised the rest of the audience! I noticed that they had commandeered the seats with the best view.

The house lights went down, and for a few seconds the room was in complete darkness, save for a few tiny red points of light where various members of the audience were smoking. Then, thundering from the huge speakers placed all around the room (one of Julian's friends was a DJ), came 'Mony Mony' by Tommy James and the Shondells, a big hit that summer. As the beat pounded relentlessly in the tiny auditorium, the stage lights were brought up very, very slowly. Moska's *corps de ballet*, naked and covered from head to foot in stage blood, crept on to the stage. The lights brightened a tiny bit more, and the audience could just make out the dark, glistening forms of the dancers' bodies writhing in time to the music. More light, and now they were clearly visible, stamping and jumping across the stage. Every breath in the audience was held. This, they knew, was a revolution.

The record died away, but the dancers kept up the same rhythm, standing in a line across the stage, stamping their feet just inches from the front row. Every breast, every scrotum, wobbled visibly in time to the beat. When Moska made his entrance wearing a white lab coat and pince-nez, there was a ripple of applause from the cognoscenti, which he acknowledged with a fluid hand gesture. Climbing on to a rostrum, he stuck his hand deep inside his coat (as the sound system struck up a deafening rendition of the death aria from *Madam Butterfly*) and produced a huge bullwhip which he brandished above his head then brought down with a crash on to the floor, mercilessly flogging the dancers who cowered and ran around the stage. After a few moments of this they fell panting at the foot of the rostrum, writhed around a bit, smeared more blood over each other then came to rest in a formation that explicitly represented a woman's pudendum.

During the foregoing, I had crept invisibly from behind the curtains into a hollow space inside the rostrum. Now, as the aria reached its crescendo and Moska belaboured the huge human vagina with his whip, I crawled under the mass of dancers and emerged – was 'born' – through a central aperture of writhing, wriggling arms. There was sudden silence, and I lay, quivering in a foetal position and slightly streaked with blood, at the audience's mercy. You could have heard a pin drop.

The dancers disappeared, and Moska once again cracked his whip. Now it was the turn of Nutter, Julian and Anna, who came tripping on to the stage dressed in nurses' uniforms: Anna and Julian as women, Nutter in white Y-fronts, stripped to the waist, with a stethoscope round his neck and a paper nurse's cap perched absurdly on his head. Between them they produced huge rolls of gauze in which they wrapped me, running round and round my body (while Moska blew a whistle) until I was completely swathed like the Mummy. There was then a completely gratuitous scene in which Anna and Julian 'simulated' sex with Nutter (although how much of Anna's performance was simulation is a matter of debate, at least from where I was watching).

I won't go into detail about the rest of the show: more scholarly minds than mine have recorded that historic evening. Suffice to say that I was on stage for the ensuing four hours, during which time I was regularly stripped, whipped, dressed in a variety of costumes (nun, city gent, Vietnamese peasant) and engaged in sexual acts with every member of the cast. In one memorable scene, I was the front end of a pantomime cow while Nutter was the back; we were violently attacked by the rest of the cast who 'slaughtered' us with chainsaws then pulled out yards and yards of innards (old sheets soaked in fake blood) from our 'stomach'. (This scene had been inserted at the last minute by Moska as a gesture to the vegetarian faction, who whooped and cheered hysterically during this scene of bizarre cruelty to an animal.)

The evening's entertainment ended with my naked body hand-cuffed to a huge wheel upon which the symbol for nuclear power had been painted. The rest of the cast then took potshots at me with handfuls of wallpaper paste into which Moska had stirred several ounces of glitter. The resultant mess looked as if someone had had a huge and very glamorous orgasm all over me. Finally, Moska appeared in a Maoist uniform, brandishing the Chinese flag in one hand and a huge sacrificial knife in the other. He held a pose for a few, heart-stopping moments, then brought the knife down across my throat. Pints of fake blood (the biggest single expense on the *Meat* budget) pumped out and the show was over.

The audience was shell-shocked. Even when the lights came up and I stepped down to take my bow, they couldn't applaud for over a minute. It's the greatest tribute an audience can pay to an actor – the homage of stunned silence. Finally, they erupted. They screamed, they clapped, they stamped their feet. Fights broke out. Things were thrown – flowers, loose change, beer glasses, lighted cigarettes. I saw one of my oldest fans (a sweet old gentleman, actually) stagger out of the auditorium white-faced, clutching his chest. We took a final bow and beat it to the dressing room. It was 10.15. I peered out of the window to watch the crowds filtering politely out of the Shaftesbury Theatre, where *Hair*'s first night had just reached its disappointing conclusion. Where was the excitement, the revolution, there? My audience was still hysterical in the theatre; finally Moska had to risk life and limb to calm them. At last, they were pacified and left to perpetrate God knows what acts of insanity in the London night.

It took me an hour to clean myself up after the show. In fact, for the duration of the run I had peculiar red stains from the fake blood inside my ears, and was forever discovering grains of glitter in the most embarrassing places. Finally, I was ready – to celebrate! I knew, and Moska knew, that together we had made history. But this was no time for analysis. This was time for a party!

Julian, that social butterfly, had arranged the first night celebrations at a club on D'Arblay Street that would entertain us 'all night, and all tomorrow if necessary'. We were mad Maenads, high on our own powers of creation/destruction. We danced, we drank, we took drugs – nothing could quench the spirit that Moska had unleashed. And I danced longer, laughed harder, than anyone else there. What was it that Moska had unleashed in *me* – an angel? Or a demon?

And I made love that night – wild, carefree love. There was a woman at the club whom I had never seen before, a tall statuesque beauty with flaming red hair (she reminded me of Rita Hayworth in *Gilda*); Nutter couldn't keep his eyes off her. But she was interested in only one person on the dance floor – me. I was delighted; I'd been having a little trouble with Nutter during rehearsals for *Meat*, listening to his endless complaints that Moska was a 'pervert' and that he hated the sexual acts that he was forced to perform. He particularly hated the sex act with Julian, and objected to a scene in which he and I had to kiss while the rest of the cast strafed us with machine-gun fire. 'I'm not gay, Marc, I can't handle it,' he told me over and over again, as if I was somehow responsible for the strange company he chose to keep. His relationship with Anna had suffered too; the pressure to 'perform' on stage had rendered him incapable of making love to her in private. And now he was hoping to 'prove' himself as a man at a party that was being held to celebrate *my* success.

'She's gorgeous, man,' burbled Nutter in my ear as 'Rita' sashayed across the floor towards us. 'I'm gonna make it with her. God, yeah, I've got to, I've got to . . .' He was a randy little schoolboy again, with an itch to be scratched. But I knew 'Rita' had eyes only for me. As she approached us, she peeled off one long, black satin glove. Nutter was practically doubled up with lust, and made to grab her. She deftly flicked him aside, wrapped the glove around my neck and drew me into a close, sensuous tango. Nutter was furious, and stormed out of the club. I didn't care; for the moment, only two people existed – me and the woman in my arms. There was something about her that turned me on. It wasn't just the glamour of the evening, the drink and drugs that I'd taken. It wasn't just her physical beauty, or the way she touched me as we danced, although those were both powerful aphrodisiacs. There was something special about this lady, something that the other girls just didn't have.

We were magical together on the dance floor. Every eye was rivetted upon us as we glided together, lost in each other's embrace, oblivious to the envious stares from around the club. We danced for – what? Minutes? Hours? I'll never know. And then, without a word, we left the club together. A short taxi ride (we could hardly keep our hands off each other), a smart apartment in Chelsea, a night that I will never forget. Had I finally found the woman of my dreams?

You could have cut the air with a knife when I reported at the theatre the next afternoon. Nutter was sullen, threatening to jump ship (he ruined the show that night with an aggressive, erratic performance). Anna was pasty-faced and tired – hungover? Or had she and Nutter had a row? Even Julian was subdued, and wouldn't look me in the eye. Thankfully, I was professional enough to rise above backstage bitchiness, and pulled the show together. It was a stunning success. But we'd lost something, the sense of camaraderie built up so carefully over months of rehearsal. Why? What had happened? I felt that the rest of the company was keeping something from me.

I found out the following day, and, once again, I had to turn to the newspapers to read the 'truth' about myself. It was Julian who sheepishly brought the *Evening News* to me; I knew as soon as I saw the familiar masthead that there was a shock in store. I expected it. I almost welcomed it. If you keep receiving blow after blow on the same bruise, it hurts a little less each time, although it never heals. And the pain becomes a part of your life.

Pinky had pulled no punches this time. There, in the centre pages, was a full-length cut-out of 'Rita', posing seductively under the headline BOYS WILL BE GIRLS!. ' "I was Marc LeJeune's sexy surprise,'' says man-about-town Crystal DeCanter, hostess at a saucy London Club,' ran the first paragraph. It was my first experience of kiss and tell – but this one had a sting in the tail. Rita/Crystal, my lover of a night, had betrayed me – and lied to me. My mouth filled with bitter-tasting bile as I realized with disgust that I had been tricked into bed by some kind of sexual freak, a hermaphrodite, a cheap drag queen.

'He was a fantastic lover, inventive and uninhibited,' says statuesque Crystal, 6′ 1″ in his stilettos. 'Sometimes he was aggressive, almost violent with me,' he purrs, 'sometimes he was so soft and tender, like a little boy.'

It ran on in this revolting vein for several more column inches, and only mentioned my triumph in *Meat* at the bottom of the page.

Marc LeJeune's checkered stage career hit an all-time low this week when he opened in the sex revue *Meat* at the Travesty Theatre. LeJeune's decision to pull out of the million-pound musical *Danish Blue* has backfired badly: not only is he facing legal action from former manager Nick Nicholls, but also has the exquisite torture of knowing that the show is now London's top box-office draw without him! Read more about *Danish Blue*'s new star in tomorrow's *News*!

Now I understood Nutter's hostility, Julian's embarrassment: they had realized what I had failed to see, that my lover of a night was a parasitic whore who was using my success to further her – his – own tawdry ends. It was a bitter blow. I had only just learned to trust my fellow man. Must I unlearn that lesson so soon?

I had to face Nutter; his good opinion was all that mattered to me. I found him sitting in the kitchen brooding over a can of beer. 'Have you had lunch?' I greeted him, intending to soothe his temper with food.

'This is my lunch,' he growled, draining his beer and scrunching the can with his fist.

'Oh, you must eat . . .' Nutter shot me a look of such contempt that I dared not go on. 'Please, Nutter, we have to talk.'

'I've got nothing to say. I've had enough of this shit. It's time to move on.' He drummed restlessly on the table.

'What's the matter?' I wanted so badly to reach out and touch him, but in his current frame of mind I dared not.

'Everything! This stupid fucking play! That bastard Moska touching me up every night! Anna trying to castrate me! And the worst thing of all . . .' He was silent, opening another can of beer and drinking deeply.

'What, Nutter?'

'The worst thing of all is that . . . I . . . I fancied that fucking drag queen!'

So that was it. No care for my pain, for the trauma that I'd been through. No: selfish Nutter was frightened by the fact that he had come so close to having sex with a man, had actually found another man desirable. I pitied his narrow-minded ignorance.

'Well, it's a good job I saved you then, isn't it?' I tried to make a joke out of it. 'From a fate worse than death . . .'

Nutter was in no mood for jokes. 'I can't take it, Marc. I'm leaving. I've got to find myself. There's nothing for me here.'

'What about the show?'

'You'll do fine without me.'

'What about Anna?'

'She's all yours, mate.'

'But Nutter . . . What about me?'

He looked into my eyes. What was it I saw in his soul? Love? Pain? I would never know. For a moment, he held out a hand as if to ruffle my hair, the way he used to when we were schoolboys. I closed my eyes, awaiting his touch. When I opened them again, he was gone.

Nutter's disappearance seemed to affect only me. Anna was philosophical. 'They come and they go, babe, like free spirits,' was her only remark. Moska was pragmatic, rewriting a few scenes in the show (I now had a new back end in the infamous abattoir scene).

Life in the house went on much the same as usual. But I was left with a terrible, empty craving. I filled that void with drink, drugs and transient love affairs.

Meat ran its course at the Travesty, and failed to transfer. It had been just too far ahead of its time. But Moska regarded it as a triumph, despite the paucity of reviews (the few that had appeared were mostly bad). 'This is not show business, Maaaahhrrrrk,' he said to me one dull winter afternoon. 'This is revolution. We are soldiers in an army of love. We must fight on.' I agreed to be in his next show; I had little else to do. Since splitting from Nick, I'd had no other offers. Life at the house was comfortable enough, and there was always something or someone to take the pain away. Moska promised me an even better part in his new 'piece', and once again we began the endless round of classes and workshops and trust exercises.

Nineteen sixty-nine was the shadow of 1968, a dark year, full of death and disillusionment. One afternoon, while shopping in Camden Town with Julian, we were accosted by a bunch of skinheads who pushed us down an alleyway and beat us up. How much of that violence was simple sexual curiosity? How much of it was the primal desire to destroy beauty? We repaired ourselves and continued, proud if bloodied, on our way. But the fun had gone.

Moska's next show was even more extreme than *Meat*. We had a better venue this time – a professionally equipped theatre, with proper dressing rooms and a pleasant foyer bar. Moska, somehow, had chased up a fistful of grants and gained the all-important backing of the Arts Council. We opened in July with a piece entitled *Shitface*, a violent meditation on the death and destruction that characterized the time. I played several roles, martyrs all: Brian Jones, Jan Palach and, most memorably, Judy Garland, who had just died. The climax of the show featured me in full Dorothy Gale drag, staggering downstage clutching a bottle of booze and diving head-first into a toilet which swallowed my entire body, leaving only the ruby slippers tapping desperately above the rim. As I died,

Moska and the rest of the company appeared from the wings in full moon suits miming weightlessness before 'Captain' Moska saluted and planted an American flag right up my arsehole.

Shitface was not a happy production, although this time the reviews were more widespread, and the hippy press at least gave us raves. But the backstage dramas reached ridiculous levels. Practically every night someone walked out, while Moska alienated everyone by bringing in his latest discovery (often alarmingly young) to fill the place. By the end of the run, I was almost as damaged as Judy Garland herself. Every time I lurched towards that toilet bowl – a welcome sight, as it spelt oblivion – I was haunted by the image of Janice Jones.

We closed at the end of November, and I badly needed to get away. Julian and some of his friends were going to Amsterdam for the Wet Dream Festival, a celebration of the 'erotic arts' that promised 'sex and drugs galore!' I had nothing better to do, nothing to stay in London for, so I went with them. They returned in time for Christmas; I stayed.

I'll draw a veil over my Amsterdam experience for one very good reason: I can't remember a thing about it. I recall a ghastly ferry crossing. I remember marvelling at the beauty of the city, its narrow houses and bridges, its endless canals. I remember sitting down with Julian in a café and ordering 'cake'. I remember nothing else for the next nine months. I survived – somehow. That's all I can say about Amsterdam.

When I returned to London at the end of 1970, I found an angry, divided city. Where once we had spoken of 'happenings' and 'good vibes', now all the talk was of 'actions'. Anna and Howard happily plotted one action after another, each more violent and dangerous than the last. They recounted with glee their recent antics at the Miss World competition, which they'd picketed dressed in the cow costume left over from *Meat*. They boasted that they were going to 'get' various leading industrialists, and hinted darkly at involvement with European terrorist organizations. Howard had taken to wearing a beret, dark glasses and a flak jacket, and adorned his room with photographs of Andreas Baader and Che Guevara. Anna had cut her hair short and was wearing dungarees: she was among the first to go for 'radical feminist chic'.

Of course, I got dragged into their dangerous games. I didn't care about my career; if anything, I wanted to destroy the part of my life that seemed only to have brought misery and despair to myself and those I loved. So I joined in their merry pranks, as they called them. We started making bombs at home – pitiful affairs that would only cause a little fire damage, and were completely uncontrollable and unpredictable. For reasons that now escape me, we planted one of these in the world-famous Biba boutique in Kensington, a place where, once upon a time not so very long ago, Anna, Julian and I had loved to shop. It went off and caused considerable damage to a rack of velvet loons. A few months later, I was roped into a 'zap' on the Festival of Light, the ill-timed moral cleanliness campaign attended by Mary Whitehouse and Cliff Richard. Dressed as a Church of England vicar (my long hair and beard looked just the part) I mingled with the good folk in the Central Methodist Hall until, at a prearranged signal, I leapt on to the stage, ripped off my dog collar and the rest of my clothes while Anna ran around the auditorium screaming, 'Suck my tits!' We escaped before the police arrived.

All of this had cut me off completely from the world I'd once known: the world of my parents, of Nick Nicholls and his 'discreet' clients, of the closeted Pinky Stevens and his tight-lipped show-business buddies. But it made me a celebrity in London's radical underground, who heralded my every appearance (whether 'scheduled' or otherwise) with rapturous write-ups in the free press. It was a strange sort of fame, an exact inversion of what I'd known before. The worse I behaved, the more they loved me.

Public acclaim demanded that I do one more show with Moska. Our names were inseparable; we had been called 'the Dietrich and von Sternberg of the fuck-you generation' by one journalist. And

Moska was desperate to milk our association to the very last drop. But I could see what his admirers couldn't: that this was a man utterly bereft of new ideas, who would flog the dead horse of avant-garde shock theatre until it dropped in its traces. 'Today's revolution', I said to him as we started rehearsals for our final collaboration, 'is tomorrow's convention. You've got to move with the times, Moska. Find new ways of expression.' He couldn't understand me. It was sad to see this man, undoubtedly talented, so blinkered in his ideas. But what was wonderful and liberating in 1968 was tawdry in the cold light of 1971.

Just as I was ready to move on, the theatrical establishment began to catch up with me. Ironically, Moska was now the darling of the Arts Council, wreathed with awards and raking in grants hand over fist (I never saw any of the money). For his next show, he had gone into partnership with the Institute of Contemporary Arts, the famous ICA on the Mall, a radical venue just a stone's throw from Buckingham Palace. In recognition of his august surroundings, Moska had decided to go highbrow, and planned a radical reworking of Sylvia Plath's *The Bell Jar*, poignantly retitled *The Bell End*. Tragic Plath's masterpiece was a favourite of mine, but once it had been through Moska's artistic mincing machine, there was little left but the hollow shock imagery of gas chambers, razor blades and the usual chorus of dragged-up ballet dancers covered in his signature stage blood.

Rehearsals plodded on through the long, hard winter months of 1971 and 1972. By the time we were ready to open, I was so confused and exhausted that I hardly knew what I was supposed to be doing. I was weary of Moska and his foolish working practices, weary of the uncertainty of the underground. I'll admit it: I was awash with drugs, embarking on one doomed affair after another, promiscuous in my choice of partners. I couldn't see any escape. 'Deadening and corrupt', Moska had called his theatrical rivals – how quickly that had come home to roost. As we approached the opening night, I was desperate.

First of all, there was another party to live through, a launch
for the ICA's Festival of Underground Theatre, of which we were
the main feature. The beautiful regency rooms were packed to
overflowing with a curious mixture of London's freaky fringe
community, respectable figures from the artistic world and, of
course, the ever-prying press hoping for a story. I moved through
the crowd, all smiles, ready with a juicy quote (a 'soundbite' we'd
call it today) for the newspapers and TV crews. But my heart was
dead. I've never felt less joy, less euphoria, about a first night – that
night that all artists live for. Yes, I could play the star, but mine
was a hollow glitter.

Suddenly, I spotted Pinky Stevens across the room. My heart
skipped a beat: it was our first face-to-face meeting since he had
started his hate campaign against me. How dared he come to the
party? Of course he was hoping that I'd make some horrendous
public scene and provide him with the copy for tomorrow's column. What appetite drove this vulture to feed on my misfortune? I
had to confront him – not in anger, but in sorrow and bewilder-
ment.

Silence fell as I walked through the parting crowds to where
Pinky stood chatting and laughing with his intimates. Soon his was
the only voice audible in the room. He sensed something wrong,
looked to his friends for guidance and saw all eyes staring in
my direction. He swallowed hard and faced me, his expression
impenetrable: fear? Or was it desire?

'I think we need to talk.' That was all I said. I turned on my
heel and walked out of the room; Pinky followed. No sooner were
we out of the room than the hubbub of voices exploded louder
than before, each one of them discussing the 'showdown' that was
doubtless imminent.

Without looking back, I led the way downstairs to the dressing
rooms. Pinky stuck to me like a shadow. I knew there was a scenery
dock where we would be undisturbed. Thither I took him. All
around us was total silence.

'So what happens now?' he asked, laughter playing round his mouth and eyes. 'Are you going to kill me too?'

Inside I was shocked, but I was an actor, and knew how to dissemble my emotions.

'Why do you hate me, Pinky?'

'It's my job.'

'But why me?'

'You're just irresistible, Marc.'

'You mean . . .?'

'You're such an easy target.'

'Have you no shame? No integrity? Is there nothing to which you won't stoop?'

'From you, Marc, that's rich.'

It wasn't going the way I had planned. I wanted Pinky to see me as a fellow human being, a brother; instead he hid behind a sneering professional mask. I changed tack.

'I wish we could be friends.'

'With pleasure!'

'No, I mean more than that . . . When I first met you, I was attracted to you. But you turned on me. Why is that, Pinky? What drives you to such cruelty?'

'I've really no idea. Now, if you don't mind, I must get back to the party.'

'You know what they say – that love and hate are two sides of the same coin.'

'Do they, indeed?'

'Yes.'

There was a long silence, our eyes locked in mutual exploration. Pinky was not an unattractive man: horn-rimmed glasses concealed penetrating, intelligent eyes, and his mouth was made for kissing as well as for sneering. I felt his desire for me beating in hot waves. I pulled my shirt off and pressed myself against him.

'Oh Pinky! Take me!'

In trying to steal a kiss, I wrong-footed him and brought us both crashing to the floor; Pinky hit his head on a pipe. He swore loudly, pushed me off and staggered to his feet. I lay there, my clothes in disarray, trying to look seductive. Pinky, the cold-blooded, uptight Englishman that he was, brushed down his trousers, adjusted his glasses on his nose and was gone.

How I got through the performance I will never know. Doctor Theatre again, I suppose. But even his sweet balm couldn't cure me completely. When the show was over I hung up my pig mask (for some reason, Sylvia Plath metamorphosed into a pig woman), rubbed a little Savlon on to the barbed wire wounds on my arms and legs and left the theatre alone. I walked for hours in St James's Park. I strolled along the river, contemplating suicide at every bridge. But life was still stronger than death, and my feet led me home at dawn. I couldn't sleep. One question went round and round in my brain: What have I done? What have I done?

The aftermath of that night was swift and far-reaching. Pinky, true to form, had ignored the olive branch and turned our poignant backstage meeting into the most lurid copy. 'Marc LeJeune threw caution to the winds last night at the ICA,' it began. 'How far will an actor go for a good review? All the way, it seems . . .' I couldn't be bothered to read any more. For once, I felt I only had myself to blame.

It was a turning point in my life. I realized just how far a man would go to protect himself – even to the extent of betraying his fellow man. Pinky and I had so much in common – far more than he would admit to his editors or readers – but was desperate to maintain his position as the pampered pet of the West End, the harmless eunuch who would flatter and fawn on those who fed him scraps. But on those, like me, who threatened to blow his cover he squandered his real talent, a talent to abuse. How much of that vicious copy was really directed against himself?

For there was one big difference between us. Whereas I had always lived my life in the open, heedless of what people thought,

Pinky was condemned by his own fear to a life in the shadows. I was one of the brave ones: those who loved and fought for the freedom to love. But privileged Pinky couldn't bear the idea of freedom. He chose to be half a man, assuaging his guilty conscience by punishing me for his own shortcomings. And it had worked, so far. His editors had their suspicions about Pinky (he was, after all, living with another man, and enjoyed secretive liaisons with boys many years his junior) but, as long as he kept churning out columns that held me up as the last word in sexual irregularity, they turned a blind eye. But now he'd overplayed his hand. True, I came out of the incident looking foolish. I'd tried to seduce a journalist, it seemed like the last resort of a desperate man. But Pinky had compromised himself as well. What, after all, was he doing in the 'sordid cupboard' with a 'half-naked, drugged-up degenerate' in the first place? From that moment on, Pinky's stock at the *Evening News* began to fall dramatically.

But there were other, more immediate repercussions. They began the morning after my exposé in the *News*, a paper that my parents had begun to read every day. There was a deafening bang on the front door of the squat, so hard that the old door finally fell off its hinges, smashing the rainbow fanlight in its descent. A second's silence, then the unmistakable sound of my father's voice raised in anger.

'Marc! Marc! Come down here this minute, boy, or I'll break every bone in your body, so help me God!'

I sprang out of bed. I could vaguely hear my mother gibbering in the background, pleading with Dad to calm down. I had to think quickly. I pulled on a pair of trousers and a T shirt, dragged a comb through my hair and slapped myself round the face. I checked myself in the mirror, practised my biggest smile and bounded on to the landing.

'Mum! Dad! You've heard already! That's brilliant!'

'Heard? I should bloody well say we've heard, you disgusting little pouf!'

'Please, darling, don't shout at him . . .'

'Oh, Dad, you're not talking about that crap in the papers again, are you?'

'Crap? I should say it's crap, boy! We've had dog shit through our letter box thanks to you and your filthy ways! Now come down here so I can belt you.'

It was a bizarre scene. I almost wanted to laugh. My father, no longer a young man, was rolling up his sleeves to punish me, when I could have flattened him with one blow.

'I've told you before, Dad, that's just stories that the papers make up to publicize the show. But that's not what you're here for, is it? I thought you must have heard my good news!'

That stopped him in his tracks. His brow furrowed, he looked confused. A pitiful light dawned in my mother's face.

'Good news, Marc?' she stammered. 'What's that, darling?'

'Haven't you heard?' Just then, Anna stumbled out of her bedroom, wearing only a T shirt with a huge female symbol painted on the front in vegetable dye. I grasped her in a bear hug and planted a huge kiss on her lips.

'We're going to be married, of course!'

CHAPTER FIVE

We decided to make a big splash with our engagement, and offered the exclusive to a number of newspapers. A frenzied auction ensued, with bid succeeding unbelievable bid as editors raced to cash in on the story. Finally – sweet irony! – we signed with the London *Evening Standard*, deadly rival to Pinky's *Evening News*. He had sown discord; now his enemies would reap the harvest.

I discussed the situation in detail with Anna. I'd undervalued her in the past: now I realized that this was a woman I could work with, an astute business head as well as a warm and spontaneous human being. When I'd shocked my parents with the announcement of our impending nuptials, Anna took the news without missing a beat; she simply stood there and beamed, accepting their faltering congratulations and even kissing them both as they left. What I'd stumbled on as an escape from an awkward jam proved to be an astute career move. Accident or intuition? Again, I just don't know.

We made a brave decision: we'd speak frankly about our plans for an 'open' marriage, our interest in other lovers – of either sex. It was unheralded, unprecedented, and it worked. We invited photographers into our home, where we posed as a loving couple, kissing in the kitchen, snuggling up in our king-size bed ('There's always room for a friend!') and walking hand in hand in the garden. The photographs were sweet and innocuous, but the copy that would accompany them suggested a world of carnal pleasure just beyond the frame.

'Yes, I've enjoyed male lovers,' admits Marc. 'I don't know any man who hasn't – or who hasn't wanted to.' And how would he feel if he came home one night and found his beautiful wife in bed with another bird? 'I wouldn't mind,' he laughs, caressing Anna's hair, 'as long as they let me join in!'

The *Standard* sold out as soon as it appeared. The phone rang so much that Anna and I had to take it off the hook – as soon as we'd negotiated a five-figure sum for the *Standard*'s coverage of our summer wedding.

Bisexuality isn't such a big deal today, but in 1972 it was front page news. I was the first major star to admit to being anything other than 100 per cent straight, and others were quick to follow my lead. An unknown singer called David Bowie suddenly popped up in the music papers claiming that he too (and his wife, for that matter) swung both ways, and the floodgates opened. Records, plays, books and even films – *Cabaret, The Rocky Horror Picture Show* – took my basic idea and turned it into gold. All I'd intended, as usual, was to be honest and to help other people live their lives more openly. What I'd achieved was a unique expression of the spirit of the age.

I looked around me and saw the lifestyle I had instinctively pioneered in the last ten years turn into the fashion of the day. So why not go along with it? I was hardly jumping on a bandwagon – I'd been riding that wagon over rough and smooth for as long as I could remember. Anna was quick to spot the potential. 'You're famous all over again, babe,' she said. 'But this time you're not going to blow it. You've got to cash in.'

I shuddered. What was all this talk of cashing in – or selling out, as we would have called it not so long ago? There was a new consciousness abroad, one that would take the fragile, crazy beauty of the sixties and turn it into hard currency. Looking back, I see that perhaps I should have resisted, remained true to myself and the grass roots whence I'd come. But at the time, destiny had the stronger pull.

Our wedding was a media circus. We'd kept the guest list small, inviting only a dozen or so friends and family (including Mum and

Dad, of course) to witness a simple civil ceremony at Chelsea Register Office. Anna and I exchanged our vows in matching white trouser suits, tailored at the waist with wide lapels and cuffs, and, of course, huge flares (very few people could wear that style without looking ridiculous; Anna wasn't one of them). We both had the same accessories: a red carnation, a red handkerchief in the top pocket and, for going away, white broad-brimmed fedoras with red satin hatbands.

As we prepared to step out of the Town Hall and face the world, we stopped and looked at each other. Anna kissed me. For a moment, I really felt that I loved her. I owed her so much. Maybe this crazy marriage wasn't so crazy after all. Maybe we could make a go of our lives together. 'Let's go get 'em, babe,' she whispered, leering and winking. She threw open the door and we descended the steps into an artillery of flashguns. It took a terrible, exhilarating half hour to make our way to the waiting car (paid for by the *Standard*). In that time we'd been interviewed and photographed by every major newspaper, magazine, radio and TV programme in the country.

The press coverage was astonishing, not so much for its volume but for its enthusiasm. Those papers who withheld their blessing simply ignored us altogether; conspicuous among these was the *News*. For Pinky it had not been a happy ending; his editors, stung by the fact that they'd missed out on the biggest story of the decade, had sacked him. Now he could rant and rave as much as he liked, and nobody would listen.

If something as simple as a wedding could cause such a ballyhoo, why not go one step further? Anna and I spent night after night (when the nation assumed we were enjoying a wild honeymoon!) plotting our next move. How could we ensure my continued success? What was the 'product' that would fit the 'brand'? The best answer, as usual, turned out to be the simplest. I would return to my first love – rock & roll. That was, and always had been, the medium in which I felt most at home.

Now those years in the underground wilderness paid off. Since 1968 I'd met no end of would-be musicians, producers and promoters, most of them struggling along like the rest of us, living from hand to mouth and enjoying themselves too much to concentrate on their careers. Four years on, many of them had fallen by the wayside, but some of them were bona fide successes. It was time to call in favours. Anna had a phenomenal memory and an address book to match it, and within a few days I was booked into a top London studio with a band and a producer to cut my first single.

It took two days, and there was magic in the air. I don't know what it was; I was off drugs, clean and sober, with both feet on the ground. But sitting in the studio singing my heart out, I felt as high as a kite. It all happened so quickly: the song was written, the band rehearsed and recorded, I 'laid down' the vocals, the whole thing was mixed and cut in a flash. *Voilà*, pop immortality, 'the first and still the best bisexual novelty record of the seventies' (*Melody Maker*) – the unforgettable 'Bi Bi Baby'.

We knew we had a hit on our hands. 'Bi Bi Baby' ('Don't be a cry bi baby, Be my bi baby/Bi bi baby tonight') had the lushness of Phil Spector, the sexuality of Elvis Presley. Even the engineers and session musicians, jaded professionals to a man, whistled it as they went about their work. All we needed now, said Anna, was the right image to launch the song. She was all for bringing Moska in to direct my stage appearances, but I put my foot down: Moska was yesterday's man. The keynote of my new image must be simplicity, the quality possessed by all truly great pop. I went back to basics: a leather jacket, tight silver trousers, 'bovver boots' and a greasy, slicked-up, larger-than-life rocker haircut. I was clean-shaven and bare-chested, with male and female symbols drawn around my nipples in lipstick. An icon was (re)born.

And of course 'Bi Bi Baby' was a hit, a huge hit, the one by which other 'overnight sensations' are measured. If only they knew the long, hard slog, the pain and loss that it had taken to get there! But pop music is about celebration, not about soul-searching, and

I was glad to be doing something upbeat and happy for a change. Everyone, from kids to grandparents, loved me, whether they understood the message or not. It was just like the old Bran Pops days. The only ones who voiced disapproval were the underground press, my champions when things had been going badly and when my work dealt in blood, slaughter and pain. Now that I was happy and successful they turned their back on me. It was their loss.

The excitement surrounding 'Bi Bi Baby' reached a climax when I made my début on *Top of the Pops*. Remember that this was the first time people had had a chance to see me on television (apart from the news footage of the wedding) since I was the Regular Guy, that clean-cut, smart-suited 'ace face' of the Swinging Sixties. How long ago and far away that all seemed! There were kids buying the records who had never heard of the Regular Guy. But for those who remembered, there was a delicious irony, a dangerous sexual charge that made the record irresistible. My performance on *Top of the Pops* brought all that together in one devastating package. There was the band, pounding out the beat. There was Anna on bongos and backing vocals, almost as much of a star with her new skinhead crop as I was. And finally there was me: 'five foot ten of leather, lurex and sweet, sweet sin' as one overwhelmed journalist described me.

The record went straight in at number 35. In those days, a hit was a hit – record sales were enormous, and you could become rich overnight. But success was never to be mine without controversy as its bedfellow. The BBC was inundated with complaints about my 'lewd performance' and its 'dangerous threat to young minds'. That was how Middle England responded to an anthem of love and freedom! And so I was banned, never again to appear on *Top of the Pops*. 'Bi Bi Baby' slid down the charts the following week, but despite the best efforts of the censors it was to stay in the all-important top 100 for months to come. You don't get that kind of lasting success without working hard for it, and boy, did I work.

Life became one long round of promotional activity: interviews on the radio (*Woman's Hour* was fascinated by the details of our unconventional marriage), TV spots, personal appearances at night clubs, and finally a full-scale rock & roll tour. It was the kind of work that I was born to do, and the audiences were always there rooting for me. Some of them came out of curiosity, expecting to see a freakshow, but they left as fans. A whole new generation was discovering my work and was eager to find out more. I gave interviews to the press whenever possible, stressing that I was no flash in the pan like some of my pop contemporaries: I had a background, a pedigree. Journalists who had done their homework were quick to draw attention to my earlier incarnation in TV commercials, but I pointed them towards my distinguished career in the theatre, my championing of the avant-garde, and most of all my crucial role in bringing rock & roll to British ears in the first place. I spoke affectionately of the tiny London clubs where I'd done my first gigs, and hinted at an early association with Brian Epstein and the Beatles.

My hard work paid off. The cheques started to roll in, and, as any celebrity knows, success breeds success. I was in demand everywhere, happy to lend my image to advertisers, to speak at formal dinners and even to open supermarkets (what memories that brought back!). After a few months, Anna informed me that we had enough in the bank to move to somewhere 'fit for stars to live'. We'd been hanging on to the squat, eager to conserve our meagre capital for the necessary expenses of my career, but now we were in a position to reap the rewards of careful financial management. Anna insisted that we should move to Cheyne Walk in Chelsea, an expensive enclave favoured by the seventies rock élite. At first I was horrified: how would we afford such staggering prices? But, as Anna reminded me, to stay a star you have to live like a star, it's what the public expects. So Chelsea it was.

We defrayed some of the cost by allowing a Sunday supplement to photograph us moving into our new home, but still there was the monthly rent cheque to consider. And I had other expenses: I had engaged a top show-business lawyer to negotiate my way out of a legal misunderstanding with Nick Nicholls, who (thanks to his ungenerous and over-literal interpretation of our 'divorce' contract) was still creaming off a considerable amount of my earnings. The thought of Nick taking twenty per cent of my money galled me excessively; every time I stepped out of the house that parasite was gaining by it. My lawyer assured me that he would get a result, but that negotiations could be lengthy – and expensive. There was nothing for it. I needed another hit.

The follow-up to 'Bi Bi Baby' proved problematic. Pop's a wayward will o' the wisp; there's no magic formula for a hit. All the signs were right: we'd reassembled the same team of producer, engineers and musicians, and we had a cracker of a song, the moody 'Swing High, Swing Low', which I still think is the better number. But this time, the magic just wasn't there. I poured my soul into making that record, I travelled tirelessly round the country promoting it to anyone who would listen, but the backlash had set in. We got radio play, and the fans loved it, but *Top of the Pops* had closed its doors on us, and the record failed to dent the top forty. Now, of course, 'Swing High, Swing Low' is recognized as a classic. But at the time I had the depressing feeling that we had a flop on our hands.

It wasn't such a serious blow. Anna had arranged our affairs so successfully that money just kept rolling in: enough, at least, to maintain our lifestyle in Cheyne Walk, where Anna loved to entertain friends old and new. (She regularly held her women's 'consciousness-raising' groups there, pioneering the feminist revolution that was about to sweep the nation.) But there wasn't quite enough money for all our needs. Reluctantly, I had to drop legal proceedings against Nick Nicholls when I realized that it would cost thousands of pounds to annul the contract I had been bamboozled into signing. I was philosophical: if Nick could live with himself as a leech, good luck to him. It was a small price to pay to be free of him. Free of him! Little did I know . . .

My career was ballooning out of control. I'd have been content with success at home, I'd never really considered markets outside the UK. But DJs in America had picked up on 'Bi Bi Baby' months after its release in the UK, and suddenly it was a hit all over again. Friends reported that it was played in the hippest clubs in Manhattan, that my posters were on every street corner, that Marc LeJeune was the talk of the town. It felt strange: thousands of miles away, people were talking about me, listening to me, fantasizing about me. An 'interview' (cobbled together from my British press) appeared in *Rolling Stone* magazine, stating that 'THERE'S A NEW BRITISH INVASION – but this time he wants to get inside your pants!' 'Move over, David Bowie,' said the ill-informed journalist, 'there's a new Queen of England after your crown!' There was only one thing for it: I'd have to go to America to set the record straight.

Anna was excited by these developments, keen for me to get out and 'develop new markets'. She arranged everything: my flight, currency and accommodation, a string of interviews and appearances, and a showcase performance at the prestigious Rascals club in Greenwich Village. She drove me to the airport in 'our' new car (I had never learned to drive, so in effect it was hers) and kissed me goodbye as a crowd of waiting photographers captured an intensely private moment for tomorrow's front pages.

I must confess, I was glad to be travelling. Life with Anna, although exciting and creative, had also been claustrophobic. She'd never pressed her conjugal rights, thank God, and there was a genuine, frank affection between us, but like so many others in my life, she wanted more from me than I could give. She wanted me always to be working, working, working. I knew that she was right to drive me hard, that it was good for my career, but I knew too that she was busy feathering her own nest. A break would do us both the world of good.

First, though, I had to face the terrifying prospect of flying. It's hard to believe that I'd lived till 1973 without ever stepping on board an aeroplane, despite my international success. But for all my sophistication, I was still a naïve working-class boy in many ways. The idea of flying terrified me. Even to board the plane I had to load myself with tranquillizers, and I took full advantage of the booze trolley as soon as we were airborne. The flight mercifully passed in a daze, but with one unfortunate side effect: I developed a nasty stomach infection, and spent much of my time in New York searching for the nearest 'bathroom'.

Manhattan was everything I'd dreamed it would be. Who can see that skyline from the plane window without wanting to burst into song? Nothing could dampen my enthusiasm, not even the surly immigration official, a gorilla of indeterminate gender who growled at me but let me through. I took the bus into town (Anna had stressed the importance of keeping expenses down) and carefully filed the ticket stub (the whole trip was tax deductible). I was staying downtown, in an apartment on Bleeker Street, right in the heart of the Village. As I walked from the bus station to my new address, I was 'rubbernecking' – gawping at the magnificent buildings that surrounded me on every side. The Village felt more like home – smaller houses, a scruffy elegance that reminded me of London. The apartment itself was tiny: one room served as bedroom, kitchen and lounge, while a converted cupboard in the hall housed lavatory and shower. It was cramped but clean and, to my relief, cockroach-free.

The moment I set foot in the door, the telephone began to ring. Anna had borrowed the apartment from an old boyfriend, and had already given the number to every paper and promoter in town. Within half an hour I had invitations enough to keep me busy for a year, even in the city that never sleeps. New York was ready to eat me alive.

I spent my first afternoon getting my bearings, enjoying coffee on Sheridan Square, watching the world pass me by. There were a few curious stares – hip New Yorkers already knew who I was –

but for the most part people left me to my own devices. After the insanity of London, this was heaven itself.

But there was little time to relax. I was booked to do my first show that very night. My itinerary had been the subject of serious arguments with Anna, who ignored my plea that I should have time to recover from jet lag. 'It's a myth, babe,' she'd assured me (she who had never been further than the Isle of Wight). 'Just take a little something if you find yourself dropping off.' So after a shower and a snack at the apartment, I made my way to the club that had been chosen for my New York début.

Rascals was an exclusive venue on elegant Christopher Street, a short walk from my front door. The agent had been vague about the details of sound-checking and lighting design, so I turned up at eight o'clock ready to run through my set and consult with the technicians. At least I didn't have to worry about a band; Anna had provided my backing music on reel-to-reel tapes. I knocked at the tiny street door for a few minutes. Finally an elderly janitor shuffled out into the daylight, looked me up and down and spat.

'You the cops? He ain't here.'

'No, I'm Marc LeJeune.' I faced the street light so he could get a better look at me.

'Nobody here of that name. Come back later, fella.'

'No, you don't understand, I am . . .' The door slammed in my face. I had yet to learn that New York operates on a very different schedule from sleepy London town.

When I returned to the club at ten, there was still no sign of life. But by pressing my nose against the smoked-glass window pane I could dimly make out a light and the thud of music. Slowly, the club was coming alive. I banged on the window, much to the amusement of a passing (male) couple who helpfully shouted 'Honey, you must be *desperate*!'

The door opened and an anaemic figure in a black shirt and sunglasses peered out.

'Hey, Marc!'

At last, somebody knew what was going on.

'Hi! I'm here to do the soundcheck.'

'No problem, baby! Come on in! You ain't on for a while. Have a drink.'

I followed him into the dark interior, glad to be off the street. The club was completely empty – at an hour when London clubs would have been bursting at the seams! A barman was casually wiping a few glasses, candles burned in coloured glass shades along the top of the bar, and the DJ crouched in a corner sorting through a pile of records. I thought, for one panicky moment, that nobody had turned up to see me.

The manager, who introduced himself as Al, handed me a drink – an enormous vodka martini. 'So Marc, whaddya need? We got lights, we got music, we got a mike for ya.'

'I'd like to see the stage, please.'

'Baby, you're sitting on it.' That was the first shock of the night: I was expected to perform on the tiny raised dais on which our barstools were perched.

'Is that it?'

'What you see is what you get. Hey, don't worry. We've had 'em all in here. Singers, strippers, the lady with the snake,' (there was a shout of derisive laughter from the DJ and the barman), 'they've worked this stage, baby, and the kids love 'em. You're gonna be fine. Have another drink.'

I'd downed my first martini already; I felt the need for a little Dutch courage. I also felt an urgent need for the lavatory.

Once I'd recovered, I began to relax and enjoy myself. This isn't London, I kept reminding myself; they do things differently here. So what if the stage was a few upended beer crates nailed together with chipboard? It would make my triumph all the greater. The friendly barman handed me another drink with a wink and a smile. 'I love that record you got out, Marc,' he said. 'We can't wait to see what you've got to show us.' My first American fan!

The club started to fill up around 11.30. At first a few shifty singles staked their place at the bar, surveying each new arrival with hungry eyes and plying my friend Larry the barman (clearly a bit of a pull) with drinks. But when the groups of twos and threes started to arrive, it was time to make myself scarce. So I retreated to the 'dressing room' (all I'll say is that I'd had better – and worse, for that matter) and whiled away the time enjoying the martinis that were regularly sent through for me and eavesdropping on the bathroom gossip. 'Hey, what time does the show start?' I heard one reveller ask his companion. 'I guess he'll be on after the go-go dancers,' came the reply.

Go-go dancers? This hadn't been mentioned. Wrapping a T shirt round my head as a disguise, I peeked into the club. It was crammed full (a good indication of my international pulling power!) and there, dancing along the top of the bar, were two young men wearing nothing but jockstraps. As they writhed their way from end to end, dodging the drinks, hands would reach up to tuck dollar bills into their waistbands and, if the money was right, cop a quick feel. It was little short of prostitution, and hardly the kind of support act I would have chosen, but 'hey, welcome to New York!' as Larry whispered in my ear when he caught me staring, open-mouthed. I laughed to cover my embarrassment, returned to the dressing room and wrapped myself around another martini.

One thing confused me: there was not a single woman in the club. At home, I'd been used to a mixed audience of every age, sex and class. In downtown Manhattan, it seemed, my appeal was somewhat more specialized. Many years later, artists from Bette Midler to Madonna to Take That realized the importance of 'breaking' themselves with the trendsetting gay audience. I was at the cutting edge yet again.

Finally it was show time: nearly three o'clock in the morning! I had been ready for hours, squeezed into my silver pants, my leather jacket open, my hair swept up to new heights. As Al announced me, I checked myself one last time in the veined, cracked mirror that dangled from a rusty nail in the dressing room. Was New York ready for me? My intro music began.

The stage, I remember thinking as I stepped on to it, looked a lot better when it was properly lit and surrounded by a crowd of eager faces. The music slammed into gear, and I went into a raunchy rendition of 'Bi Bi Baby' – possibly the best performance of that song I ever gave. Who cared that the microphone wasn't working? My vocals were clearly audible on the backing tape. The audience applauded and screamed at my every move. For the final verse, I moved off the stage and walked among them, regaining the podium with my clothes only just intact. This wasn't adulation, this was on a par with Beatlemania! Maybe *Rolling Stone* was right – another British invasion had taken place! There were even photographers at the club: news had travelled fast! One of them in particular caught my eye, a curly-haired young guy in a leather jacket that matched mine, prowling around the front of the stage snapping me from every angle. I found myself drawn to him, performing for him – but I had good reason to be wary of photographers! Later, when I looked for him to find out which paper he represented, he had disappeared.

I followed 'Bi Bi Baby' with a soulful rendition of 'Swing High, Swing Low', which met with a muted response; it's a more serious number, and I could see a number of thoughtful faces around the club, and even a few of the more romantic couples retiring to private corners to carry on their courting. But then for my finale I gave them what they really wanted: a reprise of 'Bi Bi Baby'. Suddenly everyone was up on their feet again, screaming the house down, blowing whistles, happy and laughing. It was more than I'd hoped for. New York loved me – and I *loved* New York!

I didn't get home until the commuters were streaming on to Manhattan by bridge and tunnel, the daytime people taking over from the night-time people. I'd been danced off my feet, taken from one club to the next by a group of fans who promised to be my best friends in the city, all of whom found time to give me their numbers and ask for a little private conversation. It was flattering, this new-world directness of approach, if not entirely to my taste. I wasn't ready to plunge head-first into the fleshpots of Manhattan – yet.

I slept through most of the day, adjusting to my topsy-turvy New York routine. I was roused at six o'clock in the evening by a knock at the door and the surprise announcement, by a liveried chauffeur, that my car was waiting downstairs. My car? Anna had insisted that I use public transport, and had vetoed a limo service. 'I think you have the wrong address,' I told the handsome driver, reluctantly.

'Mr LeJeune?'

'That's me!'

'I've got a car downstairs to take you to the factory.'

'The factory? Am I opening it or something?'

'No, sir. The Factory.' This time he said it with an unmistakable capital F.

'Mr Warhol is hoping to meet you, Mr LeJeune.'

Mr Warhol? It rang a bell. Warhol . . . that's right, the American artist who had been in London a few years before, who had seen me in *Shitface*, or was it *The Bell End*? I remembered seeing him on the news, heralded as the darling of the international avant-garde. Moska had been most dismissive, and I'd not bothered to find out more. But now he was courting me. I was intrigued.

'Give me a minute to get dressed, and I'll be right down.' I stepped under the shower (so powerful it practically knocked my eye out), had to go suddenly to the toilet (that bug I'd caught on the plane had woken up in a bad mood!), showered again and thought about what to wear. I decided to dress down: a skin-tight white cotton T shirt and a pair of blue jeans would do just fine, Warhol or no Warhol.

My experience of Andy Warhol and his famous Factory was brief but intense. I was ushered into the run-down old building on

Union Square, ascended in a scary freight elevator to the fifth floor and walked into a strange silver space littered with canvases, old furniture and people draping themselves in bizarre attitudes. There was no reception, nobody to greet me or introduce me to the great man, who, eventually, drifted over and stared at me in silence from behind his shades. 'Wow . . .' was all he said. He motioned me to a chair, where I sat uneasily fiddling with my quiff. Warhol disappeared for a moment, then returned with a super-8 movie camera on a tripod. He set it up, pointed it towards me and switched it on. This, I understood, was to be some sort of 'screen test', but the director himself had soon wandered off to apply a few dabs of paint to one of his outsize canvases. Eventually the machine whirred to a halt. I hovered behind the artist's shoulder as he worked, crouched on the floor.

'That's very interesting,' I said. 'Who is it?'

'Jackie,' he said, breathlessly.

'Lovely.'

There was silence again as he carried on working. I was becoming impatient.

'You wanted to see me, then?' I snapped.

'Sure . . . We're shooting a movie tomorrow, if you want to be in that. Otherwise I'm not sure what we can do for you. Talk to Brigid.' It was the longest speech I ever heard him utter.

I couldn't warm to Warhol, but like many others who came into his orbit, I wanted to prove myself worthy of his attention. I'd be back at the Factory.

Happily, Warhol had either forgotten about the limo or had omitted to mention that it was at my disposal, so for the rest of the week I enjoyed the car and the charming company of the driver until, one day, he simply stopped turning up.

That night I returned to Rascals. I felt that I'd made real friends there. I had a ball, and got completely addicted to the house martini all over again. And at every turn, I'd see that same young photographer from the night before. Was he going to sell these pictures? If so, we had to talk business. But before I could beard him, he disappeared.

I was driven to the Factory the next afternoon, and found the place abuzz with activity. In every mirror people were adjusting their make-up, teasing their hair, plumping up their busts. Warhol himself was the still centre of this hurricane of vanity, gawping into space and occasionally muttering 'Wow . . .' I tried to catch his eye but he looked straight through me. He wasn't even operating the camera, which was being loaded by one of his assistants.

At length I was hustled over to a decrepit old couch and told to sit down beside a muscular blond boy who was wearing nothing but a pair of swimming trunks. Assistants positioned the camera in front of us, while various women perched on the back of the couch and discussed our hair, the day's news, their love-life problems. I wasn't sure whether the camera was running or not. Warhol continued to stare into space.

Then one of the girls, a loud-mouthed overweight creature, smacked my blond neighbour round the ear and said, in a terrible whining New York accent, 'Well aren't ya going to suck his dick?' That was the cue for all hell to break loose. I won't go into details; it's all there for anyone to see in the famous Warhol 'masterpiece' (as it would later be called), *Beauties #5*.

I've read a great deal about Andy Warhol's 'methods' over the years, and have particularly enjoyed the wealth of speculation about the 'structure' of *Beauties #5*. Let me lay this particular myth to rest. There were no methods, no structure. Much has been written about the fact that I seemed to appear and disappear at random in the film, reflecting 'the evanescence of Warhol's sense of selfhood'. The fact of the matter is that my stomach troubles were getting worse and worse, and I had to keep excusing myself to go to the lavatory. Thus I missed out on some of the four-minute reels, of which around ten were shot that afternoon. Warhol didn't seem to care whether his star was in the scene or not.

What qualities there may be in *Beauties #5* (and who am I to disagree with critics who regard it as a milestone in seventies cinema?) were nothing to do with Warhol; they were entirely the result of my performance. I was the only professional there; I controlled the action, I gave the cues, even my accidental absence gave the film its much-discussed philosophical core. Needless to say, I was never given credit for this, nor did I ever receive any form of payment. I phoned Anna directly after we'd finished shooting to tell her to send an invoice to the Factory.

The party after the film was more fun than the film itself. At night, the Factory turned into a strange sort of night club, where Warhol's regulars would mix with whatever luminaries were in the mood for a bit of downtown slumming. That night I met Mick Jagger (who, of course, I'd known well in London) and his wife Bianca, painter Jasper Johns and even Elizabeth Taylor. I'd seen her hanging around at the side of the room, sparkling quietly in her diamonds, looking as beautiful as she did in the movies. She sidled up to Warhol and nervously, humbly asked him to introduce us. Andy beamed; this was the sort of thing he loved. He grabbed my arm and thrust me rudely at Miss Taylor. 'This is Marc LeJeune, my new star!' he said, then wandered off towards the toilets. She blushed, stumbled over her words and told me she loved my record. I hoped we'd become better friends than we did, but at that moment Liz was too shy to talk further, and left the party. I'd see her again many times over the years, and she always gave me a special smile in memory of that awkward first meeting.

After a few days, I was well into the New York groove. My schedule went something like this: get up at four o'clock in the afternoon, shower and shave, then wander down to my favourite coffee shop and diner, Tiffany's on Sheridan Square (at least I could tell the folks back home that I'd had 'breakfast at Tiffany's'!). After eating, I'd meet up with friends in the Village, do some shopping or just 'hang out', picking up ideas and tapping into that famous creative energy. By ten o'clock it was time to hit the bars or go to a party – I was never short of invitations. As dawn broke we'd head off for Chinese food at one of the fantastic all-night places around Times Square. By seven or eight in the morning I was ready for bed again.

I was having a ball. I kept in touch every day with Anna, enthusing about the wonderful times I was having, teasing her about how much money I'd saved. She was so happy for me. 'Stay as long as you like, babe! Mama's taking care of business!' It was good to know that I had such a good friend at home.

And wherever I went, I was haunted by my phantom photographer. He stalked me – that's not too strong a term – from club to club, from party to party, even to my front door. After a few days, I'd have been disappointed if I hadn't seen him somewhere in my peripheral vision, his camera clicking away, his scuffed leather jacket decked with lenses and light meters. He must be on assignment for a magazine, I concluded, and too shy to introduce himself.

But finally I was to meet my secretive lensman – and in the strangest circumstances. Larry, the barman from Rascals who had befriended me that first night, had introduced me to a members-only bath house over on West 18th St, the perfect place to freshen up after a hard night on the New York party circuit. I was relaxing in the steam room one evening, clad only in a towel, idly wondering where Larry had wandered off to, when suddenly I caught sight of a familiar face grinning in the doorway of my cubicle. For a second I didn't recognize him – the absence of the leather jacket (of any clothes whatsoever, bar the skimpy strip of white cloth around his midriff) fooled me for a second. But then it clicked – the mop of curly, dark brown hair, the critical, quizzical gaze.

'Mr Camera Man.'

'Hey.'

'So there are places where even you won't take photographs, I see.'

'Right. The steam fogs up my lenses. Too bad. You look pretty as a picture.'

'But this one's strictly for your eyes only,' I jested.

When we emerged from the baths half an hour later, I had learned a lot about John Kinnell, photographer and native New Yorker. His fashion and celebrity portraiture had been seen in all the best titles – *Vanity Fair*, *Vogue*, *New York Times*. He was on intimate terms with the stars, the darling of the downtown party set. And moreover, he was completely and utterly besotted by me.

'How old are you, man?' he asked, staring up close at my face.

'I'm in my twenties,' I replied.

'Cool. You look sixteen. That's why they love you.'

Kinnell had a true artist's eye, and had identified one of the key factors in my lasting appeal. I've always looked younger than my age; even when I first worked for Nick Nicholls, clients would slaver over the fact that I could easily pass for fourteen. What had been a curse in earlier life (I'd never forget the playground taunts of 'Baby' Young, 'Young' Young) had become a blessing in adulthood. Kinnell said I was like Dorian Grey. Did he think I had a portrait in my attic?

We walked to his studio, a ramshackle old meat warehouse down by the Hudson River. 'I want you to come and see some pictures,' he'd teased. It was the oldest line in the book. The huge room was empty, uncluttered (how different from Warhol's Factory, that hive of busy little insects), brightly lit from the skylights and unfurnished save for a mattress on the floor where Kinnell slept. A stack of tripods, light stands and cables in one corner were the only clue to the occupant's profession – until I looked at the far wall. There, stuck up all over the whitewashed brick surface, were dozens and dozens of beautiful black and white prints – all of me.

There was me on stage at Rascals that first night, my arms flung above my head, revealing my naked torso. There was me bleary-eyed at the bar, after one too many of Larry's martinis, looking (as Kinnell put it) like a lost child. There was me walking in the park, attending a formal reception in black tie, dancing at a club. There was even one of me standing at a urinal, glancing over my shoulder (I vaguely remembered the sensation of being watched that night). And in the centre was a huge blow-up of my face, tightly cropped, the eyes half closed and the lips parted as if in ecstasy. I guessed that it had been taken during a performance, but without its context it looked exactly as if it had been snapped during the most intimate moment of a man's life. The overall effect was shocking – and intensely exciting. I felt – I don't know – violated? Adored? Did he care about me as a person? Or was I just a shape in his viewfinder?

But there was something irresistible about Kinnell. He put down his camera, slipped an arm around my waist and kissed me on the lips. Before I had a chance to speak, he sat me down on his bed and tossed over a large, black leather-bound portfolio. 'I'm going to take a shower,' he said, leaving me to peruse his scrapbook. Here were pages from all the top New York magazines, record sleeves, book jackets, portraits, still lives and even nudes – beautiful, tasteful, classic nudes, compared to the harshly-lit rubbish produced by some amateurs I could mention. I was impressed.

I was also confused. I'd let a man photograph me, caress me, even kiss me, without flinching. I couldn't just shrug it off with a philosophical 'When in Rome . . .' There was more to it than that. I found John Kinnell powerfully attractive, that was the truth of the matter. It dawned on me with terrible, searing clarity. I desired him!

Poetic justice! All the coverage I'd received at home for my daring confession of bisexuality, the attention I'd always tolerated from homosexuals, the scandalous allegations that had been made about my relationship with Phyllis . . . all that had been lies, or at least distortions of the truth. But here I was, for the first time in my life, falling in love with a man. Yes, after less than an hour in his company, I was falling in love with John Kinnell. I saw the danger.

This, after all, was a person I'd only just met. The pit opened up at my feet, and I jumped in willingly.

I leapt up from the bed, filled with a sudden energy – a piquant mixture of fear and elation. At that moment, Kinnell returned naked from the shower, his dark curls hanging damp and tousled round his face as he idly towelled himself. I threw myself on him and wrestled him to the ground. We made love right there beneath my giant portrait.

When I awoke in John's embrace a few hours later, I had some serious thinking to do. I could feel my life literally splitting in two: there was the life back home, where I was not only Marc LeJeune, bisexual superstar, but also a family man, a husband to Anna and a son to my loving parents. Then there was the life right here in New York City, in this studio, in this man's arms. More divided those two lives than the salty depths of the Atlantic Ocean.

For the rest of my stay – four all-too-short days – I was never out of John Kinnell's company. We hardly left the studio, occasionally going for a walk in the park, for a picnic on Coney Island, or to visit the narrow little house in the Bronx where he'd grown up. I moved out of my Bleeker Street apartment and into the studio. I dropped my new friends, even dear Larry who'd been such a life-saver when I arrived, friendless, in the city. I didn't care that the phone was ringing with no one to answer it. Let them wait! I had more important things to do.

I was giddy with happiness! How far away they all seemed – Nick Nicholls, Pinky Stevens, Anna, Moska, Nutter . . . Even the memory of poor dead Phyllis and Janice no longer had power to move me. I was free of them all. But not for long. Even in the selfish daze of my first real happiness, I knew that I would soon be banished from Eden. I would have to return to London.

It came so cruelly soon, the morning of my departure. Kinnell drove me to the airport and kissed me goodbye right there at the check-in desk. 'You'll be back, lover,' he growled, and was gone. I stood there watching him as tears clouded my eyes. Then I had to race off to the bathroom again.

The moment that Anna met me at Heathrow, I knew something was wrong. She was drawn, haggard. There was no warmth in her greeting. 'Welcome back to England,' said her shuttered, miserable face. 'Welcome back to England,' said the grey skies, the penetrating drizzle. My heart was in New York.

'I've been trying to ring you for days, Marc. Where the hell have you been?'

'In the studio.' I wouldn't lie.

'There's a problem.'

'I thought there might be. What's up?'

'You'll see. We'd better get home.'

I felt sick with apprehension. What fresh disaster had overtaken me? What price was I going to have to pay for my few moments of happiness with John?

We got 'home' – it was home no more for me – after an arduous hour in traffic. I put down my bags and breathed a sigh of relief. There was only one thing I was looking forward to: a proper English cup of tea.

'I suppose you'd better sit down,' said Anna. 'Now try and stay cool.' She thrust a magazine into my hands – a grubby little publication with the title *Super Boys* in wonky lettering above a picture of a grinning, naked youth.

'What's this? A coming-home present?' Anna's face was stern.

'This is no joking matter, babe. You'd better take a closer look.' I thought there was something familiar about the picture. It was me.

Nick Nicholls! I knew it before Anna told me a thing. Not satisfied with stealing half my earnings, now he was trying to exploit the mistakes I'd made in the past. My hands were sweating; the cheap newsprint came off all over my fingers. I flicked through *Super Boys* – the crudest, most unimaginative sort of filth. A couple of shots – the crudest of the lot – were of the unfortunate young man who had taken my place in *Danish Blue* and had now split with Nick (Anna told me) for a successful career in a popular television series.

It looked bad, very bad indeed. My immediate concern was not for myself, but for my parents. What if they had seen the magazine? They couldn't be expected to understand that a young artist will sometimes go too far to pursue his career. And what would the press make of it? Titillating bisexuality was all very well, the flash of a chest and a shapely backside in silver pants. But this kind of exhibition? It didn't matter that I'd been forced to pose for the pictures – practically raped, in fact. That's not what came across.

My instinct was to go straight to Nick and ask him, man to man, to cease publication. Surely there was some spark of fellow feeling in him? Couldn't I appeal to his better nature? If it was a matter of money, that could be arranged: there was enough in my account to buy all the prints and negatives, the entire Marc LeJeune archive, lock, stock and barrel. But, said Anna, it was already too late for that. She'd taken matters into her own hands, with disastrous consequences. After a telephone conversation which had quickly degenerated into a screaming match, she'd threatened Nick with 'a visit' from some of her friends in the Hell's Angels movement. Nick countered by calling the police, who had 'busted' the house and found Anna in possession of a quarter ounce of marijuana. The time for civilized negotiations was long gone. Why hadn't she consulted me before stumbling into this farcical mess? Of course, it was my fault, said Anna: I hadn't picked up the phone. All I could do was try to limit the damage.

I phoned my parents to assess, discreetly, whether word of *Super Boys* had reached them. I was going to suggest that they might like to take a holiday in the sun, a cheap package tour to Spain, for instance. But as soon as Mum picked up the phone I knew it was too late.

'It arrived in the post, the filthy . . . thing . . .' she sobbed. 'Your dad looked at it, then he went funny . . . He couldn't breathe. His face went purple. I was so scared, Marc . . . He's in the hospital now. They don't know what's wrong with him. Please come home, lad. Please . . .'

I knew I had to go home, to nurse my parents after this terrible shock. But fame is an engine that needs feeding, and I just couldn't find the time: I was booked in the studio the next day to record my album. How could my mother understand that I wasn't master of my own destiny? I still believe that she resented me, resented my career, for the rest of her life. But Dad was out of hospital by the end of the week, recovering from a mild heart-attack. Those years of smoking and bad diet had finally caught up with him.

Recording my début album *Both Sides* was a nightmare. I'd planned it all so carefully: the choice of songs, the personnel, even the artwork. But we were dogged by bad luck. The musicians were churlish and slapdash, influenced by the negative publicity that had followed the publication of *Super Boys*. We ran badly over budget (thanks to a lazy producer who couldn't be bothered to turn up on time) and had to dispense with many of the elaborate musical ideas that would have made the album really special. And, I'm ashamed to say, my heart wasn't in my performance. How could it be? I was worried to death about my father, and when I wasn't thinking about him I was miles away – in a studio in New York, to be precise. The final humiliation came during the photo shoot for the cover. I'd 'art directed' it myself: I would appear with half my face unshaven, rugged and masculine; the other half would be smooth, fully made up, the hair blow-dried and teased. It was a beautiful idea (one that would be copied many times over the years) but I was working with idiots. The photographer was a fool, a cheap snapper foisted on me by the record company, and he kept up a stream of lewd banter throughout the shoot. 'Come on love, how about a bit of tit?' he kept asking. I stormed out of the studio almost crying with rage. John, where were you?

Although I was disappointed at the time, *Both Sides* has worn rather well. It's a concept album, the first of its kind. Side one contains a handful of up-tempo pop numbers, standard boy-meets-girl stuff, plus the big hit single 'Bi Bi Baby'. Side two is a slower, darker set, with lyrics hinting at homosexuality, drugs and death. It was the perfect expression of my artistic self, the two sides of my persona, and a witty reference to my dual sexuality. If it had been packaged and polished as I had originally conceived it, *Both Sides* would now rank in the top ten rock albums of all time.

But this was a rush job, recorded and released within three months. Even before it came out, I was sick of it, sick of England, sick of my life at home. Since my return from New York, Anna had changed from a loving wife and a capable manager into a strident, demanding harpy, obsessed by money and utterly unconcerned about my personal problems. And that wasn't all: I discovered to my horror that she had been unfaithful to me. Returning from the studio earlier than scheduled (the producer hadn't shown up that day, and the musicians had all got drunk) I discovered her naked on our giant bed, *in flagrante*, with another woman. It was like a sick joke, a publicity gimmick that had come back to haunt me. And Anna didn't even have the decency to hide what she was doing. 'Care to join us, babe?' she laughed, as her companion (a surprisingly attractive and feminine woman) lolled provocatively at her side. I slammed the door and left the house. How long had this been going on behind my back – in the house that *I* paid for with the sweat of my brow? I felt disgusted and betrayed.

I had few friends left in London. When I tried to cheer myself up by getting a haircut at dear old Willy Frizz's, I was curtly informed by Monsieur Frizz himself that there were no appointments available. It was no great loss: Willy had long since lost his cachet. New York stylists were infinitely superior.

I couldn't wait to get back to Manhattan. The one thing that kept me sane during this horrible homecoming was the daily (or rather nightly) phonecall from John, who heedlessly ran up enormous bills telling me in graphic detail the treats that he had planned for me 'once you get your ass back over here'. As my career had hit a sticky patch, his was taking off: a prestigious midtown gallery had offered him a one-man exhibition, in which he planned to show my portraits. There were my two lives in a nutshell. At home, photographs and photographers only brought me shame, disgrace and heartbreak. In New York, they brought me glory – and love. Can you wonder that I decided there and then to return to America, to make my home in the one place that I really felt at home?

There was one more factor that hastened my decision to leave, something that I still find hard to talk about. Despite my pleadings, Nick had continued to publish more and more photographs, each set more damaging than the last. Who cared that some of the worst ones weren't actually of me? Nick would put my name on any old filth, and people believed him. (One of his most notorious photographs, showing a young boy doing something unspeakable with a banana, was widely assumed to be of me. In fact, it wasn't; the face is partially obscured, and anyone who cares to look can see that the model's teeth are jagged and uneven, unlike my famous 'toothpaste' smile.) It seemed that there was a new magazine every week, each tackier than the last, an endless string of smutty little titles – *Young and Restless*, *Playboys*, *Hard Boys*. And somehow each one found its way to my parents.

This constant campaign of terror finally took its toll. As I lay awake one night, still aglow from the two-hour conversation I'd just enjoyed with John, drifting into dreams of our life together in New York, the phone rang. It was two o'clock in the morning. I reached out for the receiver, expecting to hear John's silky voice teasing me with yet another sexy suggestion. 'Hellooooo' I crooned.

'Marc?' It was my mother's voice.

'Mum? What's wrong?'

'You've been on the phone for so long, Marc. I've been trying and trying. I'm so sorry . . .'

'What's the matter, Mum?'
'It's your father, dear. He's dead.'

Within two days, I was on a flight back to New York City – on a one-way ticket. I left everything and everyone behind me. I couldn't even face my father's funeral. Anna was furious and shocked, but was anybody thinking of my needs? For once in my life, I put the demands of others in second place, and did what I had to do for myself. It was a question of survival.

The euphoria I experienced when the plane took off was extraordinary. No more fear of flying: once I was airborne I felt the cares slipping away from me, and a sudden rush of excitement at the thought of what was waiting for me when I arrived. Throughout the last weeks, I'd been hanging on to just one thing, the only good thing in my life: my feelings for John. It took guts to turn my back on my career and my family in England, but I believed that nothing should stand in the way of love.

I dozed for much of the flight, enjoying happy dreams of how John would meet me at the airport, perhaps with a huge bunch of red roses (he loved these operatic gestures), whisk me into town and treat me to dinner, or simply take me back to the studio that would now be my – our – home. Time flew. The anticipation was delicious.

How I survived the tedious waiting in line at the immigration desk, the slow torture of baggage return, I don't know. But finally I was free, with just a suitcase and two pieces of hand luggage – all that remained of my life in three bags. I rushed through the gate into the arrivals lounge, where a crowd of eager faces strained to see their loved ones. Any second now, he'd leap over the barriers and sweep me off my feet. I dawdled down the walkway listening for his 'Hey!' The smile was freezing on my face. He wasn't there.

What had happened? My immediate thought was that he must have met some accident. Or perhaps a job had come through at the last minute, keeping him in town, unable to contact me. I didn't care, as long as John was all right. I had to find a phone.

I called the studio. The phone rang and rang. There was no answer. He must have left already. Maybe he'd been delayed in traffic and would appear, flushed and breathless and full of apologies, and we'd laugh about how worried I'd been. I found a seat that commanded a view of the entire concourse and waited for an hour. I called again. Still no answer. Where was he?

Finally, I had no option but to struggle with my luggage on to a bus and make my own way to the city. I had just enough US dollars to pay my fare; I'd have to walk across town to the West Side. When I arrived I was hot, dirty and anxious. How could my longed-for homecoming have gone so badly wrong?

I dragged myself up the last few stairs to the studio and rang the buzzer. To my intense relief, there was the sound of movement inside, and voices. I distinctly heard Kinnell say, 'Oh shit, man!' He must have unplugged the phone and overslept. I smiled; his unreliability could be charming in its way. Eventually I heard him stumbling towards the door. He appeared, wearing only a pair of faded jeans. I fell into his arms, savouring the touch of his warm flesh. Then I looked over his shoulder and saw, sprawled on the mattress, another man.

I can't recall the scene that followed without a sense of disgust. After all my happy expectations, to be let down so cruelly, so casually, it was too much. I lost my reason. I screamed, I wept – exactly the sort of ridiculous homosexual melodramatics that I'd always despised in others. Kinnell was apologetic at first, but then turned nasty. Who did I think I was, he asked, his fuckin' wife? When I leapt across the bed and attempted to attack his new friend, Kinnell grabbed me by the wrists and pushed me to the floor where I lay grovelling at his feet. The other man dressed quickly, stepped across my prostrate form and left, remarking as he stood in the doorway, 'Hey, John, looks like you have a little problem here.'

It took me some time to recover from this hysterical attack. I think of it now as a kind of mini nervous breakdown brought on by my recent troubles. John was comforting, caressing me as I lay sobbing in his lap. I had to understand that this was not a marriage, he said. We were both free to take our pleasure with whoever we liked. There were no rules for a gay relationship – we could live exactly as we pleased, as long as there was love and respect on both sides. That was all I wanted to hear. He loved me, it was enough. For a long, long time to come, I told myself that that was all I needed in life. But can love ever really be enough?

Of course I was used to the idea of free love – it was something I'd pioneered in the sixties, after all. But I still had a lot of emotional baggage that I had to get rid of. From my parents I'd inherited worn-out patriarchal ideas about possessiveness, about monogamy and the stifling of sexual desire. I had so much to (un)learn. Sex, said John, was the life force, the spring of all his creativity. We need love and friendship, he believed, but we mustn't confuse love with sexual fidelity. To him, life was a smorgasbord of opportunities – sexual, artistic, political. This was a new way of living that we were carving out in downtown Manhattan, a community of lovers and creative collaborators bound together by trust and respect for each other as individuals. One day, he said, everyone would live like this.

It was exciting to me, a challenge. I knew that I was at a crossroads in my life. I could either cling on to my old ideas and 'chuck' John for cheating on me behind my back, or I could embrace the new, wherever it might lead me. To celebrate my decision, I took John out for dinner.

The New York years were the best of times and the worst of times. The community of lovers bound together by trust and respect had strange ways of expressing themselves, as I was soon to discover in the clubs that Kinnell had started frequenting, where there was no kick too far, no kink too extreme. In steamy back rooms, heaving knots of humanity fumbled in a confusion of hands and mouths. In basement 'dungeons', painted black and kitted out with an array of torture devices, men would inflict bizarre punishments on each other, twisting and stretching each other's extremities to a point, Kinnell said, beyond pain and pleasure. And strangest of all, there were clubs where men would go to the bathroom (to use that coy American euphemism) on each other.

At first I went along as a tourist. Then I was a nagging wife (as John put it), constantly trying to get him to leave, to come home where I'd give him the pleasure he was seeking. Then I gave up my last shred of resistance and joined in. It was sickeningly easy. Without any restraints on my behaviour – since the death of my father and the disappearance of Nutter from my life – I didn't really care what anybody thought. This, then, was freedom.

We weren't just going out to these clubs once or twice a week as a special treat. We were going every single night, sleeping for most of the day and only 'working' when it fitted around our social schedule. John's career was still flourishing, the commissions coming in faster than he could complete them. But I wasn't earning. There was the occasional cheque from England, the odd PA in a club for $50, but it wasn't enough. The lifestyle we'd chosen was expensive.

It wasn't just the usual costs of food, clothes, rent and transport. Added to that was one massive bill that overshadowed all the rest: drugs. I'd discovered how New York kept awake all night: cocaine. We'd go to parties where drugs were part of the buffet, but more often we'd have to pay for them. At the height of his career, John could afford two grams of coke a day – until the work started to dry up. He had become erratic, unreliable. Like so many artists, he felt oppressed by deadlines, deadened by commercialism. He came to despise the industry for which he was working, 'the fucking fashion vampires', he called them. They in turn took their work elsewhere, to the latest star photographer. In New York City, there's always someone younger and hotter waiting to take your place.

After eighteen months, we were feeling the pinch. John had lost interest in his career, only working when I locked him in the studio. He reserved his energy for the night life. It was all he cared about, all he lived for – the next high. In his own strange way, he was faithful to me; he never had affairs with any of his hundreds of 'tricks', and very rarely brought them home to the studio. To him, those bodies in the dark were interchangeable, just a way of getting nearer to the oblivion that he was seeking. That was what it was all leading to, the drugs, the sex, the alcohol, the pain – oblivion. Darkness. John, so full of life, seemed hell-bent on self-destruction.

I worried about him to the point that I couldn't sleep. I'd lie there night after night (day after day actually) watching his unconscious form, wondering what demons drove him to this life of excess. What had gone wrong with John? Or was it I who was in the wrong?

What few savings I'd brought with me had been used up long ago, and now John was having trouble meeting the monthly rent cheque. He didn't seem to care; we could always move somewhere cheaper. It didn't matter as long as he had somewhere to hide out and sleep in the daylight hours. But I couldn't bear to see everything we'd worked for slip away – and for what? A snowstorm of cocaine, a few nightmarish hours of sexual depravity. I was going back to work.

The opportunity presented itself in the most unlikely form: a cultured, older man I'd met at one of the bars, who sat there night after night in a blazer and cravat, sipping a drink, watching the comings and goings through wire-rimmed glasses. Occasionally he'd speak to one of the revellers, buy him a drink and give him a card. He was friendly but aloof, an amused, intelligent observer at the feast. There was something paternal about him, and I badly needed a father figure in my life at that time.

Peter von Harden (he insisted that it was his real name) had grown up in Germany, came to New York just before the war and was now a naturalized American. His interests were as broad as mine; he could talk with authority about modern art, Victorian literature, the crisis in the Middle East. He was a man of strong opinions, refreshingly critical of the clubs and their 'superficiality', a lover of the finer things in life. He spoke with enthusiasm of an exhibition at the Guggenheim, of a wonderful restaurant on the Upper West Side, of the latest Broadway openings. Talking to him was such a joy when the most you usually got in the way of conversation at the clubs was: 'Yeah, harder!'

But there was one thing that struck me as incongruous: what was this civilized European and connoisseur of the arts doing hanging around in gay sex clubs? He was candid in his response.

'I'm talent-scouting.'

'What for? A Broadway show?' That's when I knew that the old urge to work had come back to me.

'No. A movie.' A movie! Even better. I'd always longed to work in films.

'What kind of movie?'

'A porno movie.'

He was frank, I had to admit. But a movie was a movie, and I needed work, especially as I had just noticed John handing over the last of the week's money in return for a few ampoules of amyl nitrate. I swallowed hard.

'Interesting. Tell me more.' He was impressive, persuasive. Peter von Harden, it seemed, was the leading producer of erotic gay films, professionally shot on 16mm stock, using a roster of star talent that he'd recruited from the clubs under exclusive contract to his 'studio'. Now he was in pre-production for his most ambitious project to date, and was looking for a new star. There was a loaded silence. I wondered if he knew who I was? Or was I just another body?

'Do you think you could use me?'

'My God, could I? With your name on the credits,' (he did know who I was after all) 'we're practically guaranteed an Oscar!' We laughed. 'I can make you a big, big star by the end of the year.'

Where had I heard that before? But I was older and wiser now.

I knew all about the promises that hungry older men would make to beautiful, talented youngsters. I was interested only in one thing.

'How much do you pay?' He thought for a moment, scanned the ceiling, looked back at me, took a drink and finally named a figure. It was enough – just. It would enable us to keep the studio for another month. Peter gave me a card and arranged to meet me the following day at the swanky New York Athletic Club.

I took care to look as if I meant business: a smart blazer, a clean white shirt and tie, neatly pressed slacks. I didn't want my director, whatever the movie, to think that I was some starry-eyed amateur ready to be pushed around and exploited. Von Harden was equally impressive, clearly at home in the lavish marble halls and oak-panelled bar of the NYAC, where the waiters and porters treated him with a respectful familiarity. We ordered whisky sours and talked business.

I now think that, in a different time, Peter von Harden could have been one of the truly great *auteurs*. His love of cinema, his deep learning, his visual flair, could have created masterpieces. But here was a man, like me, fatally out of step with the times, a man whose vision had galloped ahead of the mainstream, dooming him to work in the despised fringes of the industry. Looking at his films today, I realize that he could have been greater than, say, Derek Jarman, a vastly overrated film-maker who took von Harden's basic ideas and watered them down for mass consumption. But Peter couldn't compromise like that.

The project that he outlined to me that afternoon was a remake of Douglas Sirk's fabulous 1958 melodrama *Imitation of Life*, one of my all-time favourite films. I remembered how shocking we'd found it back in the fifties, with its story of a brilliant young actress (Lana Turner) and her friendship with a poor black servant. Von Harden's version would transpose the basic theme of racism and inequality to a gay context. I'd play the Lana Turner figure, of course, the beautiful but vulnerable actor who embarks on a reckless affair with a poor black garage mechanic. We talked for hours about the subtle interplay of cinematic reference, the daring theme of miscegenation, the fascinating use of my public persona in this challenging new context. The film, which von Harden grandly announced would be entitled *Imitation of Sex*, would start shooting on Saturday at a friend's uptown apartment.

I must confess that, for the first time in my life, I was actually ashamed of something I'd done. *Imitation of Sex* was not what I had expected: there was little demand on my acting experience, there was no dialogue (a few 'oohs' and 'yeahs' were dubbed on later), but I was expected to 'perform' in other ways. Fortunately, my co-star was an old hand and soon set me at ease. 'Forget about the camera, Marc,' he advised me, 'let's just do it.' All I could think about was the fact that this sacrifice would enable John to carry on working.

There wasn't much plot to get in the way of the action: a rich white New Yorker is enjoying a Jacuzzi at home when the doorbell rings. He answers the door wearing only a pair of scanty briefs, to discover a tall black man dressed in oil-stained overalls. My understanding was that the visitor wanted to come and 'wash up', although this was never made explicit in the film; narrative cohesion was not one of von Harden's strong points. Soon we were back in the Jacuzzi. It took two days; I was paid half my money at the end of each day's shoot.

Von Harden had assured me that his films played on a very small, exclusive art circuit; imagine my horror when, a couple of months later, I saw *Imitation of Sex* advertised at one of the sleaziest grind houses on Times Square, with a poster blazoning my name (above the title, at least) and a still that left little to the imagination. I was mortified, but, strangely, *Imitation of Sex* became one of the biggest-grossing adult movies of its time. It wasn't the direction I'd seen my career going in, but I had no choice.

I couldn't bear to go and see *Imitation of Sex*. John, of course, went time and again and said it was 'hot', though whether he was referring to my performance or to the 'action' in the cinema itself

I wasn't sure. Years later an American fan sent me a video copy of the film which, he reported, was doing good business as a classic reissue. I watched it for the first time, and was agreeably surprised. My performance as a drugged-up New York party boy was genuinely affecting (not for nothing had I been studying the guys in the clubs!), and the frank sexual content still had the power to shock. Now, of course, we're used to nudity and sex in every medium, from rock videos to major motion pictures. Many of the ideas that von Harden pioneered in the seventies have entered the mainstream. And, of course, the 'adult' market is thriving, with entire cable channels devoted to pornography. *Imitation of Sex* and all the other films I made with Peter von Harden stand up pretty well against the trash that's churned out today. Our films weren't pornography, they were erotica. And as such, they have an appeal far beyond the crudely sexual. I see their influence everywhere.

Our next project was a remake of the popular Steven Spielberg hit *Jaws*, shot on a weekend trip to Fire Island. I played a sun-worshipper who's attacked by a shark (von Harden himself swam underwater with the fin) and rescued by a lifeguard, who drags my semi-conscious body to his hut and practises mouth-to-mouth resuscitation. It was an even bigger hit, and enjoyed massive mail-order sales in a super-8 version.

After that, we made title after title. There must have been dozens, maybe even a hundred; I can't remember most of them now. A few highlights: a remake of Hitchcock's suspenseful *Rear Window* as *Back Passage*; a tribute to Chaplin (*The Great Dick Taker*), in which I played an SS Officer who gets his come-uppance at the hands of a bunch of boisterous GIs; a rare venture into the horror genre, *Night of the Giving Head*. Fortunately for me, plans to rework the great spaghetti western *A Fistful of Dollars* were abandoned.

I was in my physical prime, working out daily at an East Village gym, taking sunbeds. I looked good. The money was coming in: good money, but not enough to keep the old studio. We were obliged to take a more modest apartment on Avenue A, and to ride buses and subway trains instead of taxis. But we survived. On Peter's advice, I placed an advert with my portrait and phone number in the *Village Voice* offering massage. I had healing hands, and soon I had a regular clientele who'd come up to Avenue A for a therapeutic rubdown.

My heyday in this other Hollywood lasted nearly two years. That's a long time in the adult market; by rights I should have received a special lifetime achievement award. But audiences are notoriously fickle, and soon they were looking for new stars. The 'clone' look was all the rage: clubs were full of men with walrus moustaches, enormous muscles and leather chaps. To me, they looked ridiculous: hyper-masculine on the outside, but all too willing to discuss the latest quiche recipe once you got them home. I decided to bow out of the industry on a high. My last film for Peter von Harden teamed me with some of the legends of gay erotica, on exclusive 'loan' from other studios: Kip Noll, Al Parker and Casey Donovan. Together we made cinema history in what I consider to be von Harden's masterpiece, a tribute to his idol Ingmar Bergman entitled *The Seventh Inch*.

When I retired from film-making, I discovered that I was quite a celebrity in New York City. It was the time of the disco boom: chic new night clubs were opening all over town, where the glitterati mixed with the street kids in a hedonistic utopia, fuelled by the exciting new dance sounds and by the inevitable shovels-full of cocaine. Free from the demands of von Harden's gruelling shooting schedules, I threw myself into the party life, enjoying my fame. I knew them all: Liza Minnelli, Truman Capote, my old friends the Jaggers, Andy Warhol ('I love your films,' he said one night as I stood in the queue for Studio 54) were all close friends. I was out every night for nearly two years.

But however hard I danced, there was one great, growing sadness in my life. John had gone from bad to worse. He hadn't worked for months, and barely ever left the flat. He didn't even go to his beloved sex clubs any more. No, John had a new love in his life: heroin.

I don't know when he first started using the needle. He'd always loved drugs – he'd take anything he was offered at the clubs as a way of loosening his inhibitions and achieving that longed-for high. But now, he was using them in a different way: to block out reality. He'd stay indoors with the curtains drawn (the sunlight made him itch, he said), making insane drawings (he could have been a great artist) or, more often, just staring at the walls. He was still beautiful, I loved him more than ever, but even I couldn't fail to notice that he was beginning to smell. Was that one of the reasons I went out at every opportunity? How many of the other revellers in New York's discos were running away from a similar sorrow?

But the party had to end sooner or later. The disco round was expensive, and money, as usual, was the one thing I didn't have. I kept body and soul together with my thriving massage business (I had taken to doing 'out' calls at hotels), and it was possible to eat and drink as much as one liked at the clubs without paying for any of it, if you played your cards right. I was having fun, but I couldn't fool myself for long. My life was going nowhere.

The day came when I couldn't scrape together enough money to get across town and into a club. Home was unbearable: John was frantic, almost violent, unable to 'score'. So I went out walking, just walking. I drifted across Broadway, round Washington Square, through the familiar streets of the Village. I remember seeing a headline on a newspaper lying in the gutter: ELVIS PRESLEY DEAD. For a moment, I thought of Nutter, the first time I'd thought about him for years. I too felt dead – inside.

I walked downtown, towards Wall Street, heading for the river and the beautiful view of Brooklyn. My heart was so heavy. I longed to go home, but where was home for me now? Avenue A, where the man I'd sacrificed everything for was now a hunted, stinking ghost? Cheyne Walk, my 'marital home', where Anna entertained her lady friends? Or my first home, where a grieving mother sat in mute reproach of her errant son? I leaned against a railing as tears misted my eyes. What had it all meant? Had I worked, struggled, for this? This . . . nothingness?

The sound of my name jolted me back to reality.

'Marc! Hey, Marc, over here!' The harsh honk of a car horn. 'Come on, kid, jump in!'

I recognized the jowly features of Danny, one of my regular 'punters', a fat man with a chronic back problem that needed my constant attention. 'Come on, Marc, let's go uptown and make babies!'

I was grateful – God, what depths had I sunk to! – for this warm gesture of human companionship. I tore myself away from the bewitching river – had I really intended to jump? – and climbed into the warm interior of the car.

I don't know what prompted me to confide in this man – he was a sleazy individual, I'd always thought – but after we'd finished the massage I poured my heart out to him. I was broke, I confessed, unable to find work, my boyfriend was a junkie and we were facing eviction from our home. I suppose I just wanted to tell somebody, and sometimes a stranger is the best person to confide in. But to my astonishment, Danny turned out to be a sympathetic listener and a pragmatic counsellor. He'd put me to work, he said ('There's always a job for you in this town') in a new club he was opening, not as grand as some I'd been used to, but a place for guys to 'hang out and relax'. He offered me the job of 'hostess' (I hated this campy talk, but was in no position to criticize), a meeter and greeter, providing a little gloss to what could easily have been a squalid enterprise. In return, he said, I'd be paid a small retainer and as much as I could make in tips, and, crucially, he'd make sure that John was kept happy with a regular, safe supply of smack. I made a deal with the devil. I agreed.

Danny's club, Diamonds, was close to home, right down in

'funky' Alphabet City. It was unpretentious – a small room with a bar down one wall, a few tables and chairs and a quiet back room. John took to it immediately, and brought a lot of his friends along with him. They sat nursing their drinks, occasionally disappearing to the back room that they had jokingly dubbed the 'shooting gallery', on account of its tiny cramped dimensions and lack of light. My job was to keep the customers happy, chatting with the loners, encouraging them to buy drinks, occasionally getting up and singing a song to liven the atmosphere up a bit. Strange to tell, I began to look forward to my nightly 'spot', thinking up little routines and putting together outfits that I thought the customers would enjoy. It gave me a purpose in life. I incorporated a few of my routines from Peter von Harden movies, a few dance moves I'd picked up from Moska. Occasionally I even mimed to my own much-requested hit 'Bi Bi Baby'! Sometimes I was too tired to go on – it was hard to stay completely sober when surrounded by drug-users – but Danny would always make sure that I made it to that stage somehow. We were a good team, he and I. And John was happy; it was so good to see him out and about again, even talking about getting back to work. If I could just keep things together, maybe I could save him. Maybe one day we'd be back at the top of the heap – and together.

But at the back of my mind there was always a terrible sense of foreboding. We were dancing on the brink of an abyss, fooling ourselves that everything was fine when we knew in our hearts that it wasn't. Did I sense the devastation that would strike at the heart of this world in just a few short years? I think I did.

But for me, the catastrophe came sooner. It was a normal night in Diamonds; the place was full, I'd given one of my best performances and was celebrating in the 'shooting gallery' with John and Danny and a few of the regulars. Suddenly the darkness was pierced by a beam of light and a harsh, barking voice. I looked up and saw a man dressed in full NYPD uniform, with handcuffs, a night stick and even a gun in a holster. It wasn't an uncommon look around the gay clubs, but this one was taking it to extremes, I remember thinking.

'Okay, fuckers,' he spat. 'Which one of you is Marc Lajoon?'

I extricated myself from a huddle. 'That's me, officer.'

'Get your clothes on, faggot. You're coming with me to the station.'

'Why? What have I done?' Was this a raid? Danny had assured us that we were well protected against police interference.

'You ain't done nothing, sweetheart. We got a cable from London. It's your ma.'

The room span around me like an awful Hieronymus Bosch nightmare. 'Mother? My mother?'

'Yeah. She's dead.'

CHAPTER SIX

The first thing I saw as I arrived at Heathrow was a newsprint poster announcing, in big black capitals, WINTER OF DISCO. I had to laugh: good old Britain, lagging behind the times as usual, had just caught on to the trend that I'd spearheaded in New York. Still, at least I should feel at home, and maybe there would be work. I felt quite cheerful. Then the coach moved off and the rest of the poster was revealed: WINTER OF DISCONTENT DEEPENS.

The journey back into London was a shock. The country was deep in snow – the worst winter for years – everything was filthy, the great grey drifts matching the lifeless, careworn faces. As we approached the city I noticed piles of rubbish along the roadside – not just a few black bags here and there, but great mountains of the stuff, stinking and obscene in the feeble January light.

The shock deepened as we came into town. I recognized the buildings – it hadn't changed that much since I'd been away – but the people! A race of aliens had landed and taken possession of the souls of the British. Some of the aliens were easy to spot: creatures in studded leather jackets with colourful spikes and plumes of hair, rings through their noses and chains between their knees. But the rest of them were better disguised: the dead-eyed, hopeless souls who shuffled through the streets, never smiling, never catching your eye. When I'd left London, it seemed like the bustling, creative heart of the universe. I had returned to a dirty, forbidding ghost town.

I knew all about the punks, of course; I'd read about them in magazines. At first I felt hostile towards these insurgents. Who were they to destroy rock & roll, I thought? But when I heard their music, I understood. They'd taken my sound from the early seventies, mixed it up with the old rocker style that we'd introduced in the fifties, and set it in a modern urban context. As soon as I saw those dismal London streets, I understood punk perfectly. I felt like a father to them.

I arrived home too late for my mother's funeral. A hideous comedy of errors had followed her death. The hospital where she died had contacted my last known address at Cheyne Walk, to discover that I was no longer there and that Anna had moved on. Drawing a blank, the hospital handed the matter over to the police, who contacted one old 'friend' after another. All of them denied any knowledge of me. They finally ran my dear wife to ground after questioning Julian who, coincidentally, they had picked up for a completely unrelated offence. He'd led them to Anna's new address in West Hampstead, and through her they'd learned of my temporary residence in New York. The case was handed to the New York police who, after an unforgivable delay, finally found me in Diamonds. How they could have taken so long mystifies me – I was, after all, a well-known downtown attraction.

I was an orphan. Why had I spent so long running from my parents? Or was it they who had been running from me? Why had we built so many walls between us when it would have taken so little – just a word of love from a parent to a child – to bring us back together? Yes, we'd fought many times, but now they weren't there any more I felt a terrible loneliness. I had no choice but to go back to Anna. And to be honest, after the madness of life in New York, I was ready to resume my life as a normal, married Englishman. After all, we were both older and (I hoped) wiser now. We'd played hard for years, and now we were both ready to take stock, even to settle down. I'd forgiven her for her last terrible betrayal. I longed for peace and stability after thirty years of chaos.

Anna had a new home and an independent income: she'd set up in business as a psychotherapist, and shared the house with a constantly fluctuating group of female patients who paid her at a handsome rate for board, lodging and treatment. Such was the success of this arrangement that Anna was now referring to the house as a 'therapeutic community'. Fortunately for me, there was a spare room when I arrived in London (I later discovered that one of her house guests had killed herself), and Anna bent the 'women only' house rule to accommodate me.

The atmosphere was instantly familiar; it was like a cleaned-up version of the good old Portobello squat. But where once we had created a gypsy camp from colourful rags and tatters, Anna had put together a carefully designed 'look' featuring natural floor coverings, ethnic wall hangings and coarse, chunky pottery. She opened the door wearing a huge bottle-green sweater, which, she proudly announced, was made from 'happy sheep', hand spun and dyed by women crofters and knitted 'in house'. She had aged in five years: the hair was now completely grey, still cropped short, and the crow's feet and facial hair went unchecked. That aside, she was the same old Anna: beaming, content, self-satisfied. The rest of the household were identical copies of her.

A waft of lavatory cleaner hit me as Anna opened the living-room door (I was later told it was eucalyptus oil) to introduce me to the group of sinisterly similar females huddled in earnest conversation. They resented the intrusion, particularly, I felt, from a man; Anna mumbled an apology and showed me up to my room, remarking that they'd just reached a crucial point in the afternoon's 'session'. This was her twice-weekly therapy group for women who had suffered abuse by previous therapists; later they would 'heal' each other with aromatherapy and massage. I offered to 'do my bit' with the massage – after all, I had years of experience in the field – but Anna chose not to hear me. Instead she left me in my room, quietly shutting the door behind her. I was glad to rest; occasionally I would hear the odd scream from downstairs, but that aside there was nothing to disturb my sleep.

I awoke, refreshed, and took stock of my surroundings. It was a plain, cell-like room, the walls white, the floorboards bare, a simple white blind at the window. The atmosphere was strangely clinical;

perhaps Anna's tenants liked to pretend they were in hospital. But there was peace in the air, and that was what I needed. Idly, I started flicking through some of the literature stacked on the bedside table: *Oral Herstory Workshop*; *Victims of Abuse: Healing the Silent Wound*; *Friendly Food: a Women's Vegetarian Cookery Course*. Then it hit me. *Bereavement Counselling: the Psychic Approach*.

I don't know why, but I suddenly burst into tears. Not the tears of rage and frustration that I'd known (so well!) during my life with John; this was from a much deeper well. I cried like I'd never cried before, great shattering sobs that left me weak and exhausted, huge rivers of snot coursing down my twisted face. What was happening to me? Psychotherapeutically speaking, I was an emergency case.

As soon as I could see for crying, I picked up the leaflet and read it from cover to cover.

Loss. Denial. Anger. Healing. These are the four stages of bereavement. Blocked energies mean that all too often victims get stuck in the denial phase, leading to depression, sickness and even suicide. The psychic approach opens channels of feeling to facilitate a full working-through of the grieving process, restoring the correct balance of emotions and the possibility for growth.

That was me! Depression, sickness ... all in the wake of my mother's death. Had I really allowed myself to grieve for her? And what about my father? Why had I run away from his death? And why, even when I forced myself to think about him, did I feel so little? Perhaps I needed therapy – I, Marc LeJeune, the great coper, the pillar of strength on whom everyone else had relied. I wasn't as strong as I thought.

I kept a low profile around the house for a few days, getting used to a quieter, gentler way of life. The women impressed me as pleasant, considerate neighbours – for that's what we were like, each in our little rooms. Anna delighted in her role as earth mother, of course, but at least she really did look after her little brood, making sure that nobody was hungry or lonely.

It took a few weeks before I could talk to Anna about my bereavement. The pain had been so sudden and intense, and it was difficult to ask for help. 'Everyone needs therapy of some sort or other,' she explained, 'it's just that most people are too shut off from their own energies to realize it. But sometimes the bravest thing is to admit that you've got a problem and seek professional help for it.' As we talked further, I began to realize that I had more problems than I'd ever suspected. It wasn't just the death of my parents that was eating away at me, it was a fundamental self-hatred manifesting itself as deep-rooted misogyny, emotional and sexual sado-masochism. Anna made me realize how much I had to work through: my own destructive relationships, my sexual compulsiveness, even (she suggested) some profound and unresolved issues around racism. The more we talked, the more I confessed, the better I felt. I wanted her to know everything – to understand me and to heal me.

I started attending a group that she was running three evenings a week, where half a dozen women (plus me) would explore their 'personal stuff' in a supportive and mutually respectful environment. At the first meeting, I sat quietly, speaking only when told to by Anna. At the second, I told a few stories from my own recent past, and was astonished by the rapacious fascination that gripped the group (whose own stories were pale accounts of sexual incompetence or thwarted love affairs). Soon my confessions had become the focal point of the group, as I spilled my guts hour after hour, weeping hysterically as I regressed further towards the ultimate source of my pain.

For I had realized that there was something, somewhere, very wrong with me. What had led me into such abusive relationships? All the friends I had known, worked with, loved and lived with, had tried to destroy me. Possessive Phyllis, criminal Nick, vengeful Pinky, mad Moska, confused Nutter, suicidal John. All of them had taken, taken, taken from me and given nothing but pain in return. Yes, even John. Far from him now, I realized that I had sacrificed everything – career, family and friends – to support a man who repaid me with anxiety and degradation.

And then there was the sexual angle; that was what fascinated the group most. Why had I become involved with all these men? I'm not gay – that much I made clear from the outset – but there was some power that drew me again and again into the destructive downward spiral of male sexuality. Male sexuality, I learned, was all about death, the desire to possess and destroy, the oblivion of the orgasm. Surely I, in seeking out these relationships, was trying to destroy something in myself.

I could feel some great revelation at hand. Three times a week, then four, then five (such was the involvement of the group) I dug deeper and deeper into my past, desperately searching for the key to the puzzle. I groped around in my subconscious, I seized on every tiny memory from childhood, I sent myself into hypnotic trances, and gradually something started to emerge. It was a memory – not even a memory, it was so deeply buried in my subconscious – from early childhood. A faint trace of a pain so great that I had repressed all awareness of it. And what was it? What was the image that returned again and again, like a nightmare struggling into the cold light of day?

My father. Always my father. Something that had happened a long time ago, that had set me off on the path to destruction, spiralling down, down into the dark, deathly hell of male sexuality. Finally, I had to face up to the truth, to the one thing that made sense of my life.

At an early age, I had been systematically, possibly ritually, sexually abused by my father.

As soon as Anna suggested this to me at the end of an intense session, everything fell into place. I could see it all as clearly as if it was yesterday: Daddy coming into the bedroom, sitting on the bed, pulling back the covers, no, no Daddy, it tickles, stop it, I'm scared Daddy, scared . . . I was amazed at how the details flooded back, tumbling over each other into consciousness. Why had I always feared my father? Why had I tried to hide from him, to prevent him from knowing anything about me? Why did I feel so little grief or remorse when he died? Now I knew. For a moment, it was too much. I would have given anything to take that memory away, to run away from it as I'd run away from everything in my life. But when I finally accepted it as the truth, it made sense of all the problems that I'd ever experienced in my life. It all came back to Daddy.

Alongside this terrible realization came another awareness. For the first time, I saw the crucial role that women had played in my life. While men (from my father onwards) had abused, exploited and sought to kill me, women had been my saviours, nurturing and protecting me. First there was my mother, who tried to stand between me and my tyrannical father. Did she know of our 'secret'? Or did she simply sense the pain in her child? Then there was Sue, the feminine counterpart to Nutter – and what a difference was there! Nutter was cold, incapable of loving; Sue was open, warm and spontaneous, an angel of light who had tried to lead me out of my adolescent darkness. Why did I spurn her?

The pattern continued. Janice, who had literally sacrificed her life for me. My new friends in the house, who had taken me in as a motherless child. And above them all, like a guardian angel in human form, my wife Anna. She who had given me so much, asked for so little, and had finally brought me to this intense personal reawakening. My life had been a battle between the male (destructive) energy and the female (creative) energy, and finally, the women had claimed me as a child of the light. I felt literally born again.

I realized through Anna that my New York years – when, incidentally, I'd been entirely bereft of female company – had almost destroyed me. As part of the healing process, she encouraged me to foreswear male friends. At first it was difficult, but after a few weeks of chastity, I felt a growing sense of relief. Rid of the constant itch, I discovered a new set of rhythms, a gentler energy that I shared with the women in the house. They too had decided to live without sex, to choose celibacy as a positive option and to channel their energies into growth and self-development. Hence the vast amount of knitting.

Life without sex soon became a positive joy. I felt – we all felt – so superior to those people outside the house who ran themselves ragged in the search for transient, humiliating pleasures. When we sat together after a meal and watched television, we'd turn over if a sexual situation arose; it just seemed to disrupt the flow of energy in the house. 'I can't believe that people get themselves tangled up in those ridiculous positions!' commented one of the girls when we'd accidentally stumbled across a love scene on BBC2. 'I mean, men just look so silly without their clothes on!'

Eventually, television was banned from the house altogether. This was the result of one of the many democratic 'house meetings' around which our home life revolved. We held meetings to discuss every issue that affected our lives, from the non-smoking policy (I had to sneak out for a walk if I wanted a cigarette) to the cooking and cleaning rota. There were meetings to arrange meetings. We'd sit around the kitchen table in a sweet haze of fruit tea hammering out the issues of the day, discussions that could become surprisingly heated, considering that everyone in the house agreed with everyone else. What excited them was the democratic process, strictly observed and minuted to the last detail. Motions had to be properly proposed and seconded; in fact, a motion had to be passed to introduce a new motion, thus doubling the amount of meeting time. Emergency motions could be introduced to veto certain discussions (for instance the suggestion by one mentally ill house member, soon to leave, that we might have a party). My role was minimal; to balance my natural masculine tendency to dominate the meeting, I was only given half a vote.

It wasn't just in the domestic sphere that I'd embraced a strong female influence. Looking around me in the months after my return from New York, I saw a city falling apart at the seams, torn by political strife and civil unrest, a city eaten alive by greed and envy. This, then, was the achievement of our great parliamentary system, that conclave of old men: to set class against class, race against race, man against woman. What the country needed, I saw clearly, was a new style of leadership, a woman's touch. Men had led the country through depression, war and long, bitter strikes; now it was time for a woman to take us into a new age of growth and enlightenment. And suddenly, behold the woman! At the general election in May 1979 I voted (for the first time in my life!) for Margaret Thatcher.

I've been heavily criticized in recent years for my support of Mrs Thatcher, mostly by trendy middle-class academics who can't understand her grass roots appeal. But for a patriotic, working-class boy like me, she was the obvious choice. I loved my country (I'd been away too long!) and it pained me to see it falling apart. The young were desperate, disillusioned ('No future!' they cried); the old, so many of them war heroes, were being left to rot. I didn't want to live in a land run by small-minded northern shop stewards! My England was a country of individual opportunity, where people with talent could rise to the top, a country I was proud to call my home. Strangely, when I mentioned my enthusiasm for Mrs Thatcher to the rest of the household, I was met with shocked silence and hostile stares. I decided to spend election night watching the results in a wine bar in Hampstead.

I'll never forget the atmosphere that evening. There was an excitement I hadn't felt since I was in the thick of the Grosvenor Square riots. And once again I knew instinctively that we were on the cusp of great change.

The bar was bustling with the typical Hampstead crowd – educated, well-heeled people with whom I felt immediately at home. They were young, smart, out for a good time – judging by the amount of champagne consumed. They were hungry – for success, for pleasure, for the chance to spread their wings and make something of their lives. How I understood that! I who had seized every opportunity, good or bad, right or wrong – it was the challenge that counted! As the results came in, it became clear that we were witnessing a landslide. Mrs Thatcher was swept to power on a wave of optimism, generously toasted by the real working people, the people who had the guts to make their own decisions in life. Goodbye, Grey Britain! Hello again, Great Britain! I felt an intense pride in the knowledge that I'd played my part in this historic event.

Throughout the evening, I'd been vaguely conscious of someone watching me. I was used to it: plenty of people recognized me, staring and whispering to their friends. It didn't bother me; unlike a lot of stars, I've always been flattered by public attention. It's part of the job. But this particular fan was taking an unusual interest, watching (it seemed) my every move. Finally I caught her eye and held her gaze for a few seconds. She smiled. She was an attractive woman of forty or so, with curly, shoulder-length auburn hair, pale white skin and dark eyes framed by the biggest pair of spectacles, in bright red plastic, that I had ever seen. She was with friends (I'd heard her chatting and laughing raucously) and obviously liked a good time: any woman of her age who wears a mini-coat in fake zebra must have a sense of humour. The waitress came over to my table and announced that 'the lady over there' would like to buy me a drink. Normally I wouldn't have gone to a fan's table (they come to me, sit or stand for a few minutes then leave happily clutching an autograph) but I'd noticed that she was drinking some rather good champagne.

As soon as I approached, she stood up and offered me her hand; she had a firm, hearty handshake. 'It's Marc LeJeune, isn't it?' she asked (she had a New York accent). The question didn't seem to require an answer. 'And you are?'

'Rosalyn Vincent. Everyone calls me Ginger. Join me! Let's see if we can talk a little business.'

All my life I've worked with the best: they just seem to be naturally attracted into my orbit. 'Ginger' Vincent was — is — a byword in entertainment circles. I soon learned that she was an agent and manager with top-class contacts in television and an impressive client roster; she mentioned a breathtaking list of names in the first five minutes of our conversation. I admit now (and we've laughed about this since) that at first I thought Ginger was a charlatan, a mouthy New York name-dropper, a practice which I've always found tedious and unprofessional. But it was nice to be recognized, and to be treated to such good wine (it had been a long, long time since I'd tasted vintage champagne). I even allowed myself the luxury of believing Ginger's suggestion that she could get me some television work. But when I found her business card in my trouser pocket the next morning, I was more realistic: just another bunch of empty promises.

I was wrong. Two days after we first met and exchanged numbers, the phone rang. I wasn't on phone duty in the house that night (like all domestic duties, the telephone was ruled by a rota), so Ginger was interrogated by one of my housemates before being put through to me. 'Jesus, Marc, who was that crazy dyke?' were her first words, before asking me to lunch the next day. 'I've got something for you. Nothing big, but it's a start. Come round to my place at about one.' She gave an impressive address in Hampstead and rang off.

The house was palatial ('Just a present from an ex-husband, honey') and Ginger ushered me into her conservatory-office, a glass-roofed sun trap that overlooked an extensive back garden with tall trees and well-tended borders. Charlatan or not, this woman was doing well for herself. She'd answered the door wearing a huge pair of sunglasses ('The party only finished yesterday morning') and opened a chilled bottle of Frascati as soon as we sat down. Lunch — a delicious selection of Mediterranean snacks — was served by a maid ('My PA, Caroline'). Ginger didn't beat about the bush; as soon as I was enjoying my first stuffed vine leaf she got straight down to business.

'It's a game show. It's not much, but it's a start. What do you say?'

I knew (and she knew) that I was going to say yes. But I didn't want to appear too eager. I asked for details of the pay, the format, the contract, all the while bursting with delight that British TV had 'rediscovered' me! I haggled. I questioned Ginger about her interest in the deal – what would she get out of it? She named her terms; I accepted. I questioned details of repeat fees, hospitality, transport to and from the studio. She was refreshingly direct.

'Listen, Marc, it's a telly job. Frankly, in your position, I don't think we have too much bargaining power. Shall we just say yes?'

I said yes.

I'd never given much consideration to game shows as a medium. At home, of course, they were the subject of derision – 'mindless soma' and 'sickeningly sexist'. But game shows gave pleasure to millions, and I've always been a performer who's happier with a grass roots audience. It's easy for academics to sneer at quizzes, soaps and sitcoms, but if that's what the people want then that's good enough for me.

And this wasn't just any old game show. *Secrets* was a radical new concept. The format's familiar to everyone now that the show's a hit (and I still enjoy my occasional guest appearances when I can afford the time – so rarely these days!), but back in 1979 it was such a radical departure that the ITV schedulers buried it in the afternoon. A panel of ordinary people are told a secret about a mystery celebrity – anything from a childhood prank to a major medical problem – and then have to guess who the celebrity is. In the last round the celebrities guess which one of the panellists is concealing the final secret. I was a natural choice for the show because, as Ginger wittily remarked, I had enough secrets to keep the show going for ten years!

I signed the contract for an initial appearance fee of £200 and was in the studio by the end of the week. And I had terrible, terrible pre-show nerves! I of all people, who had been in work non-stop since childhood, found myself practically throwing up when the car arrived. I hadn't been able to discuss my feelings about the job with any of my housemates, even Anna – I just knew that they wouldn't, couldn't understand the pressures that an actor is under when faced with a new job. So I'd kept it all bottled up inside, unwilling to admit my fears to Ginger ('It'll be a breeze, Marc, you'll be in and out in a couple of hours'). What was I so afraid of? I still don't know. Failure, perhaps? But that had never frightened me before. True, it was a long time since I'd played to a home crowd; had my English fans forgotten me?

Whatever the reason, I arrived pallid and sweating at the Teddington studios where *Secrets* was recorded in front of a live audience. I felt confused, disorientated. I didn't know where to go, who to report to; it was as if I'd never been inside a television studio before in my life! I got hopelessly lost somewhere between security and reception, and ended up stumbling across the *Secrets* audience, who were waiting in a queue to the rear of the building. Like audiences all over the world, they were helpful and supportive, and put me in the care of a friendly young assistant producer who finally got me to make-up.

I thought the smell of the panstick would bring my confidence back, but I was mistaken. If anything, it made me worse. I sat there staring at myself in the mirror, watching the familiar tan base go on, and all I could see were my own watery eyes staring back at me. I wanted to run out of the building, go home, hide. But I couldn't.

Finally I found myself in the green room waiting to go on. I sat in a corner gulping down a coffee, wishing that there was something a little stronger to steady my nerves, although it was only eleven o'clock in the morning. I was sweating through my make-up; I must have looked terrible. Then I felt a reassuring hand on my shoulder. I looked round and saw a tall, handsome, dark-haired man smiling down at me. 'It's all right, Marc. You're going to be fabulous, I just know it. I'm Noel.'

Ah, Noel, the *Secrets* host and chairman – Ginger had mentioned the name. I forced a smile and tried to buck myself up. 'I'm just preparing, you know,' I ventured, my quavering voice betraying my nerves. In reply he grinned, pulled a hip flask out of his pocket and handed it to me. It was neat vodka, strong and odourless. 'I get nervous as a kitten every time,' he said. 'Go on, have a drop of mother's ruin.'

A look of pain flitted across his face, so transient that only a seasoned observer could have spotted it. I took a deep swig and handed the flask back to Noel. Noel. Noel. The name was bugging me. And there was something familiar about the face: the big blue eyes, the dark lashes, the dazzling smile. But he was so young, in his early twenties at the very most. He would have been a child when I left for New York. How could I possibly have met this dapper young man in his sharp, double-breasted, three-piece suit before?

He read my mind. 'You haven't figured it out yet have you?' I shook my head. His eyes twinkled. 'It's Noel, Uncle Marc. Noel Jones.'

Noel Jones! Of course: the eyes, the smile, the bearing of a star in one so young. This was Janice Jones's boy, that poor little ghost of a child who had needed a father so badly. An orphan now, like myself. And a child no longer! I grabbed the flask out of his hand and took another long swig. Mother's ruin indeed! Yes, booze had been the death of Janice, that was for sure. The sweet sadness of that memory came rushing back to me. I stood and grasped him by the shoulders, gazing in wonder. Janice Jones's son! The years slipped away and it was the sixties all over again. I felt a warm rush of confidence. Everything was going to be all right. We embraced.

Buoyed up by this emotional discovery, I performed brilliantly. I was witty, flirtatious, slightly naughty. My 'secret' ('This king of the charts once played Shakespeare's queen of Egypt' – they'd certainly done their research!) was guessed after much hilarity by one of the female panellists (who, it later transpired, was the mother of a notorious child-killer – the public's lives are so much more interesting than ours!). Noel and I had a few words on camera, and I joined my fellow guests on the celebrity desk. The switchboard was jammed with calls from well-wishers, and I was rebooked.

Noel sent a huge bouquet of red roses to my dressing room ('To my favourite ever Uncle, love Noel XXX') and collared me as I was getting into my car to ask me out to dinner. I had the feeling that somehow I ought to make up to him for all the hardship he'd known as a child. Yes, he had confidence and poise on the surface, but I knew it couldn't have been easy for him. Janice had neglected him shamefully, palming him off on a series of totally unsuitable nannies and boyfriends. Like me, he was a survivor of child abuse.

From the moment I met Noel in the restaurant I knew that there was more on his mind than old times. He was dressed to kill: a tight white T shirt showed off the fruits of hours in the gym; thickly muscled, hairy forearms were well tanned and accessorized with gold bracelets. When I arrived (he'd got there early, he was half-way through a bottle of wine already) he leapt up to greet me with a bear hug and a discreet peck on either cheek. This was no ordinary, friendly dinner; this was a full-blown date. Of course, I was flattered; Noel was many years my junior, a rising star in his own right and, I had to admit, a very attractive man. His physique was offset by a light, frivolous sense of humour and, of course, a reminder of his mother in every feature.

I tried to keep things on an even keel; I asked Noel about his working life, his professional ambitions. But he wasn't interested in talking shop.

'I've never forgotten you in all these years, Marc.'

I didn't know how to reply. 'I've often thought of you too, Noel.'

'Have you? I wonder if you've thought of me in quite the same way as I think of you?'

I began to see where this was leading. 'How can we ever really know what someone else is thinking?' I was playing for time, uncertain of how to proceed. On the one hand I knew this was wrong; I was trying so hard to avoid dangerous relationships, and had even taken vows of celibacy in a ceremony back at the house. But it was sweet – oh, so sweet! – to be on the receiving end of a little romantic attention after such a long, long time.

'When I was a kid, I always dreamed that you might be my daddy,' Noel continued. 'I used to think about you when I went to sleep at night and when I woke up in the morning. And you know what?'

I wanted to stop him, but I couldn't. 'What?'

He put a hand on mine, caressed my fingers. 'I still do.' I took a gulp of wine. Time to cool things down a little.

'I was very fond of your poor mother, Noel.' If there was one thing calculated to dampen his ardour, I thought, it would be a reminder of Janice. But it didn't work.

'I found her, you know. When she killed herself.'

I gulped again. He was still stroking my hand, interlacing our fingers.

'Yes, I did hear that.'

'I went to boarding school after that, of course. I always had your picture with me. I used to get bullied about it by the other boys, until I was big enough to take care of myself.' A few muscles rippled underneath the T shirt. 'I've always had a picture of you by my bed ever since then, Marc. I even stole copies of your magazines from the local newsagent. I've still got them all.'

I knew which magazines he was referring to; he must have been about sixteen when they appeared.

'You look even better now than you did then.'

It was too much. I was only flesh and blood. Despite all the therapy I'd done, I couldn't fight against this kind of temptation. When Noel suggested that we skip coffee and desserts and go back to his flat, I agreed.

*

For the next couple of weeks, I was walking with a spring in my step. The weather was beautiful, Britain had made a fresh start – and so had I. My first appearance on *Secrets* was such a success that they'd booked me for four more shows, and the fan letters started coming in all over again. I felt reborn – and I was in love. Yes, I had fallen head over heels in love with Noel Jones, a man many years younger than me (although seeing us together you'd have thought we were the same age – my lucky looks again!). With Noel, things were so easy and pleasant. We just wanted to be together, to have fun. We went out to restaurants, to night clubs, for walks on the Heath, for long, giggly shopping trips round the West End. After all my hardships, this was a holiday.

Of course, there was trouble at home. Anna and the rest of the household were immediately suspicious when I didn't come back that first night and subjected me to a full-scale interrogation. I just said I'd been in rehearsal – how could they know any different? But something gave me away. 'I sense a disruption in the energy flow,' said one of the more intense women in the group, 'as if someone is holding back from complete openness.'

'Come on Marc,' added Anna, 'you know how we all believe in complete openness.' There was to be no privacy, that I could see! But I fought them off for as long as I could, pleaded exhaustion and retired to my cell.

Finally, though, they trapped me. It's easy to see when someone's in love, and my happiness must have been blinding to this community of embittered celibates. They were desperate to discover my 'secret' (it was just like the game show in my own home), and tried every possible method to worm it out of me – everything, that is, except a direct, friendly question. If one of them had taken me aside and said, 'I'm so happy for you, Marc, you seem to be walking on air, you must be in love, why don't you tell me about it?' I would have launched into a twenty-minute rhapsody about my new friend.

At a house meeting after my second night out with Noel, a motion was introduced regarding domestic security – in response, they said, to a recent spate of sexual attacks in the area, rendering them 'vulnerable to male violence at any time'. The 'action point' arising from this (after a general motion had been passed censuring men in general as potential rapists) was little short of a curfew: all house members would meet in the lounge at 11.00 p.m. before the doors and windows were locked for the night. 'Does anyone have a problem with that?' asked Anna. All eyes were suddenly glued to me.

'Yes, I do.' I decided it was time to speak up. 'It's an infringement of personal liberty, and it severely curtails my ability to earn a living which, as we all know, is particularly vital to the economic stability of this household. Especially,' I continued, with a beneficent smile at a couple of defaulting householders, 'as some of us are struggling to keep up with our existing financial commitments'.

The motion was dropped, but the campaign wasn't over. Various other foolish attempts were made to curb my freedom: a series of voluntary 'retreats', of which I was to be the first lucky beneficiary; a motion to introduce heavy housework penalties on 'offenders' (but none of them had the guts to specify the crime). Finally Anna collared me in my room, walking in without knocking.

'We have no secrets from each other, do we, Marc?'

'No, of course not.'

'So what's going on, babe? Who is he?'

'Is that really any of your business?'

'Well yes, I think it is. After all, you're living in my house. And yes, it is my house, whatever you may think to the contrary. And it just so happens that I don't like living in an atmosphere of concealment. So if you've got something to tell me, tell me now. Or get out. Go and live with your new friend, whoever he is. Betray the community that took you in and healed you. That's fine; it's what we'd all expect from a man, after all. They were right, I should never have let a man come and live here, even a man like you. You're all the same. Bastards.'

It was a formidable argument. Love is selfish sometimes; I didn't realize that my caring sisters had felt so betrayed by my new relationship.

'All right, Anna.' I decided to brazen it out. 'I had a few nights out, I slipped up, it's true. But there's nothing going on, as you put it. There's no need to do anything drastic. Everything's cool.'

I'd have to be more discreet in future, that was clear. At the next house meeting, Anna cheerfully introduced a motion whereby all house members would have to apply to the group if they intended to have sexual relationships outside the house; the meeting would then vote on the individual situation before granting permission. Failure to comply with this new rule would result in penalty points; anyone accruing more than three penalty points would be asked to leave the house. The motion was carried unanimously. The women celebrated with a story-telling session that lasted well into the night.

My relationship with Noel suffered accordingly. We could no longer spend the night together, despite my inventive attempts to convince Anna that I was 'on location'. She, with her extraordinary intuition, saw straight through me and replied with a withering look of disappointment. Occasionally, I'd meet Noel for lunch or afternoon tea, and we'd spend a couple of hours at his flat, but it was never enough. Noel was looking for a total commitment, and wouldn't understand that I had responsibilities that I couldn't just turn my back on. Noel, like many gay men (as I've discovered over the years), was possessive to a pathological degree. After a few months, he became depressed and emotional, and we had a big bust-up. It cleared the air, we remained friends and continued to work together, but the magic had gone. Noel found another friend, and our brief happiness was over. If only he could have made a few more allowances, been a little more tolerant. But Noel was an all-or-nothing kind of person.

Free from emotional distractions, I threw myself wholeheartedly into work. My housemates disapproved, of course, but Anna couldn't afford to argue with the money. After a triumphant first season of *Secrets*, the network decided to put it out at prime time on Saturday nights, and my career took on a whole new lease of life. I became a regular guest with a special spot of my own: each week, I'd reveal another of my 'secrets', and nothing, it seemed, was too much for my devoted audience. Sometimes it was just a bit of fun ('This star once posed in the altogether!'), sometimes risqué ('Which star got the surprise of his life when his new girlfriend turned out to be a boyfriend?') and sometimes deeply personal ('This star managed to miss the funeral of both his father and his mother'). The more I revealed on *Secrets*, the more audiences loved me and the higher the ratings climbed. It was a strange feeling: all the things that had made me ashamed in the past were now making me popular. I had a new reputation: a man that's lived and loved, a man with a past who's not afraid to own up to it. Suddenly I was an authority on all aspects of love and sex; I appeared on chat shows, on serious talk shows. I was everybody's favourite agony uncle. Total strangers would stop me in the street and ask my advice.

With this kind of success, it was only a matter of time before other producers started moving in for a piece of the action. I was offered a contract – a lucrative one, thanks to Ginger – as a regular panellist on a new game show starting on ITV in the autumn, the highlight of their Tuesday night schedule. *Get a Wife!* was a brilliantly simple idea: a team of experts (me and a couple of celebrity guests) would interview a group of six contestants (three men and three women) about their personalities, tastes and ambitions, and at the end of the show we'd pair them up for a dream date. My role was a combination of matchmaker and marriage guidance counsellor – I often thought that I would have made an excellent psychotherapist if things had turned out differently. And, of course, my reputation added an exciting edge to the show: who better than an admitted bisexual to judge these attractive young boys and girls?

I love television. After that initial burst of stage fright I felt completely at home with the cameras; I knew that this was the medium I was always meant to work in. Hadn't I been one of the pioneers of TV back in the sixties? And here I was having my third bite at the cherry. TV's like that, as Ginger explained: it's a forgiving medium. You can get away with murder – literally! (her joke) – provided that you can win over the audiences at home. I knew that they loved me, and any indiscretions I committed in the past only added to my appeal. They may have tut-tutted a little as they sat in their armchairs watching me, but every last one of them wished they'd had the guts to live life as fully as I'd lived mine.

Money wasn't the only reward for my sudden re-entry to the mainstream. Once again I was in demand for a whole host of celebrity duties: chat shows (who could forget my appearance on *Parkinson*?), phone-ins (my frank advice on sex caused headlines!), even a return to commercials. An enterprising young producer signed me up to make an aerobics video, which was fun, even though we never got beyond shooting the pictures for the cover. I looked pretty good in a sweatband and leg warmers! How that brought back my days in modern dance.

One sunny spring afternoon Ginger took me out to lunch at her favourite restaurant in Hampstead, a bright, airy place with a fashionable *nouvelle cuisine* menu, a fantastic wine list and very attractive staff. It was a delightful afternoon; Ginger was generous with her praise, happily basking in my success. The waiters were attentive and flirtatious; one of them slipped me a card and said he was a resting actor hoping for some career guidance. I felt that I'd found my level at last: I was working, proud of what I was doing, and I was enjoying the money and recognition that went with it. But there was a new challenge on the horizon.

As we relaxed with our liqueurs, Ginger rummaged under the table and pulled something out of her bag: a thick bundle of paper which she thumped down on the table without a word. I looked at her uncertainly; her eyes were twinkling behind those huge, red glasses. With a wordless, mimetic gesture I questioned her: is this for me? She laughed her loud, American laugh. 'Read it, Marc!'

A script. A comedy script. A TV comedy script, I deduced from the complicated camera directions. I read through the first few pages rapidly, laughing occasionally, enjoying the story. It was standard, high-quality sitcom material, the sort of thing audiences loved, with a central male character, a bumbling, straitlaced kind of man with a frumpy wife and a couple of trendy daughters. I turned the pages, waiting for the outrageous neighbour to appear; that, I assumed, would be my role. I read on, I skimmed, I scanned, I flicked the pages. There was nothing that I thought suitable for me. Was Ginger simply asking my opinion on a script that she meant to give to someone else?

'Yes, it seems like an excellent piece of work, well crafted, solid, an excellent vehicle for an older actor. Perhaps lacking a little brilliance in the secondary characters ... A comic neighbour, perhaps ...?'

Ginger roared with laughter again and knocked back her brandy. 'Think again, honey!' she barked. 'It's all yours!'

'Mine? You mean ... Surely you don't mean ...?'

'You bet I do! Read it through by tomorrow and call me. Hey! Sugar! Can we get the cheque?'

Ginger bundled me out of the restaurant and into a cab. My head was in a whirl. A series – for me? It was what I'd always dreamed of. But surely there was some mistake. This was a role for a much older actor, a father figure. I may have been over thirty, but I looked many years younger.

I went home and read all through the night. I began to see subtleties that had evaded me on first sight. Lester, the main character, was a middle-aged man trapped in a conventional marriage, with two teenage daughters who are preparing to fly the nest. His wife, Moira, is looking forward to a quiet retirement of seaside holidays and collecting china ornaments (there was a running joke about 'my whimsies'). But Lester longs to break free from this sentence of death, as he sees it. He feels more at home with his daughter's generation. He enjoys the lust for life of a man many years his junior. But to the younger generation he's just an old man who's trying to be hip – hence the title, *Lester's Square*.

Reading it for the third time, it began to make sense. I could easily be made up to look older (the character would be in his mid-forties), but only I could convey the young soul beneath the thinning hair, the shapeless cardigan. And what a shock for audiences! How they would hoot with laughter when they saw Marc LeJeune – the scandalous, dangerous Marc LeJeune – playing a fuddy-duddy old dad who's dying to live a wild life! It was a brilliant piece of casting against type. It would work. I wanted to call Ginger right then to tell her 'Yes!', but it was four o'clock in the morning. If Anna heard me talking on the phone at that hour she'd assume that I was 'up to no good again' and threaten me with penalty points. I waited until midday, when I calculated Ginger would be enjoying the first 'stinger' of the day, before telephoning with my acceptance.

Rehearsals and shooting for *Lester's Square* passed by in a happy six months. I was starring with a top-rate supporting cast, we were blessed with a genius producer who brought out every last drop of comedy, from belly laughs to poignant sighs. I loved the role of Lester: so unlike me, but I could empathize with his fears and dreams so strongly. Maybe, I reminded myself, that's what I would have been like without my talent.

Everyone in the team knew we had a smash hit on our hands. It's an instinct. I'd felt it before with *There Were Three in the Bed* and 'Bi Bi Baby' – everything was in the right place. I could hardly wait for the first transmission.

And, of course, *Lester's Square* was a hit, the sort of hit that an actor dreams of. It ran for three years with ever-increasing audiences; our Royal Wedding special in 1981 got the best ratings of any comedy show that year. By the end of the last series, we even had the critics on our side, although they'd tried to crucify us at first. Oh, the reviews of the first show were so cruel! I was used to rough handling by the press, but my heart bled for the kids on the team who had never seen the critics in action.

There was one review that particularly caught my eye, a clipping from *Gay News* that was brought to me by the director. As soon as I saw the byline I knew what was coming: it was my old nemesis Pinky Stevens. But he was Pinky no longer; now he was signing himself 'Paul Stevens'. The serious tone of his review told me why.

Marc LeJeune is a traitor to his lesbian and gay brothers and sisters. For years he's exploited our struggle with his bisexual posturings, perpetuating worn-out stereotypes of gay men as effeminate, immoral freaks. But now in the appalling *Lester's Square* he directly insults us. This sickening charade of heterosexist family life, with LeJeune as the overpowering father figure, completely marginalizes the les/gay struggle. Where are the positive images of loving same-sex couples? Why is the wife's ambiguous sexuality so rigidly repressed? It's a horrible vision of a right-wing, sexist, racist future.

It ran on in this vein for a full page. Surprisingly, the picture editor had chosen to illustrate the piece with an old photograph of me looking tasty in my 'Bi Bi Baby' leather jacket.

What did I care for the carpings of the critics? If anything, they added the vital touch of acidity that made my life even more piquant. Yes, life was sweet for those few years. And it was trouble-free, thanks to the calming, controlling influences of Ginger and Anna. This time I was handling fame as an adult, enjoying its fruits but not letting it go to my head. I stayed in West Hampstead; Anna maintained a strict eye on my private life, keeping me out of the clutches of the gold-diggers. For nearly three years, I was celibate – by choice (it's not as if I was ever short of offers!). And what a difference it made! I awoke each morning full of energy, looking forward to work, happy with my home life. How easy things would be if we could all live like that!

Of course, a few creepy-crawlies emerged from the woodwork to bask in the warm sunshine of my success. I wasn't surprised to receive a letter from Nick Nicholls, congratulating me on *Lester's Square* and requesting a meeting to discuss a business proposal 'that would be very much to our mutual advantage'. Typical Nick, trying to blackmail me with those old photographs again! I took great pleasure in sending him a terse reply that told him (in the nicest possible language, of course) to go to hell.

Less expected, and less easy to dismiss, was the surprise that awaited me at the studio gates one morning. I was chatting to the commissionaire when I noticed someone getting out of a blue estate car and walking over towards us. Instinctively I edged through the gate to safety; we'd been warned about the dangers of crazed fans, and I had been particularly wary since the death of poor, dear John Lennon. I was about to sprint up the steps to reception when I heard a familiar voice. I turned around, scarcely believing my ears. It was Nutter.

For a moment I was dumbstruck. The guard shut the gate between us. I could so easily have walked away, left the past behind. But I couldn't.

'Marc, it's me, Nutter! It's good to see you, mate!'

I smiled weakly.

'It's been too long, Marc. Can we talk?'

I signalled to the guard to issue him with a pass and let him through. As soon as he was past the gate, Nutter bounded up to me and grasped me in a bear hug. It took my breath away.

'God I've missed you, man. It's been so long.'

I broke away, held him at arm's length. Was this really Nutter? This affectionate friend, so pleased to see me? Could this really be the man who had walked out of my life and made no attempt to contact me for ten years? I was shocked, almost angry. But I could never be angry with Nutter for long. The years rolled away and we were best friends, brothers again. We walked into the studio arm in arm.

But there was a problem. Of course I wanted to see Nutter, to talk, to catch up. There was so much I wanted to know: he was older now, with less hair (no more Elvis quiffs for him) and a little thick round the middle. Had he settled down? Why had he come to see me? But first I had to do a day's work. And on a more practical level, I had to keep him out of Ginger's way. If she saw me with a strange man, she'd immediately report back to Anna, and if Anna discovered that Nutter was back on the scene there would be hell to pay. So I hid him in the studio audience, where he could watch me at work, learn a bit about my life and be ready to take me out for dinner (his suggestion) at the end of the day. I heard him laughing uproariously at every scene, wolf-whistling the actress who played my daughter when she came on wrapped in a towel, applauding whenever I finished a scene. The day sped by. When the studio was clear, I smuggled Nutter into the dressing room.

It was a strange evening. We dined in Soho, at a small restaurant not far from the theatre where we had made history in *Meat*. Nutter, to my astonishment, was full of nostalgia. 'Remember the birds, Marc? And the drugs? God, they were good days. Remember that time I almost got it together with that drag queen? God she was gorgeous. What a laugh!' But that wasn't the only surprise. I also discovered that Nutter was married, had been for five years, and had a young son. 'His name's Mark, mate. You see, I haven't forgotten.'

But beneath all this jollity, there was a sadness that he couldn't hide. He loved his wife, he said, but since the kid had come along they never had any fun. They used to go out to clubs, for long drives along the coast, on mad drinking sprees, but that was all over now.

'She's a great girl, my Sarah,' he said, after a few drinks. 'I want you to meet her, man. She's gorgeous. And when I met her, she was like my salvation. I mean that. She was so together, so strong, and I was such a mess after all that shit . . . You know what I mean, Marc. They were crazy times, they nearly did my head in. So we got it together, we got married, I sorted myself out and got a proper job . . . Yeah, I work with computers now Marc, it's the future, man, the real revolution, not like all that hippy shit in the sixties, this is the real thing . . . So she's good for me, you know, really good . . .'

I waited for the 'but'.

'But the excitement's gone . . . You know, the buzz. Since the kid came along, and he's a fantastic kid, my son and everything, he means the world to me, but since he was born Sarah just doesn't want to . . . You know . . . I mean we just don't seem to have the time . . . God, I miss the old days. Hey! We were the team, weren't we, Marc . . . The things we did together, you and me!'

I had the impression that Nutter was trying to tell me something. During the course of his monologue, he'd grab my arm, cuff me on the shoulder, ruffle my hair; now his leg was pressed firmly against mine under the table. I sat up, straightened myself and ordered coffee.

'I mean, I'm not old. I'm still attractive, aren't I? I can still get the birds if I want to. And the guys, for that matter. They all used to fancy me, didn't they? God, those were the days . . .' And he was off on the now familiar refrain.

It broke my heart to see Nutter, my oldest friend, in this maudlin frame of mind. Whatever had passed between us, I still loved him, I wanted to reach out and touch him, help him. His life and mine: what a study in contrasts! Nutter, so sure of himself, so wasteful of his talents, had settled for a life of embittered mediocrity. And I – how many times had I been told that I wasn't good enough, that I'd never make the grade? Fate had dealt us strange hands. I wanted to see Nutter again, to help him reach the kind of contentment that I'd found. But there was little I could do with him in his current state. I paid the bill, took him outside and started looking for a taxi.

'Hey man, we're not going home yet! The night is young! Let's go to a club. Come on, take me somewhere really naughty.' His arm was round my shoulders again; I could feel his liquory breath warm on my cheek.

'No, Nutter, I think it's time I got home to bed. Got an early call in the morning, you know!' But he was having none of it. As we passed the entrance to a quiet alleyway, one of those dark lovers' lanes that run down to the Strand, he wheeled round the corner and took me with him.

'Come on, Marc,' he said, leaning against the wall where the dim rays of a streetlight lit his face, his dishevelled suit, his loosened tie. 'Kiss me goodnight, man.' I gave him a peck on the cheek, but it wasn't enough. He grabbed me, stuck his tongue down my throat and pinned me against the wall. As soon as I could catch my breath I slipped from his arms and ran back up to the street where the late-night revellers were pouring out of the pubs. We shook hands. Nutter was grinning like a Cheshire cat.

'I'm not going to say sorry.'

'Just call me.'

'Give me your number.'

I handed him a card.

'Come on, Marc, let's go to a hotel.'

'Call me! Goodnight!' I jumped into a taxi and sped away, leaving him standing on the pavement with his arms raised in despair. I was shaking like a leaf. It was too much, too soon. But I knew that he would call.

I should have known that my happiness was too good to last. Since returning to England with nothing but the clothes I stood up in, I'd rebuilt my life. I'd had the courage to make a fresh start and had been richly rewarded. But fate hadn't finished with me yet. We had to go one final round before I reached the safe haven where now – at last! – I enjoy a lasting peace.

I don't blame anyone for what happened; I've always as a person had a strong belief that what's meant to be, will be. When I lay in that incubator, a tiny spark of life, the powers marked me down for a very special life. I've studied philosophy at the only school that counts, the school of life. And I studied hard.

The cracks started to appear the night I met Nutter again. So many old feelings coming back to haunt me, so many memories and dreams. For days, I couldn't concentrate. My work suffered; Ginger thought I needed a rest, and cancelled a string of lucrative personal appearances. But it wasn't work that was the trouble (I'm never happier than when I'm working hard). There was something else. What was it that made me jump every time the phone rang? Why wasn't I sleeping? It came to me in a flash as I woke one night from a vivid, feverish dream about that summer holiday so many years ago, Nutter and me in a tent in the countryside, all our lives before us, so close, closer than friends ... I was lonely.

That was it. I, who had given and received so much love in my time, was lonely. The life I'd chosen had its rewards, but it always ended the same way – with me, the star, the one who brought home the bacon, alone at night with nobody to comfort me. There were millions of people out there who worshipped and desired me, I knew from fan letters, but what good is a letter when you need to be held?

I lay there, staring at the patterns that the orange street lamps made on my wall, the curtains stirring slightly in a warm night breeze, a distant siren the only sound to break the dull city hum. I, Marc LeJeune, was lonely. It was a terrible confession. I felt betrayed by all the friends who had left me – by Phyllis, Janice, my parents, Noel, John. The list went round and round in my mind. And now Nutter. Since that first, strange night, nothing. Was he ashamed? Did he regret his moment of frankness, now he was safely returned to the bosom of his family? How easy for him to open his heart, to win my affections again, and to forget it all when it suited him. But I was left with nothing. Sleep wouldn't come. It was three o'clock in the morning, the very dead of night. I turned on my bedside light (how dark that made the rest of the world!)

and reached into my cupboard for a bottle of whisky and a glass – my only solace in the nights when sleep was denied.

And the phone rang, loud as a bomb in the stillness of the house. I leapt to my feet and on to the landing, concerned only that the rest of the house would sleep on undisturbed. I ripped the receiver off its cradle and whispered hello. There was a strange jumble of noise at the other end, the pounding beat of music, a jabber of voices. I said hello again, a little louder.

'Maaaaaaaaaaaaaaaaaarc!' Unmistakable: Nutter, drunk. 'Where are you, Marc?'

'You know where I am, Nutter, I'm at home in bed. Where the hell are you? Don't you know what time it is?'

'Don't be angry with me, man.' The voice now pleading, apologetic. 'I'm in a club somewhere, I don't know where, I wanted to see you.'

'What do you mean? It's three o'clock in the morning!'

'I went out looking for you, Marc, and I got a little bit pissed and I ended up in this club, right, but you're not here are you?'

'No, Nutter, I'm not.'

There was a silence.

'Nutter, are you all right?'

'I just wanted to see you, man, I'm sorry, I just really wanted to see you, that's all.' He sounded close to tears.

'Look . . . Oh shit, Nutter, it's the middle of the night.'

'Yes?'

'Look, you'd better come round. Get a taxi. You can't stay in a place like that.'

'No, I've just got to see you Marc. Please.'

I gave him the address (several times, as he was very confused) and instructed him to leave the cab at the corner of the street and walk to the house, where I would be waiting for him. I'd smuggle him upstairs, taking care not to wake the rest of the house, and he could be out before anyone else was up in the morning. It was the least I could do for an old friend in need.

Half an hour later the taxi had still not arrived. Tired of waiting, I had fallen asleep with my head on the windowsill, the curtains blowing gently about my ears. I was awoken by an ear-splitting shout.

'Hey, Maaaaaaaaaaaaaaaaaaaaarc! Where are you? Maaaaaaaaaaaaaarc!' I opened my eyes, and there was Nutter standing in the driveway, even more dishevelled than I had seen him the last time. The rest of the house was in turmoil. Lights snapped on, windows were opened and women's heads popped out all along the top storey. Nutter was oblivious to my desperate shushing. He saw me and beamed, flinging his arms wide in a drunken welcome. 'Marc, my old mate! Let me in! I'm a bit pissed, man!'

I looked to the left and saw a face dark with anger – Anna! With a warning flash of her furious eyes she sent the rest of the household scuttling back to bed. We raced each other downstairs; she got to Nutter first.

'What the hell do you think you're doing?' she asked in poisonous whispers.

'Anna! Christ! I haven't come to see you, have I? Where's Marc? I want Marc!' I was right behind her. I hurried them both inside before the whole of West Hampstead witnessed a celebrity scene.

Nutter slumped down on the settee and began asking for a drink. I thought he'd had enough, but I'd forgotten that Nutter was one of those who can drink themselves sober again. Anna pulled out a bottle of brandy from one of her secret hiding places and we all took a large swig, then another, passing the bottle between us. Anna, unused to alcohol, became drunk almost immediately. I remained sober, but the brandy took the edge off my nerves. Nutter had stretched out at full length on the sofa, his head near me, his feet towards Anna. Even with his shirt untucked, his hair thinning and his eyes red from drinking, he was still a very attractive man. I could see that Anna was thinking the same thing.

There was a long silence as we passed the brandy from mouth to mouth.

'Well, here we all are again,' I said.

'Just how we always should have been,' said Nutter. Anna bristled, unsure of herself.

'What do you mean?'

'You and Marc, baby, the two people in the world I really loved. We went through so much together, didn't we? Remember the good times, Anna?'

She was woozy now. 'Yeah . . . Good times.'

'But there was one thing we never did, wasn't there?'

I could see where this was going. Anna was slower.

'What's that, babe?'

'We never made it.'

'Hunh?'

'The three of us. You, me and Marc. You into that?' For a man who had been drinking heavily for several hours, Nutter was surprisingly in control. Anna was dumbfounded.

'Come on. For old times sake, let's do it.' He jumped up and massaged Anna's feet. 'Relax . . . Relax . . .' Anna slumped in her chair. I rose stealthily to my feet and sidled towards the door, but Nutter saw me.

'Not so fast, Marc. You don't get away this time. Come on Mister Superstar. Kiss me.' Anna watched, stunned, as Nutter held me in a deep, passionate kiss. She rose, stumbled across the room and locked the door.

And so I became trapped in a three-cornered relationship that lasted for the best part of four years. If I hadn't believed in karma before (and my interest in Eastern beliefs had begun long ago) I would now. Hadn't I been the great exponent of bisexuality, the guru of free love and open marriage? And here I was living out the logical conclusion of all the publicity, the hype and hysteria that had surrounded me in the seventies. I had so little control over the affair; it had its own momentum. We were forced into secrecy, Nutter because of his marriage, Anna and me because of our vows of celibacy and our commitment to the ideal of shared living space with the other women. Anna was distraught to discover that she was still attracted to men as much as ever – or even more so! She wanted Nutter all the time, and with each encounter she felt more guilty. As the weeks turned into months, and our occasional drunken flings became a regular arrangement, I heard her use the word 'betrayal' again and again.

And it was hard for me, too. I had prayed for love, for companion-ship, but this was not what I had in mind. I've always believed in one-to-one relationships – call me old-fashioned! – and sharing Nutter with Anna was not my idea of heaven. Many times I tried to convince him that we should pursue the path of our own relationship, which, after all, was the stronger bond. But he was adamant: he had both of us, or neither.

Of course Nutter was getting exactly what he wanted. He occasionally allowed himself the luxury of worrying about his wife (he kept these guilt attacks for me, never mentioning them to Anna) but that aside he was just as happy as he could be. He had his family life at home, his job in computers, and more sex than he could handle. 'I'm the luckiest man in the world,' he sighed one evening after a particularly extended session. I caught Anna's eye, and recognized the same weary bitterness that I felt reflected in my own.

We even met his wife and child. They had a barbecue one late summer evening at their house in Stevenage. Anna and I took the train out of town, barely speaking for the entire journey, and were met at the station by Nutter – the happiest I ever saw him. His home was comfortable, his wife Sarah (pregnant again) was charming and so happy to meet Nutter's oldest, dearest friends. 'He's told me so many outrageous stories about the old days, I sometimes feel quite jealous!' she squealed. Anna and I went off in search of drink. Two days later, Nutter was back at West Hampstead as if this was the most natural thing in the world.

I was unhappy but resilient. It was Anna who really felt the strain. The women in the house had turned against her, excluding her from their meetings and outings, muttering darkly about 'harbouring the enemy'. They'd tolerated me while I was celibate as a sort of eunuch in this bizarre, sexless harem. But now there was a greater threat: Nutter was everything that they most hated and feared. Virile, amoral, sexually active, he'd even flirted with one of the women over breakfast. She complained, at length, to Anna; I heard their conversation droning on for hours. But, I noticed, she didn't offer to leave.

The crunch came when the rest of the house was planning an outing to Greenham Common, where a brave band of women were standing in the way of America's nuclear forces with peaceful protest. Anna had worked so hard for this weekend, had spoken of little else, but now she was unsure. Nutter was coming to town; Sarah and the kids (one of them a very young baby) had gone to stay with her mum for a few days of rest and relaxation. Anna couldn't leave me and Nutter alone for the weekend, but she knew also that failure to travel to Greenham would mark a final break from the others. She decided, and the three of us spent a dismal weekend 'reliving our youth' (as Nutter put it) in a series of crowded, overpriced London night clubs. On the Saturday night Anna and I watched, horrified, as Nutter chatted up one young girl after another, hoping, he explained, 'to even up the numbers' for a weekend of complete debauchery. He failed, thank God, and was morose for the whole of Sunday. Anna spent much of the time in tears, furiously washing up in the kitchen.

Strangely, while my home life fell to pieces, my career went from strength to strength. After three series of *Lester's Square* I was put straight into a new show by the same writers, entitled *Oxford's Circus*. It was an even greater hit. I played Martin Oxford, a Cambridge professor given to wearing tweed jackets and a big moustache (I grew the 'tache that's since become my trademark for this role – and my fans loved it so much I could never bring myself to shave it off again). He's successful, popular with the students, but he's not happy. (That bit at least I could relate to.) So what does the great man do? He resigns his chair at the college and runs away to join the circus. On the road with a motley crew of clowns, acrobats and freaks, he finds fulfilment. *Oxford's Circus* had everything: slapstick, glamour, wit and pathos – particularly in the scenes when Martin occasionally returned to his wife and grown-up family. In the second series, Mrs Oxford agreed to free herself and join the circus. The ratings almost doubled.

The show was a smash; I was a smash. I was first division, solid gold British television royalty, unshakeable at the top of my profession. I was in the papers every day – attending openings, giving away prizes, posing with competition winners. The press loved me; they enjoyed the odd joke about my 'shady past', as they loved to call it, but they treated me with respect and indulgence. When British forces were sent to the Falklands, I was among the few performers privileged enough to appear at the all-star variety 'send-off' show, in the presence of royalty and Mrs Thatcher, who shook my hand backstage. I worked tirelessly for her re-election in 1983, rattling tins and speaking at dinners. I even campaigned against the miners' strike in 1984, a shameless attempt by the power-crazed unions to plunge the country back into the misery it had known in 1979.

But I wasn't happy any more. The happy days had gone when Nutter returned. Yes, I loved him, perhaps more than I had ever loved anyone. He was my oldest friend, my only link with my childhood. His enthusiasm for our affair never cooled; he visited as often as he could, oblivious to Anna's frequent depressions. If you'd asked me what I wanted, I would have said I wanted the situation to carry on, I wanted Nutter to myself. But I know now that I wanted out. Perhaps what happened next was meant to be.

The optimism of the early eighties was running out. A chilly wind of change was blowing. *Oxford's Circus* was doing well, but was the third series greeted with just a little less enthusiasm? Ginger was reassuring; 'You're an institution, Marc, they know you'll always be there,' she said, dismissing my anxieties. But was I not just a little bit more sensitive than her?

And there was worrying medical news – the first cases of a strange new disease that seemed to be striking at the American gay community. Soon we had a name for it: Aids. And, to everyone's dismay, it crossed the Atlantic. People were dying, people that Anna and I knew were dying. I thanked God every night that I had been celibate for all those years after my mother's death.

All that I could have dealt with – it was under control, as Ginger told me every day on the phone. Until the rumours began. The director took me aside one day to ask me if I'd ever made any videos, as he'd heard from an acquaintance 'on the scene' that there were cassettes of me circulating and changing hands 'for a great deal of money'. I was mystified; I could only assume that someone had got hold of my aerobics workout tape, until I remembered that we'd never actually got round to making it. A few weeks later Ginger reported that 'Marc LeJeune's videos' were the only topic of conversation at the Groucho Club. She was worried, I could tell, and demanded an explanation. I had none to give; I had never made any videos. An old tape of *Top of the Pops*, I suggested? No. These, she said, were videos of a very different nature.

And then the papers picked up the story. At first there were just a few mentions in the sniping, left-wing press – *Private Eye*, the *Guardian*, *Time Out*. They knew about my political affiliations, they (and they alone) hated my work, always on the lookout for ammunition against me. After a short story in the *Guardian* on 'pornographic tapes imported from America featuring a top-ranking British comedy actor', all hell broke loose. The *Sun* ran a cover story. The next day it was in every paper in the country, the subject of every conversation. It was a quiet week in politics, and the Sunday papers, without exception, made it their front-page lead. On the following Tuesday, Ginger called to inform me that the contract for *Oxford's Circus* had been cancelled. Ruin was staring me in the face once again. But why? And, more to the point, how?

CHAPTER SEVEN

GAY PORN SHAME OF TV'S MARC

Top TV actor Marc LeJeune, star of *Oxford's Circus*, appeared in gay pornographic films, it was revealed last night.

The *Sun* has seen video copies of films so disgusting, so perverted, that *we cannot describe the contents in a family newspaper.* In each of them LeJeune, 40, appears in explicit sex scenes with other men. The films, believed to have been made in America during the seventies, include *Imitation of Sex* and *Back Passage.* Self-confessed bisexual LeJeune was today unavailable for comment.

Now we must ask the question: how can a known homosexual and pornographer continue to appear on British television, where he is watched by millions of innocent children?

It didn't take me long to work out what was going on. Quite clearly Nick Nicholls, Pinky Stevens and Peter von Harden were in league to destroy me. Peter must have sent the tapes to Nick (they were almost certainly part of the same pornography 'ring'), and Nick would have relied on Pinky to get the story into the papers. They all had motives: I'd snubbed Nick's attempts to 'make friends' when I'd become famous again; I'd got Pinky sacked from the *Evening News*; I'd deprived von Harden of his livelihood. And they had the opportunity; a star like me is an easy target for scandalmongers. I recognized their style straightaway: the vitriol of Pinky, the vindictiveness of Nick, the sleaze of Peter von Harden.

It was all the proof I needed. Three people who hated and envied me had conspired to destroy me, fabricating lies that they knew would inflict maximum damage. And their lies bred more lies as other papers got hold of the story, piling up detail upon detail. Soon I was reading about other films I had supposedly made, scenes in which I had performed unspeakable (impossible?) acts. Some even ran 'stills'. Yes, I lost my job, but it didn't stop there. Once I was vulnerable, defenceless, they turned on me with a vengeance. New allegations appeared every day. There were no lengths to which they wouldn't go: camping out on my doorstep, questioning anyone who went in or out of the house, popping up in the strangest places (one young reporter even posed as a homosexual and tried to proposition me – for an 'exclusive', he explained – when I was out for a walk on Hampstead Heath). And it wasn't just me who suffered: Anna, Ginger, anyone who came into contact with me was fair game.

I think the person who suffered most was Nutter. At first he'd been dismissive of the scandal: 'It'll blow over, Marc, don't freak out' was his unhelpful response. But one morning he was photographed leaving the house. He managed to obscure his features, and the picture never appeared, but Nutter was terrified. He never came to the house again, and rang me constantly, imploring me not to mention his name, not to 'ruin his life'. Suddenly, I saw Nutter for what he was: a man happy to take his pleasures where he found them, but unable to face up to the consequences. Ultimately, he didn't have the courage to be honest about himself, about his real sexual nature. The affair with Nutter ended as abruptly as it began, and, to my eternal sorrow, we've never managed to repair the damage. Nutter, if you're reading this now, I hope you understand that honesty is really the only way.

At first, my response was to fight back. The whole scandal was based entirely on lies, and I thought it was time the country heard my version of events. I prepared a press release which Ginger sent out to every news desk in the country.

Marc LeJeune has never appeared in any sort of pornographic film or video. The productions recently referred to in the newspapers are a series of experimental works made by Mr LeJeune in New York, where they met with critical acclaim and ran to packed houses in major Manhattan theatres. They were adult in their themes and content but contained nothing obscene. Certain individuals are conducting a vindictive smear campaign against Mr LeJeune but have so far failed to come up with any proof whatsoever that these so-called porno videos actually exist. Mr LeJeune has never been ashamed of anything he has done in his colourful thirty-year career, but simply wishes to set the record straight.

But none of the papers would print the story. Instead they kept churning out lies about my years in New York, when (apparently) I was a 'high-class call boy', a 'drug dealer' and a 'go-go dancer'. If I'd had all those strings to my bow, I'd have been a millionaire!

If the truth was no defence, I would have to resort to legal action. I knew enough about the law to realize that the individual has some protection against this kind of attack, and I told Ginger to instruct solicitors. Nowadays it's common practice for major stars to sue the press – Elton John and Jason Donovan are just two of the celebrities who have followed the trail that I blazed. But for me it was a lonely battle.

Ginger bitterly disappointed me by refusing to pursue our case, claiming that the costs would be 'ruinous' and that anyway the lawyers had advised her that the newspapers would simply plead justification, which was an absolute defence against charges of defamation. How typical of the law! The liar is protected while the innocent man is punished.

I had no choice but to surrender to circumstances, keep a low profile and ride out the storm with dignity. My enemies had triumphed, for the time being, at least. I accepted my fate, but it was particularly galling to see that Pinky-Paul had used my misfortune to lever his way back into the mainstream. His insane rants were now appearing in daily newspapers disguised as campaigning journalism; he had obviously 'sold' my story to the papers in return for work. I knew the man was totally without morals, but this I found shocking.

So I entered my wilderness years. They weren't bad times; I'd saved enough money from *Lester's Square* and *Oxford's Circus* to live comfortably, the house was paid for and I could even afford to run a little car. Anna and I led peaceful, separate lives; the 'therapeutic community' had disbanded after our affair with Nutter, and I think Anna found it a relief not to share the house with a bunch of neurotic lesbians any more. She had taken a job at the Citizen's Advice Bureau, and was involving herself more and more with local politics (Labour, I'm afraid to say), so we saw very little of each other. We were polite, but distant.

The trauma of losing my job, losing the adoration of millions, was tempered by a new freedom. I no longer had to live up to the expectations of my fans. They knew the worst about me, and they could take me or leave me from now on. Some of them stuck by me (and I gained a whole army of new, rather eccentric fans thanks to the scandal); most of them drifted off. I didn't really care. For the first time in my life, I had to live as a normal person out of the glare of publicity. I wasn't a star any more. I was just like anybody else.

And do you know what? I liked it. I liked going round the shops not caring if I was unshaven or wearing an old tracksuit. I liked going to the local and having a drink – maybe a few drinks. So what if I got drunk? It mattered to nobody. And I found it easier to make friends. I started visiting London's pubs and clubs, meeting a new generation who had grown up in my shadow – and how differently they looked at life! These were kids who just wanted to go out dancing and having a good time; they didn't care about setting the world to rights or starting a revolution. They were young and looking for fun and they took me to their bosom.

After a few months of depression and loneliness, much given to pensive, solitary walks on the Heath, I found that I was actually enjoying life again. It was as if I'd woken from a long, tedious nightmare – my parents' deaths, the craziness of New York, the traumas of psychotherapy and success – and now I was sane and happy once more. And I was free – a dawning realization. At first it was a feeling of slight puzzlement, as if I'd lost something: a bag, a set of keys. Then it was a growing sense of euphoria. And finally, it hit me. There was nothing and nobody left to fear. My father and mother were both dead, Nutter (whose good opinion had always meant so much to me) had lost my respect, and my enemies had done their worst. For the first time in my life, I could live my life for just one person – myself.

One friend stood by me during this strange watershed. Ginger Vernon was more than an agent, she was a friend. When the scandal was at its height, it was Ginger who kept me sane, taking me out for dinner, forcing me to carry on even when everything inside me just wanted to curl up and die. And when the storm had passed, she was still there for me. She could so easily have forgotten me, moved on to other clients – she was a busy, successful business-woman in her own right. But no: she'd take me out for lunch two or three times a week, treat me to shows, films and parties, introduce me to her friends. Thanks to Ginger, I never lost sight of one vital fact: that I had the kind of talent that malice can't destroy. 'The first day that goddamn story came out,' she told me over lunch, 'I was planning your comeback.'

But when the time came, did I want to make a comeback? I'd grown to like my new life; it was easy, relaxed, and full of fun. Work, to me, was just a dim memory of hassles and headaches, and now I was on holiday. If it hadn't been for Ginger, that was the last the world would have heard from Marc LeJeune, and today I'd be a happy, wistful old man living on his memories.

But Ginger wouldn't have it. Little by little, she dragged me back into the spotlight. Whenever she took me to the theatre, she'd tell me how much better I could have played a certain role. If we saw a film, she'd mention that the director 'is dying to work with you if we can just find the right vehicle'. She'd send me tapes of new, young bands, 'just to whet your appetite!' I was ready to forget all about show business, but with Ginger around, I couldn't.

One day, in the summer of 1988, she introduced me to a talented young DJ named Dave, a rising star (he informed me) of the acid house scene. When I was a kid going out to the clubs, the DJ was just a bloke in a glass booth spinning records; now, however, the DJ was king. Dave was the quintessence of the new generation of clubbers – thin, with a stooping, shuffling gait, unkempt curly hair sticking out from a baseball cap, baggy clothes, his speech a curious argot of London and New York. His eyes bugged out, his mouth hung constantly open (giving me the unfortunate impression that he was a slack-jawed imbecile), but, Ginger discreetly informed me when she saw me shifting nervously in my seat, he was making up to £2000 a week. I was ready to listen.

Dave announced that he wanted to do a 'remix' of 'Bi Bi Baby'. At first I didn't understand – was he proposing to cover my song? No, he explained, it would be the same song but with a new, beefed up production suitable for playing in the clubs. I was thrilled – after all, I'd been practically living in discos for the last few months. I gave him my blessing, and told Ginger to sort out the contract.

The results, when they arrived on 12″ vinyl a couple of weeks later, shocked me. Instead of the carefully crafted song that was universally recognized as a seventies pop classic, I heard a long, rambling track of beeps, high-hats, whoops and screams that had never appeared on the original. My vocals were mixed way back, treated through some kind of voice processor that made me sound like an effeminate robot. And over the top of it all, right at the front of the mix, was a cacophony of orgasmic groans and moans, oohs and yeahs ('sampled', apparently, from *Imitation of Sex*). I was furious, and felt somehow violated. I ripped the record off the turntable in Ginger's living room.

'What the hell has he done to my song? It's a disgrace! I ought to sue him! I ought to . . .'

I stopped; Ginger was laughing.

'Marc, darling boy, remind me never, never to let you make any decisions about your own career.'

'What are you talking about?'

'The record's an absolute smash. It's already huge in the clubs.'

'It can't be!'

'It is, darlin'. Dave's been playing it every night for the last week. The kids love it. He says he's never seen anything like it.'

The kids love it . . . The kids love it . . . I put the record on again. And yes, this time round I heard something else in the repetitious beat, the yelps and moans – the same thing I'd heard so many years ago when I first listened to Elvis Presley – the sound of sex. The sound of revolution. Ginger, I could tell, heard nothing but the sound of cash registers. I played it again, and this time Ginger and I danced wildly around the room. Could it really be? Was fame knocking at my door all over again?

This was the deal: Dave would circulate a few hundred 'white label' copies of 'Bi Bi Baby' to influential colleagues in other clubs, creating an 'underground buzz' and a demand far in excess of the extremely limited supply. The record would then be officially released by a small, painfully fashionable dance music label, thus ensuring that it went straight to number one in the dance charts. Then, all being well, a major-label deal would be ours for the taking, scandal or no scandal. It was deliciously, deviously simple, and it worked like a dream.

The following night, Dave took us to a club where the floor came alive every time 'Bi Bi Baby' was played. I've never seen so many happy, smiling faces in one room. The kids just couldn't stop dancing. One beaming youth edged up to me at the bar, threw his arms around me and told me he loved me. That was the kind of impact that my new record was having on the people that mattered – the young. And they weren't even drunk! This new, health-conscious generation drank only mineral water and got high on the music.

Within a few weeks, as Dave had predicted, I was back on the club circuit. They couldn't get enough of me: I could have done a PA somewhere in the country every night of the week if I'd wanted to. Ginger had deliberately priced me down, charging only £50 per gig ('We've got to get you to the kids, Marc') for which I'd travel to the club, mime to the song and, if the demand was great enough, come out and do it again an hour later. I felt that I didn't have enough material – I'd already started working on a fuller set that included new versions of some of my other classics – but the kids just wanted that one song. They screamed, cheered and moaned along with every orgasmic moment.

When the longed-for deal arrived, the record entered the top 40 within a week. And once again, I had the same old problems: *Top of the Pops* wouldn't book me, the radio wouldn't play me. I was hardly surprised. After all, this was an underground record. Everything about it – the avant-garde production, the erotic content – was calculated to shock the old and delight the young. There was a time in my life when rejection by the BBC seemed like the end of the world. But now – their loss. What happened on TV and radio didn't matter any more. The buzz was in the clubs. The record was an instant, best-selling club classic. (Collectors may wish to know that there are still a few hundred 12" copies in mint condition available for £3.50 including p&p from Ginger Vernon Enterprises, PO Box 4787, London N W 3 .)

History repeated itself. Just as the record had peaked in Britain, demand began across the Atlantic. The ultra-hip Pyramid Club on the Lower East Side booked me for a show. The money wasn't great ($200) but the signs were promising: if 'Bi Bi Baby' was a hit in America I could play the New York clubs flat out for six months. I thought America had forgotten me – after all, I'd left Manhattan during a lean period in my career. But no! Even after all these years, they still loved me.

I couldn't wait to get back to New York and see all my friends. But, much as I longed to pick up the threads of my American life, I was scared. So much had happened in the last few years! I wasn't the same confused, vulnerable young man who'd loved and lived with John

Kinnell. I'd been through therapy, I'd found an inner strength and peace. And what of John? I'd heard nothing from him for all these years. I'd seen him through the worst of his drug addiction; I had no guilt on that score, even though I'd left him in such a hurry. But where had life taken him? Had he rediscovered his passion for work, as I'd prayed night after night that he would? Or had he drifted down the path of least resistance, squandering his talents? Would he want to see me again? Would he even remember me?

I didn't know where to find him. He'd left our old apartment, of that I was sure; all my letters had returned unopened. He wasn't in the Manhattan phone book. But I knew, somehow, that fate would bring me and John Kinnell back together. I stepped off the plane at Newark full of misgivings.

But my first surprise was a nice one. I picked up a copy of *Village Voice*, hoping to acquaint myself with the downtown scene so many years after I'd left it. I flicked through the pages of gossip, news and reviews, checking that my forthcoming show at the Pyramid was properly advertised. There it was, a small display ad down at the bottom of the page.

RETURN OF A LEGEND! Kitsch pop and seventies porn star Marc LeJeune in his one and only New York show at the Pyramid Lounge, 18 April 12 midnight.

One and only New York show! Little did they know: the bookings were already rolling in. Then my eye alighted on a much larger advert at the top of the page.

DEATH IN LIFE AND LIFE IN DEATH. An exhibition of photographs by John Kinnell, Weiss Gallery. Private view 16 April.

My heart leapt. John – my John! – was working again, getting shown in a prestigious SoHo gallery, and the private view was today! I felt proud and humble; after such trials and hardships, two artists were finally getting their just rewards. I would surprise John by congratulating him in person!

The Weiss Gallery was a stark, glass-fronted building, air-conditioned and almost entirely white inside. The atmosphere as I arrived that evening was hushed, reverential – the tribute of an awe-struck public to the work of a great artist. A snooty receptionist asked to see my invitation, but I simply told her who I was and she motioned me in with a respectful apology. And now for my second shock: on each of the square, white walls of the gallery hung one enormous black and white print, maybe eight feet by ten, of a hideous, gaunt skeleton of a face. Different lighting and angles told the full story: the bald, moth-eaten scalp, the bright, sunken eyes, the lips pulled taut over teeth too big for the mouth. There had always been a morbid side to John's work, but this, I felt, was too much. What had possessed him to photograph these . . . these terminal cases, famine victims, whatever they were? It was neither beautiful nor brave; it seemed to me only obscene.

And then the third shock. A familiar voice from behind me.

'Marc. They told me you were here.'

I turned, and there was John. But not the John I had left behind all those years ago. His was the face on the wall. Death in life and life in death: it was my John.

My first impulse was to scream and run. I felt as if I was trapped in a horror movie, that my life was in danger. But then everything fell into place: John, the man I had loved and practically given my life for in the seventies, was dying. I swallowed hard, blinked and held out my hand. He shook it, weakly, and leaned forward as if to embrace me. I must have flinched.

'It's okay. You don't have to kiss me if you don't want to. I'll understand. Enjoy the show!' He laughed, and tottered away. I couldn't breathe. I fell out on to the street and into the subway, sweating and sick.

As soon as I was back at the hotel I phoned Ginger and told her to cancel the show at the Pyramid; I had to come back to London immediately, for reasons that I couldn't explain over the phone. But for once, Ginger let me down. It was too late to cancel, she said, and any breach of contract would cost us dearly. But what was money compared with my peace of mind? I pleaded with Ginger, I'm not ashamed to say that I cried, but she was a rock. 'You'll do the show, Marc, and you'll be fine. Don't call me again, I'll be away for the weekend. We can fix the flight for next Saturday if you want, but it comes out of your own account. Good luck.' And with that, she rang off.

I got through the show – I don't know how – and the kids loved me. And of course I gave a great performance; I've never given anything less. I bumped, I ground, I closed my eyes and rolled my head in ecstasy. But with every beat, I saw John's giant death mask on the gallery walls. Every young, attractive face that gazed up at me in adoration was transformed to a putrefying skeleton. Each moan of pleasure sounded to me like a death rattle.

For the rest of the week, I stayed in my hotel room arranging my early return to London. I was scared to step out on the street. How many more ghosts would I see, faces that I'd once known as beautiful young men? And, absurdly, I believed that death was waiting for me on the streets and in the clubs of Manhattan. I had escaped once, but it wouldn't let me slip through its bony fingers again. I had to go home.

Back in London I threw myself into the night life, dancing my life away, anything to exhaust myself and escape from the nightmares that plagued me. I discovered a new side to the clubs that had once seemed so innocent and joyful. The drug-dealers had moved in, supplying the kids with ecstasy and amphetamines – and I got a taste for them. On ecstasy, everything was fine: you could forget your troubles, you could love your fellow man without seeing him crumbling away into a shrivelled corpse in your hands. And the speed kept me awake and buzzing, going from pub to club to party, talking and walking sometimes for days on end without sleep – and without the terrible dreams that came with sleep.

Sometimes I'd drink a bottle of wine and pass out for twenty-four hours, but then it was back to the clubs and the drugs, running, running from death.

But it was catching up with me. In a nightmarish repetition of history, Pinky was on my tracks again, hounding me through the papers just as he'd done twenty years ago. Every day he published a report 'outing' a show business colleague, dragging the most personal, intimate secrets into the public arena. 'How can these rich, privileged hypocrites continue to deny the truth about their sexual preferences while thousands of their gay brothers are dying of Aids?' asked one column, seeking to add a moral dimension to what was clearly a campaign of hatred and revenge. 'Marc LeJeune is sending dozens of young men to their graves,' he claimed one day.

By refusing to speak out about his sexual preferences he is perpetuating an atmosphere of fear and ignorance which can only lead to the spread of HIV and Aids. It is time he was stopped, and if he and his closeted co-conspirators don't have the courage to speak out then others must do so for them.

And he didn't stop there. In a full-page feature headed WAR CRIMINALS, SEXUAL TRAITORS Pinky named his top ten 'closet killers in the Aids wars' (I was in good company: it was a who's who of top entertainers) and listed our various 'crimes'. Mine included voting for Mrs Thatcher, failing to speak out against anti-lesbian and gay laws, doing a benefit for our troops in the Falklands and releasing a record that failed to promote bisexuality in the context of a safer sex relationship.

Marc LeJeune is personally responsible for the spread of Aids among young people in Britain. We invite him to make a personal statement of his own commitment to safer sex and fund-raising for HIV research.

God, I knew it was lies – how many years had I spent listening to Pinky's insane lies? But this time, I couldn't ignore it. The words seemed to pursue me as I ran from dancefloor to dancefloor: Marc LeJeune, a killer! A killer! And every time I saw John's face, laughing as he turned away from me in the gallery, laughing because I'd shirked his kiss. I threw myself into an even more punishing round of clubs and drugs, finally, when all the clubs had closed, wandering Hampstead Heath where the party carried on all night. I couldn't be alone: I had to have company to feel that I was still alive, still sane. I'd go anywhere with anybody, back to sordid flats in the worst parts of town – anything to avoid the terrors that overtook me when I was on my own. But there were the nights when I passed out drunk, waking in terror in a strange room or even, I'm ashamed to confess, in a doorway near Embankment station. And at last it caught up with me, the thing I dreaded most: I became ill. I collapsed one night with a fever, dragged myself out of the club and into a cab that took me to Ginger's. She put me to bed and called a doctor who ordered two weeks total rest. I had a serious chest infection.

I've always, thank God, been a healthy person: like all actors, I know that my body is my livelihood. And for forty years, I'd looked after myself. But now a combination of bad diet, lack of sleep and too many late nights out on the damp Heath had conspired to give me a nasty respiratory problem. I lay there for days, unable to eat, seemingly not getting any better. I lost weight: without exercise, proper food or fresh air I was bound to. But gradually, with rest and care (provided selflessly by Ginger) I recovered. Now there was only one thing left to fear: myself.

I dreaded each lonely day in bed, when Anna had gone to work and Ginger's visit was many hours away. There was nothing – no drink, no drugs – to take away the pain that had brought me to the edge of madness. But finally, in those dark days of recovery, I faced up to my fear. Yes, John was dying, hundreds were dying, but I was alive. I was one of the lucky ones: I had survived. I realized what had terrified me, what had driven me through the hell of the night: guilt. I felt guilty for my good fortune. Fate had claimed others, perhaps as talented and beautiful, but had spared me. Why? Why leave me to grieve? Why not just take me! But no: mine was a different destiny. I had escaped from New York with my life: now, I realized, it was my duty to make the most of it.

There was another important factor that contributed greatly to my recovery. Pinky Stevens had continued his crusade against his many show-business enemies, pouring down fire and brimstone from his newspaper pulpit. And finally, his 'outing' campaign hit the big time: a major, well-established British star about whom there had always been rumours (strenuously denied) was finally caught in the act. Photographs, quotes, the lot. It was on the front of every paper for a week, Pinky was on television justifying himself with his mad, fundamentalist rants, the whole country was talking about him. He must have been so happy. But then the worm turned. The star in question (whom I won't name – why rake over other people's dirt?) marshalled his resources, engaged the best lawyers in the city and mounted a counter-attack, suing Pinky and his paper for defamation. The papers went into overdrive, reporting every detail of the trial, and Pinky lost. He was personally liable for damages in excess of £1 million, and the paper had to pay punitive costs. Pinky lost his job (again) and disappeared from the public eye. Ginger's spies kept us informed of his rapid downward spiral: he was arrested for a physical attack on a member of the clergy at a demonstration outside Westminster Abbey, was tried and found guilty not only of grievous bodily harm but also of contempt of court, and was finally sentenced to three years in prison. Serving his sentence was probably the happiest time of his life: at last, he would really have something to complain about. And that was the last I heard of Pinky Stevens.

I was so delighted that I ignored my doctor's orders and went out for one grand celebration. Details of that night are sketchy in my mind: I started off at my favourite drinking club in Wardour

Street, then went for dinner and on to a West End disco, where I took a couple of tabs of ecstasy. When the club closed, I took a cab to the Heath to walk myself sober. I was found unconscious the next morning by a jogger, with blood pouring from wounds in my wrists where I had cut them falling on some broken glass, and my foot firmly (and painfully) lodged down a rabbit hole into which I had tripped and stumbled, knocking myself out in the process. It was not, as was widely reported at the time, a suicide attempt.

I was taken to the Royal Free Hospital, where I lay unconscious for several days. The first thing I saw when I came round was a television camera sticking straight in my face.

The ward where I had landed up had just become the subject of a 'fly-on-the-wall' documentary series for BBC television. For several days, I had 'starred' without even knowing it. Cameras had recorded my unconscious state, the nurses and consultants clustered around my bed, the other patients whispering excitedly about a celebrity on the ward. When I finally regained consciousness, there was great rejoicing, and there was Ginger by my bedside, urging me to sign a release form allowing the BBC to screen the footage of my admission and recovery. 'It's a guaranteed ratings-topper!' she beamed as I weakly scrawled my name at the bottom of a form.

But before I could adjust to my new stardom, I had to scotch the ugly rumours that were spreading about me. My accident on Hampstead Heath – a simple matter of a sprained ankle and freak laceration of the wrists – was misinterpreted as a botched suicide. That was ridiculous enough, but nothing compared to my supposed motives. I was a has-been, some papers said, unable to cope with living in obscurity. I was a drug addict, reported another 'news' paper, making much of the fact that I'd been associated with acid house 'raves'. All that was harmless enough, but there was one story that outraged and upset even me.

I had attempted to kill myself, the rumour went, because I was dying of Aids. They'd done their homework, I'll give them that: they'd dug up my relationship with John Kinnell, they'd 'linked' me to various other Aids cases, famous and unknown (of course I'd already lost several friends to the disease). They even reported that I'd been laid up with a minor chest infection. The inference was clear: LeJeune must be dying.

Now, I knew that this was impossible: thanks to my Guardian Angel, I'd been completely celibate during the crucial years when I might have come into contact with the virus. But that wasn't the point. How would the public react to the news that Marc LeJeune – the eternally young, fun-loving Marc LeJeune – was the victim of an incurable, wasting disease? Who would want to employ me then? No, I'd become at best a figure of pity, at worst a leper, shunned and feared by an ignorant society. People with Aids have my greatest respect and sympathy, but I couldn't allow such a malicious falsehood to destroy my career. So I settled upon a plan.

In return for using my name to boost their ratings, the BBC would allow me to make a short, dignified statement quashing the rumours about my health, supported by the testimony of one of the hospital doctors.

With this understanding, I set about making the most of this marvellous opportunity. The cameras loved me; instead of hovering around the ward watching the various admissions and emergencies, they spent more and more time by my bed recording my views on life, my hopes for the future, my salty anecdotes about a lifetime in showbusiness. When *Intensive Care* hit the airwaves a couple of weeks later, I was an instant smash. Viewers were shocked by my pitiful state on admission, distressed by the ugly rumours, moved and inspired by my courage as I fought my way to recovery. What had set out as 'a fly-on-the-wall documentary with unprecedented access to one of London's busiest hospitals' became, in the words of one television critic, 'a tea-time dose of homespun philosophy, gushing gossip and enough gore to keep the kids happy'. And yes, the gossip did come gushing forth – and the jokes, the stories, even a few tears as I remembered friends and family who had gone before. By the second week of transmission (it went out for twenty minutes five nights a week) my bed was surrounded by flowers and cards from well-wishers; by the fourth week there was such a frenzy of attention that we had to have a police guard on the hospital doors to keep the press and fans at bay. My daily flower delivery ensured that every single bed in the hospital was brightly decked.

In truth, I felt well enough to go home after a couple of weeks in hospital, but by then *Intensive Care* had a momentum of its own. The producers were adamant that I should stay with the series for the full six weeks, and booked me into a private bed. The catering certainly improved: soon I was having my meals brought in from a Hampstead trattoria by a selection of delightful Italian waiters, whose lively renditions of tenor arias and duets became a popular nightly feature.

I thrived on the exposure. I'm never happier than when I'm working, and now I could work all day, every day, without even getting out of bed. But of course it couldn't last forever. The day came when the film crew departed and *Intensive Care* came to an end, closing a remarkable chapter in television history. I returned home, feeling better than I'd felt in years, expecting to resume my quiet, low-key life where I'd left off, happy in the knowledge that millions of people still loved and remembered me. But of course this was not to be. I hadn't been out of hospital for a month when I was back in again, but this time the 'ward' was in the BBC Television Centre, and I wasn't just one of the patients – I was one of the *Patients*.

It was the first show of its kind: a drama series set entirely in a big-city hospital, with each episode revolving around a series of exciting adventures and romances as they developed against the thrill-a-minute medical background. There would be new characters in each instalment, some of them lasting a few weeks, some of them dying dramatically on the operating table. And then there were the real stars of the show: the regulars who watched and commented on the action, like a Greek chorus to the triumphs and tragedies that were 'business as usual' for the staff. I had been pencilled in for the part of Geoffrey, a terminal patient receiving hospice care. And that wasn't all: Geoffrey was dying of Aids. Did I dare accept the role? There was never a moment's doubt in my mind.

Ever since I'd last seen John in New York City – or before that, when I'd seen young kids wasting away in the early eighties – I'd felt that I needed to do my bit to fight the prejudice and ignorance surrounding this devastating modern plague. When the press reported that I had Aids I was naturally furious; but there's a big difference between having Aids and playing a person with Aids, and I felt that if I as an actor could do something to help it was my duty to do so. Ginger put it so well when she outlined the offer to me. 'They want you to play a guy who's dying of Aids. It's the only role for you in the show. What do you say?'

How right she was: it *was* the only role for me, and I was the only actor for the role. Who else could bring such compassion, such courage to the part? And I'd done my research in New York City: nobody could know better than me the conflicting emotions that come with this sentence of death.

Patients wasn't due to start filming until after Christmas, but I was keen to get cracking – and so was Ginger. She hustled the producers like a woman possessed, phoning every half an hour to insist that deadlines were brought forward, that pre-production time should be ruthlessly cut in order to start shooting right away, 'to capture the immediacy', she explained. And Ginger, once she's got hold of an idea, is impossible to shake off. Even the might of the BBC couldn't withstand her: we went into rehearsals at the end of August and were shooting the first episode in September.

The schedule was more gruelling than I had anticipated. Some *Patients* fans have jokingly said that I must have the easiest job in television: I spend my whole time in bed and occasionally potter off down the corridor or disappear for 'tests'. And I take that as a compliment: the hardest thing in the world, as anyone in the business knows, is to make it look easy. But the challenge of playing Geoffrey – a man different from me in so many ways – was great indeed. Here was a character so light and frothy on the surface, always ready with a bright remark, a joke with the nurses, a compassionate ear for the other patients, who, underneath, is facing a lonely death. Geoffrey never has any visitors. At one script conference it was suggested that he should have a male friend who came to see him, but this was vetoed. That was right: Geoffrey is essentially a lonely character. He hides his pain. He pretends all is well when really he's scared. His reaction to illness is one of complete denial. As we galloped through rehearsals, I realized that I'd taken on more than I expected.

But the answer to a challenge is always yes. Even when I discovered that *Patients* was to be twice weekly, thus doubling at a stroke the number of lines I had to learn and the hours in the studio, I took it in my stride. After all, I'm still young and capable of hard work – and, as an actor, I'm in my prime. I threw myself into *Patients* body and soul. Once shooting was underway, I was working ten- or even twelve-hour days, with weekends totally given over to learning lines.

But it was bliss! *Patients* was an instant success, and my perform-ance was singled out for special praise. I won't repeat the reviews – they've been reprinted enough times in any case – but I was thrilled to see that people had taken tragic Geoffrey to their hearts. When, after a few weeks, he became sick and hovered at death's door, the BBC was swamped with letters from fans demanding his recovery. I became a permanent invalid superstar. My fan mail from real-life hospitals and hospices was enough to convince me that I was doing important work. 'You've given me a reason to live,' wrote one fan. 'I survive from Tuesday to Thursday to Tuesday again. Thank you.'

Yes, there was some criticism of *Patients* – I expected it. 'Morbid' and 'voyeuristic' were the terms most commonly used, and Geoffrey was singled out as 'a sickening stereotype of the gay man as victim'. Yes, there would always be those who resented my success. But they couldn't argue with the ratings: two million by Easter, five million by the end of the first year, ten million by the end of the second. *Patients* became the show that everyone talks about, a microcosm for the health of the nation – and Geoffrey's right there at the heart of it. We received the highest form of flattery: a host of new medical dramas seeking to imitate our success. That was nice, but not as nice as the secret visit of Her Royal Highness the Princess of Wales to the studio, where she quietly sat and watched the taping of an episode and afterwards found time to chat for a few minutes.

It's things like that that kept me going through my gruelling schedule. After six months, I was desperate for a holiday, but no sooner had we finished shooting the first series of twenty-three programmes than we were in rehearsal again. I would have carried on working, sacrificing myself to satisfy the public, but, to my intense dismay, my health broke down as winter drew on. Simple exhaustion brought on a recurrence of my bronchial problems.

The second series went ahead without me; Geoffrey was 'in California' trying out some alternative therapies for six weeks. When I finally returned to the show, the ratings soared. The papers commented on my 'drawn, emaciated' appearance – actually a combination of careful diet and a brilliant job by the make-up department, who could make me look quite cadaverous with deft use of panstick.

Ginger was by my side every step of the way, making sure I received the best medical attention available during my illness, ferrying me to the studio every day. She fought for me at every turn, persuading the producers to give me more lines and bigger scenes, negotiating an increased salary for me when the ratings reached certain crucial levels. And as if that wasn't enough, she engineered a career for me outside the series: I became a non-executive director of a number of charities, medical and research companies, drawing a salary simply for the use of my name on the letterhead and a certain amount of free publicity. I made personal appearances at fund-raising galas, attended conferences and even gave an interview to *Hello!* magazine, for which Ginger negotiated a handsome fee. I blessed the day I met her, way back in 1979. Ever since then, she's devoted herself to 'making the most out of you, kid', as she puts it.

And it's Ginger that you have to thank for the book that you're now holding in your hands. No, I would never have thought of writing a book if it hadn't been for her insistence, her vision. My life's been exciting, of interest to a few historians and die-hard fans, perhaps, but I'd never have imagined that my little struggles to earn a living in show business could be of major literary importance. Ginger persuaded me otherwise. 'You're unique, Marc. You've blazed a trail through the twentieth century that others have followed. You're a survivor, an original. You can't let that amazing life of yours be forgotten. You owe it to us to tell your story for posterity. It's a best-seller, I just know it!'

Gradually, I came round to Ginger's point of view – as I've said, she's a very forceful woman. I started carrying a notebook, jotting down memories on the set of *Patients*. The more I wrote, the more I remembered. Soon, a notebook wasn't enough: Ginger bought me a tape recorder into which I'd whisper my reminiscences about my childhood, the madness of the sixties, my years at the top and the tough times when life seemed to be against me. Yes, I began to realize, I have lived a unique and important life. Soon the process of remembering and recording began to absorb me, to obsess me. Those voices from the past! How loudly they called to me. When Ginger presented me with a contract from a leading publishing company, I was eager to sign. By that time, I would have written the book money or no money. It had become the last challenge in a life full of challenges. To the long list of my achievements – actor, model, singer, dancer – add Marc LeJeune, author!

*

Three months have elapsed since I wrote the above, three months in which I've had plenty of time for reflection. Overwork brought on another bout of that tiresome chesty cough (I put it down to the filthy London air – what are we doing to the planet?) and I was out of action, too poorly even to dictate my memoirs to the secretary that Ginger has provided for me, a charming young chap called Simon, an aspiring actor, reminiscent of the young Nutter. What stories Simon has heard! He knows more about me than anyone else now (yes, there are stories that even I won't publish!) and has become a dear, dear friend. Could Simon's life turn out to be as exciting as mine? *Can* life be that exciting as we hurtle towards the end of the millennium? Whatever the young do today, there's always someone who's 'been there, done that' as the T shirts say. I feel sorry for them. I suppose I was just in the right place at the right time.

But where was I? Yes, indisposition has required that I take another short break from *Patients* – much to the distress of my legions of fans (they've been so kind) and the producers, who would have taken me to the studio in an ambulance if they thought they could get another day's work out of me. They'll just have to get along without me, even if the ratings dip when Geoffrey's 'having treatment'. Ginger's promised them that I'll be back in action by the end of this week. I can't wait! I hate inactivity – 'resting', as we actors call it. I certainly feel well enough to get back to the studio, as long as I can take it easy. I'm a bit shaky on my feet but that's just lack of exercise. Simon's got me doing a twenty-minute aerobics session every day with his Cher tape, and I can feel my energy levels returning. A friend of Anna's comes in twice a week for aromatherapy sessions, and she works wonders! My doctor is sceptical ('At least it can't do any harm,' was all he'd say) but I know I've stumbled across something important. I've always been willing to try new things, things that the establishment frowns on. Wouldn't it be funny if, this late in life, I were to discover a cure? A cure for chronic chest complaints would be of universal benefit.

So, I've spent a lot of time thinking about my life recently. Simon's been reading over the chapters that I've already written – a strange experience, hearing my life unfold like a story book. So much love, so much pain. But in the end, it all came out for the best. At least my story has a happy ending: I'm at the top of my career, surrounded by people who love me. How many can say that?

But the greatest gift of all is the lesson of humility and forgiveness that life has taught me. Yes, there were people in my life who hurt me, but now at last I can understand them, even love them.

First there were my parents, typical products of a sexually repressed generation, narrow-minded and afraid. In them the warmth and spontaneity of our working-class heritage had been ground away, leaving me with a deadlier legacy – the terrible memories of satanic abuse. How many others hide this secret? And yet when I try to think of my parents now, I can hardly see them in my mind; just a vague picture of cold, loveless people, forced by prejudice to betray the one person who truly loved them.

Then there was Nutter, my dearest, oldest friend, who never had the courage to face up to the one thing in his life that he really wanted – me. His youthful dreams of stardom washed away in a flood of drugs and booze and cheap sex, he sold his soul in adult life for grim, crushing respectability. Frightened of his own desires, he let his one chance of happiness slip through his fingers.

And Phyllis – I was a mere child when I fell under his spell. Perhaps he loved me; I sometimes think he's the only one who ever really did – after all, he sacrificed his life for me. But it's a shock now to listen to these cold, clinical accounts of our life together, as Simon reads them back to me with a tremor in his voice and a flush on his cheek. How open to misconstruction! Ours was in fact an innocent relationship, although I see now that in the world's eyes it looked irregular, even criminal. Oh, I didn't care in those days! I was young, innocent, with no thought for tomorrow. And suddenly: a friendship cut short, a burden of guilt that I would carry for the rest of my life, the parting gift of a sick old man. Even now I can see the glimmer of suspicion in people's eyes. I did not kill Phyllis! Will the past never let me go?

Nick and Janice, my twin satellites through the madness of the sixties. Janice was a tiny talent who wanted so much more from the world than she deserved, and ended up destroying herself rather than letting go of her dreams. And Nick, who turned all his energies to a grasping, unprincipled quest for money, but who created almost by accident something wonderful, who launched my frail bark on the stormy waters of show business, and gave the world a handful of photographs – little enough in themselves – that record a beauty that time and sickness can not destroy. Recently I surprised Simon with a gift – a vintage copy of *Super Boys* – so he could see me in my prime. I watched him as he turned the pages, his excitement writ large. He said I was 'hot'. I still am! Where is Nick now, I wonder – an old man as he must be. Smaller, frailer, still sporting that chestnut wig, unaware to this day that people laugh at him in the street.

I know perfectly well what's happened to Pinky: he remains at Her Majesty's pleasure for a few more years. Poor Pinky: a vindictive 'closet queen', so envious of those of us with the courage to live our lives openly and without shame. I wonder if they're allowed to watch *Patients* in their cells.

And finally, poor John Kinnell. Simon (who knows about these things) tells me that John ended his days a superstar in the art world, the subject of long eulogies in highbrow magazines. His photographic work from the seventies to the nineties is highly regarded – and yes, those portraits of me, taken in the first flush of our affair, are his masterpieces. Strange to see a snapshot of one's life held up as an icon. We were both young then and very much in love. But our paths diverged: John embraced the dark side, promiscuous, amoral, daring fate to do its worst. And John, alas, died last year; may he find peace at last. But I chose life. I'm still here.

And here's Ginger, always by my side, always encouraging me to work, work, work. And she has news for me, news that I can exclusively reveal through the pages of this book! Yes, I am sad to announce that this is to be the last series of *Patients* – for me, at least. The time has come for me to move on to my next (my greatest?) project, but more of that later. First of all there's the news of my dramatic exit from *Patients*. Ginger promises 'a television event that will be talked about in a hundred years!' What could it be?

I have been back at work now for – a number of weeks, I think, although the days are so busy that I've little opportunity to count the passing time. And less time than I'd like to finish my autobiography! But finish it I must, for the next challenge is awaiting me, the project that will finally vindicate me, that will ensure my immortality. Ginger announced with delight that a major film production company has picked up the option on this book – before it's even finished! – and now Simon and I are happily working on draft 'treatments'. Of course, there are things that will have to be changed. Truth and honesty have always been my watchwords, but I know (who knows better!) that there are just some things that won't 'work' on screen. Chapters of this book will have to be rewritten before publication. There are certain episodes in my life that I do not want paraded before cinema audiences as some cheap form of entertainment. Print the legend!

Patients goes from strength to strength. Now that I'm back in the saddle it's once again the most popular show in Great Britain, and I believe that it's successful all over the TV-watching world as well. And I'm the star of the show. I have so many lines to learn these days. It's as if my whole life is given to the show. I'm Geoffrey twenty-four hours a day, seven days a week! It's enough for me, as long as that's what the fans want. And I'm preparing to give them something unique, perhaps the greatest and most daring piece of television they will ever be lucky enough to witness. Yes, Geoffrey will die on screen. Finally, my audiences will be forced to go through the grief and pain of death, a pain I've known so many times in my life. They've begged me over and over again not to let Geoffrey die. But nobody lives forever! And it's time for me to move on. To tell you the truth, living with the character of Geoffrey is dragging me down. I've spent so much time in a sickbed, I've almost come to feel at times that I'm sick myself. Geoffrey has become a terrible weight around my shoulders, like the Old Man of the Sea. Thank God I've got Simon beside me to help me learn my lines and keep a grip on reality.

And yes, Simon is always beside me. At first he was a secretary, then a friend, a confidant – and now a lover. All my life I've been drawn to the young. And Simon, so full of promise, recognizes a kindred spirit even in an international superstar. We're soul brothers. We're two peas in a pod. At last, I've found a kind of happiness I dreamed of all my life. How Simon's eyes mist over with pride when I talk of the things we'll achieve together, just as soon as I've 'got rid' of Geoffrey (almost as if I must murder him before I can get on with my life!). We'll revise the book, we'll work on the screenplay, then – I have decided – Simon will star in the film. Not as me (I'll play myself in later life; we'll find another young talent to play the earlier scenes) but as the romantic lead, the great love of my life: Nutter. Yes, that's the real story, I can see it so clearly now: the love between comrades, denied, misunderstood, but finally flowering when two mature adults throw off the shackles of the past and face up in an honest and loving way to the truth of their passion. Nutter – our Nutter – will not be the lily-livered coward who chose a life of dismal obscurity. No! My Nutter is a hero who breaks free from the chains and runs to the light! I long to see that story up on the screen.

And Ginger! What can I say of a woman so full of energy, so full of life! Without her I might never have got back to work. I might still be lying in my hospital bed – I mean my sick bed at home, not my hospital bed, the hospital bed is work. Without her

I'd have been in the wrong bed, instead of the studio bed where I now lie in readiness to start shooting our film! That is, just as soon as we've finished with Geoffrey. It's hard to concentrate on lines when all I can think about is the next project – my mind's running ahead of me so fast! It was ever thus! Give me the new, the exciting! But Ginger has kept me in line, working on scripts, finishing the book, even when at times I felt it was too hard to go on with my memories. Ginger always knows when I'm feeling down, and smiles brightly: 'Deadlines, Marc! Deadlines!' It's her joke. She knows there's nothing better than hard work for getting me well. Doctor Theatre! Still the best medicine in the world.

And so I work on with dear Simon always near me, and Ginger by my side ready to take the pages out of my hand as soon as I've read them. 'I want the book on the shelves in time for Christmas!' she says – which must mean next year, I need time to revise the manuscript, to tell the story the way I want it to be told. This literary lark is hard work, I must say – harder work than I would have believed! The memories don't come out as easily as they used to. So many friends and faces that I don't remember any more. But there's so little time to work! The cameras are always around my bed, ready to roll for that last, greatest scene. My greatest challenge! Am I ready, Ginger's asking me as we get ready to 'roll'. And the answer – as it always has been – is Yes!